RISING

DRAGON BONES BOOK II

CELESTE HARTE

Immortal Works LLC
1505 Glenrose Drive
Salt Lake City, Utah 84104
Tel: (385) 202-0116

Cover Art by Ashley Literski
http://strangedevotion.wixsite.com/strangedesigns

This book is a work of fiction. Names, characters, businesses, organizations, places, events and incidents either are the product of the author's imagination or are used fictitiously. Any resemblance to actual persons, living or dead, events, or locales is entirely coincidental.

ISBN 978-1-953491-18-3 (Paperback)
ASIN B091T318Q3 (Kindle Edition)

As a writer, I do a lot of story-telling, world-building, and make-believe to say something quite simple in the end. This is a book of fantasy, dragons, and fire. But essentially, all I want to say is this:

This is to everyone on a journey of growth, love, and power. Keep rising higher.

PART I:

ROYALS

SHEDEREI MANOR RAID

A year ago, I would watch reports of the rebels on the news, shocked and appalled at their audacity to steal from the nation's most prestigious clans for something as arbitrary as relics.

Now, my gloved fingers ran along the edge of a yellowed page as I sat cross-legged on the ground, open books littered around me on the floor. The glass cabinet I'd taken it from had a circle cut into it, a little wobbly as it was my first time with the glass cutter, but efficient, nonetheless. My eyes carefully scanned over the words in the book in my lap. Holding my place in the first one with one hand, I switched to another tome laid out on the floor beside me, skimming the words. My gaze then drifted to a third. Deciding the first one held the most relevant information, I turned back to the first one.

I glanced over my shoulder at my lookout, a rebel by the name of Jonis. His eyes were trained on the driveway to the house and at the skies as—disgustingly—the owners of this manor owned several ZST-trained dragons. He'd warn me as soon as he saw any trace of them, so I tried to focus on my part of the job.

I flipped the pages of the book in front of me, tracing my finger over a few key words, trying to commit them to memory. The book was obviously old, clear by the yellowing of the pages and the faded text. But this part was especially worn, decay blossoming in saturated umber spots all along the page, letters faded beyond recognition in some areas. I waited a second, and the glasses I was wearing showed a scanner starting up in the lower-left corner of my vision, having detected missing passages. Within a few moments, the missing words on the page fluttered to life in my vision, shifting slightly as I got a better grip on the book and started reading.

It was a device the rebels had given me that pieced the words together based upon complicated algorithms that calculated letter and word fragments, context, and the cause of erosion to piece together what the text originally said. The technology was fairly new, acquired from making some choice trades with a rebel country, so I couldn't be seen with it on in public. But it worked great. I would never have been able to get through this book without it, and it was proving more helpful than I thought.

I squinted at a certain line, running my finger beneath the words.

Try as I might, I could not establish the bond.

I flipped back a few pages. This book wasn't specifically about dragons like I'd hoped. It was a biography of sorts, of a general in some previous Faresh's army. From the looks of it, the book was old. I wasn't good at calculating ages, but from the kind of language the book used, I guessed it might have even been from one of the older eras, like the Azure or Crimson Age of K'sundi.

However, though the book wasn't about dragons, it seemed the army general rode dragons rather than horses to battle, so they were detailed in the book. I'd have to ask Kahmel, but if I was right about who this was, I remembered him even being mentioned in a couple books we had at the palace. He was famous for his fierceness in battle and his ability to tame almost any dragon.

His biography was a gold mine.

Ever since last year, our main goal had been to find the remaining Dragon Kings and convince them to support us in eradicating the Equalizers. But finding information to even know where to find them was a slow and steady process. The rebel agents Kahmel could trust—Rand, Arusi, Khes, Asan, and me—spent whatever time we could spare pouring through data found in old books and scavenging what hints could be found in relics and artifacts. Other rebel agents retrieved information in raids, though they weren't always told what it was for—not until we had more conclusive reasons for them to believe our impossible mission.

It was easy to feel like we'd never accomplish it. The demanding Courts and Zendaalans always requiring Kahmel's time and energy made progress all the more stagnant. They were always pushing against his constant fight for progress for more humane dragon laws.

But still, we pushed back.

"What are you doing?" Kahmel's voice came through my earpiece, making me jump.

"Reading," I whispered.

His tone was unamused. "*Where* are you reading?"

"Now, that's a different question entirely."

Even without seeing him, I knew he was kneading the space between his eyes as he always did when I exasperated him.

Which was often.

"When you said you were going on the Shederei clan mission, I thought you were going to attend the *dinner* to distract the Shederei clan, not the *robbery* of their manor."

"Serves you right for assuming."

"Jashi..."

I sighed, then hissed, "How did you even get access to our comm link anyway? This line is supposed to be for rebels on the Shederei clan mission only."

"I'm the rebel king; do you think there are any rebel missions I *don't* have access to?"

Fair point.

Groaning, Kahmel continued. "Jashi, how many times do I have to tell you..."

Whatever he was complaining about was drowned out by a passage in the book that caught my eye as I scanned the page.

The author was describing how one of his best dragons had died and that he needed another one for an upcoming battle. He found one, but it was a rowdy dragon that he couldn't "bond" with, and he was recounting how his luck had changed when he was taming a group of dragons for his soldiers.

Ever since the Dragon King advised us to investigate the Drake Bond and Kahmel set me on researching it, I was determined to see it through. Despite his concerns, Kahmel didn't understand I *needed* this.

Politicians and news outlets had no shortage of opinions about me. They saw me as an incompetent street-rat who somehow managed to sneak her way into the palace. There was no telling anyone what the real reason Kahmel had for marrying me was, and people not knowing things was a homing beacon for rumors.

It wasn't like I could disagree with what they were saying; they were right. I had no idea what I was doing in the palace. I was by no means anyone's idea of a proper Faresha, so I used these missions to serve my people in a different way.

I could at least do that much.

Focusing on the words and tuning Kahmel's nagging out, I held my breath. This might have been exactly what I was looking for.

...but this one was different. The strength and power it wielded were clear in its eyes, and I knew I had to try again with this one before I bought the dragon that Sir Jendathi was offering me. I attempted the Drake Bond.

"Jashi, are you even listening?" Kahmel asked.

"I won't be able to finish if you keep interrupting!"

There was a sigh, thankfully, of resignation. "Just be careful."

I closed the book, a small smile on my face. I was almost done here anyway. I knew which book to take. The other ones were interesting, but not nearly the well of information that this one was. This book, the autobiography, was the most important.

"I will," I assured Kahmel.

A tool the rebels gave me was in the pack by my side, so I slipped it out, then lifted the little machine on the floor beside me, extending the legs so it would stand. I set the book down in front of it on the designated tray. As I turned it on with a touch, the tool sparked to life silently, little blue lights switching on. Then it went to scanning the pages with a special X-ray tool that could detect where each page began and ended, displaying its progress with a little screen on its back that showed the pages it was going through. It could scan several a second, so the process wouldn't take long.

I toppled a lamp onto the ground, the bulb smashing as it hit the marble floor, aglow with silver light spilling from the moon outside through the windows.

"What was that?" Kahmel asked, worry apparent in his tone.

"Sorry," I apologized, knowing he must have assumed the worse. "Just setting the scene, you know. Really, Kahmel, I would think you of all people know how a raid goes."

"If I get white hairs, it's going to be because of you."

"Ah, lighten up a little, old man." I pulled drawers out of the desk in front of the window, careful to check if there were any eyes outside before stepping in front of it.

"Old?" I could hear him stiffening, and I suppressed a chuckle. Then Kahmel was mumbling something to himself, something about me aging him early. Whatever.

The machine let out a small *beep* to indicate that it had finished the scanning process, and I picked it up, folded it back, and stowed it away in my pouch, knowing the information was safely copied inside. When I got back, I could read the pages as often as I liked from my eWatch. But now that I'd gotten used to it, I enjoyed the feel of holding a book in my hand, turning the pages for myself, so I'd have it printed and bound by the rebels and brought to my and Kahmel's private library if they had the resources and time to do it for me.

I looked at the scene and nodded to myself, satisfied that it looked like a believable break-in. Finally, to really sell the story, I swiped a few valuable-looking trinkets here and there, just to throw the scent off the rebels. The Zendaalans might figure it out eventually once they pieced together that the Shederei clan was very fond of ancient book relics as part of their decor, but the initial investigation would still point to thieves, giving the rebels a head start before suspicion was thrown their way.

"Will you be back home soon?" Kahmel asked, and I caught the way his voice softened slightly. He *missed* me.

As we had an unspoken mutual agreement not to speak about the status of our relationship, I didn't want to linger on the gentle affection in his voice. The slightest change in his usually stone and level voice reminded me that he didn't see our marriage as just convenient.

At least, it was convenient for someone, but it wasn't me.

Now that I didn't need to be as careful, I strode out of the library and tapped Jonis on the shoulder, nodding to indicate we should leave. I knew our movements were being captured by security cameras, but a mask covered my features, and I wore platform shoes that made me seem taller, my shirt and pants with padding that made me look heavier. I looked nothing like the current Faresha of K'sundi.

"I should be back within the hour," I estimated, wanting to get out of the conversation as quickly as possible. It took me a second to realize the awkward silence that followed must have been Kahmel saying something to someone else. And not because he was about to break the unspoken rule.

Of course, there was no reason to believe he would. It had been months since our interaction with the Dragon King, Aithel, and he'd never broken it since. A raid mission was hardly the place to discuss it, and Kahmel would never be so rash.

Still, my heart raced because of that small pause before his voice came again.

"All right. Just be careful, Jashi," he repeated.

"Yeah, yeah, yeah," I said shortly.

At the same time that Kahmel went silent, Arusi came from the other hall, giving me a thumbs-up. Looked like we'd finished at around the same time. Her mouth was covered, but by the creases around her eyes, I could tell she was grinning. I gave her a thumbs-up as well. Today looked like a good day for raided information.

Together, the three of us arrived at our exit—a guest bedroom with a draft coming through, wind gently swaying the curtains because of the window Arusi cut open with a glass cutter. The section she had cut away had crashed to the floor, leaving glass shards twinkling white with the moonlight.

Kneeling at the edge of the windowsill, I looked out into the desert night at an expanse of sand. The city lights glowed in the distance. The chilly wind cut through my clothes and touched the skin around my eyes with icy fingers. Below, there appeared to be nothing more than a plummet straight down into a shrub. But a voice came into my ear. Not Kahmel's, thankfully.

"You're clear."

Without a second thought, I leaped straight down.

A breath later, the air beneath me split, revealing a hatch that had slid open to a stealth vehicle waiting beneath the window. Having practiced the landing, I managed not to hurt my knees or ankles like I did the first few times I practiced the jump earlier today, hopping from a wall of a similar height in a hidden part of the garden. The other operatives who came with me followed, and the hatch above us closed.

We were in a vehicle built like a small spaceship. It was round, with room for at least ten people to stand around comfortably. The driver had a seat in the front. I gripped a bar that poked out from the floor in a loop and pulled it up, revealing that it was a seat, retracted into the floor to make more room for the landing.

The rebels having access to things the Faresh could slip them unnoticed was one of the reasons now was one of the best times to be a rebel. High-tech camouflage vehicles, disguises, and virus technology that disabled security systems made raids much safer for everyone involved. Which was why I allowed myself to come on such excursions. I couldn't risk it if it were a threat to my position.

It was still a risk, but I would go stir-crazy if I just sat around *having dinner* for my assignments all the time.

Arusi taught me how to find and read rebel messages and mission statements. There would be some indication of a claw somewhere around the message. Whether it was drawn, a sticker, a cut-off from an advertisement, or whatever. The claw would be encrypted with a message that could be read with the decryption code on my eWatch. I would discreetly scan the air above the claw, and the message would appear on my eWatch for me to read later. The message would destroy itself five minutes after opening it. Any rebel in the area could find the mission and report that they'd attend it.

When I read this one, I knew it was something I could take a chance on, given that there'd be all the preparations necessary for me to disguise my identity.

The other two rebels pulled up seats as the driver set us on our way back, charting the path and then turning to us.

"Great job," Khes said as he turned around, grinning, the scar over his right eye twitching with the motion. Now that the war was over, Kahmel's war general was able to spend more time with rebel missions like these. A good thing, because it made Kahmel feel better when I told him I went with one of his close friends. *Our* close friends, now.

Arusi peeled off her mask and smiled. "This place was a well of information."

The rebel beside her nodded, taking off his mask as well, revealing a soft face and an easy-going expression. I'd only met Jonis a few times, and he always smelled like bubblegum since he always had a piece in his mouth. He wasn't K'sundii—he was from the now-rebel country Vahdel, but he lived in hiding with the rebels here. His hair was wavier than the tight coils of the K'sundii, a brown that tinged with bluish light from the control panels surrounding him.

He sat in his seat with his legs crossed, a lopsided grin spread across his face. He admired a jeweled necklace he must have swiped to help with the burglary set-up as he made popping sounds with the gum in his mouth. "A well of other things, too."

I chuckled. The burglary angle was necessary to throw the scent, but I didn't feel sorry for the owners. The Shederei clan was always complaining about something Kahmel did and was one of the groups pushing for the Court to eradicate him.

Arusi shook her head and shoved Jonis playfully. "That's not what we were here for."

He laughed and pretended to be shaken from a stupor. "Oh, right, right. Information."

Khes chuckled with them. "That's right, Jonis. Reduce the resistance to common theft."

Jonis put the necklace away. "I'm just kidding. But still, it's entertaining to see these greedy people squeal like pigs when you take their precious things."

That was true. Whenever raids happened, the best part was hearing the rumors about it afterward—all the wrong guesses and people sounding like it was their very life taken away from them rather than small treasures that were insured to the teeth.

One other rebel had come on this mission, Jonis's brother, Michan, who assisted Khes with keeping an eye on the area while we went in. He nodded out the window.

"Just in time, too."

I stood to look out with him and watched as the couple came home. I thought they'd traveled in their car, but I was mistaken— they'd taken their dragon. It landed on the driveway with robotic stiffness, following the commands of the man guiding it with a holographic control panel. It was odd how a sight I'd gotten used to seeing all my life—rich people owning dragons like they were exotic cars—now turned my stomach. It was like seeing with new eyes, and what everyone else saw as a machine was now a tortured creature in agony to me. This was what the K'sundii reduced the dragons to because of their folly. This was our fault.

But we were making it right now. We would figure out how to save them, those of us in the rebellion. And we would make the rest of K'sundi see reason, too.

We had to.

CAVES

Not too long ago, the very thought of being around a dragon would have sent me running in the opposite direction. Now, I was itching for any opportunity to go, especially now. I watched as a dozen old men tried various intimidation tactics on Kahmel, a man who sincerely couldn't care less.

Some part of me feared the fact that nothing fazed my husband these days. But then again, his lack of arguments in these meetings meant I could get back to my dragon faster.

It wasn't like he'd tell me what was bothering him anyway.

"We just fail to understand the need to maintain the presence of all these wild dragons if the war is over," one of the council members complained.

That part caught my attention.

Straightening my back, I narrowed my eyes. But since I wasn't paying much attention before, I wasn't even sure which council member had said it. Light poured into the room from windows that reached the ceiling on either side. As Faresh and Faresha, Kahmel and I sat at the head of a long table with the council members lining the sides—a bunch of old men who had nothing better to do than dress up in their lavish robes and cluck like hens all day.

"How can you say that?" I blurted as Kahmel opened his mouth to answer. He looked at me, surprised. Probably thinking I wasn't listening.

Which I wasn't, at least not until they mentioned taking my dragons away.

"What harm have they done? The dragons in the wild are just existing peacefully; leave them alone! They haven't even caused any accidents lately, right, Kahmel?"

Kahmel had his dark face in his hand but looked up at me and nodded, his tinted glasses covering his eyes. "Er, yes, that's correct."

"Well, there you go," I said, leaning back into my seat. "Leave them alone."

The council members looked to Kahmel as if pleading with him to save them from my random outburst. However, Kahmel offered them no such thing, raising his eyebrow, challenging them to vocalize any of what was obviously passing through their minds.

One of them cleared his throat. The bald one with the glasses. I forgot his name.

"That may be the case, er, Your Majesty," he added politely. "But that doesn't change the fact that the people don't *feel* safe with these monsters—"

"Dragons," I corrected, cocking my head to the side and daring him to oppose me. I supposed I'd learned something from Kahmel in our time together.

"*Dragons*," the council member ground his teeth, "lurking around in the mountains."

I crossed my arms, leaning back into my chair. "Says you," I mumbled.

"What?"

"I think what my wife's trying to say," Kahmel finally stepped in, "is that it hasn't become a serious enough problem to have to change anything. There's no real need to get rid of them, and while we're no longer at war, it always does well to be prepared. We've already learned the hard way what happens when we're not."

At that, all the council members fell into silence. It was almost funny since I knew the real reason Kahmel kept the dragons around had nothing to do with war, but since we almost fell so severely in the last one, no one could object. Especially since they were the ones who were unprepared and Kahmel was the one who saved them.

"If that's all of the issues you want addressed for today, I believe the meeting is adjourned," Kahmel said. No one objected, so he stood. "You are dismissed."

The council members all rose from their seats and neatly lined out the door, and as soon as they were gone, I breathed a sigh of relief.

"Finally." I stretched out the kinks that were forming in my back from sitting in the same position for so long, the big earrings hanging from my ears swinging as I did. It had only been a few months since Kahmel and I were married, so wearing all these luxurious things was still foreign to me. The lavender robes that hugged my figure made it a little difficult to rise from my seat, but Kahmel stood first and offered me a hand.

"Thank you," I said as he gave a small smile.

Despite the glasses that masked his expressions, and though we really didn't feel like a couple, in the few months Kahmel and I had been married, I'd learned how to see through those glasses, that stone face he always wore.

His mind was miles away from here.

Sighing, I adjusted the bracelets that had slid up my arm, so they fell back to my wrists, where they weren't so tight. "What now?"

I wasn't expecting the way he pulled me into his chest, his cloak draping over me as he swung his arm over my shoulders and walked with me to the door. "Now we have dinner. I've been meaning to talk to you for a while now, but we've been so busy."

"Yeah, I know." I hated when he put me in these sudden, awkward situations. Where part of me wanted to instinctively pull away, say we were only married on paper and in the eyes of the country because we had to do it.

But the other part of me liked the warmth radiating from his chest and arm.

And I didn't understand that part. Not at all.

Still.

I didn't pull away.

Together we strode into the courtyard of the palace where a fountain spewed into the evening sky, colors lighting all along the artificial pond.

I didn't think there was any amount of time that could pass that would get me used to the magic of this palace. The way time stood still, back when K'sundi was known as a nation of brutal warriors, led by the tribe of "savages." Tiles lined the way to the dining hall, pillars flanking our way. Desert plants flourished all around the court, potted palms placed sporadically.

Outside of these walls, K'sundi had changed a lot. But knowing what I now understood Kahmel and I shared, I wondered if things had really changed at all.

Maybe *savage* wasn't the right word for us, members of the dragon tribe, but we were resilient and determined to make this nation strong enough to rise against its hidden enemies. And that started by making sure they had the dragons to do it. Kahmel and I may not have agreed on a lot of things, but we at least agreed on that.

Then again, maybe we *were* savage.

In all the best ways.

I scowled as Kahmel made us both skip the dining hall. "Aren't we going to have dinner?"

"Yes," he said, stroking his short beard. "But we're not having dinner here."

I groaned. "Are we having dinner with some rich clan family again? You should have warned me; I was prepared to pig out, not eat fancy."

Kahmel chuckled. "You're going to like it, trust me."

I wasn't convinced until he led me out of the palace's grand doors and down the long stairs, toward the dragon stables.

"I get to ride Comet?" I asked, a grin spreading on my face as I pulled away from him. I was planning to read the book I'd acquired from the Shederei manor raid, but it was worth putting off if this involved riding Comet.

Kahmel grimaced. "Not quite."

Groaning again, I crossed my arms. "Why give me an Elemental dragon as a gift if you won't ever let me ride it?"

He sighed. "Why ask me if you can ride him if you regularly go riding, whether I say yes or no?"

I looked away, trying, and probably failing, to hide the way I flinched. "I don't know what you're talking about."

What I really wanted to know was how he always found out about my little secrets.

"Sure, you don't," he drawled. "Regardless, as long as we're going together and I can do something about it, we're not riding on Comet. As I've said many times already, he isn't trained enough to be safe for riding. And we can't afford any unfortunate accidents."

I tsked. "Being a Faresha is complicated. I can't ride my dragon just because the Court would rise up in protest against all dragons everywhere if one little accident happens."

We reached the stables, a huge structure Kahmel had installed to be part of the castle shortly after the war ended. He grabbed some mandatory earpieces from where they were held in a shelf to the side —so the dragon's roars wouldn't leave us deaf—then, to open the doors, he pressed his thumb to the fingerprint scanner and gestured for me to go in before him as he handed me my earpieces.

"I'm not talking about for the sake of the Court. I'm talking about for the sake of your safety. You're my wife, and I don't want you to get hurt."

It wasn't a serious comment, but Kahmel's words worried me.

He really didn't care anymore about the Court.

"Come on, Jashi, you wouldn't want Huntress sitting around here all alone, feeling neglected," Kahmel said, a smile crawling up his face as he approached his dragon's stable.

"If she does, it's your own fault," I quipped, taking me from my previous concerns as I slipped in my ear protectors.

The dragon whipped her head up as if she knew we were talking about her. The stable wasn't like a horse's stable, with wood doors to hold the animals back. These were dragons. Huntress rushed up toward us until she hit the force field that created the barrier between us. Her stall was more like the size of a small house, with vaulted ceilings that gave her room to float up a little when she got antsy. Being a Wingless, she didn't exactly flap up into the air, but she still appreciated the space to set flight.

Kahmel put his earpieces in. "You know that's not fair. I'd spend much more time riding her if I had the chance." He took my hand and flipped up his sunglasses, revealing his pleading tangerine eyes underneath. "I'm sure she'd appreciate it if you spent a little more time with her in my place."

I snatched my hand away from him, turning away and pressing on the button to release the force field, then walked toward the dragon. I was being baited into forgetting our disagreement. And it was working. Rather than let him win, I changed the subject. "If we have to take your dragon, I at least get to take the reins."

"Are you sure you're ready for that? You haven't gone much farther than a few circles around the palace so far."

I tilted up my chin. "I can do it."

He shrugged. "Fine by me." Then he stroked Huntress behind the ear, earning an eager roar in response. She kneeled so we could climb her.

I swung myself over, a little uneasy on the landing, but then again, it had only been a few months since I started riding. Kahmel said I was a quick learner, but I couldn't tell if it was true or if he was just so eager about me warming up to dragons, he would have said anything.

Kahmel climbed on behind me, slipping his hands around my waist. He took me by surprise as he leaned in behind my ear, his breath hot as he spoke. "We're going to go talk to the others. There's something we need to discuss."

Oh. It was just about the rebels.

I leaned forward and took Huntress by her whiskers, shaking off the initial reaction of bristling when he got close. I flicked Huntress's whiskers, then lurched as she shot into the air.

A quick tap to my watch activated the ceiling, sunlight breaking through the crack as it opened.

Huntress let out another roar that made me glad for the earpieces. It'd been weeks since Kahmel was probably last able to ride her, so no wonder she was anxious. Guilt gnawed at me as I considered Kahmel's request to spend time with her when he couldn't. I supposed it wouldn't hurt anything, despite it being a ploy to keep me from riding my more wily, untamed dragon.

Still didn't change the fact that Huntress needed to be taken out occasionally by someone who cared. And the stable hands certainly didn't care much at all. Everyone in the palace only obeyed Kahmel out of a sense of duty rather than respect.

And now, that applied to me, too.

Huntress rocketed into the air above the palace, wind rushing through my hair and undoubtedly sending it into Kahmel's face, but I couldn't care less. The breeze provided needed relief from the dry, hot desert air. Adrenaline rushed through my veins as the ground vaulted away from us, the city of Hashir becoming smaller in the distance. Unfortunately, the Court wouldn't budge on the opinion that dragons without ZST training couldn't enter the innermost parts of the huge city, so we could only take the dragons out toward the desert.

But there was no way we would ever allow our dragons to be electrocuted into submission, so the desert would have to do.

Now that we were in the air, I knew it was safer to talk. The walls had ears in the palace, so Kahmel and I never allowed ourselves to talk about the rebels there.

"So, what do we have to discuss with the others?" I wanted to know, calling over my shoulder so Kahmel would hear me over the wind. "Did something happen?"

"Nothing new," Kahmel called back. "We already knew we were

running out of time. Now we're at the point where we have to do something about it."

My gut twisted at that. "You mean T'shan."

Kahmel squeezed a little tighter. "Yes. But I'd rather discuss the details when we're all together."

A million other questions bubbled up, but I stowed them all away and asked, "Where will we be meeting?"

"The usual place, at the foot of the mountains."

Sighing, I tried to breathe out the unease that settled in my stomach as my mind flew to all kinds of possibilities for what could go wrong if we slipped up. T'shan was a fellow Half-Drac, and with only two months to his eighteenth birthday, we didn't have much time left to save him.

Just a few months ago, I nearly made a royal mess of everything just because Kahmel was trying to save me from the very same thing we were trying to save T'shan from. Who was to say he wouldn't do the same?

Heat rose to my palms, and I breathed out again to dissipate it, embers flying from my nostrils.

My stomach jumped into my throat as Huntress went from smooth flying toward the mountains to suddenly deciding to swan-dive. My shrill screams rivaled the roars of Huntress as she went down, her serpentine form slithering through the air as she arced downward.

"Jashi!" Kahmel shouted.

I twisted to push Huntress's whiskers into his hands. "Do something! I never should have tried this."

But to my surprise—and horror—Kahmel pushed my hands back, shaking his head. "You have to take control of her, or we're going to crash into the ground."

He said it so calmly, the same way he might have said, "It's raining, take an umbrella." If it weren't for the fact that we were hurtling toward the ground, I would have pushed him over in that moment.

With little other choice, I desperately tugged at Huntress's whiskers to try to get her to budge.

To no avail.

"Kahmel…"

"You can do it," he insisted.

With a growl of determination, I yanked at Huntress's whiskers one more time. "Come on, get up!"

As if in response to my pleading, Huntress immediately straightened, hovering over the ground and making a series of strange noises between growls and hisses.

If I didn't know any better, I'd say she was laughing.

Kahmel chuckled and patted my back. "See? I knew you could do it. Huntress is just having a little fun with you; she does it to me all the time."

"And you freaked out over me riding Comet every once in a while." I shuddered, trying to steady the shaking in my hands.

"One, you never ride Comet for more than a couple minutes at a time," Kahmel objected. "Going out farther distances is the real test because that's when they get bored. And two, so you admit you rode Comet."

"How much farther is our meeting place?"

"Should be just up ahead."

Looking up, I realized he was right. The area of the mountains was starting to look familiar. I tugged on Huntress's whiskers until she began her descent, cautious of another sudden skydive. But Huntress did no such thing; rather, she lowered peacefully to the ground.

The desert expanded on either side of us, dunes coming up in soft peaks in the distance. The Dharian Mountains loomed overhead, the natural split between the desert and the forest of K'sundi. Our meeting point was at the mouth of a cave in the mountain, about ten minutes away from the palace and facing away from the main city. The perfect location for secret meetings.

Huntress landed on the ground with another excited snarl as

though she were quite satisfied with herself. Sighing, I released her whiskers and dismounted.

"Crazy dragon," I muttered as I started walking toward the entrance to the cave.

"Aren't you forgetting something?" I heard Kahmel dropping down from his dragon behind me.

"No...?"

He came to walk beside me. "And I suppose you know someplace we can get another dragon if she flies off."

I stopped short, shooting him a look. "You could have just said I forgot to tell her to stay put." Running back, I saw that Huntress was already about to take advantage of my folly, crouching down and readying herself to take to the skies again.

"*Hat sud!*"

Instantly, she snapped to attention, then curled up into herself, tucking her head into her arm. Her escape attempt was foiled.

I sighed. "Why are dragons so much trouble, anyway?"

Behind me, Kahmel laughed. "Because otherwise, they wouldn't be dragons. Your pronunciation of dragon command words is getting better, by the way."

I nodded. He was right. Huntress didn't just flat out ignore me like Comet had many times before when I tried simple commands. *Hat sud* was used to keep the dragon in one place, but there were many other instructions I could issue. To breathe fire, to take flight, even to find someone. Comet rarely understood when I tried any of them, so I typically just took him flying and decided to leave command word practice to my dragon training days with Kahmel or Rand.

Kahmel pointed to a white Draconian perched outside of the mouth of the cave, right next to three flyers. "Looks like the others are here already."

"Good. We won't have to wait to get things started. You weren't kidding about dinner, were you? It wasn't just code for us to meet?"

"Arusi brought barbecue."

Music to my ears.

The cave yawned open before us, darkening as we went in deeper, but Kahmel solved the problem. A flame lit across his palm, throwing reddish light across his face and illuminating our path.

Before long, the end of the tunnel got brighter, and we could hear voices.

"How much longer are we going to have to wait for them?" came Asan's voice.

"Shh," said Rand. "I think that's them."

When we turned the corner, there was no longer a need for Kahmel's fire, so he clenched his fist to extinguish it.

This was one of the rebel's hideouts, so lighting was already arranged with crude lightbulbs strung up along the walls. A fire burned in the middle of Kahmel's most trusted agents, Rand, Arusi, Khes, and Asan.

"There they are!" Khes's deep voice bellowed through the caves.

Arusi was turning over some meats that were roasting on a wire rack over the fire. When Kahmel said she brought barbecue, he wasn't kidding. The savory smells wafted through the air.

She smiled. "Welcome, Your Majesties."

Kahmel's twin threw his head back as he watched the two of us enter the room. "Took you long enough."

"Sorry," Kahmel apologized as he took a seat around the fire, "the Court held us up in meetings all morning. We just barely got away."

Asan chuckled. "I hope you didn't say anything stupid to get out of it. I'm tired of cleaning up after your political mess-ups."

I enjoyed the atmosphere of ease here, even though our gathering was for serious reasons. They always found a way to enjoy themselves—and each other's company—in the middle of it all, and I loved that about them. They were my friends as much as they were Kahmel's now. It was nice being away from the pressures of the palace and among people who understood me. They knew about my fire abilities, and that fact alone was freeing and comfortable in a way I was never able to explore all my life.

"Forget about that." Kahmel accepted a plate full of grilled meat and skewered vegetables from Arusi as I sat down next to him. "I had a reason for calling you all here."

I deflated a little. Some part of me hoped that hearing some words of caution from his PR manager and close rebel soldier would snap him out of...whatever mood he'd been in.

But no.

"Are you okay, Jashi?" Kahmel stirred me from my thoughts, drawing the attention of the other four around the fire.

I supposed my worries were a little more obvious than I wanted. "I'm fine, just hungry," I grumbled.

Arusi pulled off more meat and vegetables from her makeshift grill and put it on a plate, pushing it to me. "Then eat up; we have plenty."

I accepted the food and fork I was offered and ate glumly as Rand leaned forward.

"So, what's this about, Kahmel?"

"It's about T'shan."

The circle grew quiet as we all knew what it meant. We were running out of time, and we needed to move forward, whether T'shan was ready or not.

"From what you've told me," Kahmel continued, "he's been doing well in the dragon-riding lessons, right, Rand?"

The twin nodded. "Absolutely. The kid's a natural at it."

It was true. T'shan was much better at dragon-riding than I was, along with his friends Jemmorah, Ashed, and Kent. We all learned in the same "class" together, with either Rand or Kahmel as the teacher. Rand most days, since Kahmel rarely had time.

But then again, T'shan had more practice than me since he trained directly under Kahmel during the last few weeks of the war.

Kahmel sighed. "We only have two months until he turns eighteen, and we have another problem."

"Problem?" Arusi asked, frowning.

Asan shifted his lanky body, pointing to Kahmel and me. "These two are leaving the country soon, and we'd rather tell T'shan what he needs to know while they're still here. He's more familiar with them; it'll be better coming from one of them."

I held up my hands to stop the conversation. "Wait, back up. This is the first I'm hearing this. Leaving the country?"

"That's because we only just found out where we need to go," said Kahmel.

At first, I didn't understand what Kahmel was talking about, and then it dawned on me. "We know where the other Dragon Kings are?" I said in a whisper, not used to Kahmel talking about it anywhere. He didn't even bring it up at the rebel meetings he conducted. Only him, Nana, me, and the other four present were allowed to know about it. But no one outside of us was ready for it, either. Even with all the dedication the rebels had toward a better Hemorah, what the Dragon King Aithel told us in his realm was a lot even for us to handle.

There were three more Dragon Kings we had to convince to help us in our fight to free Hemorah of the Equalizers. Kahmel and his men were spending every waking second researching on where the others could be, though the rebels outside of the five of us only knew to look for certain keywords in ancient books and artifacts around K'sundi.

Khes grinned. "We hit a gold mine of information even the Zendaalans couldn't have known existed."

My brow furrowed in confusion. "Where could that be?"

"New K'sundi," Kahmel answered, grinning.

Suddenly, it all made sense. The area that used to be Omani before the war hadn't been cleared so heavily of old information as it had in K'sundi during the Equalization. K'sundi's punishment for being the nation of "savages." Their excuse was they didn't want us to ever go back to those old ways of being, so our records and artifacts, other than antiques cherished by the wealthy, were purged more than that of other countries. Except for the written word, which was the only resource we really had left for information.

"You found new information?" I asked, perking up. It had been starting to feel like we'd never figure out where the other Dragon Kings were.

"We did." Khes leaned forward like it was a secret. "Near the caves you and Kahmel explored."

"And what did you find?"

Khes opened his mouth to answer, but Kahmel cut him off. "We'll get into that another time. The main thing is, T'shan is running out of time, and so are we. We have to get moving on the Dragon Kings now that we have the information we've been looking for."

I'd noticed the cover-up, but I decided not to question it, pushing my food around with my fork. By now, I was used to the familiar feeling of Kahmel hiding something from me. "So, what do we do?"

"*You're* going to talk to him," Arusi said. "And tell him everything."

I raised my eyebrow. "Everything?"

Asan nodded. "Well, everything except about the Dragon Kings, but that goes without saying."

I huffed. "Why do I have to do it? He's closer to Rand and Kahmel."

"But he sees you as an equal," Arusi chimed in. "And you know how he'll feel, trying to take it all in all at once. Your own transition wasn't more than a couple months ago."

I put another piece of meat in my mouth to bite down my doubts. I understood their point, but I wasn't sure if I was the right person to handle this kind of thing. I was going to flip T'shan's world upside down. Tell him he had to join the rebels for his own safety. Possibly smuggle him away to hide him from the eye of those that would insist upon his eighteenth-birthday blood test. He wouldn't be able to tell his friends or anyone else for that matter.

As if reading my mind, Kahmel added, "If things don't go as planned, I have a back-up plan. But you won't like it."

"Which is?"

A hardness shadowed his features, the kind that unnerved me. "T'shan's safety comes before anything else. We'll be able to protect him much better if he is solely in our care. Like if he was incarcerated."

I blinked, but I knew Kahmel wasn't kidding. He could pull all kinds of strings both as Faresh and as the leader of the rebel group. It wasn't like getting rid of his family members or Court members, who were too high up and important to simply dispose of. T'shan was a regular citizen. If Kahmel wanted it done, it would be done.

I clenched my fists. If I didn't like his solution, I'd just have to make sure it wouldn't be necessary. "All right then. I'll convince him somehow."

Rand slapped his hands together, startling me out of my thoughts. "Well, now that that's out of the way, let's have some of those cookies Arusi made."

Arusi narrowed her eyes at him. "How did you know I brought some?"

Kahmel rolled his eyes as his twin winced. "Well..."

"How many did you eat?" she demanded.

"Who said I ate any?"

Khes laughed and then wrapped a thick arm around Rand's neck and shoulders. "You better have left some. I'm a big man with a big appetite." He squeezed so Rand gagged a little. "Now, how many did you eat?"

I laughed at the display, forgetting my worries for a minute while Rand made an idiot of himself. But Rand was good at loosening up a tense moment. With Kahmel being so busy all the time, I spent more time with Rand than his twin. But he was good company.

Somewhere between all the bickering and eating cookies, Asan scooted next to me while the conversation transitioned off to Rand and Kahmel arguing about proper dragon care.

"Daunted by your mission?"

Daunted. That was a good word for it. I hadn't realized it until Asan said it, but he was right. I had the experience of a few rebel missions under my belt now, but this was different. There was so much riding on this, and if I messed it up, the repercussions could mean someone's life. And it had my gut twisted in all kinds of knots.

I nodded, finishing off my plate and looking for one of those cookies Rand was talking about.

Seeming to know what I was looking for, Asan offered me one.

Grilled meat, cookies—this was why I loved Kahmel's friends.

"Look, you're still a new member of the rebellion, and we all start off a little rocky," Asan assured me, patting me on the back. "But you don't become one by accident. You have all of our confidence, and for good reason."

I smiled, accepting the cookie and the advice. "Thanks."

He returned the smile and chuckled. "You should feel sorrier for me having to deal with that guy all day." He gestured to Kahmel, who was rolling his eyes at something Rand said. "It's like he doesn't even care about the political headaches he causes these days."

At that, I dropped my gaze.

That's because he doesn't.

TRUST

The ride back to the palace was awkwardly quiet between Kahmel and me. He took the reins this time, as I wasn't in the mood to deal with Huntress's antics.

Besides, by the time we left the cave, it was a lot darker than any of us expected. I trusted Kahmel to conduct us better in the dark than me. I wasn't sure how he did it; he didn't use any fancy gear, he just... knew where he was going somehow.

I had my arms wrapped tightly around Kahmel's waist, watching the desert drift by us as Huntress flew at a lazy pace that let us admire the starry expanse that covered us.

I watched with more than a little envy at how naturally he carried himself with his dragon. "I don't know how you feel comfortable steering Huntress after dark. You can't see anything; she could crash into anything she wanted to."

"I know," Kahmel answered, the wind throwing the curls in his hair to the side. His hair had gotten longer, and I kind of liked it this way better than when he was cutting it closer. "And a couple months ago, I would have agreed with you. But I choose to trust Huntress now. And that's a big part of dragon-riding, Jashi. You're somewhat at the mercy of the beast at times, especially after dusk when the dragon can see much better than you ever could. But it has to come to a point where you trust it enough to believe it won't take that opportunity anymore. I can understand that you and Huntress aren't at that point yet, but I know her now."

The dragon purred as Kahmel scratched her behind the ears.

"Do you trust me?" I blurted without thinking.

He squeezed my hand, glancing back at me before turning back to the desert. "I always have."

I bit my lip as my cheeks warmed. A few beats elapsed before I steeled myself enough to say, "But I've betrayed your trust once before."

"Like I've told you before, Jashi," Kahmel said as he guided Huntress to turn toward the palace. Now that the night lights were on, it practically glowed. "That wasn't your fault."

"I know." I knew that was what he *said*. But that didn't make it true.

I looked up at the skies, feeling the cold desert air pull all around us, but Kahmel's warmth seemed to banish the chill.

I didn't know why I wanted to know now, of all times, but I couldn't hold it in anymore. "If that's true..." I took a deep breath and forced the rest out. "Then why are you always hiding things from me? Are...are you afraid I'll betray you again?"

Kahmel's voice softened. "No, that's not it at all." He sighed, breaking Huntress off from her course toward the palace and directing her to the air directly above it. "*Codis*," he told her.

Instantly, she started circling the palace like a serpentine vulture, unflinching from her circuit.

I had to learn more command words.

Kahmel shifted his position on the dragon to face me, taking my hands in his. He pursed his lips. "I'm sorry I have to keep things from you, b—"

"But it's for my own good," we finished at the same time, and he winced. I rolled my eyes. "Mine or yours? You say you trust me, but you never tell me anything! You treat me like a child." I tilted my head up. "I may be five years younger, but you don't have to coddle me."

He hesitated, and I looked away, gazing at the palace beneath us. I pursed my lips. "Then you don't trust me," I concluded.

I knew all that talk about everything that happened last year meaning nothing to him was a bunch of baloney. Whether he wanted to admit it or not, he had to have been hurt by it all. I told his enemies about his every movement every day for weeks. And he expected me to believe he just didn't care about all of that?

"We found out how to reach the other Dragon Kings," Kahmel said all of a sudden. "More or less."

I cocked an eyebrow at him. "Yeah, I know that. We just came back from talking about it with the others."

"One is in the country of Gheres," he went on. "But what we found is a little hard to decipher on what it means for the other two."

This was what he was keeping Khes from saying earlier. I cocked my head. "But...?"

He scratched the back of his head. "It's like what happened last year when we were looking for the entrance to Aithel's realm. We were searching fruitlessly in K'sundi because the maps that existed for K'sundi at the time are now outdated. We should have been looking in Omani because part of it used to be K'sundi."

"So, you're not sure which country you should be looking in?"

"Something like that, yes. For one of them, we're not sure if the entrance to the dragon realm is in current-day Endir or Vadesh. Both countries were named the same a couple hundred years ago until they split up in the Great Peace Agreement that happened between them in the last century."

I drew breath through my teeth. If one of the Kings presided in Vadesh, I wasn't sure how we'd get to his or her realm. Vadesh was just pronounced a rebel country last year.

Kahmel nodded, reading my reaction. "Our sentiments exactly. And the last one is just strange." He closed his eyes as if he was reading lines from behind his eyelids. "*The bellowing one that trembles from wayward, send a message to him forthwith.*" That's from a letter from a K'sundii Faresh to his subjects during a hunger crisis in the Crimson Age."

Once he opened his eyes, he must have noticed the glazed look in mine as he started to go into history and ages. I hated the ages of K'sundi. They were so confusing. The Azure Age, the Crimson Age, the Opaline Age, the Age of Knowledge, they all blended together to me, and I couldn't for the life of me remember what order they were in. All I remembered was when the eras all became standardized for all countries, in the Age of Equalization.

Which was why I failed history many times in school.

"What matters is," Kahmel said, breathing out, "we've found a lot of vague mentions of a 'wayward' dragon, and if a Faresh was requesting that they seek it out, it had to have been a Dragon King. All this time, we thought there was only one, so we got passages like this one confused. Now we think one of two things. One, 'wayward' could mean north, like somewhere in a cold northern country. At the time, the northern countries were still a mystery, so they could have considered them 'wayward.' The other possibility is it's on the moon."

I laughed, honestly thinking Kahmel was telling a joke until I realized he hadn't cracked a smile.

"Are you serious?"

He pursed his lips and shrugged. "As you already know, interpreting ancient texts is a finicky business, and it's hard to tell what these old stories could mean. But 'wayward' generally means something they couldn't reach easily at the time, and therefore thought it was 'wayward.' The moon is definitely a contender."

"But come on, Kahmel." I scoffed. "How would K'sundii from way back then even reach space? K'sundi wasn't capable of space travel until…" I drifted off as I tried to remember the name of the era.

"The Opaline Age," he supplied.

"Right, that."

"I know it's far-fetched." Kahmel scratched the back of his head again. "But then again, so is the existence of another realm where Dragon Kings reside. To be honest, we still don't know the full potential of the dragons of *this* realm. Especially since I haven't been able to deal with the dragon laws and handle the ZST usage in

K'sundi. Who knows what they're capable of if properly motivated? But either way, you see how confusing the third one is, so we're leaving that one for last. To give us time to better interpret it."

I did know. Just researching the term "Drake Bond" was taking me months, and every time I thought I figured it out, I'd find another book that contradicted me. I couldn't imagine how Kahmel dealt with it as a hobby.

Sighing, I shivered at the chill of the night air, rubbing my hands together as they started to feel like icicles. It was getting cold quickly, and now that I wasn't holding onto Kahmel's back, I felt it.

Kahmel grasped my hands and held them between his, diminishing the cold with his touch. "We should be getting back soon. I'm sorry; I didn't think we'd be out this late. I would have brought something warmer."

I studied him as his hard features hovered over our hands. He breathed hot air into them and rubbed them together, warming them even further. If we weren't directly over the palace, he might have used fire. It wasn't like either of us would be burned by it.

But I noticed that the longer we were away from the palace, the looser he allowed himself to be. He joked with Rand, opened up some to me. Whatever that...change...was didn't happen as much when he was away from the palace.

It wasn't like I didn't understand him; there was a lot waiting for him at home. The Court trying to get rid of him. His family lurking around. Zendaalans, too.

But of all the things he was trying to avoid at home, it was easy to wonder if I was one of them.

"I don't keep things from you because I don't trust you, Jashi," he said unexpectedly. "There's just so much going on at once, and I don't want to scare you." He looked up at me, his eyes glowing against the night like fire. "A lot happens you don't know about. Things that keep me up at night and give me nightmares. I don't want you to have to deal with that."

I swallowed as I remembered the conversation we had last year that scared me. Toward the start of the darkness that shrouded him now. "Threats from Zendaal?"

Kahmel tried to hide the expression, but I saw his eyes flicker away from mine. I was right. "Just issues you shouldn't have to worry about."

I bit my lip, searching his gaze. "All right, keep those things to yourself. But you've got to remember that you have limits, too, Kahmel. You shouldn't be shouldering all of this on your own. Most Fareshes have entire clans full of support for their reign, neighboring clan families in their favor. You have no one but Rand and the others."

He cupped his hand, hot from his breath, around my cheek and gave me a small smile. It felt good against my cold skin. "I appreciate your concern, but the fact remains that if anyone else had become Faresh, they would have come into the palace with clans full of support already. Most clans are already well connected, and if not that, they'd have the members of the Court that favored them on their side. I became Faresh by law, not by election. I have to build my relationships from the ground up. It's not that simple."

"Hm," I muttered, not quite convinced. "You know, just because you say it isn't simple doesn't make it true. Even if you did have to build relationships from scratch, you're not even doing that right now. No one knows anything about you. You're distant. And you're always on the HoloScreen arguing with someone. Maybe if people saw other sides of you, you'd have more allies than you assume."

He fell silent at that. He knew I had a point.

As silence settled between us, it seemed we both realized he still had his hand on my cheek and how close we'd gotten as the cold air pushed us together.

Kahmel cleared his throat, dropping his hand to his side. "I'll think about it. For now, let's just get home, or else we'll freeze out here."

"Agreed," I said, and he repositioned himself to ride the dragon properly, flicking her whiskers to break her from her circuit in the air and start her descent toward the stables.

DRAGON-RIDING LESSONS

I had such a good time laughing with Kahmel and the others, I almost expected him to be there, lying in the bed next to me when I woke up in the morning. But when I opened my eyes, the retractable bed he used was gone, like it usually was, and it reminded me.

Kahmel spent more time anywhere else than at home. It was the reality of being Faresh as well as one of the least-trusted men in the kingdom.

Sighing, I pulled the covers from my bed, glad to have them off since the chill of the night had long worn off and the heat of the afternoon was already settling in. Looking at the clock on my nightstand confirmed that it was almost noon.

I bit my lip. Not too long ago, waking up at almost noon meant I was woefully unemployed. But now, I woke up like this every day, living...well, like a queen. I felt undeserving, but when it was Kahmel who chose me, not the other way around, it was hard to say it was my fault. This was Kahmel's doing. Still, I couldn't help but think of Lora, who was still working her butt off to cover college payments and keep her grades up to finish her degree.

I'd done nothing to get here, but we both grew up having it rough. Didn't that make me a cheater of some sort?

Getting up, I put those guilty thoughts behind me, going into my closet to pick out a robe to go about the palace in.

I knew if she were here, she'd admonish me for having those

thoughts. Growing up in an orphanage, we both knew and had seen how good fortune tended to make the receiver feel bad for it. Like they shouldn't have it when others were still suffering.

Survivor's guilt, of a kind.

The Lora in my head told me to be grateful for what I had and not to feel bad about enjoying it.

I finished getting dressed, clad in bronze robes that billowed around me, silver bracelets clanging gently as I walked, my fingers decked with rings.

Even though Lora was too busy to have a conversation with these days, finals and all, imaginary Lora's advice made me feel better.

Besides, it wasn't like this blessing didn't come with a curse of its own.

I walked into the dining hall for breakfast. As usual, Kahmel wasn't there. But Rand was, munching on a slice of toast with an avocado spread on top.

My footsteps echoed in the empty halls as I sat next to him.

Rand looked up from the screen glowing in front of him from his eWatch. "Oh, good morning, Jashi," he said, flashing a smile.

Where Kahmel always wore tinted glasses to hide his bright orange eyes, Rand had deep brown ones that he took no steps to conceal. Not that he should—he actually had nice eyes. Especially since he smiled a lot more than Kahmel, which made them twinkle.

Casting my eyes down, I decided to focus on my plate. Servants came to my side on cue, putting down hot platters of sausage and eggs.

"Good morning, Your Majesty," greeted one as he poured a cup of orange juice at my side. He was one of the few servants brave enough to actually greet me when he was in my presence. I made sure to remember his name.

"Thank you, Armeen," I said, being extra friendly in appreciation. He nodded with a chipper grin at the acknowledgment and backed away along with the others.

I stabbed my fork into the sausage and nibbled at it.

Rand poked my cheek. "Come on, what's with the glum face?"

Rolling my eyes, I cracked a small smile at him, watching him pout, his expression ridiculous enough to make me laugh. "Just... thinking." *About how I'm a wife, but not really. And a Faresha, but just barely. And married to a Faresh, but he's never here. So he sends his brother.*

But none of those thoughts were appropriate breakfast conversation. Or for any conversation. Ever. I barely felt comfortable enough to talk to Kahmel about it, and he was my "husband." Much less Rand.

Even if he was fun to be around.

"I know what'll cheer you up," Rand insisted.

I raised an eyebrow, taking another bite of sausage. "Oh?"

"I bet you forgot today is dragon-riding lessons day."

I sat up straight. "I did!" I grinned. "I get to ride Comet today!"

Rand scoffed, then said in a lower voice, "Not like you don't every other day, anyway." He continued munching on his toast and scrolling through his projected screen.

"That reminds me," I hissed, slapping his arm. "Did you tell Kahmel about me taking Comet out for rides?"

Rand laughed. "No, but you're not exactly the queen of stealth. Let's not forget you weren't a good spy either," he added even more quietly.

I smacked his arm again and scowled. But he had a point. "Serious, Rand, then how does he know? I wait until he's busy; I'm careful to avoid all the cameras in the stables."

Rand shrugged, grimacing as he returned his attention to his screen. "I don't know if I should tell you. I already shouldn't be letting you ride Comet in the first place."

Now it was my turn to pout. "Come on, Rand. You and Kahmel do dangerous things all the time. Sneaking out to ride Comet isn't even that bad. It's no different than what you told me about when you and Kahmel seized those dragons from—"

"*Shhh,*" Rand sat straighter, looking up as if begging the heavens for guidance. "And you wonder why you didn't make a good spy," he hissed. Then he leaned in close. "You know where *most* of the cameras are. But there are tons of others in this palace you don't know about. *However*, the cameras are monitored by palace guards, and we're not sure—"

"'Which ones can be trusted,' blah blah, blah. That, I already know. Gosh, sometimes you're just like your brother."

Rand slapped his chest like I'd stabbed it. "Don't insult me like that."

I laughed. "Says his twin."

"Come on," he said, winking. "We both know I'm the better-looking one." He finished his meal and downed a cup of orange juice. "Hurry up and finish breakfast. We'll start riding in half an hour."

"Okay!" I continued eating with restored vigor as he slid his chair back and started for the door.

"I'll round up the troops. Oh, by the way." He stopped. "Don't forget."

I knew exactly what he was talking about, and it soured my mood all over again. I didn't need the reminder. I still had no idea how I was going to start my conversation with T'shan. "I know."

"Good," he said, exiting the room, leaving me to quickly finish my breakfast so I could get back to my dragon.

Maybe today we could teach him to stop trying to electrocute me.

By the time I found Rand in one of the palace gardens, the "troops" had already been rounded up. That was what he called his and Kahmel's dragon-riding trainees, though lately, Kahmel hadn't had the time to make the class, so he'd left it to Rand to carry on.

Just like everything else.

T'shan, Jemmorah, Kent, and Ashed were standing at the ready in the middle of the clearing. Behind them were the dragons Kahmel had given them, a mix of Draconians and Wingless. And there was mine, the only Elemental in the group, a neon-yellow Draconian with a rubber muzzle around his mouth. He growled at the air as I approached.

I still didn't know if that meant he was happy to see me or just the opposite.

"Glad you could join us, Your Majesty," T'shan said, smiling as he bowed, the rest of his friends also bowing in turn.

All these months, and I still hadn't gotten used to people doing that around me. I tried to look anywhere but at them.

Rand stepped in for me. "Her Majesty wouldn't miss her lessons for the world. When else would she get the opportunity to try taming her Elemental headache over there?"

I narrowed my eyes at him, severely tempted to stick out my tongue as well. But the trainees didn't need to know their Faresha was that unprofessional and petty.

Instead, I chuckled. "Right, what he said."

Kent clapped his hands and rubbed them together. "What are we learning today?"

"Today?" Rand stroked his bare chin. "Nothing. Today, we review."

The pupils groaned, but I wasn't complaining. They were already ahead of me in spades, and review days gave me the opportunity to catch up at least a little.

"Oh, good, you haven't started yet," a familiar voice purred. It made my skin crawl. Dralus came from out of the palace halls and stood on the sidelines with his arms crossed, the chrome on his skin flashing blinding light in the sun. His red eye glowered at us. "I do love watching these displays."

There was clear discomfort running through all the trainees, but Rand cleared his throat, drawing their attention away from the unwelcome spectator. "Run through your drills," he commanded.

We all turned to our dragons, not needing further instruction. My hands clenched at my sides. Dralus was always lurking in the palace, like a vulture ready to snap up the bones of the weak. As Chancellor of the Zendaalan presence in K'sundi, he had as many rights as a K'sundi royal, a fact that made my blood boil. Zendaalans had as much authority over the countries under their rule as the rightful leaders. Sometimes more.

Pushing my frustration back, I climbed onto Comet's back, securing myself into the saddle. Normally, I didn't like using them, but Kahmel wasn't wrong about Comet being unpredictable. Better safe than sorry, especially with Dralus always watching. He would leap on any excuse to have our dragons banished from the palace grounds.

My feet locked into the slots on the side of the black, curved saddle. With a press of a button, Solid Light reins appeared, connecting from his muzzle to my hands, glowing a gentle cyan color. Another "training wheel" feature that was necessary for a dragon whose mouth you didn't want to get near for fear of electrocution.

I whipped the reins, and Comet took to the sky. Jemmorah, T'shan, Kent, and Ashed did the same, their dragons roaring with excitement.

As usual, mine just made vague growls that might have been acceptance or aggravation.

I guessed I'd just have to find out.

ELECTRIC

A funny fact about dragons and me:
I was still afraid of them.

The way they radiated power and ferocity as they beat the air with their wings. The way the air tingled when they roared. The killing stare that looked like it could penetrate your very soul. I couldn't help but be amazed by it. But it also scared the hell out of me.

Every day I climbed on Comet, there was this mix, this simultaneous rush, of freedom and fear. And every minute of the ride was trying to balance on a tightrope between the two. As my hands shook as they gripped the reins, I could never tell which one it was. But when the wind clawed my hair and the ground free-fell beneath me, I knew I belonged up here. I didn't even have a reason why. It just pulsed through my veins, rushed up to my head, and I just *knew*. When my dragon roared, I wanted to roar with him, let the whole country know we staked our claim on these skies, and not even my own fears would take that away from us.

Nor could the Zendaalans.

I heard Rand's whistle blow from my earpiece, signaling our first drill.

At once, we all tugged on our reins, leading our dragons higher into the sky, straight as an arrow. As gravity tugged at my back, I knew all it would take was for Comet to lean backward by two degrees, and I'd be hurtling toward the ground.

But instead, he spread his wings like he was supposed to and dipped sideways, then flapped once to start spiraling downward.

Rand whistled again, so we began our next command.

I bit my lip as I pulled the reins and slowly leaned from side to side, my heart leaping into my chest as Comet tilted with me like a kid pretending to be an airplane. With a sigh of relief, I realized Comet might be willing to cooperate a little today.

Still couldn't trust the sneaky lizard, but it was something.

I stole a glance to admire the other, more skilled fliers around me. Kent, Ashed, Jemmorah, and T'shan. All of them guided their dragons with an elegance I could only dream of right now, hooting as they executed each command.

Meanwhile, I just didn't want to get thrown.

Then again, their dragons were already mostly trained. Mine was still getting used to being ridden. Not to mention it didn't have the most stellar temperament in the world.

Rand whistled again, and this was where it was going to get tricky because it involved command words. Of which my pronunciation was getting better, but still wasn't perfect. Especially with my nerves on end.

But dragon-riding was a game of confidence, and I couldn't allow my lack of it to hinder me now. *Even if you aren't sure of yourself, convince your dragon that you are,* I remembered Kahmel told me once, on the rare occasion he was able to teach the dragon-riding class, and I clutched those words to my chest.

Our dragons flew abreast in the air, so there was no fear of accidentally hitting one another. I shouted, *"K'mhet!"*

For half a second, I thought Comet would do little more than yawn, but he responded with a roar and what would have been a huge arc of lightning flying from his mouth, though the effect was dampened by his muzzle. For the moment, the command was just for practice, not execution. Even *with* his muzzle, little blue arcs of light buzzed through the cracks like electrical hairs coming out of his mouth.

The air warmed even hotter than it already was as pillars of fire shot from the mouths of the other dragons in unison.

Another whistle, and this time we separated. *"Hos vihenal,"* I struggled to pronounce. The dragon, as I expected, didn't recognize it and kept flying straight.

"Hos vihenal!"

Comet may have yawned, but it was hard to tell with his muzzle on.

I groaned. "Come on, Comet, you know I'm no good at these command words. You know what I'm trying to say. Land!"

Comet shuddered, and I frowned. He sometimes did that when we were flying at certain angles against strong wind, but it wasn't even windy today.

Then I realized.

"No, no, no, please don't—"

Comet had no regard for my pleadings. He shuddered again, then free-fell. My stomach lurched into my throat as we spiraled toward the ground, Rand shouting something in my earpiece, but I didn't have the mind to understand what he was saying. Wind rushed in my ears and whipped around my face. I pulled desperately at the reins, but Comet was indifferent. His body rumbled, and if I didn't know any better, I'd say he was chuckling.

"Jashi, abort!" Rand repeated.

I sighed, really wishing I could have gotten Comet to straighten before we hit the palace garden grounds. But Rand was right. Hitting a button to unlock my feet from the saddle, I stood and jumped from Comet's back, activating a paraglider that extended from the pack on my back. Arm handles extended from either side to give me the ability to steer, and I watched as Comet plummeted to the ground in a great plume of dust.

"Dang it, Comet," I mumbled. There went his streak of days without accident.

"Are you all right, Jashi?" came Rand's voice.

"I'm fine, I'm fine."

Jemmorah's voice came next. "Should we stop the routine?"

"Go on without me," I said before Rand could object. One of the actual perks of being Faresha: what I said went. I didn't want anyone's sympathies right now. Or to hold anyone else back from their practice, for that matter.

Rand said, "All right, I'm on my way, Jashi. Steer yourself away from Comet in the mean—"

"Yeah, yeah, yeah, I know procedure," I grumbled.

Just as I started directing my glider for the castle, Comet's grumbling and jerking caught my attention. My mouth fell open as I noticed what he was clawing at. The pieces of his muzzling lay at his feet, and a hungry look shone in his eye as he set his gaze on me.

"Uh, Rand?"

"What's going on, Jashi?"

Before I could respond, Comet leaped back into the air, bounding straight for me. I only had time to scream before I felt a tug at one wing of my glider and then the jerking that followed as I was towed to the ground. We landed with a thud. I crashed hard on my arms and side, my glider well beyond broken.

Comet loomed above me, his yellow form eclipsing the sun, mouth sparking with electricity.

Then a stream of light wrapped around his neck and yanked him back, earning a yelp from the dragon.

"Jashi, get away!" Rand roared. He was digging his heels into the ground just to keep the dragon back with his laser whip wound around the dragon's neck. Guards were swarming in from all sides. I caught Dralus looking on. It was clear from his expression that he'd never let us live this down.

I struggled to my feet and had every intention of listening to Rand's advice, but looking into Comet's eyes somehow changed my mind. He was whimpering now, staring at me like he was pleading, thrashing desperately against his restraints.

I cursed, feeling like I'd gone crazy for even considering what I was about to do.

Then again, being married to Kahmel, it was bound to happen someday.

"Let him go!"

The guards froze, looking to Rand for guidance. Even he looked at me like I had lost my mind. I still wasn't sure I hadn't.

"Jashi, come on, this isn't a game."

"I know that," I snapped. "Just let him go."

He still didn't look like he believed me, but he had no choice but to nod to the guards. They took a couple steps back, though they still had their laser pistols at the ready. After a moment's hesitation, he removed his own laser whip from Comet's neck.

Comet finally stopped struggling, centering his attention on me again. I flinched as he rushed toward me but decided to hold my ground. The dragon stopped mere inches from me, his head almost as big as my body, then he lowered it to look me in the eye. Arcs of electricity flew from his mouth like glowing whiskers, though none of them touched me.

"Jashi..." Rand said, doubt obvious in his tone.

I shook my head, not taking my eyes off of Comet. "Don't interfere."

The static radiating from the dragon was making all the hairs on my body stand on end. But I took a chance and placed a hand on his snout. Comet breathed out like a sigh, his intense eyes finally closing as if in bliss.

I heard the whir of weapons powering down as the guards saw Comet was no longer volatile.

Rand came around, looking between the two of us and shaking his head. "Well, then. I suppose that settles that."

I gave a shuddering breath of relief, barely able to believe it worked.

Comet opened his eyes, finally, and nearly knocked me over as he nudged my legs with his head.

There were clicks and the whirring noises of lasers powering up ringing through the air as the guards pointed their weapons again, and instantly Comet was growling and hissing at them, the electric arcs coming from his mouth getting brighter and longer.

The dragon took a few steps in front of me, as though he was protecting *me*.

Rand wagged his head, waving the guards away. "You heard Her Majesty. She said to stand down."

"But sir..."

I cocked my head. "Or will Kahmel have to hear about this?"

That got them all to stow their weapons away completely. Seemed no one wanted to be on his bad side. Standing on the sidelines, Dralus looked like he'd eaten a lemon. I wasn't sure what kind of repercussions my actions today would have, but I relished in the small victory.

Once the weapons were out of the way, Comet threw one more hiss at the guards and then went back to my side, this time successfully throwing me to the ground with another nudge. "What the hell does he want?" I asked, hoping Rand was more used to this than I was. I'd never seen Comet act like this before.

Rand grimaced. "That, uh, means he wants to ride again. I think he finally likes you."

I glanced at the eager yellow dragon and narrowed my eyes as he nudged my legs again. "Then what was all that throwing-me business about?"

"I think that was his attempt at playing."

Remembering my ride with Huntress the night before, I realized Rand might be right. "I think we need to set some ground rules as to what 'playing' is," I said, stroking Comet's nose and hoping that would abate him for the moment. Because I *definitely* didn't feel like riding again right now.

"Look at it this way," Rand offered. "I think you earned some major respect just now. I mean, you stared down an Elemental dragon—that's huge!"

My cheeks warmed at the compliment, and I had to admit, I was surprised at myself.

"Um, sir?" T'shan was coming forward with a spare muzzle. The other dragon riders were beside him, cautiously looking in on what was going on. They'd definitely broken off from their routines when they heard all the raucous.

Comet started hissing at him immediately, and I held up a hand to stop him, making T'shan freeze in his place. I stroked Comet to calm him down, which only worked to a degree. Electricity wasn't flying from his mouth, but my hair was standing up, and if looks could kill...

"I don't think he likes being muzzled," I said

Rand sighed. "The Court is going to love that," he mumbled. He waved the guards away. "Anyway, there's nothing left to see here, thanks, men. We'll handle it. Come on, Jashi. You and Comet have had enough excitement for today. Let's have Comet taken back to his stable, and you can watch the other trainees while you practice the pronunciation of command words."

I nodded and followed after him, Comet close at my heels without needing instruction.

Did my confronting him really change his attitude toward me so drastically? Feeling like I'd earned that respect made me puff out my chest a little.

Perhaps I wasn't so helpless with my dragon after all.

Looking at Dralus, though, I knew Rand was right. Comet was a dangerous dragon that nearly killed me and now refused to be muzzled.

The Court wasn't going to be pleased.

PROMOTIONS

"*Hat sud, k'mhet, At mure, shog asun...*" I muttered what I had written on my practice sheet. Rand had given me new words to practice while the others continued flying, in addition to correcting my pronunciation on the ones I already knew. I'd been repeating them to myself and practicing since then, at first sitting in a chair in the middle of the garden and then later pacing the area.

Dralus had left shortly after the incident with Comet, but I wasn't convinced that was a good thing.

I didn't notice T'shan in front of me until I bumped right into him.

We both stumbled, T'shan jumping back like he'd been lit on fire and bowing deeply right afterward. His friends were by his side, too, standing like they didn't quite know how to react. They had their riding gear in their hands since they must have just finished up training.

"It's okay," I said quickly. "It was my mistake for not looking where I was going. I'm sorry, T'shan."

Only then did T'shan look up from his bow, albeit timidly. His orange eyes seemed to almost glow. "Is Your Majesty all right?"

Laughing, I waved him off. "I think I'll be fine. So how was dragon-riding?"

"Nothing in comparison to what you did," Kent said, grinning. The neckline of his shirt was drenched in sweat as drips streaked from his wide head. He held his riding gear flush against a broad chest, occasionally wiping moisture from the top of his head, which was close-shaven and glistening with it. "That was amazing, Your Grace."

"Oh, stop," I said, averting my gaze to the ground.

"Please, don't be modest, Your Majesty," Ashed said, with his usual calm demeanor. "What you did took a lot of bravery. That's not to be underestimated."

"The kid is right." Rand came up behind them, patting Kent on the back as he did. "What you did took guts, Jashi. You should be proud of yourself."

I smiled at him, feeling sheepish. "Thank you."

He smiled back. "No problem. You deserve it." Turning to the rest of them, he added, "Good work today, everyone. I'll be telling Kahmel you're all doing well. Very well. He'll be pleased."

Too bad he's never here to see that for himself, I thought.

"Go put your gear up in the stables, and you're free to do as you like," he finished.

T'shan, Kent, Jemmorah, and Ashed all stayed near the palace in suites with their families, now working as full-time dragon-riding trainees. We only had riding days twice a week, but the rest of the days were spent either studying old material for reference or my least favorite part—dragon care. Giving a dragon a bath was a punishment I wouldn't wish on my worst enemy.

Well, except maybe my in-laws.

The four ran for the stables, hooting. Just as I was about to join them, I felt a firm hand on my arm. Rand gave me a knowing look.

Dang it, I completely forgot about talking to T'shan with all the drama with Comet.

"Right, thanks for reminding me," I whispered to Rand. Then I jogged after the four. "Hey, T'shan! Wait up!"

T'shan turned as the others ran ahead, his orange eyes full of obvious curiosity. "What is it, Your Majesty?"

"Can I talk to you for a minute?" I came a little closer, lowering my voice a little. "In private."

He frowned but nodded. "Of course."

If anyone saw T'shan and me wandering through the garden almost aimlessly, alone, they would assume all kinds of things.

I was sure if Dralus was around, he would have a field day. But we had to talk business where prying eyes wouldn't be able to see. Kahmel had shown me all the palace's blind spots, so we could talk in private whenever necessary, so our seemingly "aimless" trek wasn't aimless at all. But if worst-case scenario, someone was looking, it would look fairly innocent. Though I did notice a few lingering stares from servants.

I laughed at something T'shan said as we made small talk on the way but sobered up when we passed a tall rose bush that perfectly blocked the palace from view.

"So, T'shan. About what I brought you here for."

The conversation had deviated so much from the reason I invited him, he probably forgot I'd mentioned it.

"Right, what is it, Your Majesty?"

I opened my mouth but realized that after the whole walk here, getting in position and preparing for this all night, I still had no idea what to say to him.

Hey, great job today. You're going to die in a few months if you don't become a rebel.

How are things? I know you can manipulate fire, and so can I. Join the rebellion.

Have you ever heard of the Half-Dracs? You're one of them!

Nothing seemed appropriate for ripping this poor kid from everything he knew and sending him plunging into the world of uncertainty I lived in every day. Sure, I was safe now that I was with Kahmel, but I still worried about everything else. The Zendaalans finally getting tired enough, Kahmel's promise to the Dragon King, not to mention all the other Half-Dracs that we now knew existed and needed rescuing as much as T'shan did.

And more than anything, I felt grossly inadequate to fill the role I was supposed to fulfill. Kahmel wanted me to train with T'shan and his friends so I could get close to him, but I felt like I'd failed that already. T'shan was always so dutiful and shy around me.

How could I explain everything and get him to let us protect him? Not only that, but convince him to go against the peace-bringers?

My mind went blank, and T'shan was staring at me for a response I couldn't provide him.

I decided to change tactics. "Kahmel is really impressed with how your training is going."

It wasn't a lie. Kahmel was very satisfied with how things were going. With T'shan and the others, too. Was it what I was supposed to talk about? No, but it made me look less ridiculous than I felt. T'shan bought it. He smiled from cheek to cheek, his orange eyes twinkling. "Did he say that?"

I nodded, scratching the back of my neck. "Oh, yeah. He thinks you're doing such a great job." I hesitated. Kahmel was going to kill me for this. "He thinks you should move on to more of a challenge."

T'shan's eyes became disks. "You mean join a dragon-recruit team?"

I grinned and hoped it didn't look like a grimace. "It wouldn't be all the time; you still have to work on your dragon-riding skills. But every once in a while, you can join the recruiters as Kahmel deems necessary."

T'shan bowed, and I bit my lip. I was going to be in *so* much trouble. But I remembered Kahmel mentioning it to Rand recently enough, and they were considering letting all of them practice being recruiters. So hopefully it wouldn't be too hard for Kahmel to make it happen to cover for me. Recruiters just went around the mountains looking for dragons and tagging them if they seemed like good riding material. If they were too rowdy, it would be too dangerous to try to tame them, so that was why recruiters were necessary to sift through the "okay" ones.

Because wild dragons still didn't get any better than "okay."

I felt like a complete coward, but right now, all I wanted was to get back to the palace.

"Thank you so much, Your Grace," T'shan said, finally coming up from his bow. "And for going out your way to tell me yourself. It's truly an honor."

"Don't mention it," I said through my teeth. *Literally.*

RAND HADN'T SAID anything to me all through dinner. There was just the cling of utensils scraping against our plates as we ate.

Kahmel was late again, so it was just us. Someone mentioned him being at a speech or something; all his reasons for being away blurred together at some point.

I just stared at my mashed potatoes, scraping peas around with a fork.

"More water, Your Majesty?" Armeen's question stirred me from wallowing in self-pity. At his encouraging smile, I mustered a faint one to match and nodded, grateful to have a friend. He filled my cup and walked away.

I wanted to accredit the silence to the servants standing around, but I knew Rand was mad at me this time. When he was mad it was hard to tell the difference between Kahmel and him. The same hard expression that looked calm from the exterior but hid a storm of anger underneath.

I bit my lip, wondering if I could speak vaguely enough for the servants not to know what was going on but still get my point across.

"Listen, about what happened earlier—"

"Let's not get into it right now."

I grimaced. No jokes? No hint of a smile, or even an annoyed sigh? I really messed up this time.

I went back to pushing my peas around. There was no easy way to get around this.

"His Majesty Faresh Kahmel and Secretary Zuwei," one of the servants introduced. I lifted my head to see Kahmel coming into the dining hall, dressed in a smart suit fit for the camera, and his sunglasses, Arusi beside him, elegant as always. A green dress hugged her short frame nicely, her hair in a bun. Kahmel took off his sash and placed it in the waiting hands of another servant.

"Sorry we're late," he apologized.

Rand and I just shifted uncomfortably, the unspoken contention hanging between us.

"Nice to see you all, too," Kahmel remarked at the silence as he and Arusi sat down.

Rand looked up at him and sighed, shaking his head before going back to his food.

Arusi's eyes drifted between the two of us. "What happened?"

I cleared my throat, my eyes on my mashed potatoes as I made swirls with my fork. "Well, I talked to T'shan like you asked, Kahmel."

Kahmel's forehead twitched, and I knew he was wondering why I was mentioning this in front of the servants. But I continued before he could respond.

"I told him about his promotion." I smiled like I was reliving the moment I told T'shan, partially for the servants' benefit and partially hoping a cute smile would make Kahmel more lenient. "He's so excited about joining the dragon recruiters. I'm so glad you decided to let him."

Kahmel looked to Rand, his confusion neatly hidden behind his glasses.

Rand nodded, his lips pressed into a tight smile. "T'shan's been so ecstatic, he practically told the whole palace." Glaring at me, he added, "Now he's wondering when his first outing's going to be."

I didn't meet Rand's gaze; instead, I turned back to my food and reluctantly pushed some potatoes into my mouth.

Arusi nodded in understanding. "Well...a new recruiter. I'm happy for him."

"Obviously," I said, smiling at Kahmel again, though, at this point, I just wanted to cry. My first and only mission as a rebel and I'd already messed things up. "He's happy, but I think you should talk to him yourself. He really needs to hear the words of praise from you."

Please fix this, I mentally begged.

"I...see," Kahmel said, his expression hard to read.

In other words, mad.

Rand sighed, turning to his twin. "And then there was the incident with Comet."

Kahmel's eyebrows raised in concern, and Rand told him everything that happened. I just wanted to sink into the floor. I'd made a mess of everything.

I was hoping Kahmel would give me a second chance with T'shan. I was going to tell him. With his birthday coming up, I had to.

But then again, Kahmel may not give me that chance. I chickened out this time—what reason did he have to believe I wouldn't do it a second time?

Dinner soon ended, and, thankfully, Arusi was going to stay at the palace a while, so she retired to her room. She always had good advice; maybe she could help me now.

Rand went toward his room, and as I stood from the table, I pretended to remember something. "Oh, Kahmel, go on without me. I wanted to tell Arusi something."

"Actually, I wanted to talk to you. Would you mind putting it off until tomorrow?"

I turned to see Rand was already too far down the hall to rescue me. And probably too upset with me as well. "All right, I'm coming," I relented, following him down the hall to our room.

FORMING BRIDGES

I took as long as I possibly could to change into my pajamas in the closet. With so many layers of robes and jewelry and makeup, it was easy to pretend. Kahmel even knocked once, and I assured him I was coming.

And then continued to pull my nightgown on very slowly.

However, I soon ran out of things to do in the closet and eventually had to come out.

My mission should have involved procrastinating. I was a professional at that.

Peeking out the door, I saw Kahmel sitting on the edge of his bed, looking at something on his eWatch. Work-related, probably.

I swung the door open carefully, treading lightly to my bed.

Kahmel turned to me and switched his screen off. "Listen, Jashi—"

"I'm sorry! I panicked, okay?" I cut him off. "It won't happen again, I promise. I'll tell him next time we have a dragon-riding lesson together. I just...I'd already told him I wanted to talk, and I was nervous and needed a reason to bail, and since I knew you and Rand were talking about it anyway, I figured—"

Kahmel sat on my bed. "Jashi, calm down, it's okay."

I turned away, my head down. "No, it's not. You gave me a simple task, and I messed up. I still have no idea what to say to him." I breathed out. This was an issue much bigger than my need for validation. Priorities needed to come first. "I'd understand if you wanted someone else to do it."

Kahmel laughed, surprising me. "No."

Sometimes this man infuriated me. "What do you mean, 'no'?"

He got up and slid under the covers of his own bed. "Like you said, it's a simple task. You'll get to it eventually." Laughing again, he added, "Just try not to give T'shan too many more promotions; we don't have too many positions left to give him."

I frowned. What just happened here?

I got up and marched to his bed, plopping myself down beside a surprised Kahmel. "So, you're going to let him keep the position?"

Kahmel spread his hands to either side. "I don't have much choice, do I?"

"I suppose not. But...so you're not mad?"

He put a hand through his hair. "I know that even though this is a simple task, a lot is riding on it. And you're nervous, which is understandable. So it's okay."

I could barely believe I was being let off so easily. "Okay," I said in a small voice.

"Besides, it's not like T'shan is undeserving of the position. He's got a natural skill for riding. The others, too. You might have to tell them they've all got the job. And you're improving fast, too. What happened with Comet proves that. I think you've finally earned your dragon's respect, which is a huge part of training him to be ridden. Your training is always twice as hard because you're breaking in a new dragon and learning at the same time, but look at how far you've come."

My cheeks warmed at such high praise. "Thanks."

"Listen, I've been thinking. Schools should be out soon for winter break, right?"

Frowning at the change in subject, I had to think about it for a second. "Yeah, I think so."

"Well, we've got about a month before we have to go abroad, you and me. Why don't you invite your friend Lora to the palace for her vacation, if she can come?"

My mouth dropped open. "Are you kidding? You wouldn't be able to stop her!" I laughed. "The issue would be getting her to leave."

He smiled, though I could tell it was a tired one. "Good. Tell her to come whenever she's available."

"But why? What made you think of her?"

"Palace life," he said, yawning. "It's bound to make anyone feel out of sorts when you don't have a sense of familiarity. And I know you've made friends with us, but you've got to be lonely for what you're used to."

I had to admit he was right. The idea of Lora coming for a few weeks at the palace made the stress of talking to T'shan dissipate a little.

I hated when Kahmel was right.

"If that's all, Jashi." He blinked slowly. "Would you mind going to your bed so I can sleep?"

I smirked. "I'm supposed to be your wife; you'd think you'd ask for the opposite."

He pulled his covers further up his shoulder and closed his eyes with a smile on his lips. "You can stay if you like; you'd get no complaints from me. I'm tired of getting an extra bed out every night, anyway."

Getting out of his bed, I tsked. "Yeah, you'd better go to sleep. Maybe it can happen in your dreams."

"You're the one that offered."

"I did not!"

"Goodnight, Jashi."

I climbed into bed and tucked myself in, surprised at how much better I felt about everything already. I could just imagine all the things Lora and I could get up to if she came. Kahmel may regret his decision to invite her in the end.

Looking over at Kahmel, I knew he was asleep by the way his chest rose and fell.

I pulled a silk cap over my hair and sank into my pillow.

"Night, Kahmel."

RAND WAS WAITING for me as I came down to breakfast that morning. He looked up from his eWatch screen and swiped it away.

I sat down beside him. "Rand."

He sighed. "Look, I'm sorry for getting so mad at you yesterday. I talked to Kahmel, and he's right. I should cut you some slack, especially considering everything. You're far from home, and everything is still new. So, I apologize," he concluded.

I pursed my lips like I had to consider it. But truth be told, I was still shocked Kahmel let me off. And that he told his brother to get over it, too.

Cocking my head, I let a sly smile crawl up my lips. "All right, I suppose I can let it slide this once." I pulled a piece of toast onto my plate. "I can't stay mad at you, anyway. You're the nice twin."

Rand chuckled, almost nervously. "Yeah, but you don't want to say that around Kahmel too loud; he may get the wrong idea."

"What? You're the one always saying you're the handsome twin; why get mad when I agree?" I asked coyly, deciding to make him squirm as a small revenge. Kahmel and I weren't in a relationship in the real sense. Rand knew that, and I knew that. And who knew? Maybe if given the option, I might have chosen the other twin, anyway.

It was an entertaining thought to imagine how Kahmel would react if I voiced that opinion out loud.

Rand sipped at his orange juice innocuously, then cleared his throat. "Yeah, I guess I do. Anyway, what's on the agenda for today? Arusi and Kahmel are in a meeting right now, but it should be over soon, and she'll be available to do whatever."

"What about Kahmel?" I asked, slathering strawberry jam on my toast and taking a bite.

He shook his head. "He's got more meetings after."

"Hm, oh well." I noticed Rand squirming as I looked up at him. "I guess that just leaves us more time together." A slow moment passed before I added, "You, me, and Arusi, of course. Maybe we'll do some reading in the library. I need to practice my command words."

"Haha...yeah. Sounds good." Suddenly there was something that needed to be addressed on his eWatch, which he promptly set to work investigating.

It took everything in me not to laugh.

I finished breakfast quickly, standing and letting my robes twirl around me as I spun. Out the window, Hashir bustled from afar, cars dotting the air, the train snaking through the buildings with ease. Maybe I would put off studying. It was such a nice day, and I could spy out places to take Lora before she came.

That reminded me, I had to tell her she could come. She was going to be so excited.

Rand got up from his seat, too. "Happy to go to the library?"

I laughed. "No, I was just thinking—"

"Oh, Your Majesty." A servant came in. I was still getting used to placing everyone's faces, but I was pretty sure she didn't work at the palace. She must have been representing someone else. She bowed deeply. "I was looking for you. They told me you were having breakfast."

I looked to Rand, wondering if he knew what this was all about. No one was ever looking for me about anything. Rand looked just as confused as I was.

"What is it?" I asked.

The servant finally lifted from her bow but kept her head down. "I'm here on behalf of Lady Omah. She's in town and would like to know if you'd like to come with her to lunch this afternoon on her property. She'd like to apologize for her...less-than-embracive behavior."

I wasn't quite sure how to respond. I hadn't heard from any member of Kahmel's family for months. He'd told me he spoke with them one day, then we didn't hear from them again. Not since Sokir was imprisoned and then "went missing." We weren't on the best terms.

Whatever the reason for the invitation, I knew I had to accept. The clan family of the Faresh was almost as important as the Faresh and Faresha themselves. At least for appearance's sake, I had to be cordial.

Judging from Rand's tight-lipped expression, he wasn't happy about it either.

But I smiled and said, "Tell her I'd be honored to come."

The servant smiled and bowed again, backing out of the room.

Scrunching my eyebrows together, I turned to Rand. "What was that all about?"

He scowled as he flicked open the screen to his eWatch, typing something. "I don't know, but we'll get to the bottom of it."

"I thought Kahmel said he handled them. What would they want with me?"

"Can't say for sure, but I wouldn't be surprised if this had something to do with intimidating you. Still, they must have a lot of gall to try speaking to you after Kahmel...uh, spoke with Dad."

I groaned as we both started for the door. "I guess I'll have to put off going to the city for later."

"We're going to the city?"

"Yes, you're taking me to the city to find places Lora would like. She's coming over."

He looked confused at how the subjects changed so quickly. "Uh, yes, ma'am?"

I huffed and smirked at him. "Damn straight."

TO THE WITCH'S HOUSE

Arusi cocked her head and held her hand out, making a "so-so" gesture. "Do you have any other pink robes?"

I pursed my lips and stared in the mirror, having to admit she was right. I liked the blush pink color, but the robe wasn't fitting me like I wanted. It cinched my stomach strangely and made my shoulders look huge the way it draped around them. There must have been a reason I hadn't worn this one out yet.

"I think you're right. I'll look for another one," I admitted.

Arusi leaned on the vanity in my closet, the thin braids she had put in her hair cascading over her shoulders. It was a nice look on her. I thought she should wear her hair like that more often.

Rand and Arusi were taking me to his mother's house as unofficial chaperones. They would be hanging around the outskirts of the property in case I needed them. Besides being pretentious and snobby, we did also have to be concerned about my safety as my in-laws posed a certain threat. Rand and Kahmel's younger brother, Sokir, blackmailed me just a few months back, so the whole family was suspect.

Sokir had been in league with the Zendaalan, Attican, who had been sentenced to death a few months ago. It was odd, knowing how much I was against all the executions Kahmel ordered during his reign. But when he ordered Attican's, I realized how wrong I was about his paranoia. It was justified.

I crossed my arms as I examined my pink robes. "I still don't understand why you can't come to lunch with me. I can't stand that woman; I'd hate to be alone with her."

"Sorry, Jashi," Arusi apologized, leaning over to look past me at something. She pointed. "What about that one? It's not pink, but it's been a while since you've worn it."

The robe Arusi was pointing to was a bright yellow one that I only remembered wearing a few times, but now that she mentioned it, I remembered liking it a lot. It had patterned borders on the sleeves and the end of the skirt. "Ooh, you're right, this one's nice. Anyway, quit dodging the question."

Arusi started sorting through some bracelets I had in a drawer of the vanity she sat at. "It's not proper etiquette. Your mother-in-law invited you to a private lunch, and you're a royal clan now. Certain things just aren't proper, like inviting extra guests to a private gathering intended only for family. Especially when it's Kahmel's parent that invited you. It would be different if it was something grander, like a luncheon with fifty people. Then it wouldn't matter so much who you invited to come with you. But this isn't the case, unfortunately."

"Gah, so many rules." I started putting on the robe we'd picked.

"You get used to it," Arusi said. She pulled out several bangle bracelets as well as matching earrings and rings. "Here, I think these would go nicely with it."

As I finished dressing, I accepted all the jewelry. It still felt strange, putting it all on and knowing it was mine. "I doubt it. I still pinch myself sometimes to see if this is all just one big crazy dream. Me, living in a palace? Psh." I started putting my earrings in, looking in the mirror and seeing Arusi chose well. She had different tastes from Lora, for sure, but she had a very classy style I liked too. "I just try to make as little of an impression as possible. Follow Kahmel's lead and try not to mess anything up." I laughed. "I don't belong here."

But Arusi didn't laugh with me. She rolled a bracelet back and forth on the vanity. "I disagree. I think you should stop trying to shrink into the background behind Kahmel and letting him reign the country on his own. You are his Faresha." She stood up and untied the sash around my waist, adjusting it and tying it better than I had. "You're loud, you don't have much of a filter, and you have a bit of a temper. But I think the palace could use a breath of fresh air. And you may think Kahmel's the more logical one, but the man has a temper of his own." Then she did laugh. "And sometimes he needs a fresh perspective to snap him out of a bad idea."

I didn't quite know how to respond, and Arusi had finished with the sash around my waist. I realized that she had always treated me like I was meant to be in the palace, not like it was an accident or the luck of the draw.

And more than that, I felt like she was talking about something specific. Like something she wanted me to talk Kahmel out of.

Could it have something to do with the dark mood I'd been noticing him in?

Either way, the admonishment warmed my heart. To know she believed in me.

Arusi started as I rushed forward and hugged her, then slowly closed her arms around me.

"You're welcome, Jashi."

"All right," I said, pulling away. "We've got to drive to the witch's house."

Arusi cackled.

We left my massive closet and went out to where a limousine was waiting. Rand joined us soon after, ducking into the car with a HoloCall with Kahmel.

"Yeah, I have her right here," he said as he got in, and the chauffeur closed the door behind him. He turned to me. "Kahmel wants to talk to you."

I leaned closer to Rand—which I noticed made him stiffen. "Kahmel? Don't you have meetings to get to?"

Kahmel looked livid, even behind his glasses. He had people

clamoring to ask him things all around him, so I knew he was out somewhere special. Probably just outside of the Legislation House of the Court. He dismissed all of them and stepped into his own car to get some privacy. "I do, but Rand told me my mother summoned you."

"Gosh, you make me feel like some kind of demon your mom is calling out or something."

"Though that would make her a witch," Arusi muttered, chuckling.

Kahmel was unamused. "I'm serious, Jashi. And her servant didn't say anything about why she wanted to meet with you?"

"No. I thought you said your family was 'handled,' by the way. I seem to remember someone assuring me 'they won't be a problem anymore.'"

"I know, I know. I'm sorry, I have no idea why she's come back like this. But like Rand's already told you, even though you have to keep up the appearance, we're keeping them at arm's length." He clenched his jaw. "I'll have to have another talk with them after this. Just try to make it through the afternoon."

"Whatever, I guess."

I leaned back in my seat and huffed as Kahmel and Rand went on to talk about other official matters. They weren't long, though, because Kahmel really was in the middle of something. And soon we were off to visit the witch.

The limousine pulled into a long driveway that led up to a mansion. I'd never been to Kahmel's family house before, so the topiary bushes, marble statues, and reflective pool were all new to me. It had Rand rolling his eyes, though.

"Did you and Kahmel grow up here?" I gawked at a topiary bush of a dragon, actual size.

"Somewhat," was his offhanded answer. "We were fourteen when we moved here after the assassination of the last Faresh. Only another four years until we turned eighteen and had to leave. After Kahmel's blood test."

All of a sudden, the topiary forms and marble statues no longer looked as whimsical. More monstrous, sinister. It sent a tingle up my spine to imagine the kind of people they had to be to sell out their son like they did. And now that they were all royalty, they had to pretend like none of that ever happened. That they hadn't left their son for dead.

My stomach churned, and I lost my appetite for eating anything.

"We're here," Arusi announced.

Looking out the window, I saw we'd pulled up to the house already.

The chauffeur opened the door to Arusi's side, and I maneuvered around her to leave. I bit my lip, looking back into the limo and wishing I was leaving with it.

Rand gave me a lopsided smile. "We'll be close, okay? Don't worry about it."

"Remember what we talked about," Arusi said with a wink, leaving me somewhat confused. Was she talking about our conversation about me being Faresha? What did that have to do with anything?

But she closed the door instead of explaining, and the chauffeur stepped back into the car.

My safety wasn't something I was really concerned about. Rand and Kahmel were pulling out all the stops. The "chauffeur" was really a rebel that was in on everything. And they were going to ditch the limo and take up a strategic position somewhere in the dunes behind the mansion where they could keep an eye on things.

I just wanted to know what all of this was about. I had the feeling Mira didn't just want to catch up.

But since I'd get no answers just standing here, I started for the house, several servants coming up behind me and going into the house before me to announce my arrival.

I stepped inside the home, a huge expanse of grandeur. White tiles lined the floors, an iron chandelier leaning down from overhead. A few palms grew in pots along the floor, breaking up the stark black and white color scheme. But it didn't succeed in making the place feel any warmer.

But then again, my assessment was probably biased. I just imagined Kahmel and Rand being chased out of here by Zendaalans, and suddenly, the whole place looked ugly. There was a time I envied Kahmel for having parents that knew about his abilities. But that feeling was long gone now that I really understood his history. And I felt bad for ever being jealous of him.

Mira came down a grand staircase, and the way she held her head up, you'd think she was the Faresha rather than me. She was dressed in a lavish red robe and gold jewelry that clanked with every step. Her hair was swooped in a tall updo that resembled a bird's nest. Her eyelids were coated in purple and laced with thick black lines. Lips painted violet spread into a grin. She gave a flourishing bow.

"Your Majesty. I'm so pleased that you've come. You'll have to excuse Kolin for being out."

I smiled stiffly. "Thank you for the invitation."

"The pleasure's all mine, really. Please, right this way."

She and an army of servants led me to a patio out back, which gave a splendid view of the dunes of the Shosho Desert. She must have had environmental systems around the patio. I didn't feel the smoldering heat I should have felt when we stepped outside. But I could see the shimmering outside of the limits of the concrete, exposing the reality of the desert.

A servant pulled out a chair for me and then for Mira. The servants put themselves to work arranging the table, pouring two glasses of water, setting out plates, and placing before us two servings of fish with lemon wedges beside them.

"So, Your Grace," Mira said, smiling like the first and last time we'd seen each other hadn't been a disaster. But then, they were all good at pretending in this family. "Tell me, how is palace life treating you? Are you adjusting well?"

"It's all right," I said, briefly scanning the dunes and wondering which one Rand and Arusi were hiding behind, watching the conversation closely.

"Hm, difficult is it?" Mira cocked her head, making me wonder if her heavy earrings would topple her over.

I shrugged. "I wasn't raised to be a royal, that's for sure. But I'm learning."

She plastered on another cheesy grin. "Oh, that's wonderful. It's good to have such a go-getter attitude." She picked at her meal with her fork and started eating. "I couldn't imagine being in your shoes, all those people having so many expectations of me when I have absolutely no idea about anything. But you don't let anything discourage you!"

All I could do was chuckle politely and grind my teeth as I swallowed several statements that were not part of Arusi's crash course in etiquette.

I took a bite out of the fish in front of me, finding it was disappointingly tasteless. I wasn't sure what the lemon was for, but I didn't think it was going to help much with this.

Mira watched with disdain as I reached for the salt, but I didn't care.

She took a deep breath. "I wanted to apologize to you for our first encounter."

Finally, we were getting to what the heck I was here for. "Oh?" I said, raising my eyebrow like I had no idea what she could be talking about. Even if it was for a fake apology, I was going to make her work for it.

Mira nodded, grimacing. "I was rather harsh in my reaction to your addition to the family, and I realize I was wrong for that, Your Majesty. It was just all happening so fast, you understand."

"Yes, of course," I said with mock sympathy, taking another bite of fish. Even with the salt I'd added, it still tasted bland and overly flaky.

Mira took a sip of her water and said, "Yes. And the way you and

Kahmel said not one word to us since you ascended to the throne, you must admit I couldn't have felt very welcome to even make up for my folly."

"Not one word?" I repeated, taking up my own cup of water. "I was sure Kahmel said something to you."

I enjoyed the dangerous look that flickered across Mira's face. "Hmm, true. He did speak to us once after the wedding, some months later. But we've chosen to ignore the words he spoke in anger. He'd just come back from the war, newly-married, it could make anyone say some regrettable things."

It didn't look like Kahmel had wasted time with pleasantries when he spoke with them. Could he have threatened them?

Whatever he said, it looked like they'd gotten over it.

"Tell me, Great Faresha," Mira said, pulling away more fish with her fork, putting it in her mouth as she paused. "How does that feel, being called Faresha? Different, isn't it?"

My palms were warming, and I took a deep breath to keep it from getting worse. She was just a lot of words, and she was trying to get under my skin, dancing around the subject like this. I shouldn't let her get to me.

"It is a little off-putting sometimes," I admitted, my insides simmering, which I tried to smother with a bite of the bland food.

"I hope it isn't too much for you, all of this. I really wish Kahmel hadn't put you in this situation as fast as he did. No formal training, no idea about laws, or even the foggiest on how to lead or inspire a nation."

"I—"

"I can only hope you're attempting to provide him an heir."

I almost choked on my fish. "Excuse me, I really don't think that's any of your—"

"You may have Kahmel fooled into thinking you can be his Faresha," she hissed, her eyes narrowed. The niceties were over. "Maybe he relates to you, with that wretched fire curse of yours."

My eyes widened. She knew about my fire?

"He may even think he loves you," she went on to say, her voice low. "But despite Kahmel's little *talk* with us, Zendaal assures us that they're exhausted with the fire-breathing circus performers who've taken over the palace, and your days on the throne are numbered."

So that's where she got her information. The Zendaalans. I stood up. "I didn't come here to be insulted."

Mira tilted her head up, looking down on me, even from a seated position. "You should be grateful. You weren't meant for this role. The Zendaalans just want to alleviate you from a pressure that should have never been yours."

"Just get to the damn point. What is this really about?"

"They offered you an out, once. They're offering it again. Disappear, Faresha. Retreat to some no-name town with a new identity, and don't look back. With you out of the way, maybe Kahmel will marry someone sensible enough to talk him out of the ridiculous decisions he's making. Don't force them to take matters into their own hands."

No. I would never go down that path again. I wouldn't be Kahmel's traitor again, no matter what they threatened. "I'll pass." I turned to walk away.

I heard her stand behind me. "Why? Because you like dressing like a royal and pretending to belong? So you can eat fine dining and rub shoulders with important people? Don't be selfish, *Your Majesty*. Your people deserve better than that. Better than you."

Tears brimmed my eyes as I clenched my fists, breathing out embers. Is this what Arusi was talking about? Did she expect me to defend myself?

How could I when Mira was right? I had nothing to offer anyone. The only purpose I could find for myself was doing work with the rebels, and it was clear I couldn't even do that right.

"I can't say you're not right," I said, my chin trembling. "But I didn't ask for any of this. I didn't ask for Kahmel. I didn't ask for the palace. And I certainly didn't ask for you."

"But you can fix this."

I chuckled sadly, still unwilling to face her. "Kahmel has a mind of his own; let him 'fix' it if he wants to."

As I walked away, I couldn't deny that some part of me wished he would.

BEHIND THE THRONE ROOM

"Jashi!" Arusi called behind me, but I just wanted to put as much distance between me and everything related to this palace as possible. As soon as the limo had stopped out in front, I'd dashed away from Rand and her.

Their quick footsteps resounded through the halls behind me, but I knew the palace a lot better than I had a few months back. Racing through the corridors, I soon found what I was looking for. There was a line of patterned tiles along this wall, and I pressed the middle one, releasing an entryway that slid open. Their footsteps passed me by as I slipped through and shut the entrance behind me.

This was the secret passage that led to the throne room—one of the many such shortcuts in the palace. Kahmel and I used them all the time now when we needed to talk in secret.

Hiding in the folds of my robe was a lighter. I took it out and tried to create a little flame to push back the stifling darkness but found that the fuel must have been running out. The first few tries didn't even make a spark. I tsked. Of course, now of all times it would run out on me. I wished for the umpteenth time I could create flames spontaneously like Kahmel could. But according to him, it would come with more practice with flames, which we weren't able to do as much with him being so busy.

Finally, a flame sparked to life. My heart raced as I eased it from its place on the lighter and into my palm, a brief elation rushing through my body as I made it bigger, casting light onto the walls and illuminating the corridor.

I slid my back down the dusty wall until I reached the floor and cried.

I didn't ask to be here. I didn't ask to be Faresha or to make people upset with me being here. As much as I hated her, Kahmel's mother was right. I'd had my doubts about him at first, but Kahmel was a good Faresh. He only worked so hard because he wanted the best for K'sundi, and he was doing his best to change it. To save it. *I* was the one that didn't fit in this picture. What qualified me to be Faresha? I couldn't claim to be a good one. Or even a decent one.

It was starting to get strenuous maintaining the fire, and I didn't want to be left in the dark. I wasn't sure where I would go. The servants would notice me if I left, and they'd tell Arusi and Rand where I'd gone for sure.

Sweat beaded down the side of my face, my breath quickening as my flame started to die down. I growled in frustration. If I were better at my fire, I wouldn't have this problem. If I were more capable, I wouldn't need Kahmel to save me from my own mistakes all the time.

Mira was right. The people didn't need someone like me as Faresha.

The fire flickered, now no bigger than a lit candle. Tears streamed down my face as it wavered.

I jumped and bumped into the wall behind me as it roared to life again. I frowned at it, having to hold it out away from me just to keep my clothes from catching.

"Jashi?"

Kahmel was coming from the hall in the other direction. He wore some of his more exquisite cream robes, his royal sash about his chest. He was even still wearing his sunglasses. He must have come straight from a meeting with the Court.

Ah. The re-birthed fire was his doing.

I looked up at him, too tired to care that I was probably covered in dust. "How did you know I'd be here?"

He shrugged. "Rand and Arusi told me they'd lost you. I was in the throne room, so this was the first place I checked."

Damn it. I hadn't considered if he'd come home and continued work in the throne room.

"I'll be all right; I just need some time alone for a while."

He fell silent. "I'm so sorry my mother insulted you like she did."

The fire had shrunk to a more manageable size, and I messed with the end of my hair with the other hand, twisting it around my finger. "I'm all right," I repeated.

He crouched down, studying my face. "You don't look it."

Turning away from him, I said, "Any reason you came here, or you just want to set the passages on fire?"

"I wanted to apologize." He straightened. "And to tell you something. You know I had a talk with them before. Essentially, I told them it was in their best interest to leave us alone, or I could arrange for an unfortunate accident to their property. It worked at first, but judging from what my mother told you, it looks like they're being backed by the Zendaalans to give you hell. But I won't stand for it, and I don't care what the Zendaalans do."

That's what scares me, I thought. *You don't care. But I do.*

I squeezed my eyes closed as tears came down again. "Oh, just leave them alone. I don't care enough, anyway."

I could feel the confusion on his face, but I refused to look at him.

"You think she's right."

I laughed. "Of course I do!" Groaning, I clenched my fist and extinguished the fire he maintained in my hand. "What am I doing here, Kahmel?" I said into the darkness. "I'm not smart. I'm not clever. I'm not even royal. I'm here because you needed to save me, not because I'm fit to be Faresha."

"And you think I'm a fitting Faresh by anyone's standards?"

"No, but you *are* a good Faresh, Kahmel." I looked down, guilt gnawing at me as I remembered the year before. How wrong I had been about him. "You care. You want to make us a better people. You're fighting to get rid of the Equalizers, so we can be free again.

Us and the rest of Hemorah. The Court hates you because you're actually making a change."

He hesitated for a few beats. "But who else would want those things as much as I do? Who else wants K'sundi to change, Jashi? Or knows we need the dragons back? Or is willing to acknowledge that we need to be rid of the Equalizers?" His voice came closer as he spoke lower. "We're going to find more Half-Dracs all over K'sundi, if the Great Spirits help us. Who else will they relate their struggles to?" His hand went to mine. "I know it's hard because, believe it or not, I understand how you feel. All the ways you're helping this country can't be exposed just yet. It won't even feel helpful. All the things you mentioned I do? No one even knows about them. I'm the ruthless tyrant, remember? Even you thought that at first."

My heart sunk, and I nodded, forgetting that he couldn't see me because of the blackness that surrounded us.

As if reading my mind, he added, "I don't even blame you. That's as far as I'm allowed to appear to anyone with the Court breathing over my shoulder. As for you, you *can't* act as you would as Faresha because I'm not around as much as I'd like to be to help you."

Wiping my cheeks, I realized he was right. Whenever I did do anything "official," it was much easier with Kahmel around. Like when he let me speak at the last meeting we held together in the throne room.

"We're both limited right now," he continued, breathing out. "Though maybe I can help you feel a little less restrained, at least. You do a wonderful job of keeping yourself contained not to ruffle anyone's feathers, but...you don't have to."

I whipped my head toward him, or at least where his voice had come from in the dark. "What are you talking about?"

"I try to make sure no one asks much about you because I know the pressure to act refined makes you uncomfortable. But it's about time they got used to their Faresha. This has proven to me now more than ever they need to realize you demand as much respect as I do."

Clenching my fists in my lap, I said, "But Kahmel, I could get you in trouble. People already think I'm a laughingstock as it is."

That deadpan tone took over his voice. "Don't worry about that."

I didn't want to ask, but I couldn't stand this scary attitude anymore. "How bad has it gotten with you and the Court?"

"It's not the Court," he finally confessed. I could hear the heaviness in his voice. He paused. "It's what Zendaal's telling the Court. They haven't said anything officially, but I know K'sundi is heading toward the rebel country list. They're just waiting for an excuse to do it."

"Then why tell me you don't care all the time?" I demanded.

"Because it doesn't matter. That's another reason you and I have to travel while K'sundi's still on the good list. We're going to look for the Dragon King realms that are available to us, but we're also going to form alliances where we can. We're not the only ones disgruntled with Zendaal; we're just the only ones willing to talk about it. I know of a few world leaders who might side with us. When Zendaal takes away their alliance with us, we should have several things: other countries on our side and more freedom to free the dragons, meaning I'll be fulfilling my promise to Aithel."

I heard him pull up his sleeve, and he took my hand to trace where the marks were. They pulsed like a faint heartbeat. I winced because I knew it must have hurt him a lot more often than he showed.

Aithel had burned into Kahmel his promise to make K'sundi a better place for the dragons, and until that promise was fulfilled, the marks still hurt. How much, I didn't know.

"As long as that's still happening, my job isn't done," he said. "I just hold the Court off as best I can for the time being because we still need to make our trip. But you can't do anything bad enough to send us over faster, believe me. I'm the one they're watching with a magnifying glass."

I wasn't sure I believed him. I'd heard the kind of things Zendaalans and Court members said about me. They feared the integrity of a nation led by a warmonger and a dunce. Still, it seemed like there was a lingering reason why there was such a dark cloud over him these days.

"I didn't tell you because I didn't want to scare you," Kahmel said. "But I suppose my ideas to keep things from you have never worked, have they?"

I laughed, sniffing. "No, they haven't."

He chuckled. "You know, I talk to Matron Taias often enough to convey messages to the rebels in her area. She calls me a bonehead."

Typical Nana.

"Well, you are," I said, nudging him with my elbow. "And a horrible communicator."

"All true, I admit." He let silence fall between us for a moment. "I'm fine with the Court hating me," he admitted. "The Zendaalans, my family, I'm used to it. I'm used to not caring. But the closer we come to K'sundi being severed from the Equalization, the closer I know I am to where I *have* to care. And it won't be about the government, who I'm used to being against me." He laughed. "I'm king of the rebels." I felt him stiffen. "It's the people I'm worried about. They won't want me. They don't want me now. They most certainly won't want me when everything goes to hell. And I'll have to somehow convince them to believe I've done it all with their best interests at heart. Not only that, but come with me and rise against everything to fight for everyone else. And you know..."

He stopped so long, to the point that I tried to focus on his face in the dark. I could just barely make out his head turning away from me, his hands clenching at his sides. "You won't have to stay after K'sundi is dropped from the Equalization if you don't want to," he finally forced out.

My heart stuttered. "What?"

"Right now, getting a separation would be too dangerous because Zendaal could use it to make me seem like an unfit ruler with no hopes of an heir."

I thought about Mira's concerns on the same subject. No one needed to know how that wasn't happening.

"But after they cut ties with us," Kahmel went on, painfully, it seemed, "you won't have to stay. Not if you don't want to." He gripped my hand. "I don't want to see you go. But I also would have preferred our relationship to have happened more naturally, instead of as rushed as it was. I hate knowing how uncomfortable you are with the situation." He took a deep breath. "Suffice it to say, when Zendaal does as we predict, I'm in for a lot of changes. And it's going to be difficult. Figuring out how to win these people over. And potentially saying goodbye to the woman I love."

The air was thick with emotions. I'd never seen him so vulnerable about how he really felt. So that's what this was all about. I realized how true what he said really was. He was used to fighting the world, not making himself relatable or lovable to anyone. That was what he'd need to do if he wanted people to trust him when he finally finished fighting everybody off. And he was perfectly willing to make up reasons to keep fighting to avoid that. He may not have even realized he was doing it, but he was. Sure, the Court kept him busy, but as Asan could surely tell him, his public image was woefully neglected in comparison.

So was mine, to be honest.

I stood up and scoffed. "Oh, so that's it then."

A fire banished the dark over Kahmel's hand as he looked up at me in confusion. "What are you talking about?"

"I could have helped you with this a long time ago."

"With what?"

"Everything!" I said, putting a hand on my hip. "You want people to trust you? Then quit being this brick no one can talk to. No one knows anything about you; of course they don't like you!"

"Wait—"

"And you can start with taking these off." I snatched the sunglasses off his face.

He shot to his feet, trying to get them back, but I held them away, and he couldn't get any closer with the flame in his hand. "Hey! No one can know about my eyes, you know that."

"Why? You just said what the Court thinks doesn't matter anymore. Your eyes being a secret helped you when you cared. But the Zendaalans can't get rid of you over being dragon tribe."

He scowled, opening his mouth several times but not seeming to find a good enough response. "But what will showing my eyes do?" he finally asked.

"Haha! Then you admit it has nothing to do with the Court anymore."

"Well—"

"You just don't like feeling vulnerable."

"I didn't say—"

"And guess what?"

He sighed, kneading the space between his eyes. "What?"

He probably regretted telling me to speak my mind now. "I think that vulnerability you're afraid of showing is exactly what would get your people to like you better."

Kahmel frowned. "That doesn't make any sense. How does me being vulnerable make people like me more?"

"When we start looking for Half-Dracs, don't you think they'll be more willing to show themselves when they see their Faresh is dragon tribe? One of them?"

He shut his mouth at that.

"Ha!" I grinned triumphantly. "You know I'm right."

"I still don't understand how the conversation ended up here." He tried clumsily to change subjects.

"Fine, keep your glasses," I said, tossing them to him, watching as he scrambled to catch them so they wouldn't fall. I turned to leave but stopped short. "Oh, and about the other thing you mentioned." I pulled at the sleeves of my robe, looking into his deep orange eyes. "You're right that it would have been better if we'd got the chance to pursue our relationship slower, if at all."

His gaze fell.

"But who's to say we can't do that now?"

His face twisted in confusion. "I don't...?"

I shrugged, knowing he didn't know what to do with me. But if I stopped to think about this, I might never say it. "There's no law that says we can't date while we're married. Unless you want us to separate," I added in a small voice.

"No! I mean, no, but—"

"Then why not?"

Kahmel stopped. "Well, we've never had the chance to really talk about...*us*. You...you want to?"

He was right. I had just broken our unspoken agreement. But if I was being honest with myself, I was willing to give this a try. A coy smile slid up my face. "When did I say I didn't?"

He clenched his fist to put his fire out, then came closer. In the dark, he put his hand into my hair for a second before pulling my lips against his. He kissed softly as if he was scared I'd evaporate between his fingers. Then he pulled away slightly, tentatively, before drawing away completely.

"I don't think I'll ever understand you," he muttered.

My heart raced, and my face flushed with heat.

It was an odd first kiss—a real one anyway—swathed in emotions thick enough to cut through and in the darkest crevices of the palace. But it still felt like a sweet date.

"Hm," I hummed, stepping away and sliding the wall open, pouring light into the small cavity onto a Kahmel that looked frozen in his place. "I'm surprised you ever thought you could."

WELCOME TO THE REBELLION

My bracelet sounded like a rattle as I walked into the dining hall with Rand and Arusi, the little beads that dangled from it jingling as I went. But for once, I didn't feel as awkward as I usually did in all my majestic apparel, my feathery earrings down to my shoulders, hair styled in braids that trailed halfway down my scalp, and the rest allowed to curl freely around my head.

Rather than feeling like a child in their parent's clothes, I finally felt suited for them.

I studied the food laid out before me on the breakfast table, then went to the door of the room where servants were standing outside of it. "Excuse me, can someone bring out a box of cereal, please?"

Most of the servants looked like they didn't even know I could speak, but Armeen nodded with a smile and hurried off to fulfill the request.

Happy, I sat down and smiled at Rand and Arusi as they sat down with me.

Arusi picked up some sausages and eggs from the table. "You seem to be in a good mood."

I shrugged. "I suppose I am."

Rand took a sip of orange juice as he pulled out his eWatch and studied the screen. "Good, about time you actually start speaking up around here. And by the way," he put down the watch. "What happened between you and Kahmel, anyway? He's been acting weird all morning."

I took a glass of orange juice and started sipping it myself. "Who ever knows with that man?"

Rand looked dubious, but the servants came in at that moment, along with Armeen, bringing out several boxes of cereals from several brands.

"Now this is what I'm talking about." I pointed at one of the more colorful ones and waited eagerly as Armeen poured. "Thank you very much, that will be all."

"Shall I...leave the box with you?" Armeen asked, looking like he was trying not to laugh.

I considered it. "Actually, yes, thank you."

"Would you, er," he hesitated, "like the toy inside as well?"

I grinned. "Ooh, I didn't even notice it had one. Just set it there," I said, pointing beside my bowl.

Armeen took a plastic yo-yo out of the box and left, wagging his head, leaving Rand nodding in approval. "Finally, a royal I can get behind."

"Oh, that reminds me," I said, pulling out my own eWatch. "I need to call Lora and tell her she's spending her winter vacation here. By the way, Arusi, would you mind helping me plan out a few places for us to go? Preferably nice places to eat and shop."

"Gladly," she answered, smiling. "It's about time you had some fun around here."

For once, I finally was.

LORA and I had spent every minute she wasn't studying or in class talking about her visit on HoloCaller. When I'd given her the news almost two weeks ago, she looked like she was going to cry. And now that the date was almost here, we were both so excited our calls were now little more than squeals that more closely related to a couple of clucking chickens than actual conversations.

But before she came, I had one more order of business I was determined to see through.

As promised, Kahmel gave me all the liberty I needed to muster up the courage to have the conversation. Not even Rand brought it up anymore. And knowing I had my best friend coming to visit in a few days was just the boost I needed.

Ever since the last incident with Comet, he'd been too excitable for riding. Kahmel told me Huntress sometimes did the same thing when she was in a mood, and I supposed something about our last ride together set Comet off somehow because now I couldn't even get close to the stables without him going into a frenzy.

Though, this was a much-preferred frenzy to his usual variety. Normally, he looked agitated, vexed. But this time, it was like a huge dog that didn't know his own size, looking for a hug like a puppy would but weighing about a thousand times more.

Somehow, I felt confident that, despite all the time we were spending apart, Comet and I would have no problems getting in sync the next time we rode.

I spent this week's riding lesson on Huntress, giving her the exercise she needed as I promised Kahmel I would. She rode beautifully, and I only flubbed a few of the command words when it came to it. Even I knew a big part of it had to do with my confidence improvement. Maybe Huntress felt it, too, because she didn't even try to take me on a joy ride like last time.

After the lesson and everyone had their showers, I winked at Rand to let him know what I was doing and told T'shan, Kent, Jemmorah, and Ashed that I would be joining them for lunch at their cafeteria, much to their surprise and delight.

"You were amazing, Your Majesty," Jemmorah gushed. "You've improved so much from last time you rode."

Ashed nodded, neatly separating his vegetables with his fork, probably not even conscious he was doing it. Ashed was a neat freak like that. "Your last interaction with Comet probably has something to do with it. Faresh Kahmel taught us that dragons can smell fear and that they respect a rider that doesn't have the stink of it when they're riding."

"Yeah, so what does your dragon think of you?" Kent said, patting Ashed on the back. "I mean, you just plain stink."

Jemmorah laughed as T'shan rolled his eyes. "I'm sorry, Your Majesty. The one time you eat with us, and they have to act like morons."

"Hey!" Ashed objected.

Kent grinned. "Oh, Her Majesty is cool like Faresh Kahmel is. They know we're not acting; we're just regular morons."

"All right, that's enough out of you two," Jemmorah finally admonished.

I laughed. "Really, it's okay, guys. This is fun."

Kent raised a glass of water. "To Her Majesty and her impressive dragon-riding skills."

The other three laughed and raised their glasses. I giggled and rose mine as well, clinking it together with the others, spilling water onto the table.

They settled into conversations about what they'd do with the rest of the day, and, once we'd finished our meal, I waited until they were all headed to their rooms to single T'shan out.

"Hey, can I talk to you?" I said as they started back.

"Oooh, you're in trouble now!" Kent jeered.

Ashed scoffed. "Last time she talked to him, he got a promotion. You're just jealous."

"No, I'm not!"

I rolled my eyes and ignored them as Jemmorah stepped in and smacked them both upside their heads. "Anyway, follow me, I do need to say something rather sensitive."

T'shan nodded and followed as I led him toward a grove of palm trees that swayed with the winds. We were far enough from the palace not to be heard, and not enough guards made their rounds here to worry about, either. It was another spot Kahmel and I sometimes used to talk.

"I'd just like to say," T'shan started, "that I really appreciate my new responsibilities, Great Faresha."

I chuckled. "I'm really glad to hear you say that."

And even gladder that Kahmel let him keep the position. From what Kahmel told me, he was seriously considering giving the others the same positions as well. Just like what was happening with T'shan, their duties wouldn't change too much from what they already were. They would get slightly different subjects to study and sometimes be sent out on tasks with recruiters as well. But later down the line, they would be able to wrangle up dragons like pros, and it would be essential to Kahmel's plans for more dragons to be allowed to live in the wild.

Four trustworthy dragon recruiters weren't much, but they were more than Kahmel had before. And, hopefully, that number wouldn't stay small for very long, as they would also eventually become teachers to other young dragon riders.

And then suddenly, a small drop would become a ripple.

But now was not the time for promotions.

"What did you want to talk to me about?" T'shan asked, raising an eyebrow.

I took a deep breath. But I was ready this time.

"To tell the truth, I should have told you sooner, but I didn't know how to say it." Suddenly, I felt like Kahmel, all those months ago, sitting in front of me, telling me we were going to be married and that he knew about my fire. I knew how daunting this was going to be, but, hopefully, I would also be able to help T'shan know he wasn't going to go through this alone, that he would have friends who would have his back. Because, honestly, I didn't know Kahmel well enough back then to know that the same had been true for me. Which was why I ran away.

And if I'd known back then what I knew about him now?

I might have run toward him.

"Listen, we know who you are," I started. T'shan furrowed his brow in confusion, but I held up a hand to stop him. I took out the lighter Kahmel gave me—it felt like years ago now. The flame sprung from the lighter as I started it, and I quickly gestured it into my palm and let it grow, my heart rate going up and energy rushing through my body as soon as I did. It had been a while since Kahmel and I had the chance to practice, but holding the flame in my hand felt as familiar as always.

T'shan took startled steps back, but he held my gaze, confusion, understanding, and apprehension battling for dominance in his expression. But he had enough of his senses together to take note of my choice of wording. "Who's 'we'?"

I bit my lip, not sure if I should mention Kahmel yet. Maybe save that for after I saw how he reacted. "Me and more like us," I answered instead. I closed my fist. "You're not alone. And if you want to live, you'll listen to me and let us protect you."

T'shan looked like he wasn't sure what to believe, taking another half step away from me as he frowned. He paused for a few beats. "I've never shown my abilities to anyone but my parents. How could I be in danger?"

Now for the complicated part. I closed my fist, stepping toward him and lowering my voice an octave. "You're due for the eighteenth-birthday blood test. You take that test, you'll find yourself strapped to a hospital bed, getting ready for a lethal injection."

He shook his head in disbelief. "Th-that's not possible. That's not *legal*."

"It's what they almost did to Kahmel," I finally decided to reveal. Mention of the name of the man that'd earned his respect for more than half the year made him solemn.

"He's...?"

I nodded.

T'shan paused but then scoffed, shrugging like the answer was obvious. "Well, if he knows what goes on and he's the Faresh, I've got nothing to worry about. He'll put a stop to it."

I pursed my lips. "It's deeper than you assume. You know how hard he has it just trying to get laws on the dragons passed. He's working at it, believe me; he works his ass off. But between the Court and the Zendaalans, he's fighting an uphill battle. He needs our help."

T'shan's Adam's apple bobbed as he swallowed. "Zendaalans? The Court?" He crouched on the ground, his head against his knees. "Why? What do they want with me?"

That was the question, wasn't it? With an answer that would take much longer than we had time for. I crouched to meet him. "T'shan, I don't think you're ignorant about how things run in this palace. They hate Kahmel. They hate me. They don't want us here. It has nothing to do with Kahmel's upbringing; it's because he won't be their puppet. I can't tell you what they want with us, but I can tell you we sure as hell won't go down without a fight. Now, we can protect you, but you'll have to go against everything you know from here on out. You said your parents know about you, so we'll protect them too. But we—*I* need to know you're with me."

T'shan didn't answer for a while, and I was afraid I'd blown it somehow. That maybe Rand was better at this whole motivating thing.

But then he finally looked up at me, his eyes shimmering with moisture that he tried his best to blink away. "You've stood by me, Your Highness. You and Faresh Kahmel." He put his fist to his chest. "I'll stand by you."

I grinned, nearly tackling him in a hug. It was partially because I was excited, but it was also to get close.

Close to his ear, I whispered, "Welcome to the rebellion."

DRAGON HISTORY

I was combing out my hair, still dripping wet, when Kahmel stepped into the bedroom, taking off his sunglasses as soon as he did. He grinned. "You did it."

Half-smiling, I dipped my head down. "After stalling for I don't know how long."

"Hey, all that matters is you did it." Kahmel took off his sash and sat on a plush chair in front of my bed, watching me do my hair.

I frowned and looked at the holographic clock that hovered over the bed. It wasn't even dinner time. "Wait, aren't you home early?"

Kahmel nodded. "To make arrangements, but—" He scratched his nose, indicating that we would talk about it another time. But I could surmise what he meant already. The rebels were making accommodations for T'shan and his family. Rand and I only had a quick moment to update each other, but, after I had finished relaying my and T'shan's conversation, Rand told me that not only were the rebels going to make accommodations for T'shan's family, but they were considering offering membership to the dragon riders as well. They could easily learn all the skills of dragon recruiters within the rebels, and they'd attain the same goals as before. But Rand assured me it was an issue for another day. In the meantime, we were going to tell a story about T'shan needing separate training to the remaining three and split them apart, unfortunately.

"Well, it's nice to see you home before dark," I said, starting a thick twist in the section of hair I had in my hands. "You usually don't even get home in time to have dinner with us."

Kahmel scratched his head. "Yeah, I know. But I'm going to try to be here for when Lora gets here tomorrow morning."

I lit up. "Yeah, I can't wait. And she's bringing Talad with her!"

At that, Kahmel's face fell. "Talad? You didn't say he was coming before."

"Yeah, it was a last-minute thing," I said, frowning at how frizzy the twist was getting. I smoothed it out and tried again. "He was free, she was free, they decided to come together." I turned to him, smiling, thinking he was kidding. "What, can't he come?"

"It's...not that," he hesitated.

I tsked, realizing it wasn't a joke at all. "Bull."

Kahmel looked away, sighing. "Well, he's not the most trustworthy character. He did help you get into all that mess last year."

I narrowed my eyes, dropping the piece of hair I was working on. "He was helping me because some strange brute had arranged my marriage, and I wanted out. He was being a good friend."

He shook his head, waving my statement away. "That's not what I meant."

"Yeah, it is what you meant."

He stopped. "I'm sorry. It's just, I know Lora, she's a sensible girl. And this is still the palace. I don't trust just anyone to be let in here."

I huffed. It wasn't like I didn't understand his perspective. Talad had questionable connections, and he had the tendency to get mixed up in trouble, but he was still one of my best friends growing up. I wanted some way to repay him for the help he did try to give me last year.

Being Faresha made everything so complicated.

I shook my head, picking up my hair where I left off, finding most of it had undone itself, and I'd have to start from the beginning. The woes of long hair. Untwisting, I said, "Fine. I'll just tell him he won't be able to come. Some other time."

After a moment, Kahmel sighed. "No, no, don't do that." He kneaded the space in between his eyes, where his glasses usually sat. "Look, why don't you let him stay at a hotel near the place. I'll pay for everything. Just tell him it's because I'm being paranoid or something."

I grinned. "You mean because you are?"

He made a face. "Just tell him."

Finishing the twist again, I got up and hugged Kahmel, pecking him on the cheek. "Thank you."

His body went from rigid and surprised to relaxed, his arms wrapping around me in return. "I'm sorry I can't allow more than that."

"It's all right, I understand."

I didn't even notice how long we stayed like that until Kahmel said in a low voice, "As much as I'd love for you to stay in my lap, I think it's time for dinner."

Realizing the position I was in, I hopped up, my cheeks burning. "You could have said something!"

"And let it end?" he said as he stood up with a smirk on his face. Then he put an arm around my waist and pulled me closer. "Besides, you left me on a pretty confusing note last time we talked."

I unwrapped myself from his arms. "Yeah, I decided it was our first date. And you've got a lot more before we do anything...anything."

Embarrassingly flustered, I was ready to run for my closet to change back into something more suitable for a Faresha for dinner, but Kahmel grabbed my wrist before I could.

"All right, I can agree to that. But there's just one more thing I wanted to clear up about that conversation."

Surprisingly, my body warmed. My fire was coming, and I wasn't even sure why. It only ever reacted when I was extremely angry or scared, and at the moment, I was neither.

Breathing out embers, I asked, "What?"

Kahmel, if he was surprised, didn't flinch. "It's about what you said then, and also what you said to T'shan. About helping me."

I blinked, having to think back to my conversation with T'shan to even remember what he was talking about. Then I remembered I'd told T'shan that Kahmel was fighting an uphill battle and needed our help. I vaguely remembered relaying that detail to Rand when I told him how the conversation went. That must have been how Kahmel heard about it. But with such a minute detail, I didn't see where he was going with this.

"You're right," Kahmel said. "I do need help. I'm too used to being alone. Having to figure things out between my brother and me, and then later with Arusi, Asan, and Khes. I can't afford to run myself to the ground, trying to do everything without support." He laughed. "Even T'shan, I wouldn't have him or his friends if he wasn't brave enough to tell me to my face when I was wrong. I'm going to try to be more open with myself toward people."

A sly smile crawled up my face. "Does that mean you'll take off your glasses in public?"

Kahmel scoffed. "One step at a time. But," he closed the space between us, his features hovering above mine. "I see what you mean now, that I can't do this alone. You're right, I need help. My people's help." He took my hand and kissed it. "Your help."

I shrugged, trying to seem standoffish. "I barely remember what I said to get through that hard head of yours. But I'm glad it helped."

I was going to move away, but he took my chin in his hand and tilted it up. But he stopped, like asking for permission, and I let him. Closing the gap, he kissed my lips, staying there for a few soft, slow moments before pulling away. "Now, let's get ready for dinner before Rand sends a search party."

I laughed, trying to shake off the hotness in my cheeks. "What, because he's worried?"

Kahmel shook his head. "Just hungry."

Lora gasped and pointed at everything we passed by in the limo, and though I was enjoying her over-dramatic reactions to everything, I was also very conscious of Talad sulking in the corner, poking at the stitching in the seats and eventually shifting his gaze to the drinks in the cooler.

I had tried my best to explain why we couldn't allow him to stay in the palace, but that apparently didn't stop him from being mad at me.

It was nice to finally be in regular street clothes, though, garbed in my disguise for being among the public. Synthetic braids came down to my elbows, an airy tangerine scarf around my neck, matching the rosy pink top and ankle-length skirt I was wearing. Though showing up in a limo was a little less than discreet, I'd already instructed the driver to park a good distance from our destination.

Sighing, I returned my attention to Lora, who was pointing and demanding I explain something else to her from outside the window. Not that she was listening to my assertions that I still didn't know the city well and that she was better off asking Kahmel when we went out to dinner with him later. He promised me he'd make sure to come on time for my friends' sake. But I also had a suspicion he wanted to assess Talad for himself.

Which may not have been a bad thing. Maybe he'd finally decide all this security was silly and let Talad stay at the palace.

"You finally ready to tell us where we're headed?" Talad asked, though there was more impatience to his voice than teasing.

But I grinned anyway, plopping next to him and nudging him with my elbow. "Come on, I told you it's a surprise."

Lora looked up at me with begging eyes, clasping her hands together. "Will you at least give us a hint?"

I thought about something vague enough not to make it obvious, but something clever enough to tease them further. Smirking, I said, "It's one of the only things I'm proud about from my time in Hashir, I can tell you that. And it's about something I didn't think I'd be interested in a million years."

Lora bit her lip, thinking.

Talad just looked out the window and propped his head up with his fist, jaded.

I sighed. I just couldn't win.

"Look, I'm sorry, okay?" I said, just as Lora opened her mouth to take a guess. I tried to laugh it off, maybe lighten the mood Talad had hanging in the air around him since he'd arrived. Kahmel had given me a free card to throw him under the bus, which I'd done when I'd explained it to Talad when he'd first arrived. I threw my hands up in the air. "You've seen on the news how paranoid Kahmel can be! I kind of have my hands tied here."

"It's just," Talad sighed, finally facing me, his arm leaning on the door of the car, hand balled into a fist. "I can't help feeling like you've changed, Jash. I mean, what happened to the girl I knew before she got married? Two minutes in the palace, and it's like suddenly you think you're better than me or something. Fancy limos, expensive hotels, and restaurants to make up for the fact you can't let your own friend in your home. Nice, Jashi."

"What?" Lora said incredulously. "She just told you —"

"No, it's okay, Lora," I held up a hand to stop her. Some of those words clung to me, I had to admit. But no matter how much they hurt, I still had the heated need to remind Talad that some things never changed, including my temper. "Maybe I have changed some, Talad," I said, keeping my voice level. "But no one can stay the same forever. It's called being human."

"Does that include leaving your friends behind?"

My palms were starting to warm up. How could he not understand that being in a palace made things *completely* different? It wasn't like I could just kick it and hang like I used to; I was Faresha now. And even being Faresha, I was doing my best to give my friends what they were never able to enjoy growing up, so how dare he accuse me otherwise?

"I haven't left anyone!" I insisted. "You're here, aren't you?"

"All right, fine," he said, holding up his hands as if in surrender. "You're right; I'm sorry."

The words were spat out and didn't feel authentic, but I sat back in my seat and let it go, breathing out embers as Lora and Talad turned their gazes out the windows. The car stayed heatedly silent until the limo stopped a few blocks from a museum that stood high above the streets.

As we stepped out of the car, I grinned up at the sign, proud of the one thing I could say I helped Kahmel with.

MUSEUM OF K'SUNDII DRAGON HISTORY AND STUDY

"You took us all the way out here just for a museum?" Talad drawled.

I shot him a glare. "It's not just any museum." Without more explanation, I continued to lead them toward the massive building.

Lora shot a couple of glares his way too, and though I was trying to stay impartial, I never felt prouder of my friend for taking my side.

I had to admit I felt special as we walked past the long line waiting to get tickets, and I led us straight to the reception desk where I told the receptionist that we were the "special four o'clock." Kahmel had arranged for the visit ahead of time, informed the staff of who I was, and that they were to keep the utmost discretion when I arrived.

The face of the receptionist reflected an understanding of all of this. She grinned and nodded, gesturing to the exhibits behind her. "Please. Enjoy."

Glossy marble floors spread across the entirety of the building. Vaulted ceilings gave room to the immense life-like projections of dragons that stayed still for a few breaths and then came to life with tail wagging, head shaking, and even fire-breathing actions.

"Wow," Lora breathed.

"Whoa." Even Talad had his neck craned just to see the heads of some of the beasts being displayed.

I grinned at their reactions. "And this is just the beginning. I can't take too much of the credit, but I did help Kahmel do the research necessary to put all this together."

Lora walked up to the display that showed the kind of dragon that stomp-walked in place in front of her like it was on an invisible treadmill. Talad came to look over her shoulder, and I joined him, though I already knew what it said.

Red Draconian:

A typical dragon type. Fire-breathing. Antsy, somewhat coy, nature in the wild. Will not approach unless challenged or threatened. Highly territorial. Makes its home in the caves of the Dharia Mountains. Can be tamed if approached with extreme caution and willingness to leave and return another day if the dragon proves to be too hostile. Persistence has been proven to be key in proper taming. This is the easiest dragon to tame!

I wasn't sure if the infographic made people less or more afraid of dragons than they were before, but I still felt like informing the public was the best way to get them used to the idea. Knowledge was power, right? Hopefully, this would be the first museum of many. My dream was for there to be one in Kohpal, so Nana could take the kids at the orphanage without having to pay a huge cost for transportation. Though now that Kahmel was helping with orphanage funds, it wasn't as much of a problem as it was before.

Lora whistled. "Damn, girl, this is amazing."

Looking warily up at the giant above him as it simulated flying, Talad said, "Those things really are lively when they're not on a collar, huh?"

I playfully shoved at his arm. "Come on, you're not scared of a hologram, are you? Besides, we haven't even gotten to the Elementals section. And then you'll see holographic dragon riders and tamers in action!"

Lora squealed in excitement, but I could tell Talad was only smiling politely. What was *with* him?

I played tour guide across dozens more exhibits and gorgeous holographic displays. I even took them to a "ride" where visitors could see what it'd feel like to ride a dragon. Lora was stoked, but Talad was not, no matter how much I joked, kidded, or teased. I found myself distancing myself from his gloom and being more excited with Lora and her enthusiasm.

When I did that, I realized there were a lot of people excited about the exhibits. Tour guides who were walking viewers through the museum were earning gasps and eager grins. Kids rushed into the dragon-riding simulators and argued over who would go first. People were asking questions. I'd even overheard a couple mumbling a question about the purpose of electrocution collars if natural dragon-taming was possible.

It reminded me that changing wasn't an insult. It was far from it. These people were being changed. Their views were changing.

As it should. Nothing should stay the same forever. And if I'd changed into someone that inspired a place like this, then that was a person I was proud to have become.

As we continued through the exhibits, a sense that I'd seen this before crept in. This sticky feeling, being at odds with Talad while he was in some impossible mood, was oddly familiar.

I didn't always like things like this, museums, learning new things. Not perfect, but striving to do a little better than I did the day before. I was too lost in my own emotions and being mad at the world, sulking in the corner with someone like Talad while Nana was trying to reason with me, with us. Talad was always the one I could depend on to relate to my struggles because we hated the world all the same.

But on the days I was finally willing to listen, when Nana would coax me out of my corner, she would get me to see the beautiful things in life, remind me there were things outside of the hell I was living at the time, and to enjoy the things I did have, like Lora, Nana, and the little kids that came to look up to me in the orphanage. Those days, Talad would still be in that corner, refusing to join, refusing to come out of himself. That was how he started running off alone and got caught up in the things I was no longer willing to get lost in.

I wanted to think this feeling was new, but it wasn't. It was the same feeling I'd get when he'd run away without me, right before he accused me of taking "their" side. Whoever "they" were. The difference between us now wasn't Talad at all. I *was* the one who had changed. But that was a good thing.

I couldn't shake the feeling that I'd outgrown him.

The three of us left the museum, Lora and I laughing and falling into our typical routine as if no time had passed at all. Talad brought up the rear, but I didn't care anymore. I'd chosen to evolve. Talad could too if he wanted to.

When he was ready to do that, I'd be there for him. Even though right now, he couldn't even be there for me.

FRIENDS AND FOES

"Faresh Kahmel is supposed to meet us at the restaurant, right?" Lora asked as we got back in the limo.

"Yeah, if he can make it." I slid in beside her. I was hoping the restaurant would be as good as Kahmel promised because I was famished.

Talad went in next. "He's always busy with something, isn't he?"

Lora narrowed her eyes at him. "Because he's running a country? Maybe if you did something for a living, you'd know what it was like to be busy."

I resisted the urge to snort. "All right, all right." I broke them up instead. I was done with this whole thing and didn't feel like anything but a smooth ride. "And yes, Kahmel has a lot of important things to address all the time, so he's busy most days. You should feel lucky; he's making an exception for the both of you."

"Huh." Talad broke eye contact and looked out the window. "Seems like you two make a lovely couple after all. Good thing our attempt to get you out of it failed, right?" He mumbled the last part, but I caught it loud and clear.

Lora scowled, which was a triumph for her, seeing as the most serious I'd seen her get was when someone tried to tell her she couldn't return something at the mall. "Look, I've had about enough of you. You're just jealous."

Talad scoffed. "Please. Of what? Museum dinosaurs and having to go out in disguises? Or maybe it's becoming the country's biggest laughingstock that appeals." He laughed darkly and turned to me with a lopsided grin. "Tell me, Jashi, which is it?"

My hand flew before I even realized I'd slapped him. Talad glared at me with a hand on his cheek, and Lora's eyes were wide. My hand was still suspended in the air; I couldn't even believe I'd done it.

But it felt *good.*

Breathing out, I put my hand down and slid the partition open between the driver and us. "Take us home so I can change."

I closed the partition and glanced coolly at Talad. "I've put up with a lot for the twenty-four hours you've been here, but enough is enough. You may not like that I'm here. Join the club. But now that I am, there's no getting rid of me, so you might as well get used to it. I *am* your Faresha." I couldn't help but feel a little powerful and maybe even dangerous as I chuckled and grinned at him. "And if you thought *I* was bad back at Nana's place, you don't want to meet my husband when he's in a bad mood because I've been keeping you from the worst of him. He knows who almost helped steal his Faresha away last year, and he hasn't forgotten. So if I were you, I'd be careful."

That seemed to finally let Talad understand who he was addressing, and, frankly, he was right to be afraid.

Lora's eyes glittered with approval, but we gave each other looks that meant we'd talk later when he wasn't around. The rest of the limo ride was once again silent, but it was much more comfortable this time.

After we got back to the palace, Lora and I tried to get ready quickly while Talad was taken back to his hotel to get dressed, but it inevitably ended in failure because we spent it completely in all the words we couldn't say in the car, wagging our heads and even laughing at the situation, even though it enraged us.

We relived the slap many times over.

When we were finally dressed and ready, it was evening. Talad would meet us at the restaurant, and so would Kahmel, so Lora and I had the limo to ourselves.

When we arrived at the restaurant, the sun had almost set, the night turning dark hues of purple, and the stars sparkling faintly behind the blue that remained. A dry, dusty air carried the last of the heat from the morning, dragging a slight chill behind it that meant it was getting ready to transition to the frigid night temperatures. I hugged the shawl that hung around me a little tighter.

The outfit Lora finally approved of me wearing was a tangerine silk wrap. My royal sash was wrapped around my shoulder, and a sparkly shawl the color of the insides of a grapefruit protected me from the chill that was on its way.

Lora could have easily passed for royalty on a regular basis, but even more so tonight, with a deep blue dress that hugged her curves and cascaded down her long legs with a short split on one side. She fluffed the back of her bouncy hair as she stepped out of the limo, sliding out smoothly despite the high black heels that would have easily sent me toppling back in. She adjusted her black cardigan better on her shoulders.

"I'm so excited. I hope the food is as good as the Faresh promised," she said, her glossy red lips spreading as she grinned.

Kahmel had promised this restaurant was good, but I'd yet to try it. Still, if the food at the palace was any indication, he didn't have bad taste, so I trusted him.

Another car pulled up, and Talad stepped out of it. He was wearing a tux—one I instructed servants to buy and leave at his hotel since I knew there was no way he owned one already. But he didn't even glance our way as he strode toward the restaurant, leaving his chauffeur to shut his door behind him.

Lora tsked beside me. "Now I kinda want to see what would happen if you did tell Kahmel."

I laughed and slapped her playfully on the arm. "Come now, you don't want our friend to meet an untimely death, do you?"

"He's asking for it," she mumbled as we started walking. "But whatever. We haven't been able to hang out like this for a long time. Let's enjoy it."

Those words were underscored when we went inside, where a massive crystal chandelier hung above the entrance. Delicate music drifted through the air, bright white marble floors making the room seem to glow. Even the waiters looked immaculate in black tuxes and bowties. Windows stretched all the way up to the huge ceilings on all sides except the front, giving a view of the stars from every table. A catwalk wrapped around the walls about halfway up the building, lined with tables that surely had an even better view than the ones at ground level.

He had stormed in first, so Talad was waiting for us before the host stand.

I stepped up. "Reservations for the Omah family."

The host lit up. "Ah, yes, His Majesty Faresh Kahmel is already waiting for you."

He guided us to a glass elevator to our left. With a flourishing bow, he gestured for me to go first. I went in, followed by Lora, Talad, and the host himself. He hit the only button on the panel, and we glided up until we were level with the catwalk, a clear glass banister serving as a gleaming barrier to the side. With a grin, the host took us to where Kahmel was sitting, right beside a window. All the tables on this level were farther apart than they were on the ground level, so it gave us privacy. Here in the outskirts of the city, the entire desert expanded before us, and where our table was, we overlooked an oasis just behind the restaurant, a sparkling lake in its center, palm trees and tropical foliage stretching out toward the rising moon.

Kahmel rose as we approached him, and Lora and Talad instinctively gave brief bows.

"Your Majesty," they both greeted.

As usual, his expressions were masked by his sunglasses, the sash wrapped around his shoulder, demanding an air of respect. But he managed a small smile for my friends as he gestured for them to sit. "Please."

Lora smiled as she sat down at the circular table, shaking her head. "Even knowing it's true, it's still hard to imagine the guy that lived in the fancy spooky house a couple blocks down being Faresh now. And married to Jashi!"

Kahmel chuckled as he pulled out a chair for me beside him, and Talad sat down, looking uninterested. "Am I the same as you remember?" he asked as he sat back down.

"Secretive, protective, and hard for most to get along with. Yeah, I'd say you're about the same. The hard part is imagining you with Jashi," she added with a laugh. "But believe me, I'm glad for it. She needs someone responsible making sure she doesn't get into too much trouble, and I'm tired of doing it."

I pretended to be offended, ignoring Talad as he muttered something to himself.

The host placed menus in front of us and asked for our drink order, all of us asking for water, except for Kahmel, who ordered a wine he'd chosen especially for the occasion for the table to share.

"You're the one I don't know much about, Talad," Kahmel said as warm loaves of bread were placed on the table. "You must have come to the orphanage after I left town."

Talad nodded. "That's right. I've only ever heard of you after you became Faresh."

I tugged at a piece of bread, tearing it apart carefully as it was quite hot, and getting a sliver of butter from the tray beside me. From the mood Talad was in, I was curious if I'd even have to bother telling Kahmel anything.

"You, Jashi, and Lora must have made good friends for all of you to still be in touch after so long."

I smirked as Lora made a so-so face but tried to dissimulate it with a sip of water.

Talad poked at the napkin that was folded into the shape of a swan. "If they wanted some good old-fashioned troublemaking, sure."

"Hm, so I heard," Kahmel said with an edge of danger in his voice. That made Talad shift in his seat. I had to suppress a laugh as Kahmel had no idea how effective that slight acknowledgment really was.

"We should order," Kahmel said, changing subjects. He picked up his menu.

Remembering I shouldn't get full on the bread, I put it down and picked up my own menu. All the options looked good, and I still wasn't used to fine dining like this. The menu items didn't even have prices.

I didn't like how Talad's words snuck up on me at that moment. About being the laughingstock of the nation. Feeling stupid didn't help.

Seeing how lost perhaps all of us looked, Kahmel made a few suggestions for what he liked, and we all finally settled on something we were content with. It took a little convincing, but Kahmel got me to try something I'd never even heard of. A desert vegetable that came from a particular species of cactus he was certain wouldn't kill me, so I took a leap and ordered it.

"If this cactus thing kills me or gets me hallucinating, it'll be on your head," I told Kahmel as I handed the waiter my menu once we'd finished ordering.

Lora laughed. "Do we need to call Nana, tell her you're not eating your vegetables again?"

"Shut up," I retorted. "Don't tell Kahmel all my secrets."

With a devious look in her eyes, she took a sip of her wine. "You mean like the times Nana found vegetables stuck to your butt from you hiding them under your seat to pretend you ate them?"

"Lora!"

Lora cackled as Kahmel was obviously holding in his own laughter, and I crossed my arms. "Off with your head," I seethed.

Kahmel leaned back in his seat and wagged his head. "Sorry, that fell out of style a couple centuries ago, Faresha."

"Damn it."

"Well, you're bringing everything else back, Faresh. Some would wonder if you even drew the line anywhere," Talad quipped, and the table fell silent. Like the fatal seconds before a lion leaped from its hiding place and pounced.

Or, in this case, a Half-Drac.

Kahmel's forehead creased as he raised an eyebrow behind his glasses. "Oh? I have earned that sort of reputation, yes. The barbarian Faresh. I suppose you would agree."

The challenge sounded lethal, and I wasn't quite sure it wasn't.

Talad shrugged. "I wouldn't say that. Looks like you're doing a fine job so far." He raised his wine glass and winked at me. "Marrying someone like Jashi, you must be doing something right, right?"

"Is there something you'd like to say? Because really, I'm all ears." The way Kahmel said it, it almost sounded like an option. He folded his hands together and cocked his head to the side like he was really intrigued. But the vein throbbing in his temple said otherwise.

Inwardly, I cheered him on.

"I just find it funny that you joke about something being out of date when a lot of traditions some people would think you'd keep in the past are being brought up again. Dragon-riding without collars, research through books, arranged marriage."

Lora's eyes went to her drink, which she sipped with nonchalance as if already declaring that if anything happened, she was fine with claiming she didn't see a thing.

Strangely, Kahmel eased up, his hands unclenching from each other. In a lower voice, he said, "I can understand you being dubious about me marrying your friend. You grew up in the same house with her, after all. That's why I'd like to offer an opportunity for us to all get to know each other better. I don't like this stiff air we have between us over this." With a deep breath, he added, "Things wouldn't have been as rushed as they ended up being had it been up to me, but a series of binding situations wouldn't allow it. This isn't the way I wanted it to happen, but it's happened all the same. I love Jashi, and I intend to make her happy here."

The sight touched my heart as realization dawned on me. Kahmel set all this up so he could get my friend's approval. I may not have had any family I could claim, but they were the closest thing to it for me. I was currently mad at Talad, but the sentiment was still sweet, all the same.

Talad blinked, fidgeting and not seeming to know what to do with his hands. Finally, he clenched them, squaring his shoulders back. "I'm happy for her," he said, with no emotion to the statement at all. He laughed darkly. "Forget the classes Lora's slaving herself over, the life I've had to crawl through to get by—you've let her skip all the way to the front of the line when you barely even remembered her! Believe me. I'm incredibly happy for Jashi. Lucky little—" whatever he was going to call me, it looked like Talad had reached the limit of bold statements he was willing to say in front of Kahmel.

Rising from the table, Talad bowed again. "You'll have to pardon my abrupt departure, but I suddenly feel sick."

Talad walked away, and I forced myself not to watch him leave.

PLANS ON THE PLANE RIDE

Music drifted in the room from Lora's eWatch on the dresser. We laid on her bed, tired from all the loud singing and dancing. Our hair was splayed on the sheets, entwining with each other's strands, our feet dangling on opposite ends. Two weeks had passed like the wind, but they were full. And now she had school, and I had rebel duties she would never know about.

But it was nice to know that we always had this. No matter what had changed.

"I really appreciate you having me over," Lora said.

I sighed placidly. "Just like old times."

She laughed. "Yeah, you in lavish robes and your own museum, just like old times."

Laughing, I turned over. "Well, like old times, but even better."

"Absolutely!" she turned to face me, then pursed her lips. "Are you worried about Talad?"

I looked away, listening to the upbeat tune that played.

After Talad's outburst at the restaurant, his driver took him to his hotel, and no one had seen him since. Kahmel asked me if I wanted him to send a search party after him, but I said no. It was sad but unsurprising. This was what Talad did best. Disappear. Gosh, it was what *I* did.

Most likely, he'd go crash with someone or go home. I wasn't worried.

Just hurt.

"I'm fine," I said, finally. "You know how he is. He did the same thing at Nana's place, remember?"

"Yeah…" Lora said, turning onto her back and touching her cheek in thought. "Psh, some people never grow up. Not worth your time and energy worrying for people not worried about you."

I nodded. "Yeah. Better I learn sooner than later he's not the friend he used to be to me."

"Agreed." The music floated between us, and Lora chuckled. "Too bad he didn't get to see Arusi. I remember how he looked at her when you came to visit Kohpal with her a few times."

Smiling, I remembered the same. I thought they'd be nice together at some point, but now I scoffed. "He wouldn't have been able to handle her. Arusi is too no-nonsense for him."

"His loss."

There was another pause before Lora said, "Hey, Jashi. I know this palace life stuff is…definitely a big change for you. But I'm proud of you. You're finally in a place where I feel like you're okay, and I don't have to worry about you so much."

I scoffed and chuckled. "You don't have to worry all the time. I'm fine."

Lora didn't laugh with me. Instead, she sat up all the way. Surprised by the change in the mood, I sat up with her. Her eyes were twinkling. "I mean it, Jash. You've always been like a little sister to me." She huffed as a tear escaped down her face. "And you were always getting fired, you moron. You always said you were fine, but…" Lora got choked up and just shook her head. "I'm just so glad you're all right now. And you're obviously with someone that cares a lot about you, looks after you. I feel like I can rest easy now."

I tried not to let my own eyes sting, but soon stray tears were sliding down my cheeks too. Words felt inadequate. Instead, I let my actions say all the words I couldn't say, rushing forward and pulling her into a hug, sniffling.

With that, with words unsaid but understood, our diversion was over. She had to pack up and go back home. And it was time I started acting in my role as Faresha. The farewell sobered me up but left me feeling armed for what was to come. Armed with support, understanding, and newfound wisdom that came with knowing I had matured. Kahmel was handling matters with T'shan and his family, I'd seen Lora and made peace with the situation with Talad.

It was time for me to leave, as well.

Though, thankfully, it seemed this trip out of the country would prove to be much smoother than my first.

I WAS sad to miss my dragon-riding lessons, but at least it was for a good cause.

Kahmel, Rand, Arusi, Asan, and I were all boarded on Kahmel's private plane, and it felt good to finally have a space to be able to talk about things with no fear of eavesdropping. Khes wasn't coming on the expedition because there wasn't much need for a war general at a friendly meeting between countries. Asan, being head of PR, was a necessity, even if he wasn't a rebel. Kahmel tended to leave enough messes of his own.

Hashir shrunk in the distance behind us, and I held words of comfort in my heart. From Arusi, Kahmel, Lora, and T'shan and his friends. All the ones that mattered.

I could do this.

Kahmel's hand squeezed mine, and he gave me a small smile, flipping back his sunglasses, his tangerine eyes full of warmth.

I turned away from him and went back to reading the book I'd snuck on the plane. The rebels had been able to print and bind the book we'd copied from the Shederei manor, but I was hitting a wall already. Nothing the book detailed about the general's life helped me piece together *how* he used a Drake Bond, only that he did it. Which didn't help much.

Rand clapped and rubbed his hands together. "So, shall we begin?"

I frowned. "Begin what?"

"We're officially on our mission," Kahmel explained. "We have to pool information with another rebel leader to get our bearings straight before anything else."

Arusi poured herself a glass of bourbon from the wet bar, whirling it slightly so the ice clinked around the glass a few times. "Which, in this case, is Matron Taias," she said before she took a sip.

Sometimes I forgot the little old woman who raised me had this whole double life she never told me about. It was crazy to wrap my head around her sneaking immigrants into the country, plotting with Kahmel and his associates in secret HoloCalls, then going back to stirring a pot of her famous beef stew by the time all the kids got home from school.

But I was glad to be able to talk about things without pretenses now. We really hadn't had a candid conversation since we talked in New K'sundi, right before Kahmel and I set off for the cave of the Dragon King. Ever since then, all I could ask about was the orphanage and for a recipe I wanted to make here and there.

Asan got up and moved to the center of all of us, starting a HoloCall, Nana soon appearing on the screen. I put my book away.

Rand held his hands to either side, closing his eyes. "Matron Taias, we summon thee."

Nana tsked and rolled her eyes. "I'm not dead yet, you idiot. But you will be, you keep testing me."

It was strange seeing Nana in this setting, yet oddly familiar. She handled Kahmel and his friends like a grown-up version of the kids she managed at the orphanage. Rolling her eyes, telling someone to straighten their back, and giving them the agenda for the day.

Only difference was this wasn't our list of chores. This was our plan to change a nation. Still, I liked seeing some things never changed.

Nana lit up as her eyes came to Kahmel and me. "Hello, Jashi! I see you and Kahmel are getting comfortable finally."

Self-conscious and embarrassed, I removed my hand from Kahmel's and put my face in it, my cheeks burning. "Nana!"

"Oh, quit complaining. He is your husband, after all. Not like it's anything strange. Anyway, how have you been? How was your visit with Lora and Talad?"

Interrupting the flood coming from Nana's mouth, Kahmel cleared his throat. "I think we should probably stick to business first. You and Jashi can always catch up later."

"Whatever you say, *rebel leader*," Nana teased. Becoming more serious, she said, "I believe I'm already aware of your intentions. Meet with the emperor of Gheres so you can get close to the assumed location of the entrance to the Dragon Realm. And it would be nice if we could get him on your side about bringing the dragons back. With their right minds intact, that is. It'd certainly help Kahmel with his promise to the Dragon King."

Kahmel subconsciously stroked his arm, and it made me realize I didn't even know how he was holding up with that, what with us rarely seeing each other these days. I found myself tracing lines on his bicep, imagining the black lines that coiled up his arms underneath the thin fabric of his buttoned shirt. Realizing what I was doing, I dropped my hand.

Nana was still watching and gave me a knowing look. Thankfully, instead of focusing on it, she went on to say, "I'd recommend prodding Daoliu Kun for loyalty. K'sundi has been good to Gheres over the years, and Daoliu can appreciate that. If Kahmel can live up to the friendship he had with the previous Faresh, we might have an ally we can depend on if worse comes to worst."

Rand asked, "Which reminds me, how much do we want to tell T'shan?"

Kahmel had decided that the best way to keep T'shan away from prying eyes was to keep him close. A secret take-off would be happening soon enough with T'shan and his parents being flown by a small team of rebels in another, smaller, private plane so that they could accompany Kahmel and me as "entourage." T'shan's new cover was that he and his family were stable hands for our dragons.

"Good question," Arusi mused, watching the ice cubes in her drink. "I don't think anyone is ready for the truth about the Dragon Realm until we have everything together already. But him knowing we're trying to win over other nations to our side shouldn't be too harmful. He's already extremely loyal. So are his friends."

Kahmel nodded. "I'd like to tell them whenever we can as well." He turned to me. "And I'd like the both of you to continue your dragon training as much as possible while we're away."

I grinned. Learning that Huntress and Comet would be coming with us was the best part of my evening. Transporting two dragons across the country wasn't easy business, but being Faresh had its perks.

Asan poured himself a drink next to Arusi. "I think that's the short and skinny of it. Anybody got anything else to cover?" When he was met with silence, he said, "Then I guess that's it. We'll contact you with status reports, as usual, Taias."

"I'd appreciate it. May the Great Spirits be with you all," she said before winking at me and turning off her transmission.

"Well, I'm hungry," Rand announced. He walked over to the bar, opening and closing cabinets, apparently searching for something. He tsked. "Damn it, Kahmel, you packed this place to the brim with booze, but you forgot the peanuts? What kind of rich Faresh flies around in a plane with everything but peanuts? Even flying coach, you get peanuts."

Kahmel rolled his eyes and ignored his twin as he continued his noisy search for peanuts.

I laughed, looking around at my new group of unexpected friends. Appreciating those that could grow with me. Feeling more comfortable than I had in a while.

It felt good.

GHERES

When we landed in Gheres, Kahmel and I were greeted with flashing cameras and reporters everywhere as we stepped down from the plane. The sun was settling behind the mountain range in the background, turning the skies a bright orange hue. The reporters were all chattering in K'sundii and Gheresan alike. Amid them was Daoliu Kun, Emperor of Gheres. He was clad in a dark suit with gold shoulder tassels and black shoes. He stood with his back completely erect and shoulders squared, almost military-like. His dark hair was slicked back, coming down to the nape of his neck. He had an olive complexion and dark eyes that angled at the ends, crow's feet crinkling his skin.

He greeted us with a whisper of a smile, offering his hand to Kahmel and then shaking mine in turn with a grip like wood. Arusi, Rand, and Asan were being escorted away behind us.

"Welcome to Gheres," the emperor greeted in slow K'sundii.

Kahmel pressed a button on his earpiece, reminding me to push mine, activating the instant translator. "Thank you for having us," Kahmel responded, his words translating to Gheresan through the speaker on the device.

Emperor Kun had a similar device. Even through the translator, he sounded stiff. "All of your arrangements have been made, so you have but to settle into your rooms. Your entourage will be accommodated as well."

Kahmel gave a slight bow of respect to the emperor. I followed his lead, keeping mostly silent. This was much more important than stupid arguments with the Court. Making Kahmel look bad now would be detrimental to the respect he had, not only from Gheres but also from all the other countries in the world.

"It's greatly appreciated," Kahmel said. "I look forward to continuing K'sundi's good relations with Gheres."

Kun's half-smile widened ever so slightly. "Likewise. Please, follow the servants to your living quarters and make yourselves comfortable. You have had a long journey to get here. Tomorrow we can all have lunch together."

Kahmel was silent, and it wasn't until I felt everyone's eyes on me that I realize that it was because he was looking to me to answer.

Confused and feeling out of place, I stammered, "Th-thank you. Very much. We'll do that!"

It was a choppy response, and I felt like a moron, but Kahmel was apparently satisfied as he gave the emperor another bow, an example I followed, and then did as Emperor Kun had instructed and started after the servants and assistants.

Once we were out of earshot, I hissed to Kahmel, "What'd you put me on the spot for?"

He chuckled, and I narrowed my eyes at him further. "We made a deal," he said in a low voice, as cameras were still flashing us at every corner as we made our way down the runway. "I'm just helping you stick to your end of it."

"I don't know how to talk to world leaders!" I insisted.

"It's easy—you open your mouth and speak." Seeing me scowl, he added, "You have to start remembering who you are. If you were a commoner, you might have a problem, but as a royal, you have to stop seeing yourself as beneath everybody. You are Daoliu Kun's peer and my wife, not my sidekick."

I sighed. This was going to be a hard habit to shake.

We were escorted to a waiting limo and then driven to the palace. The way there was magnificent—a rolling countryside lush with greenery and forest life. The humid area allowed for varieties of plants with huge, shiny leaves and brightly colored flowers, fruits hanging from almost every tree we passed.

Getting to the palace itself took my breath away.

We stepped out of the limo to find a structure painted a rich green, with gold-colored eaves wrapping around every floor. The driveway was lined with topiary cut with acute precision into jungle animals. Looking closer, I noticed that animatronic technology made them move slightly: stomping feet, raising heads into silent roars, and trunks waving in the air. A reflecting pool mirrored the palace, reminding me of the ethereal feel of the Dragon King's realm, and the thought filled me with an unexpected sweet feeling, like smelling a detergent that reminded you of home—somehow familiar.

We were escorted up the stairs that lead to a long patio that wrapped around the whole building. Emperor Kun's limo arrived shortly after ours, so he and his entourage were there to show us to our room themselves. It was essentially another wing to the main palace that was only accessible from the outside. Almost a separate house, like the suite I stayed in before Kahmel and I were married. They explained that Kahmel and I could have any personal entourage, like bodyguards and close family, stay with us here, which was perfect for keeping T'shan close.

Our luggage had been sent ahead of us, so we found all our things already in place in the drawers when we came into the building. Plenty of gowns and robes for me to change into, Kahmel's suits, his extra sunglasses. Since Rand and the others came ahead of us, they were already settling into the rooms they'd chosen.

"I trust that everything is to your liking?" Kun asked.

"It's wonderful," I said, still gazing at my surroundings. It was so elegant. Dark wood floors stretched across the room, plush furniture adorning the ornate feel. Urns with intricate patterns painted into them stood on the ground. Beautiful paintings hung around the walls that had to be as old as some of the art back at home. The space was huge, with a living room that had direct access to a garden behind sliding glass windows. There was a hall to the side, and, as a servant was telling us, four beds and baths. There was apparently no kitchen because all our needs would be attended to by calling a servant with a little android that would alert them to our requests and deliver it immediately.

"This will be perfect," Kahmel noted as well.

Kun nodded in acknowledgment as if confirming what he already knew was true. "I would like to remind you that whatever you need, do not be afraid to ask. There will be servants outside your door at your disposal at all times."

Kahmel thanked them again, and Kun gave a slight bow before leaving the room with an air of grandeur. I found it hard to imagine myself leaving a room with that kind of presence.

Rand came from out of one of the rooms. "Hey! This place is swank, right?"

I chuckled as Asan came out with him, shaking his head. He was dressed with the utmost professionalism, as always. A dark suit enveloped his wiry frame, his goatee and mustache combination making him look a little diabolical, but, then again, he was Kahmel's political side of the team, so that was probably a good thing.

"Here's the plan for the schedule," he said. "Tomorrow, you'll meet with the emperor for a few hours after noon for lunch. Then, around evening, Kahmel has a meeting scheduled with the emperor to discuss business."

"Jashi and I," Kahmel corrected, and Asan's eyes flickered over to me doubtfully for a moment before he conceded.

"All right, you and Jashi. Anyway, the day after, you'll be able to get some time to go on a nice 'hike' in the jungle in the morning. But don't take too long, because His Imperial Majesty wants to hold a very fancy soiree in honor of your visit, and you'll need time for preparation, believe me. Emperor Kun is known for his extravagant parties."

Arusi came from her room and leaned against the wall, crossing her arms.

I knew, like before, Kahmel and his men had already done a lot of research on the general area where the entrance to the Dragon King's realm would be, but still, it seemed like an awfully short window of time, given the fact that their information was still thousands of years old. "Do we only have the one day to go 'hiking'?"

Asan grimaced. "I don't know. The emperor isn't the best at keeping to an itinerary, and he's known to change his mind at the drop of a hat. The rest of the week looks relatively clear, but if you end up leaving an impression on him, he may want to change plans. And you don't want to appear so anxious to leave his company by declining if he does. We'll have to play it by ear."

Knowing that made me more than a little anxious. We were running out of time every day with Zendaal holding potential rebel status over our heads, and with Gheres on the good list, there was no way we'd get a second chance to come here if that happened.

Kahmel rested a reassuring hand on my shoulder. "All right, so we have our plan for now. Let's have something for dinner and rest up for tomorrow."

At that moment, T'shan came in, gaping at everything. "This place is amazing!"

His parents didn't seem to know what to do with themselves but smiled in acknowledgment at Kahmel and me, then retreated into their room. I understood what it meant.

Thank you for saving our son.

The feeling of accomplishment warmed my heart.

Rand clapped his hands together. "I don't know about you guys, but I'm ready to eat. Who do we ask for dinner?"

Asan showed us by using the little android sitting on the kitchen counter. We were soon brought a feast fit for, well, a king. I'd only had food the kind the servants brought in Gheresan restaurants, and I didn't visit those often for how high the prices of the food usually were.

There were several noodle dishes, bowls of rice, sauces, meats, chopped pickled vegetables, and more. The food was a mix of salty, sweet, and bitter, but it all somehow blended perfectly. Some of it was a bit spicier than I was used to, but it tasted heavenly, so I fought through a flushed face and teary eyes to finish it.

Once we were done, servants came to take our dishes away, and we retired to our rooms. Mine and Kahmel's was every bit as grand as the rest of the house, with a huge mattress, opulent curtains fringed with gold trim and elaborate patterns framing the windows. Warm wood extended into this room as well, not even creaking as we treaded on its firm surface. A huge rug with red and orange patterns swirling in it centered the furniture in the room and felt plush against the soles of my shoes. There was a folding screen with flowers painted over it against one wall, giving the room a taste of the jungle outside.

Noticing there was no closet, I ducked behind the folding screen to change into something more comfortable, glad to have my glamorous robes off after the long trip.

When I came back, I found Kahmel already in his t-shirt and underwear, looking at his eWatch and frowning.

"What is it?" I asked.

Seeming to have just realized I was there, he shook himself. "Oh, it's nothing."

I crossed my arms. "What happened to sharing things with me more?"

He hesitated, then sat on the edge of the bed. "All right, all right, you're right." He swiped to bring what he was looking at on his eWatch in the air before me. A news article glowed in my face.

DRALUS QUESTIONS THE COMPETENCY OF THE FARESHA

Troubling incidents in the palace call into question the Zendaalans' leniency in having untrained dragons in the palace.

"Oh," I said in a small voice.

"We're not going to worry about it," Kahmel said, standing.

"They huff and puff at me all the time. Until they decide to do something, they're just empty threats."

I tried to take solace in his words as he started rifling through some of the cabinets. "Oh good," he commented. "There are extra sheets and pillows here."

I shook my head. "No, no, we're not going back to that. At least at home, you have your own bed. You're not sleeping on the floor."

"Then...what do you suggest we do?"

"Should be obvious," I said, averting my gaze and climbing into bed like my heart wasn't beating a thousand miles an hour. I slipped on my silk hair cap and tucked my hair under it. "We'll sleep together."

Kahmel probably stopped dead, but I didn't look at him to find out. Instead, I scooted over to one side of the bed and flicked off the lamp, tucking myself under the covers.

There was the soft sound of Kahmel hesitantly pulling back the sheets. I knew he had to be wondering if I was going to take it back. The bed dipped as he eased himself into it. He flinched as I turned over, then watched in confusion as I took two of the many pillows on the bed and created a mound between us.

"Oh," he said, understanding dawning on his features.

I raised an eyebrow, leaning over our pillow barrier and watching his eyes take me in as I did. With all the meetings, work, friend problems, and rebel business, I realized I hadn't seen much of this side of Kahmel. The part that simmered under that calm exterior, just waiting for the opportunity to claim what I already knew he wanted. "What kind of girl do you take me for? We've only had the one date."

Kahmel laughed. "Ah," he said, stroking his chin, and his eyes went to my lips as if he was reliving the moment we kissed. "I'd almost forgotten. Such a romantic setting." His hand moved to the back of mine, tracing circles and then trailing up my arm. "So, if we're dating, how long before we're married? Do I have to propose again, too?"

I laughed, tilting my head back. "I haven't decided yet."

"Oh, then we'll just play it by ear, then." He placed my hand in his palm, thumbing my wrist.

"Definitely."

His eyes went to the mound and then back at me. "But you won't take the pillows away."

Taking my hand away, I crossed my arms and looked at him sideways. "Nope."

He laughed. "Fair enough. I owe you a second date, though. That's one thing I actually look forward to on this trip—we have more time to be together."

A smile tugged at my lips. "That's true."

"And Jashi?"

I groaned like he was being a nuisance. But I was having fun. "Do you understand the concept of sleep?"

He chuckled at me, then paused. "I know the process of this arranged marriage has been messy, and a great deal of playing with chance. But the time we've had together... The way you've supported my dreams, as crazy and risky as they are...I've fallen in love with you. I love you."

The words made me remember that night I left him, crying, feeling like a traitor, his arms around me. The words I'd left unspoken then.

I pushed him back down and turned over with more force to exaggerate my point. "You're totally missing the point of the pillow mound," I said. "Good night."

"Good night," he said, finally rolling over and tucking himself in.

I love you, too, I said to myself. As I'd wanted to say way back then.

CIRSSA KUN

I woke up, blissful in the soft sheets. Light poured into the room through the parted curtains, breaking the darkness behind my eyelids. Frowning, I turned over, happier to be turned away from the sun. I felt something shifting at my side. Confused, I cracked my eyes open, finding Kahmel awake, turned toward me.

I forgot he was sleeping with me.

Shaking myself, I sat up, yawning and pulling my silk cap off. "Oh, hey."

"Hey," he said simply.

At a loss for anything else to say, I slid out of bed and started getting clothes ready. "I'm calling shower first."

"That's fine."

With a start, I realized this was new for both of us. This was the first time we had the opportunity to be alone together, with no demanding meetings and Court appointments to separate us. We had to act like a couple now.

After a refreshing shower to wash the sticky humidity of the region off my skin, I got dressed in my typical ensemble and tied up my hair, knowing someone was going to come in and professionally style it later. Then I dove out of the shower, avoiding Kahmel, and going straight for the living area, where everyone else was already gathered.

Rand waved to me, holding up a small bag of something he was snacking on. "Finally got peanuts."

I chuckled and shook my head at him. One-track mind.

Arusi rolled her eyes and turned to me. "When Kahmel gets up, we'll all have breakfast together."

Asan snapped his fingers like he just remembered something. "Also, I was able to arrange that ruin visit Kahmel asked me for this morning."

I frowned, confused. "What ruin visit?"

"You really have no idea how to keep a surprise, do you?" Kahmel said from behind me, a towel around his shoulders to protect them from his dripping hair.

Understanding dawned on Asan's face, and confusion rested on mine. Asan made a locking motion over his lips and said, "Oops, sorry, I guess I can't say anything more, then."

Before I could ask, Kahmel hit the button to the ovoid android resting on the counter and asked for breakfast.

T'shan came in at that moment. "Hey, all. What are we going to be doing today?"

"*We* aren't going to be doing anything," Asan corrected. "*You* have to keep a low profile, remember? The nameless stable hand that's already nineteen and has had his blood examination."

T'shan looked dismayed. "Well, that's not fun."

"Living is more fun than being dead, I can tell you that."

"Quit being so overbearing," Arusi admonished. She turned to T'shan. "We'll be busy today, but we'll try to find a moment to do something to make sure you don't go stir crazy being hidden."

T'shan smiled at her. "Thank you, *Arusi*." He glared at Asan.

I laughed at the display. "Come on, guys. Let's quit fighting and have breakfast already."

We decided to eat outside on the patio that overlooked the garden. I liked all the beautiful foliage, but the sticky heat was going to take some getting used to. And I could do without all the biting bugs.

After a filling meal and the inevitable bickering of the twins, we were visited by a servant who informed us that we were invited to a tour of the grounds to bide our time until lunch, which was the earliest time the emperor could see us.

We obliged and got the chance to see all the exotic plants with which the emperor adorned his grounds. There were pungently sweet-smelling flowers with waxy petals that looked toxically beautiful. Some plants were carnivorous, with seemingly innocent exteriors but wicked spires that snapped shut when prodded by the very biting insects that were quickly becoming the bane of the visit for me. There were even monkeys swinging through the nearby trees, and birds painting the skies with streaks of every color in the rainbow.

As we passed a natural pond with cranes dipping elegantly in for a drink, I noticed something familiar streaking through the sky.

"Is that a dragon?" I asked, pointing.

Our tour guide, a woman that introduced herself as Obssa, frowned at the sky. "Apparently so." She looked to us with clear discomfort in her mannerisms. "It isn't...yours?"

I realized where the apprehension came from—us having uncollared dragons.

Kahmel shook his head, his sunglasses glinting off the light from the sun as he looked up. "No, ours are in a special stable."

Horror slowly crawled up her features, and though she did her best to control it, I noticed the slight tremble in her hands. "Oh, I apologize for this, Your Majesties. This is highly irregular here, you understand. We will have the matter investigated immediately."

"Hm," Kahmel hummed, but I noticed the slight upturn of his lips.

I watched the dragon as it circled in the air for a while, then streaked across the sky as it darted away.

We continued the tour, Obssa looking rattled, stealing looks at the sky every now and then.

After we were finished, it was almost afternoon, and our servants were at the estate, ready to get us prepared for lunch. They changed my robes to something cooler, a thinner green fabric that wrapped around my form. It was much better than what I'd put on, and it blew easily with the wind. They applied a heavy layer of makeup, suitable for making a good impression on Daoliu Kun, and pulled my hair into a high bun.

When the servants were done with me, I emerged into the living room to see Kahmel already dressed, his sash about his waist, his edges freshly cut. Rand was slumped on the couch, frowning out the window.

"Where's T'shan?" I asked after looking around.

"Tending to the dragons," Arusi answered. "And his parents are in their room."

I nodded at Rand. "What's wrong with him?"

Arusi shook her head. "Don't ask."

"I never get to go anywhere!" Rand answered anyway.

"Oh, quit being a baby," Kahmel reprimanded.

Rand tsked. "Easy for you to say; you're the one who always gets to sit in the limelight. I'm just your 'entourage' all the time."

Kahmel and Rand went back to arguing, and Asan took one look at them as he entered the room and came to me instead. "I suppose I'll have to tell the only responsible-acting royal in the room that you're late."

"I'm responsible!" Kahmel and Rand objected at the same time.

Ignoring them, Asan went on. "Also, the emperor wanted you to know his wife decided to come at the last minute, so she'll be joining you. For the rest of the visit, as it seems."

Kahmel raised an eyebrow at that. "Cirssa? I thought she was in Med Mali."

"Oh, so now you want to be a royal," Asan deadpanned. "To answer your question, yes, but she heard you all were visiting and took the first express flight to be here. Apparently, she's eager to meet Jashi."

I frowned. "Why me?"

Asan leaned against the table. "You have a lot in common."

I waited, expecting him to tell me what exactly it was, but he didn't.

Arusi came forward and adjusted a stray strand in my hair. "Do you not remember anything you were told about Cirssa Kun?"

I pursed my lips, vaguely remembering Kahmel giving me a long lecture about world leaders and their family members and not paying attention to a word of it.

In my defense, I had a lot of rebel information to memorize, as well. I made mental space for the important things and discarded the rest. I never did much talking at these important world affairs anyway, so I didn't see a point in caring.

Seeing the expression on my face, Arusi laughed.

Rand said, "Well, it's not a big deal, it's just—"

"No, let her find out," Kahmel said, mischief dancing in his eyes. "Trust me, you'll figure it out as soon as you meet her."

Rolling my eyes, I said, "Let's just get out of here. You heard Asan; we're late."

Kahmel and I rushed out of the room and were escorted to the palace by the same guide who took us around earlier, Obssa.

The inside of the palace didn't disappoint.

Opulent marble floors stretched across, interrupted only by the green wood pillars that held up the tall ceilings. Urns decorated the floors, all with intricate patterns and paintings on them. Snake statues slithered across the walls like they were alive, coated with a metallic gold paint that made them look regal.

We were escorted down a massive hall of pillars and a long corridor until we came out into another area of the garden. There, a table awaited us under a beautiful red awning. And so did the emperor and—

Was *she* the empress?

The emperor stood and gave us a slight bow. I still wasn't quite sure if the woman beside him was his wife, but she gave a slight bow, too, and a wide smile. Dressed as she was, she couldn't be anything less than royalty—she wore a pink gown with a red sash crossing around her at angles, her ears swinging with large gold disk earrings. Her gown brushed the floor, her wide sleeves tucked against her body as she hid her hands inside them, folded. She carried herself with a certain regality. The confidence in her smile. The elegance in the way she poked out her chest and squared her shoulders as we approached her. A presence I had yet to master.

But she was my age, maybe a little bit older.

"I trust your guide has given you a sufficient tour of the grounds?" Daoliu Kun asked through his translation device.

"Yes," Kahmel said, looking to me and clearly enjoying how hard I was trying to mask my confusion. He turned back to the emperor. "Very much so."

Daoliu nodded. We needed no translation for what he meant as he gestured to the chairs before him.

As we sat down, servants flocked around us, setting down cups and promptly pouring tea from kettles into them.

"My wife was eager to meet you," Daoliu said. "She's returned from her trip in Med Mali to be here. Your Majesties Kahmel and Jashi Omah, Empress Cirssa Kun."

Daoliu gestured to his wife, and she grinned eagerly. So, this was the person I had so much in common with. We gave polite bows to each other, and I internally wanted to kick Kahmel. I knew he'd warned me, but still. I felt like he got pleasure from me being surprised, and I didn't like it.

Cirssa was a beauty. Her thick charcoal-dark hair was swept up the sides and came flowing down her shoulders in many waves, with a braid going around her crown. Her soft, olive-toned features were lightly dusted with colors, but not so intensely that her natural beauty didn't shine through. Dark doe-like eyes looked at both Kahmel and me with a friendly twinkle to them. While her husband had only barely smiled the entire time we were here, she proudly displayed pearly whites as she greeted us. It was hard to believe Daoliu was the one who threw extravagant parties for his guests. She seemed more the kind to party. Or, perhaps, she was the mind behind the gesture in the first place.

"Such an honor to make your acquaintance," I greeted.

Cirssa spoke for herself, a light accent twinging her words. She had no translator device. "And I, you. I have heard so much about you and have wanted to meet you for some time."

I resisted the urge to let my face fall. What could she have possibly heard about me when Kahmel and I had scarcely been together a year? And more importantly, what about anything she heard made her want to meet me?

"Please, enjoy your teas," Daoliu said. "The food will be brought out shortly. I hope you enjoy seafood."

If it was anything like that nasty fish Kahmel's mother fed me, the answer was a big fat *no*. But that wasn't appropriate for the occasion, so I just smiled and nodded.

Kahmel sipped his tea and said, "I regret that this is our first meeting, Emperor, but since I've entered the palace, I've been plagued with unhandled problems that demanded my attention before I could make niceties. I know you were close to the previous Faresh."

Cirssa's face fell with concern. "Yes! Faresh Adisoh died before we were married, but Daoliu has told me how close they used to be. And he was very troubled by the status of your nation in the wake of his family's death. So tragic."

Daoliu nodded in agreement, both to us and his wife.

I was surprised to see her so liberal with her opinion. Most of the wives of the important people Kahmel hung around were about as talkative as mannequins and just as lively.

"I know my predecessor left behind quite the legacy," Kahmel noted. "I can only hope to fill his shoes half as well."

Daoliu clasped his hands together. "I cared very greatly for the previous Faresh and his family, and, as such, I care very much for the nation of K'sundii, you can be sure. You had me particularly concerned with that war, especially after the Omanians surrendered. It almost seemed like you were after something in particular." Daoliu leaned back. "But then, I understand that a man must make a name for himself when he ascends the throne. Especially in a unique case such as yours, with not an ounce of the former Faresh's family blood running through you."

Even through the interpreter, the emperor managed to maintain a commanding presence and an authority to his tone. I felt like we were trying to acquire the acceptance of some disapproving grandparent.

And more than that, the emperor most certainly had his wits about him. I supposed I wasn't used to the life of politicians that had to carefully study each other's movements and intentions, but still, with as allusive as Kahmel famously held himself to be, I was astonished Daoliu was so close to the mark.

Still far from the truth—looking for legendary dragons in magical caves—but still, closer than most.

"Yes," Kahmel said, nodding slowly. "I have a lot of work ahead of me in that regard—gaining respect, that is. As my wife tells me," he looked at me, and my eyes widened in a *what-the-hell-are-you-mentioning-me-for* way. "The more mystery surrounds me, the more speculation rises in place of factual knowledge, and I lose trust in the process. Slowly but surely, I'm trying to rectify that. Like becoming more acquainted with more world leaders like yourself, Emperor."

Oh, that. I used a bunch of less complicated words, but yeah, that was the gist.

"Oh?" Daoliu said, raising his chin. "And how will you demystify yourself today, Faresh Kahmel?"

At that moment, a steaming pot was brought in and set in the middle of us, the liquids inside still simmering, the bubbles juggling vegetables, stringy noodles, and crab meat to the surface. A symphony of side dishes was brought out, and a small bowl of rice was given to each person at the table. They gave us large plates that curved upward, seemingly to hold it all in.

Part of me was embarrassed to admit I had lost all interest in the conversation when I saw the food, but not embarrassed enough. The only thing that prevented me from digging in was the fact that we were also here on rebel business, and, therefore, it would be bad form to ask Kahmel to re-explain everything to me later.

Besides, Nana might kill me if she found out.

A servant began serving us portions of rice with heaps of the side dishes piled on, dragging a good amount of noodles and soup into more bowls and bringing them to our sides.

This was much better than the lunch I had with Mira.

Cirssa clapped her hands together. "Let's eat! I haven't had anything since I boarded my plane. I am very hungry." She seemed completely unbothered by the exchange between the men, and I was starting to greatly appreciate her laidback mentality and how she eyed the food.

Perhaps she was a girl after my own heart, after all.

"Please, enjoy," said Daoliu.

I picked up a spoon and started sipping at the soup, finding it to be just as spicy as the food I could barely tolerate yesterday, my mouth exploding with heat and pungent flavors. It was good, but it was making me sweat already.

One of the servants standing by must have read my expression and came with a pitcher of hot water to water it down. I wanted to be ashamed, but I couldn't. It was hot.

Kahmel, always the showoff, took a big bite without a problem.

Cirssa smiled at me. "It is a little spicy. We know your palates aren't quite adjusted to ours, so we came prepared."

"Thank you," I said sheepishly, earning a nudge from Kahmel at my side. I straightened my back and smiled back.

Gosh, did this have to feel so much like Nana telling me to behave at the dinner table? Only now, I was being told to be *bolder* instead of the opposite. It felt strange.

Kahmel ate some of the rice with one of the vegetable side dishes, returning his attention to Daoliu. "I do want to demystify myself a bit. Like with explaining the change I'm trying to make in K'sundi with the dragons."

"Bah," Daoliu waved the topic away. "Yes, I've heard of your inordinate obsession with dragons. You must be dealing with many matters on your hands, recuperating from the war, dealing with your country's Courts. Why waste time concerned about dragons of all things?"

Despite Daoliu's words, Cirssa's eyes lit up with excitement. "Dragons! And uncollared, no less. How exciting. I heard you brought two here, is that true?"

She was looking at me, which turned the attention of the table in my direction, leaving me feeling very self-conscious with the trail of noodles leading up to my mouth. Finishing it quickly, I said, "Uh, yes, it is. We both have dragons, and we didn't want them to miss out on getting their exercise while we were gone."

Seeming to have forgotten the discussion between the men, she swooned. "That must be thrilling! I've always thought about getting a dragon, but," she shuddered, "the idea of the collar has always bothered me. I love what you're doing."

"It's strange," Daoliu objected.

"It's daring!" Cirssa countered. "Just what the world needs these days!"

"I agree with you," Kahmel said. "I think it reconnects people to a part of themselves they'd all but forgotten. Dragons are in your history as well."

Daoliu shook his head, frowning. "Yes, yes, everyone has dragons. But not wild!" His eyes narrowed. "It seems even the Zendaalans are beginning to question your methods. Have you seen the news?"

"Our dragons aren't wild!" I argued. "You know, everyone has assumptions about dragons without collars, but you know what? If you've never experienced it for yourself, how can you know?" I leaned back into my chair, hoping it would make me seem more confident than I felt. "How would you like to see for yourselves how well our 'wild' dragons behave?"

"Well—" Kahmel started but was cut off by Cirssa's happy squeal.

"I would love to see!" She grasped Daoliu by the arm, pleading with him. Daoliu looked reluctant, but as Cirssa pouted, it soon became clear who would have their way in the end.

"I suppose there would be no harm in seeing them, but—"

Cirssa smiled triumphantly. "You could show us after lunch?" she asked, then added, "Oh, if it is possible! I do not know if on such short notice?"

"Of course!" I said, only realizing after I'd said it that Kahmel was sending me warning looks.

"Perfect! I am excited," Cirssa said before diving again eagerly into her food.

Kahmel discreetly moved his hand so that his spoon fell to the ground. "Gah, dropped my spoon." He slid his chair back and looked to the ground. "Jashi, do you see it?"

Catching his hint, I leaned in closer, and he hissed to me, "Only *one* of our dragons is tame enough for royalty, Jashi. What are you going to do about Comet?"

Oops. What *would* we do about Comet? The two dragons were being kept together.

But, feigning confidence, I whispered back, "Relax, Comet trusts me now, silly. You haven't seen us since we had that incident, him and me. We'll be fine."

"I hope you're right," Kahmel said before announcing that he'd found his spoon and placed it in the open hand of a waiting servant.

That made two of us.

DRAGONS IN THE JUNGLE

There were two possibilities of how this could go: it could end up being a great idea, and we'd have started the first steps toward warming up another country to the idea of wild dragons. Or it could end in a horrible tragedy with someone getting either burned or electrocuted.

But I decided to be positive and only think about the former.

Positive, foolhardy, either one.

Dragon stables were common enough, especially among the rich, but they were created with little more thought than a car in mind. The standard stables simply weren't enough for my and Kahmel's dragons. Not enough room, and not even close to strong enough walls. We had to use a more portable solution that didn't require us to rely on someone else's stable, but that also meant having our dragons stay together since we only had one portable stable. Which wasn't a problem at the time, but now it had Kahmel sending me wavering glances every time I grinned at him like I knew what I was doing on our way to the stable. Close behind were Daoliu and Cirssa, their entourage in tow.

I was glad I'd had such a nice lunch. It might've been my last.

We approached the temporary structure. Metal poles held hard plastic panels together with hinges on every edge that showed it could fold back down as quickly as it was erected. It had a hexagonal shape and came to a point at the top. The idea behind it was not unlike the way the K'sundii armies built up army bases on the spot when need be.

There was no war anymore, thankfully, but the concept was equally as serving, especially dealing with two dragons on the inside.

Almost hesitantly, Kahmel opened the door to the stable.

The ceiling wasn't as high as the stables at home, but they were still accommodating for our dragons, who were chained to the walls on opposite ends of the room. A protective force field detected our presence and allowed us through as we stepped in, being humans. However, it hummed resistant against the antsy beasts that couldn't control the way their tails thrashed against the walls in their excitement.

I grinned. Both were eager to see us.

Cirssa gasped in awe. "Look at them. They're so...lively!"

We met a surprised T'shan, who was cleaning Huntress's scales. He bowed when he saw us.

"Y-your Majesties," he stammered. "What brings you all here?"

"Sorry to catch you unawares like this," Kahmel said, stealing a glance at me and then back to his protégé. "Can you prepare the dragons for us right quick? We want to do a sort of demonstration for the emperor and empress."

T'shan gave another brief bow. "Of course!"

T'shan went to a rack and pulled down basic dragon-riding gear —a belt carrying a laser whip and protective earpieces.

Daoliu was still looking grouchy and unconvinced, but his wife's eyes had stars in them as we were all handed protective earpieces. Daoliu held a hard expression but flinched as electricity arched from Comet's mouth and he roared with excitement. His entourage looked uneasy as well.

"Is that...supposed to happen?" Daoliu asked, trying and failing to hide his apprehension.

I smiled and nodded. "Comet's an Elemental; that's what he does when he's happy."

That was also what he did when he was upset, sad, mad, and bored, but I didn't bother to mention those minor details.

"Why don't I introduce you to Huntress?" Kahmel intervened, guiding the group to the other side of the stable, careful to keep us along the edges as we walked away from Comet, I noted. Probably a good idea, nonetheless.

"Is she an El...Elemental, too?" Cirssa asked, her accent coming out more on the word.

"No," Kahmel said as we came nearer to the dragon that was puffing out flames as we spoke, barely letting T'shan sling a harness around her.

She was supposed to be less excitable than Comet, but at the moment, I wasn't sure which one looked least likely to leap into the skies and start after the closest city as soon as we loosed them from their restraints. Were the dragons more excited than usual today?

"Huntress is more of a standard kind of dragon, solely fire-breathing. Elementals have more unpredictable abilities."

"Interesting," Daoliu said. "Are they safe to approach?"

"Completely," Kahmel assured him, though he quickly muttered to T'shan to put a muzzle on Huntress. Seemed like he noticed the odd mood of the dragons, too.

I hoped I hadn't picked the absolute worst day to go dragon-riding.

Like a natural, Kahmel swung onto the back of his dragon, her onyx scales making it look like she'd swallowed the light in the room. He offered the emperor and his wife a hand. "Would you like to try?"

Daoliu looked less than convinced, but Cirssa took his hand eagerly. "I'd love to!"

"No," Daoliu said. Coming between Kahmel and Cirssa, he said, "I insist on going before Cirssa. To make sure it really is safe."

Cirssa rolled her eyes as even members of their entourage chuckled at the emperor's sudden burst of bravery after seeing his wife was more eager than he was.

Kahmel shrugged. "That's fine; come on."

T'shan helped the emperor onto the dragon, then hit a button on the wall beside him to open the ceiling.

Daoliu hollered as Huntress took off into the sky with the two royals. Even from here, I could see Kahmel's eager grin. The emperor trying to keep from looking freaked seemed to only encourage him further.

Once the Huntress was out of sight, I turned to Cirssa. "Let's go outside and watch them."

Cirssa pursed her lips, then eased the words out, "Yes, or…"

I frowned. "Or?"

Then she grinned. "Or you could take me on your dragon, and we could follow them!"

One of her guards immediately stepped in, his words translated through the speaker in my ear. "Your Imperial Majesty, are you sure that's the best idea? These dragons do seem…temperamental. At least wait until your husband returns."

With the toss of her head, she dismissed the idea, turning back to me, mischief in her eye. "Come on; I'm not letting him hog all the fun. He always thinks he has to protect me from something! I'm tired of being treated like I don't know what's best for me. You understand, don't you? You're new to the throne, too!" She wagged her head. "These husbands mean well, but we have to show them that we can make decisions for ourselves, too."

Her words hit more at home than I expected them to. Some part of me screamed all the words Kahmel would be saying at this moment, but I ignored it and smiled. "You're right, Your Imperial Majesty." Maybe I did need this, even to prove to myself that I was capable. If she wasn't afraid and didn't know a thing about dragons, why should I be?

Her smile widening even further, she started toward Comet with me, placing her hand on my arm. "Please, call me Cirssa. I think we'll get along just fine, Mrs. Omah."

"Jashi." I returned the sentiment.

Her guards weren't so excited. "Y-Your Imperial Majesty—"

"I don't want to hear it," Cirssa interrupted, the authority in her voice effectively shutting up the waiting objections that obviously showed in the guards' faces.

"T'shan!" I called, and he chuckled as he ran after us and started saddling Comet.

"Already on it, Your Majesty."

T'shan made quick work of getting Comet ready, and several arcs of electricity were flying out of his mouth in excitement.

"Easy, boy," I said as I approached him. He did seem to calm as I neared him, lowering his head far enough for me to stroke his snout, earning a steamy sigh in response. "Good!"

I hadn't even been sure if that would work a second time. It was nice to know it did. I slung myself over his back, then reached down to help the empress up. "Get on!"

Cirssa glowed with excitement as she took my hand and awkwardly made her way up the beast.

A guard cautiously approached us. "Are you quite sure, Your—"

I was in the middle of grabbing Comet's Solid Light reins as Cirssa dove forward and grasped them from behind me. "HI-YA!"

Flicking them on my behalf, she set Comet into the air, and he eagerly caught onto her enthusiasm, soaring through the open ceiling and embracing the wide sky like he was born for it. Once we were in the air, Cirssa leaned back again.

"Sorry, I just didn't want to hear all the complaining anymore," she apologized.

I laughed. "You're my hero."

"Oh, look!" she said, and I had to turn a little to see her point to where Kahmel and the emperor were flying. They had their backs to us with no idea we were in the air.

Smirking, I said, "Are you ready to surprise our husbands?"

Cirssa held on to my waist for stability, but she didn't even tremble. "Let's go!"

I flicked Comet's reins again, and he eagerly beat his wings to gain speed, the wind clawing at our hair. Wanting to add a touch of flair, I tugged at him so he'd tilt upward, and soon we were literally on top of Kahmel and Daoliu.

Our shadow eclipsed them, and the two looked up, shocked.

Cirssa waggled her fingers. "Hello!" she shouted above the wind.

At that moment, Kahmel was giving me a look that was a combination of wondering if I was stark-raving mad and how fast he should be ready to save the situation if things went wrong.

But I wouldn't give him the opportunity.

To me, Cirssa said, "Come on; I have someplace I want to visit. I'll tell you where to go."

"I'd be happy to be your chauffeur for the afternoon."

Cirssa pointed in the direction of a line of trees that looked like the border leading into the jungle "That way."

Kahmel didn't even say anything. His face just fell with dismay as I led my dragon in the direction Cirssa indicated, and even through the muzzle, I could hear Comet's roars of excitement as he took us flying faster.

Cirssa cheered, and I felt exhilarated. Not only was Comet cooperating, it was like he was feeding off my energy, and I was feeding off his. It felt like ever since we had a sort of understanding that one time, we wouldn't have any hiccups like that again. We were in sync now. I was starting to understand what Kahmel said about trusting the dragon and letting it lead. Comet and I were at that point now, and I could feel it.

That, and something about driving Kahmel crazy just felt right. Couldn't have him thinking I was predictable or anything.

"I could just stay up here for hours," Cirssa said, sighing. "You were right. This is nothing like the dragons with collars on them. There's not nearly the same amount of...of spirit! The heart and soul have been cut out of dragon-riding. It's a crime."

Nodding, I smiled to myself. "Now you're getting it."

We flew in the direction Cirssa indicated for a while, soaring over emerald jungle flora like it was green carpet beneath us. We finally reached a point where she asked me to land, a rocky area that gave way to a stream and a small waterfall that led down a deep chasm that yawned open beneath us. A lake revealed itself in the crater in the earth, only visible once we came close enough to notice.

"Wow," I breathed.

"I love it here," Cirssa said as we landed. "But we don't get to come much these days."

Cocking my head as I slid down and helped her down as well, I asked, "Why is that? Seems like a tragedy to leave this place unappreciated."

"It is!" Cirssa pointed down the chasm. "But those have been moving in for the past few months, out of nowhere! And Daoliu said they were too dangerous to be around."

To my surprise, I noticed both Wingless and Draconian dragons circling the air above the lake and diving into crevices in the rock wall randomly. There weren't a lot, maybe four or five, but still. It was surprising to see any at all. But then again, I remembered what happened when we were taking that tour with Obssa. Maybe they were migrating more to the area for some reason. I'd have to ask Kahmel about it later.

"If it's possible," she said, crouching on the ground and just looking out into the crater, "I'd like you to arrange for them to be taken home with you. I'm sure you could find a place for them."

I sat next to her, admittedly a little unnerved by the wild dragons being so close but also amazed by how unfazed she was. "But why? If you agree with Kahmel and me, it probably won't be long before you can have someone learning to train them for you. Maybe you'll even learn to train dragons yourself."

She certainly had the courage for it.

But Cirssa shook her head. "No, I'd prefer it if it were you. Our people—they aren't ready for this. They need more examples, more time. They're not as eager as I am to see something change. Not yet at least, and these dragons are here now. Immediate action will have to be taken, and it won't be pretty otherwise."

That was certainly true. The Zendaalans were always breathing down our necks about our wild dragons, and we already had Watchtowers in place to regulate them. Since wild dragons weren't a thing anywhere else, neither were Watchtowers. Gheres wasn't equipped to handle this new development.

"All right then, I'll ask Kahmel about taking them off your hands when I get the chance."

"I don't think you'll have to wait very long."

Cirssa stood back up and turned just as I noticed Huntress snaking through the sky above us and coming to land.

Since his translator was still on, I heard Daoliu asking Cirssa what she was thinking, going on a volatile dragon like that when he specifically asked to go first. Cirssa didn't look like she was paying much mind.

As Kahmel approached me, I suspected I was in for a similar speech.

"What were you thinking?" he hissed.

"She asked me to take her! What was I supposed to do? Say no?"

He looked at me like it should have been obvious. "Yes!"

I waved him off, striding toward Comet and slinging myself on his back. "We managed fine. Oh," I leaned forward, resting an elbow on Comet's scaly neck, "and we just adopted a few more dragons. I'm not sure how fast you can send someone out here to catch them, but Cirssa tells me the sooner, the better. They hang out down there." I pointed down the crevice, and it seemed like Kahmel only just then noticed, his mouth falling open when he saw what was flying around on the inside of it.

Daoliu and Cirssa were too busy arguing to notice us, so I took the opportunity to mention, "By the way, Cirssa says these dragons have been appearing only recently. And I don't think this region usually has them."

Kahmel wasn't even looking at me; he was still looking down the chasm, stroking his chin. "No, it doesn't."

"Any idea why they'd suddenly show up like this? It's unusual, right?"

"It is." Kahmel drifted off into thought. He finally turned back to me after a moment. "I'm not quite sure. But let me know if you find out anything else. This might be a good opportunity to have T'shan take on his first field mission as a recruiter. I'll have some rebels help him with it."

I nodded just as Cirssa and Daoliu turned toward us. Cirssa explained, "I think it's time for us to head back. I think my husband has had all the excitement he can put up with for today."

Chuckling, I said, "No problem. Here, I'll help you up."

Cirssa accepted my hand as I offered it to her, and Kahmel went back with Daoliu on Huntress.

"I wish you luck on your journey, Faresha," Cirssa said. "Regardless of what people may say of your supposedly strange views, today, you have made a friend in me."

DRIVING FORCE

Going out with Cirssa was fun, but socializing was draining. Especially since we were also invited to dinner at a fancy restaurant in the city, along with a few other politicians and important members of the Gheresan government. They weren't nearly as fun as Cirssa, so it was back to plain responses, wide smiles, and shaking lots of hands.

I made an effort to speak up a bit more, which earned me more than a couple cases of wagging heads, whispers when I turned my head, and people talking down to me like I didn't understand anything. Which to a large degree, I didn't.

Thankfully, Kahmel covered for me and scared the table to silence whenever it got overwhelming by mentioning dragons and other related politics. It was a topic that often sobered everyone up and made them argue, and though it seemed like a headache to me, it did take their attention off, making me feel no bigger than a tick. And besides, they were arguing more with Kahmel than with me at that point.

I was glad I was finally done with it all and in my room. Once I was in comfortable clothing, I crawled into bed and sighed.

Kahmel sat down on his side as he was taking his sunglasses and eWatch off, smirking as he looked from me to the bed. "So, no pillow wall tonight?"

Giving him a look, I promptly stacked the pillows just like they had been the night before. "I just forgot, that's all."

"Hey, you weren't going to get any complaints from me."

"Hardy, har, har."

Crossing his arms and resting them on the pillows to look over at me, he said, "You did well today. I was impressed you handled yourself so well with Comet. And the empress, for that matter."

"Hm, thanks," I mumbled.

Kahmel brushed his finger across my cheek. "Hey, I mean it. Don't let a room full of old people get you down. You're adjusting quite well, I say. Especially only having ascended the throne barely a year ago, I think that's more than most could ask."

Breathing in, I tried to accept the compliment. "Yeah, you're right."

"You and Cirssa seemed to get along well."

I grinned when I thought about how eager she was to go earlier. "Yeah, she's great. She was even braver than I was when I first started out. I was surprised."

"She's something, all right. I bet you wish you were paying attention when we told you about her the first time, huh?"

I laughed. "Well, to be fair, her showing up was a last-minute thing. For the most part, I had all of the details I absolutely needed to know memorized."

Kahmel chuckled. "You had all the details you were excited about memorized. Regardless, I couldn't have asked for things to go better today. Daoliu may have been somewhat rattled by the whole experience, but you had Cirssa sold on the concept. And he may not look it, but I know for a fact he gives in to most things she wants."

"Huh," I said, tapping my chin pensively. "A guy that doesn't show his emotions much, so it's hard to tell he's actually a big soft ball in the middle. Gee, I wonder if I know anyone like that."

Kahmel picked up one of the pillows and whacked the side of my head. "Subtlety is not one of your finer skills."

Laughing, I picked up a pillow and whacked him back. "Anyway, we should probably go to sleep. We have our 'hiking trip' tomorrow, remember?"

"Sure, I remember. I also have a surprise for you tomorrow."

I remembered whatever Asan wasn't supposed to tell me earlier and supposed it must have been related. "All right. Will you give me a—"

"No."

I tsked at him. "Your surprises are the worst."

This time when he picked up his pillow, I grabbed it, trying to pull it from his grasp, ending up in a sort of tug of war full of laughing and straining. Finally, Kahmel showed how easy he was going on me by pulling the pillow, and me with it, until I was lying on top of him. Heat pooled between us as we breathed like that for a few moments, light dancing in Kahmel's eyes. Then I pursed my lips and slid off, yanking my pillow away from him and putting it back on the stack.

"Good night."

IF I THOUGHT the first trek Kahmel and I had taken to find a Dragon King was bad, this time was much worse.

Bugs treating my skin like a ten-course meal, humidity that made my clothes stick to my back, jungle animals that skittered, crawled, and jumped across the forest floor at random—this was hell.

Like last time, we had a general idea of where the entrance to the Dragon King's realm was supposed to be, but no clear direction. According to the research Kahmel's people had done, there was mention of something similar to "the Trembling One" in some old translated documents from New K'sundi. They were stories of disappearing travelers and people who believed that a horrible monster lived in the jungles behind the palace of the emperor. We figured, hey, we want to be disappearing travelers, so that sounds about right.

Kahmel's men didn't put it in so many words, but that was the gist.

As far as the rebels knew, we were only going here to research more about K'sundi's past and in hopes of finding more relics. Kahmel still didn't want them knowing about the Dragon Kings. The whole thing was a lot to handle, and the rebels already had many different tasks involving helping rebel nations, researching dragon techniques to help the Dragon Watchtowers, and more. For the moment, Kahmel just sent them on tasks to research things he knew would lead to what we needed and would fill them in later. When we thought they were ready.

"You know," Rand said after taking a swig of water from his canteen, "as hard as those Dragon Kings made it to find their realm, I'm starting to think they didn't want folks finding it."

"Come up with that on your own, did you?" Kahmel deadpanned as he swung a machete through the fauna to make a path for us.

Arusi was with us, too, taking up the rear, suffering quietly.

Asan had to hold down the fort back at the estate and tell anyone asking that we went sightseeing. Not to mention keeping T'shan company.

In the bright sun, the marks snaking up Kahmel's arms stood out all the more. I realized it wasn't often that I got to see him in short sleeves like this, other than at night before he went to bed, but the lights were always dim. I didn't get to see them in broad daylight like this.

"Do they still hurt?" I asked as Kahmel cut away more leaves and vines blocking our way.

He glanced over his shoulder at me and shrugged. "Sometimes. It hurt a lot more in the beginning, though." With a curve on his lips, he added, "I got a whole day of relief the day the museum opened."

That made sense. It was fulfilling his word to the Dragon King to make people more aware of dragons and, therefore, less abusive. Still, I frowned. "A whole day? You mean it's every day? That's a lot more than sometimes."

Again, Kahmel seemed nonchalant about something that was starting to deeply disturb me. "Frankly, I've gotten used to it. It's like it has moods. Days my work has nothing to do with dragons, it hurts worse. We open the museum, we promote T'shan to dragon recruiter, we fly to Gheres, I get relief, though I know it's going to come back in a day or so."

I wasn't quite sure how I felt about knowing that he'd been living with this constant pain without me knowing it. I supposed I never exactly asked, either, but still...

Rand cleared his throat, pointing up at the sky. "Has anyone noticed that happening every once in a while for the past half hour?"

Looking up, I caught the tail-end of something long and dark slithering across the sky before it disappeared behind the leaves of the towering trees above us.

While I had my mouth agape, Kahmel nodded calmly. "I noticed." Looking to me, he said, "Remember the first time. I think it means we're going the right way."

Arusi said, "Or we're going the wrong way, and that particular dragon just wants a quick snack."

Kahmel wagged his head and chuckled. "Thanks, Arusi. Nice to know I can always rely on you to keep things positive."

"What are friends for?"

As I swatted at something buzzing near my ear for the umpteenth time, I settled into the fact that things weren't about to get much more entertaining than this. So, fishing out my lighter from my pocket, I remembered that this was the perfect opportunity to practice using my fire, finally away from public eyes, hidden cameras, and secrecy.

The jungle was good for privacy if nothing else.

I cursed, fumbling with the trigger. I forgot it was near-empty.

"You know," Kahmel started, pulling out his canteen and sipping from it, "you should really start learning how to create fire on your own. I just haven't had the time to teach you, for obvious reasons."

I stopped. "Really? I'm finally ready?"

To my dismay, Kahmel shrugged. "Not sure, we haven't practiced together in a while, and I don't know what you've done on your own. But you might as well do something while that lighter's out."

It wasn't exactly encouraging, but it wasn't like I had anything better to do.

"All right, so what do I have to do?"

Rand imitated Kahmel's stern composure—easy, being his twin. "You must appear agitated and irritated at all times while being silently angry at the world. Only then will you conquer the power of the flame."

Rand and I burst into laughter while Kahmel scowled.

"I am holding a machete, you know," he said, hacking another vine with emphasis.

Arusi came up to meet him, chuckling. "Don't listen to your brother. Please, educate your wife so we can stop having 'accidents' in the garden when she's practicing on her own."

"Accidents?" Kahmel asked, raising an eyebrow at me. "I know I haven't been home much, but no one went out of their way to tell me, either."

I laughed, lightly punching his shoulder. "Never anything major or anything. And Arusi always covers for me so nicely."

Looking between the two of us, Kahmel sighed. "Yeah, let's get started as soon as possible. What triggers your fire most of the time?"

My brow furrowed. "You would know better than anyone."

"Not exactly. I noticed your fire seems to be slightly different from mine when it comes to the triggers. Yours usually seems to come when you're anxious, upset, or scared."

I nodded in thought. I'd never really seen Kahmel breathing out embers to keep himself contained, so I didn't know his was different. "What usually triggers yours?"

"Anger."

The statement was underscored with another swing of his machete.

Rand nodded at me knowingly, as if to say, *You have no idea.*

"All right...so yeah, you're right. Anxiety, fear, things like that."

Kahmel said, "Think of the kinds of things that make you feel that way. Visualize them."

I tried to think of the kinds of events that caused my fire to come up. None of them were happy. Back when I feared Kahmel catching me working against him, my flames came all the time. Before that, whenever I was around Attican. Before that, when someone made me mad enough at an old job, and before that, when I would get emotional and upset about my life situation at Nana's orphanage.

Not thoughts I liked to linger on.

"Do you have them in your head?" Kahmel asked.

My enthusiasm to start the exercises was dwindling by the minute, but I muttered, "Yeah."

"Good," Rand butted in, back with his imitation of Kahmel. "Now get agitated and irritated about it and stay like that forever."

Giggling at him made me feel a little better. Even Arusi chuckled.

Kahmel's hand lit up in flames, and Rand ducked behind a tree before a fireball catapulted toward him, then vanished before it could touch the foliage.

"Jashi, focus," Kahmel reasserted, and I straightened my face.

"Okay, okay."

Kahmel sighed as he continued to lead our trek, potentially to nowhere. "Are your hands on fire yet?"

I chuckled. "I think you'd notice if they were."

"That's right. Those thoughts alone won't do a thing to help you now. That's because those things only start your fire. They don't control it. You do. If you want to control your fire, you're going to have to initiate it a different way."

Oddly, that made sense to me. Whenever my fire came unintentionally, there was a sense of recklessness to it. It was like my emotions were the spark, and my body was kindling. It wasn't controlled at all—it just *reacted*. There was nothing to control; I could only contain it, or, as Kahmel taught me, redirect it now.

"How do I initiate it differently?" I asked.

Kahmel shrugged. "That's where I become less helpful."

I began to wonder why I missed being taught by him. His style was always frustratingly abstract and vague. He could point me in the right direction but then more or less left it up to me to figure out how to get there.

"How is this a lesson again?"

"Sorry," he said, pursing his lips. "It's not really an experience I can describe to you. It's like..." He paused, putting his machete away. "I still remember the day it happened. I was angry. We were still living with my parents, but it was getting close to my blood test, so it wasn't too long after that we had to leave. Anyway, growing up, I had a lot of pent-up frustrations with always having to stay hidden, and then the odd family dynamic of always being separate from Rand when he was the closest brother I had. I mean, he's my twin."

Rand scratched his head; even he was sobered up by the memory. He took a seat on a particularly big boulder beside Kahmel. Seeing we were taking a sort of unannounced break, I sat down on the ground, too. Arusi took her place beside me, completing our circle.

"Rand and I had a rare moment in between me coming home from high school and him on a sick day, and we got a chance to talk, and the conversation ended up in those frustrations coming up again." Kahmel reminisced. "And Rand was yelling at me to control my anger because by that time, he already knew what kind of circumstances started it. And we really didn't need me blowing up our house and giving my parents another reason to keep us apart."

Rand chuckled beside him, but the usual humor was gone. It pained me to think of their dark times together. They argued all day long, but it showed that they'd been through hell and back together. They would never get mad at each other in the real sense. I was sure both of them would have an easier time parting with an arm than each other.

Kahmel continued, "It was a simple enough statement. Control your anger. But I don't know why something clicked at that moment. There were a lot of times when I felt like my anger controlled me. It was easy to feel that way because there was so much going on, and I couldn't control it in the slightest. I realized my fire controlled me, and I couldn't live like that. I said to myself, 'I have to do better. For me *and* the rest of my family.' I had to decide to stop being driven by my fire and start being the driving force.

"For the longest time, I kept thinking it had to be my anger that started the fire. And that's what I tried to do whenever I tried to start it on my own. Be angry. But in that moment, somehow, it made sense—my anger *was* controlling my fire, just like it was controlling me. But *I* was not my anger. I had to reclaim the reins on my fire for myself, and, suddenly, it all came together. From that moment on, I could start my fire on will. I've never had problems doing it since." He snapped his fingers, a flame the size of a candle's hovering over them. "Which was helpful when I did go in for my blood test and needed to escape. And ultimately for protecting Rand and me when we had to go on the run after that."

The sounds of frogs, crickets, and birds spanned between us as no one said anything for a while.

"It's getting late," Arusi finally said. "I think we should start heading back. The emperor might want to invite us to some dinner or event, especially given how well Cirssa got along with Jashi. We don't want to be unavailable for too long."

"Good thinking," Kahmel noted.

I frowned. "But what will we do about finding the Dragon King's realm?"

Kahmel spread his arms to the jungle. "Do you see it here? There are a million different directions to go in, and we only have a vague idea of where to go. We'll come back later."

"Will we even have an opportunity?" I tried to keep panic from my thoughts.

Kahmel took a deep drink from his canteen. "I'll make one if it comes to it."

Sighing, I stood and dusted off my butt from the moist dirt that clung to my clothes. I supposed he was right. We wouldn't want the royals to get the wrong impression of us if we were missing for half the visit.

A screech ricocheted through the air and made us all flinch and cover our ears in response, but the coverage wasn't nearly enough to protect my eardrums from the piercing pain that shot through them until the shriek was over. Glancing up, it looked like the same dragon from before, and I watched it fly over and away.

I pursed my lips but followed after Kahmel as he led us in the opposite direction.

"Come on," he insisted. "Let's go before that thing takes Arusi up on her offer of a good snack."

THE EMPEROR

Kahmel Axon Kai of the Omah Clan

By the time we got back to the palace, there were already two invitations waiting for us from the emperor; one for me and one for Jashi. It seemed Cirssa wanted a day out with Jashi alone while Daoliu talked more official things. It was perfect since Jashi wouldn't be interested in the things we'd be talking about anyway.

After I showered and dressed in my usual formal attire, I thought about the things I'd told Jashi before. Some part of me felt stupid, rambling like I did. I didn't often talk about the dark days—the days before the palace—with Jashi. Rand and I didn't even discuss it much. It was just part of us now. We didn't need to talk about it because we both knew what happened. I'd never really spoken about it out in the open like that to anyone.

But then, I didn't quite know anything else to tell Jashi to help her. I could only teach her what I'd learned through experience, and I didn't have anyone to teach me. It was a bit uncomfortable revealing that part of my past, but that was when I learned the most.

Shaking off those memories, I adjusted my tie and pulled my sash over my shoulder. Instinctively, I reached for my sunglasses but hesitated as I brought them toward my face. Jashi's words ricocheted through my mind. I clenched my fist. She was right. There was no reason to keep these on; I was Faresh already, and the war with Omani was settled. The Court couldn't stop me any more than they already tried. At the time, the Court learning I was dragon tribe and dealing with the prejudices that came with it would have been a distraction I didn't need when I still had to regain the old K'sundii territory.

Still, was there really a reason to stop? I wasn't sure she was right about people feeling more comfortable around me with them off. People were intimidated by my eyes more than anything.

I put them on.

Straightening my jacket, I winced as my arms throbbed again. I thought about the horrified look on Jashi's face whenever I talked about the reminder of my promise to the Dragon King to save her life. But that was also part of the reason I didn't like mentioning it. I could live with pain. I was going to fulfill my promise, and that was that. And if this was what it took to win over the Dragon King and gain his favor when we needed it most, it was a small price to pay.

I stepped out the door to my and Jashi's bedroom and came into the living area where Jashi sat, laughing at something Asan had said. T'shan was watching a show on a HoloScreen. Jashi looked lovely as always. Her hair was now put up in a bun with two strands allowed to twist in front of her face. I loved how she looked in the formal robes her position called her to wear. She was plenty beautiful before, but now she looked so regal and elegant and like a true Faresha. Today she was dressed in a blush-pink robe made of a billowy material that swayed easily with the wind. It seemed that Cirssa wanted to take Jashi out to a garden park that was about a half-hour ride from the palace, so she dressed in something that would keep her cool. A matching gossamer shawl covered her bare shoulders and complimented her nicely.

She tossed her head back to look at me. "Are you ready to go be cranky and boring with the emperor?"

Yep. Cute, elegant, with a very short attention span.

"If you mean talking about important issues that are the second biggest reason we came here, then yes."

"Hey, I'm sure all that boring stuff is important. I'm just glad I don't have to go."

Arusi said, "I'm glad the empress has taken such a liking to you. Who knows, the alliance you've made might just be even more important than Kahmel's."

"Ha!" Jashi proclaimed, crossing her arms triumphantly.

Asan chuckled. "Hey, Jashi, I'll be the first to tell you—you're a much easier royal to deal with than that man over there."

I rolled my eyes. "Whose side are you on, anyway?"

"Just saying," Asan said, raising his hands in surrender.

Jashi chuckled as she rose from her seat and pecked me on the cheek. "Anyway, you have to go; we don't want to make you late. Go impress the emperor."

I wasn't entirely sure where this suddenly cozy mood of Jashi's came from. She went from flinching every time I came near her to kissing me in the secret passages of the palace overnight. I was glad, but damn, this girl gave me whiplash with her moods sometimes.

"Uh, good luck to you, too," I muttered, not quite sure how to react to her acting like this was a casual thing for us. Even Arusi, Rand, and Asan seemed surprised, and rightfully so. I wasn't even quite sure what the rules were. I'd play along with this "dating" idea of hers for as long as she wanted, because I wanted to respect her comfort zone.

But as far as I was concerned, we were still married, and everything in me wanted to act like her husband and treat her like my wife.

I cleared my throat. The emperor. Focus on the emperor.

"I'll see you all later," I said as I left.

A servant was outside waiting for me. He grinned and bowed, then took me toward the palace. Once inside, he took me to a room I hadn't been to before. Emperor Daoliu was waiting for me, seated on a cushion on the floor, looking out at a small garden behind sliding glass windows where water trickled in a system of drips, dips, a wheel, and a miniature stream made completely of bamboo. Whereas the rest of the palace boasted grandiosity, this room spoke of simplicity and stillness.

So was the face of the emperor—still and unmoving as I entered the room, gave a slight bow, and sat on the floor before him.

"Thank you...for coming," Daoliu said in halted K'sundii. Apparently, his translator was turned off.

I could tell he was really trying for every word he could remember, so I gave a small smile to show I appreciated the effort. Truthfully, he knew more of my language than I did of his. The most I knew were simple phrases to get around in an airport, so, by comparison, he was already much better off. I nodded to him. "Thank you for having me."

"I was good friends with Faresh Adisoh," he said, switching the device back on, "and though some of your ideas may appear foolish, you remind me of him." Daoliu gestured to the room around us. "These are my more private chambers where I prefer to hold more intimate discussions not fit for staff members. As you'll notice, there are none here. And you, sir, have made more enemies in your short years as Faresh than most make in their entire lifetime. I'm not sure whether to congratulate you or give my condolences."

Surprised by the sudden change in tone, I wasn't even sure how to respond. Was I gauging his alliance, or was he gauging mine?

"I'm honored," I said, deciding to stay mostly quiet and see where this conversation would go. I was prepared to discuss and potentially argue politics, but something about the tone in Daoliu's voice and his pensive mood made me wonder if maybe I should just follow rather than lead today.

Daoliu went back to looking out at the garden and sighed contentedly. "This is my meditation room," he said. "I do my deepest thinking in here. Adisoh and I had many discussions in this room." He chuckled. "And many arguments as well. Mostly arguments."

I nodded, pursing my lips. I knew he and the late Faresh were close, but it really showed how close they were as Daoliu's eyes gleamed, and I noticed him taking more interest in the fountain at that moment.

"He was a good leader," I noted.

"That he was." Daoliu turned to me again. "He had a lot of ideals I disagreed with, and I'm sure he disagreed with many of mine. But what made us steadfast friends in each other was always our honesty. I spoke frankly of my opinions, and there was nothing Adisoh thought that he did not say. That was both his greatest strength and his weakness."

I wasn't sure where Daoliu was going with this, but he seemed to have a point as he took a deep breath, and his eyes steeled, so I stayed silent. Daoliu went on, "I believe if he had the ability, he would have been much like you. I understand you have a lineage of historians in your family. History is a powerful tool. It was what Adisoh lacked in his fervent desires for the nation—the history to help guide the future. He fought for a lot of things, mostly involving keeping K'sundi on good terms with the Equalizers. But he knew it wasn't enough. He just didn't know what was missing. How could he when he didn't quite know what was wrong? Though he did as the Equalizers asked, always, he still disagreed with their principles, and he was an idiot for being so transparent about it."

Frowning, I raised an eyebrow. "What do you mean?"

"I mean Cirssa told me yesterday that she felt something when she was up in the air with your wife. Damned if I know what she's talking about, but I believe her. She said she believes you're on to something with these dragons and that the area has been alive with them ever since you and your wife became more active with fighting for them. And if that's true, I'm warning you to be careful. If there is something to this dragon nonsense, and I'm sure you would know what it is, being a man with his nose always in history texts, I don't want to have to speak at another funeral for another royal clan family of K'sundi."

I was shocked. The emperor...was expressing his concern? And warning me to be careful?

"I...understand," I said, still not quite believing it. The hardness in his face hadn't changed at all, and if not for the interpreter working, I would have guessed he was cursing my name, not telling me to be careful.

"As I said," Daoliu went on, stroking his chin. "My old friend's greatest strength—and also his greatest weakness—was in his frankness. He was a wise man, but he was much too trusting. *They* used that to their advantage."

I knew what Daoliu meant and was surprised for a second time this evening. He meant the Equalizers.

"They rarely ever do their own dirty work, Faresh Kahmel," the emperor continued. "They always work through someone else. Someone that can get close."

I worked my jaw, clenching my fists at my sides. Like they used Jashi.

"What happened at the palace all those years ago happened from the inside. I would swear by it." There was an intensity in Daoliu's eyes. "Don't let it happen to you. I do not want to bury any more friends or their families." Daoliu offered his hand. "And as those are the only ones allowed to step through these doors, you can consider yourself and your wife as friends of mine."

The gesture almost seemed strange, given how hard I always had to fight for everything.

Sighing, I gave in to what was nagging me in the back of my head.

I took off my sunglasses, and gave the emperor a firm handshake in return. "I appreciate that. Truly, I do."

Instead of being shocked, the emperor's eyes lit up when he saw mine. "You are like Cirssa!"

Nests in the Old Village

Jashi Anyua-Omah

Servants came through the door, introducing Empress Cirssa not too long after Kahmel left. Cirssa entered with a wide grin, her wavy hair pulled into a high ponytail above her head, dressed in an elegant yellow dress that came down to her ankles, but the material looked breezy enough to not be hot.

"Ready to go?" she asked.

I grabbed my purse and my eWatch in case Kahmel needed to contact me. "Yep." Turning to the rest, I said, "I'll see you guys when I get back."

"Enjoy yourself, Faresha," Arusi said with a smile.

T'shan waved. "See you later, Your Majesty."

I waved to them all, then left with Cirssa, who took me to where a limousine waited for us.

"I'm so glad we could get away while the men talk about official things," Cirssa said as she ducked inside. I went in after her. With a few words to her driver about where we were going, she turned back to me. "I'm glad I left Med Mali to be here! I feel we get along so well." She giggled. "We have a lot in common."

I chuckled, thinking about how I'd missed that little detail when it was first explained to me, and curious about just how much she knew about me. Or rather, *what* she knew about me that made her want to know me better. The news basically called me a dunce.

"So, how did you two meet each other?" Cirssa wanted to know.

I almost wanted to laugh. I realized my and Kahmel's story would always be a doozy to tell anyone. If we could ever tell anyone the full story.

"It was an arranged marriage," was the simplest answer. "But I knew him a little beforehand. He lived in my neighborhood."

Cirssa nodded with understanding. "You make such a lovely couple."

That was a first. I never really thought about it, but most people commented on how unfit Kahmel and I were for each other. Either they questioned my background—or made up stories about it—or they questioned his legitimacy for the throne, period. We hadn't been complimented as a couple—ever, really.

"Thank you," I said, not knowing how else to react to hearing a compliment I didn't hear often.

"I met Daoliu at a dinner party. My family has always been close friends with the emperors of Gheres, so we were always invited, though we have no official status in the court. At first, I thought him a grumpy old man with no aspirations, but as we got to know each other, I realized it was the furthest thing from the truth." She leaned in like she was telling some deep secret. "It's all a façade. He can be the kindest man sometimes. And as I'm sure people do with you, they assume I married him for his status since I was a commoner before we married. Or, in our case, that he married me to replace his first wife."

Admittedly, I should have been better at keeping up with the families of the royals and world leaders, but I was terrible at it. Now that she mentioned it, though, I vaguely remembered Kahmel telling me that Daoliu's first wife died of a fatal disease of some kind a few years before he married Cirssa.

"That must be hurtful," I said, sympathizing.

Cirssa shrugged. "People will always make assumptions. What matters is that Daoliu and I know what we are to each other. Daoliu is surprisingly compassionate—when he's in the mood to show it," she laughed, then tilted her head back proudly. "And he admires my tenacity."

That, she had in spades, it seemed.

"And you!" Cirssa said, giving my arm a gentle shove and looking at me knowingly. "With the dragons! You are so inspiring with your passion for them! I've already told Daoliu that I'd like to visit your museum for myself sometime soon. And I want him to come with me. He's much too afraid of this dragon business. He needs to be properly educated. Like you're trying to help people to become!"

So that was the reputation I was making for myself. A Dragon Queen of some sort.

I didn't quite mind it.

"I hope we didn't scare him too much yesterday."

Cirssa made a dismissive gesture. "Don't worry about it. He needs a little excitement every now and then. It gets his blood pumping. Besides, if we always stay afraid of dragons, we'll never get to know them better! And from what you've shown me, I'm convinced we need to."

I was surprised Cirssa was so excited. Smiling to myself, I felt the swell of accomplishment in my chest. This was going better than expected. And though her husband seemed absolutely nothing like she described, I also knew that Kahmel was the same way in the shielding-one's-own-emotions department. If Cirssa said he could be convinced, I believed her.

Cirssa and I chatted until we reached the gardens, which were a huge expanse of rich green foliage and palm trees. Though, unlike the jungle Kahmel and I had visited just this morning, there was no need to hack our way through. It seemed like the entire garden was one big jungle maze with a cobblestone path blazing a way through the controlled chaos. Every corner offered several options for ways to go, and I didn't notice a map.

Seeing my concern, Cirssa laughed and said, "Oh, don't worry. I know this garden like the back of my hand. We won't get lost."

"Good, because I have absolutely no sense of direction," I said, relieved.

"Neither do I."

For half a breath, I thought Cirssa was being serious until she burst into a fit of laughter. I shook my head at her.

"Come on," she said between breaths.

We went on to talk and laugh about more things, observing things in the garden, talking about palace life, but my thoughts kept drifting back to the entrance to the dragon realm. We were missing something in our trek. If we'd had just half an hour more, I felt like we would have found something. My mind retraced our steps a million times, but I couldn't think of anything we might have missed —no hints or indications that we were getting closer or farther or anything.

Nothing except for one thing.

Part of me wanted to ask Cirssa. She seemed so interested in the jungle, maybe her knowledge of the area would prove useful. We still weren't sure what the entrance would even look like. Would it be a cave entrance like before? Or something different altogether?

"Your mind seems miles away," Cirssa commented, stirring me from my thoughts.

I opened my mouth to apologize, but the idea kept nagging at me, and I bit my tongue, wondering how much trouble I could get in for doing it. Probably *big* trouble if I did it wrong. But if I didn't outright *tell* Cirssa what I was looking for, everything should be fine.

Ignoring the Kahmel in my head begging me not to do it, I spun on my heel to face Cirssa. "How would you like to go dragon-riding again?"

Soaring over the palace on Comet—the way the wind whirled around me, Comet roaring in pleasure, making the air tremble around us—almost made me forget the fact that Kahmel would kill me when we got back. Electricity arched from his mouth as we flew higher into the air. Cirssa squealed as she held on tight to my waist.

I separated T'shan from the rest before they could ask any questions, and though he gave me a few wary glances, he saddled Comet for me. No one would know until I was ready to tell them.

Now just to make this whole forbidden excursion worth it.

I loaded up my previous coordinates from earlier this morning on my eWatch and easily found the jungle we'd explored.

"Okay, no more mystery! Where are we going?" Cirssa had to shout over the wind.

"Well, you know how my husband is a historian?" I asked. As Kahmel liked to tease me about, I was a terrible liar, so I figured the best way to go about this was to stick as close to the truth as possible without giving any of the sensitive parts away.

"Yes!"

"He was telling me about a jungle a little way from the castle that has a lot of historical significance. Particularly to do with dragons."

"Ooh!" Cirssa sounded genuinely engaged, which was perfect.

"The area used to have a lot of dragons, it seems like. It also used to have a lot of dragon nests that were hundreds of years old even before the Equalization." All of that was true. It was another reason why this area was so prime for what we were looking for. It had all the signs. I learned a lot of additional dragon facts both in my dragon training with Rand and the research I had to do for the museum. Dragon nest locations often lasted hundreds of years, as dragons revisited them, and their young reused old nests when they matured to mating age. That was part of the reason it was so important Kahmel didn't destroy the dragon nest caves in our mountains.

"I was thinking about what you said about there being more dragons in the area than usual," I said. "I thought, what if there were some remnants of the old dragon nest caves in the jungle behind the palace? For whatever reason they've shown up, it might even be one of the places the dragons you've been seeing are making their homes." It wasn't exactly *untrue*. Yes, the area used to have dragon nests.

They were destroyed after the Equalization, but there were probably old traces of them. And if there were any nests left at all, there was a possibility the new dragons hanging around the area might make use of them again.

That wasn't why I wanted to go, though.

"Hmm, you could be right, Faresha."

"So, if there's anything like that around here, it would be useful to find the data to bring back to Kahmel. He might be able to tell us where the dragons are coming from and why." This was where the fib came in. I inwardly laughed at how Kahmel would feel about me saying all this. "Think of him as your dragon pest control."

"But we could always send someone to check," Cirssa said, giggling.

"Ah, but what would be the fun in that?" I said, waving the idea away. "I don't know about you, but I get sick of everyone doing things for me. There are just some things you want to do yourself, especially when it comes to dragons, right?"

"That does sound exciting." Cirssa was back on the excited train. Good.

"So, you get to see old dragon remains, and I get to brag to Kahmel that I found a lot of important information on my own."

"What a splendid idea!" Cirssa raved.

Great. One obstacle down. Now just to do the hardest part, which was finding the damn place.

"Do you have any idea where it might be? Maybe someplace an old village used to be?"

Cirssa paused as we arched across the skies, dancing above the clouds and looking down at the landscape below.

"Maybe..." she muttered, and I barely heard her, but it sounded like good news to me.

"Yes?"

"Take us a bit lower. I think I might know where such an area might be. Ooh, just wait until our husbands find out!"

Yeah, just wait until they found out.

SHRINE

We had descended to where Cirssa indicated, and I gave Comet the command word for "stay" so he wouldn't wander off while we explored. Sure enough, we found ourselves in an area where jungle mixed with old stone, as if the jungle was doing all it could to swallow the ancient structures whole. It had nearly accomplished its goal; the only remnants left here were bits of cobblestone left in the jungle floor and some sections of what must have been a stone wall almost completely covered in greenery.

"Do you think dragons might have made nests here?" Cirssa asked.

"It's a strong possibility," I said. Again, not a whole lie. Dragons preferred to make their nests in caves, but they also didn't mind old ruins and even abandoned houses to make their homes.

But did I expect to find some ancient dragon bed for us to find? Not necessarily.

However, this was the kind of thing that matched what Kahmel's men had found, which was a small village where there were rumors about people disappearing in the mountains. If this was the village, or even part of it, we might be on the right path.

"Now what do we do? What should we be looking for?" Cirssa said as she rolled over a fallen chunk of an old wall to see underneath.

Good question.

"I'll know it when I see it," I said, glancing up at the sky. "Come on, let's keep going."

Cirssa led me deeper in, and we found more evidence of an older way of life. The traces were very faint—an old piece of wall here, the remains of broken urns there. It certainly wasn't enough to put on any map or even for anyone to remember it was here. But that was why I needed Cirssa. She would know about this kind of forgotten secret in the jungle, and that was just what we were looking for.

"Do you do this kind of thing often, or—oh!" A roar shot through the air, and it wasn't Comet's. I was glad we were wearing our protective gear this time.

I grinned. "I think that means we're getting closer."

Now, just because I was doing something I wasn't supposed to didn't mean I was stupid.

"*Hos vihenal!*" I called, the command word for "come." Comet flapped through the sky over our heads, then landed before us.

"Impressive!" Cirssa exclaimed.

"As a precautionary measure, Empress, it's best you stay close to Comet as we proceed further. Dragons are very confrontational, but Comet is an Elemental, so he demands a certain respect from other dragons."

Cirssa looked disappointed. For an empress, she certainly had an appetite for adventure. "All right, then, if you think it's best, Faresha."

We continued farther with Comet in tow. The air felt charged as we pushed forward, alive with energy. Everything in me just *screamed* we were going the right way.

"We'll only go a little bit farther," I promised her. "If there's anything to be found, I think we'll have discovered it by then."

We found ourselves in a part of the jungle with a totally different canopy of trees. These trees soared above our heads, tall enough to compete with the Gheresan palace. A faint trail lay at our feet, leading up to where stone structures lay in various stages of decay.

"Ooh, this certainly seems like a place where dragons might make their nests, right?"

"Absolutely," I confirmed. And exactly what I was looking for.

It looked like this used to be an old village. The thought was confirmed by the crumbled well that occupied the northern edge of the cluster of dilapidated buildings. The trail we followed ran through the middle, like a main road. The village couldn't have had more than a few dozen structures, maybe less. We spanned the length of it in moments. The trail continued away from the village, a distance out.

"Should we stay here and check for the dragon nests?" Cirssa asked. "This is the kind of thing you were looking for, right?"

I pursed my lips. This may be enough for us to go on if we wanted to investigate the area later. But it was still helpful having someone who knew the area. I wanted to make sure I exhausted this rare opportunity while I still had it.

"We'll come back. I want to see where this path leads," I explained, and Cirssa followed without complaint.

We followed the trail for a few more minutes before we rounded a bend.

The trail led to what looked like a shrine. Two pedestals with bowls on the top sat in the middle of stone walls and a rock floor, broken up by sprouts of grass erupting all along the ground, moss and vines crawling down the walls like a veil. The path leading up to it was more clearly laid out, the grass completely cleared, revealing rich soil beneath it.

Cirssa drew a breath. "So beautiful. You were right to come here, Jashi. It looks like dragons are in this area after all."

Cirssa said it so calmly, I almost would have thought she hadn't said it at all. Dragons paced the jungle floor in the distance, barely visible through the trees except for the constant shift of motion. Their mottled brown and green scales blended in with the environment so smoothly that, if they hadn't been moving, they could have snatched us up unseen, easily. Looking closer, I realized they even had tufts of skin protruding with green frills that resembled grass and hard skin that grew in perforations that looked like stone.

My body froze in fear before I realized why they hadn't come any closer than dozens of yards away. Comet still circled the air above us, following obediently. His presence warded the rest off like a force field. No, probably even better than a force field. Dragons broke those all the time if they were determined enough.

The thought gave me an idea to tell Kahmel about later.

But I was smart enough to know when to call it quits.

I whistled for Comet, and he came to my side, crouching for us to climb on.

"Let's go. I think we found what we were looking—"

The ground shook, like it had at the last Dragon Realm entrance. Another confirmation that I'd found the spot.

With a few gestures on my eWatch, I put a virtual pin mark on the location and told it to save it for later. I'd be able to lead Kahmel directly back here when the opportunity arose.

Cirssa clung to me, exclaiming in shock. I helped her onto Comet, unfazed by the shaking. I knew it wasn't an earthquake, not in the real sense. The best thing for us to do was to leave here. The Dragon King could sense us, and the pedestal was responding, just like last time.

I slung myself on, then flicked Comet's reins and guided the dragon up into the clouds.

"Are you okay, Cirssa?" I asked once we were in the air.

"I-I'm fine," she stammered, looking down at the ground. "What was that? Gheres never gets earthquakes!"

"Who knows," I said, hoping I wouldn't get in too much trouble for sneaking out with Cirssa. The empress was shaken but fine. I was a little surprised the empress was more startled by the trembling than the dragons that surrounded us, staring, pacing the ground like hungry cats.

And to top it all off, I *found* the entrance to the Dragon Realm. And without Kahmel's help.

I smiled smugly to myself. I changed my mind. It didn't matter how much trouble I was in. Nothing could beat that.

Breathing out, the empress steadied herself behind me. Her grip around my waist relaxed a little. "Well, that was certainly an adventure," she laughed.

I grinned. Laughing was good. Seeing it as an adventure was good.

"Thanks for helping me be able to brag to my husband," I said earnestly.

Twisting to look at her a moment, I saw Cirssa was grinning just as widely.

"Please, let's not go home just yet," she begged.

I was surprised but shrugged. "That's fine. But where can we go with a dragon?"

"The garden from before. There's a big empty lot next to it, a distance from the main trail. No one will notice us. I go there to be alone sometimes."

Ah, the days of being alone in big empty lots. I knew them well.

"That sounds good," I admitted, then turned Comet to follow her directions to the area she indicated.

We landed in a field of grass and wildflowers. A big wall separated the garden from this little area of paradise. Trees hugged the edges of the area and surrounded us where the field gave over to jungle. But here, it was pleasant and unobstructed by vines and jungle tangles.

Even Comet looked content as he turned in a circle and then lay down in the grass, head tucked under his forearm.

Cirssa and I sat down in the grass, appreciating the sunshine, despite how hot and sticky it was. Somehow it just didn't matter anymore. I did it. I found the Dragon Realm entrance. The accomplishment made me realize I wasn't as useless as I usually felt. I could do a lot when I put my mind to it. I even had Kahmel running across countries to find me because of what I was capable of when I was determined.

Cirssa pulled her knees up to her chest and hugged them, turning her head to look at me. "I've had more fun in the last few days than I have had in a long time. You don't..." she struggled with the long word, "underestimate me like the rest do. The people in the palace. I'm sure you know. It's hard being in a high position at a young age. Too many people ready to declare you don't deserve to be there."

I nodded. I knew exactly what Cirssa meant.

Tilting her head, Cirssa commented, "You have such pretty eyes."

I chuckled at the sudden and foreign compliment. My *eyes?* Instinctively, I held my head down to hide them. I never liked bringing attention to my eyes. So bright orange, they almost glowed. It was the first thing anyone ever saw when they met me. I could count on one hand how many times someone had actually complimented my eyes.

I chuckled awkwardly. "Thank you. I don't really hear that often."

"I know. Silly superstitions. I've always had to hide mine, but that was more for politics than for myself. I've always loved my eyes."

I frowned, not quite understanding until Cirssa reached up to her eye and pinched off a dark contact lens and then the other, revealing bright orange eyes. I gasped.

Cirssa chuckled at my shock, putting the lenses in a small pack she had hidden in the folds of her dress. "My grandfather was K'sundii. No one ever knew he carried genes from the dragon tribe until I was born." She smiled, her bright orange eyes twinkling.

Slowly, I started to notice how her features faintly reflected the K'sundii—the slightly curly texture to her hair, the shape of her lips, her bronze-olive complexion, and now, obviously, her eyes. They all bore ghosts of K'sundii features.

Still, knowing she was dragon tribe was incredible.

Cirssa exhaled, looking out at the field. "Well, I know you'll have to go back to your busy life, as I'll have to go back to mine. But know you will always have a friend in the palace of Gheres."

It was a heartfelt sentiment I felt from the depths of my spirit. All these politics had gotten me used to a lot of hate. It was nice for one of these relations to turn into a real friendship.

"And you will always have a friend in the palace of K'sundi."

If K'sundi would have me, that was.

FIRE AND SUNGLASSES

When I got back to the estate, I was surprised to find that Kahmel still wasn't back.

"He's still out with the emperor," Asan explained. "He hasn't sent me any messages to indicate how it's going, either."

My gut twisted a little. It wasn't a rational fear, but what if everything was going wrong, and Daoliu ended up wanting nothing to do with K'sundi anymore? We would need all the help we could get when we eventually challenged Zendaal.

Asan seemed to sense my worry and gestured for me to calm down. "Don't worry, Jashi. Kahmel knows how to handle himself. There's no use worrying before we even know what's happened yet."

I knew he was right but couldn't help being concerned.

Perhaps it was for the better.

I didn't want to explain quite yet how much I teetered on the edge of getting in deep trouble today. I wanted time to get my story straight.

Rand came through the door at that moment, panting like he'd been running. "You guys—you won't believe it—Kahmel—"

All thoughts of figuring out my conversation with Kahmel left my mind as Asan and I focused on Rand. Arusi came up behind him, laughing.

My brow furrowed. "What are you talking about? What's going on?"

"I never thought I'd see the day," Rand said, straightening as he caught his breath.

Asan rolled his eyes. "Just spit it out. What are you talking about?"

T'shan also appeared in the doorway, laughing.

But there was no need to explain as the clamor and murmur of nearby servants drew my attention outside. Coming out to look, I saw servants all huddled together, chattering in the clipped language of Gheresan and pointing at Kahmel in awe.

Kahmel wasn't wearing his sunglasses.

He strode toward us like it was nothing, as if it wasn't basically the first time in history he had ever gone out in public with his eyes uncovered. Daoliu walked beside him, a small smile on his face.

Kahmel was out without his glasses.

Daoliu was smiling.

Perhaps these were the signs of the times everyone was always talking about?

Kahmel smiled and came to my side, then turned to wave at the emperor. "Thank you for your time, Emperor Kun. I enjoyed our conversation."

The emperor's small smile had faded, terminating its short life span, and he nodded in respect to Kahmel. "And I, you, Faresh Kahmel of the Omah clan. May your days be prosperous."

The emperor walked away with dozens of servants wearing questioning faces in tow, leaving the rest of us utterly confused.

Kahmel smiled and nodded at us. "Are you going in, or are you just going to stay outside?"

"What was that?" Rand demanded, going inside. Arusi, T'shan, and I followed. "Since when do you go out without your glasses on?"

Arusi was still chuckling. "I'm sure the servants will never forget it. I wonder how long it'll take to reach the gossip columns."

I gave Kahmel a knowing look and crossed my arms. "About time."

Rand looked at me in confusion. "You knew about this?"

"I recommended it. Wasn't sure if the idiot would finally do it."

"I'm happy for you, Your Majesty!" T'shan chipped in.

Asan frowned, sighing like his soul was weary. "What I want to know is *why* you never consult me on these things. You want to take off your glasses? Fine, take off your glasses. But there's a way to do it without creating heaps of content ready for gossip columns, reporters, and tabloids to tear into like starving hyenas!"

Kahmel, as he always did when Asan scolded him, shrugged. "All I did was take off my glasses."

Asan sighed again, muttering to himself—something about a royal pain in the ass.

I smiled up at him. "How does it feel?"

Kahmel looked around like he was seeing the world for the first time, jokingly. "Not bad. A lot easier to see when I'm indoors, that's for sure."

Arusi pulled up a chair at the kitchen counter, and Kahmel sat beside her. The rest of us joined them.

"How did it go with Daoliu?" Arusi asked.

"And why didn't you text me?" Asan demanded.

Kahmel smiled, the mischief in his eyes showing how much he was enjoying everyone's shock. I rolled my eyes. He lived for being unpredictable.

"Very well, actually," Kahmel said, ignoring Asan's question. "Surprisingly well."

Over the next few minutes, he explained how the conversation had gone. After the major portion of their talk, it seemed like Kahmel and the emperor just chatted for a while.

Arusi grinned. "That's fantastic!"

Frowning, Rand asked, "What about all of that made you feel the need to take off your sunglasses?"

Kahmel looked at me as he said, "Daoliu was opening up to me, and I felt like it was only right to do the same. Someone mentioned not being so distant and such."

I chuckled and wagged my head.

"You mean this will be a regular thing?" Asan wanted to know, sighing for the third time as Kahmel nodded.

"Oh," Kahmel exclaimed as he seemed to have remembered something. "He told me that Cirssa is one-fourth K'sundii! She'd dragon tribe. She wears—"

"Contact lenses," I finished for him. "She told me. She actually took out her contact lenses in front of me." Crossing my arms, I looked at Kahmel. "You know, I realize how weird it is that you've never worn contact lenses all these years. It's so much easier than wearing sunglasses every time you go out!"

Kahmel shuddered. "I hate contact lenses. Besides," he said, a smirk crawling up his face, "they're not nearly as intimidating."

That was the real reason for it.

Rand asked, "How did it go with Cirssa? How did she end up telling you she was part K'sundii?"

Everyone looked at me, and I supposed that my time for coming up with a good way to approach the story was up. I told them everything, starting with the visit to the garden, watching their faces raise with objections as I went on to describe my thinking behind taking her to the jungle and then telling them that I did it.

Kahmel had his face in his hand. "You took the empress...to the jungle."

"She didn't mind," I assured. "She liked the adventure! Besides, I took her on Comet, and he warded off all the dragons."

"Comet? So, you got T'shan in on it, too."

"Of course not. He has no idea why I asked him to saddle up Comet."

The exasperated look on his face said, *Right, like that makes it any better.*

Before anyone else could object, I said, "The main thing is, nothing happened to Cirssa; she thought it was great fun, and I found it."

Asan arched an eyebrow. "You found...?"

I grinned, enjoying my moment to feel smug. "The entrance to the Dragon Realm. I can take you all whenever you want." Tapping my eWatch, I pulled up the location that I'd saved on it. The map hovered over the table, and I zoomed in on the location, gesturing with two fingers. "Here."

They all looked on in awe.

"And you're sure this is it?" Rand asked.

I nodded. "It's in the middle of the jungle, but it couldn't be clearer. I saw the metal bowls we're supposed to set on fire just like the one from before."

Even Kahmel looked impressed. He breathed out a chuckle. "All right. I can question your methods, but I can't question your results. And it seems you went about doing it with caution. You did good, Jashi."

Arusi nodded in approval. "You did a lot more than all of us put together with all the information we gathered."

I breathed out. That didn't end as badly as I feared.

Closing the map, I asked, "What next?"

When Kahmel looked at me, his orange eyes were piercing. I got to see him without his sunglasses often, but somehow, they seemed different this time. Like they were on fire, burning with intensity. "We go back to the jungle," he answered. "And we win over the next Dragon King."

Now that we knew exactly where the Dragon Realm entrance was, there was no need to bring anyone else on our excursion. Kahmel and I rode Huntress, the dragon zipping eagerly through the air like she was excited for what we were doing, too.

Kahmel let me steer her, holding onto me from behind as we soared through the air. The wind flapping through my clothes relieved me from the heat, if only momentarily. But even the heat couldn't beat the buzz running through me now.

With my hands on Huntress's reins, it reminded me of Kahmel's analogy from earlier. About taking the reins on one's own emotions—the things that triggered my fire, like my anxiety, my fear, my anger. To take the reins of those emotions and finally control my fire for myself. Could I do that?

In this mindset, I finally felt capable, finally felt like I didn't have to be looked at as no more than a stain on a lavish carpet in the palace.

I felt more like K'sundi's Faresha.

It helped to have Kahmel. He had believed in me since the beginning. Even when I shocked him yesterday, he was surprised I'd made such a bold decision, that was sure. But I saw the pride in his eyes. He wasn't surprised I found the entrance to the Dragon Realm on my own.

It was almost like he expected it.

There was a warmth in my chest, and it wasn't from my fire.

Kahmel snapped me out of my thoughts as he pointed and said, "Look, there it is. You were right, Jashi."

I looked down at the jungle below us. There was the shrine I discovered with Cirssa the day before, half-hidden in its shawl of vines and shrubbery. I directed Huntress to the ground. "*Hat sud,*" I said, the command to make her stay where she was.

Kahmel grinned in approval. "You just do it naturally now."

My cheeks warmed at the compliment and I looked away. "Come on; we've got a big mean dragon to wake up."

"We're most definitely in the right place." Kahmel pointed to the dragons that I didn't realize had us surrounded. Since Huntress was a regular dragon like the rest of them, they had no reason to stay away. They blended so perfectly into the environment; it was impossible to notice them unless they moved. The reptilian giants slinked between the trees, pacing the ground around us and staring at us warily. A few growled and hissed. One Draconian stood behind the shrine, towering over it and snarling. But none of them approached.

Kahmel's hand went to mine, intertwining our fingers. He squeezed it and gave me a reassuring look.

I squeezed back, but I wasn't afraid this time.

We approached the pedestals with the metal bowls on top. Like the last one, the inside was laced with ashes, but since this one was out in the open, it was also covered in dirt and pale marks from dried rain.

Kahmel tossed me a lighter, this one brand new, keeping his eye on the dragons that hadn't stopped staring at us since we approached. "To replace your old one."

Then he let go of my hand to approach one pedestal, and I approached the other. His hand lit up in flames, and he tossed the fire into the bowl, setting it ablaze.

I turned the lighter between my fingers.

I thought about what Kahmel had said, and it was tempting. Not letting my emotions control me and to control my fire on my own. I wanted control. I had proven something to myself on this trip. I was just as useful as anyone else, and I shouldn't underestimate that.

I imagined my fire like it was my dragon, and all I had to do was take the reins.

Reaching my hand forward, my heart raced as fire shot from my palm and into the bowl, my arm pulsing with power, energy, and excitement. It wasn't strenuous like when I'd practiced maintaining fire above my palm before. This came naturally, more relief than strain. Like I had released something that was waiting for me to let it out all along.

The fire stopped when I pulled my hand back, and the flames in both bowls roared toward the skies.

Kahmel looked at me with pride from the other side.

But there was something else in his uncovered eyes. A smoldering warmth that made me smile and look away. Was it awe? Appreciation?

Then my cheeks burned harder. *Attraction.*

The ground started shaking like it had when Cirssa and I were here, though the intensity was magnified. It was enough to nearly knock me to the ground, but I reached for the podium, grasping the bowl by the lip to steady myself.

Kahmel hadn't been so quick to react, falling to the jungle floor as a flock of startled birds flew above our heads. The dragons around us stomped the ground with nervous excitement, hissing and snarling as they seemed completely unbothered by the trembling.

The ground itself seemed to pulse as the shaking intensified. The leaves of the trees shuddered and whispered against the wind as the trees quivered.

A sharp cry shot out from the distance. A glowing white dragon emerged from the trees and darted through the air toward us.

The dragon of in-between.

Elegant as a bolt of lightning, the dragon grabbed me with one clawed paw, then went around and picked up Kahmel,.. We arched toward the sky, between the pillars of fire shooting up from the podiums.

We raced up to the clouds, pushing past towering trees and vines and tangle. The sky darkened, and the trees melted away. The sound of leaves stirring was replaced by hushed silence, and the darkness blinked with stars. Swirling colors of blush pink, crimson, and indigo glowed against the darkness like clouds, clustering the stars in its folds. It seemed dark, but the stars lit our faces like the light from dawn. I grinned at Kahmel, and he grinned back. We made it.

Now all we had to do was survive the encounter.

GAIENA

A black slate stood against the darkness, and I recognized it from last time.

The dragon of in-between carried us closer, and the features of the floating island came more into focus. Lush trees covered the space, but even they could only come up part of the way to the castle's full stature. The castle was made of polished black stone that almost blended in with the background, shimmering and flickering against the darkness. It looked smooth as marble.

The dragon of in-between dropped us off at the lip of the floating island and flew off into the heavens, becoming nothing more than a white speck that disappeared among the stars.

Kahmel took a deep breath and looked at me. "Are you ready?"

Realizing my hands were shaking slightly, I clasped them together. "I hope so. Do you think the Dragon King will be angry with us like Aithel was?"

Kahmel took my hands in his, and the trembling melted away. The determination in his eyes settled my unease before he even said anything. "Aithel was angry at our history. And he tested us. This Dragon King will do the same. But if we stand firm, we'll be fine. They're only trying to protect themselves from what happened to them the first time. We have to prove ourselves, and there's nothing wrong with having to regain the trust our people lost."

Our hands entwined, we strode through the trees and found the door to the palace—a huge wooden gate that swung open easily as Kahmel pushed against it.

Onyx stone lined the floors and walls, glimmering darkly with our reflection as we walked by. It almost felt like we hadn't left the jungle. Tall grasses, plants with wide leaves and red edges, and luscious flowers grew in pots on the floor along the walls. Lit sconces threw warm light on the dark rock. Vines crawled down from hanging pots positioned like chandeliers in the ceilings of the halls. The pots were glossy, earthy colors: brown, brick red, sky blue, and green with black-painted patterns.

We moved through the halls, finding ourselves in the middle of a foyer also filled with plants. Bushes grew in huge pots placed in mirroring positions at the entrance, the corners of the room, and the base of the twin set of grand stairs that twirled up to a landing, then joined into one as it went up farther to the second floor. At the top was a set of double doors. The rails of the stairs were covered in flowering vines that filled the room with a pungently sweet aroma. A chandelier hung overhead with lit candles and vines wrapped around the base in a hard embrace.

Something about the palace had a silent majesty to it, and Kahmel and I said nothing to each other, solemn as we started up the stairs. We reached the top.

This was it.

Kahmel and I pushed the doors open.

The room itself took my breath away. If the rest of the castle felt like a jungle, it was like Hemorah itself had wrapped her arms around this room and manifested herself in it. We stepped on a gray stone path that acted like a bridge to a stone circle in the floor. Around the platform was a dirt ring that wrapped around the floor, allowing trees to grow along the walls. The vaulted ceilings gave room for the trees to soar dozens of feet high, their branches and leaves arching overhead. The trees lined the walls like columns, close together and in a perfect line. In contrast, the stone platform in the middle wasn't neat but was beautiful in its imperfection. Breaks in the stone allowed various plant varieties to grow: succulents, clovers, little patches of wildflowers, and grasses.

Before us was a pool of water, a huge gnarly tree growing just behind it, the branches dark and bare. On the sides of the pool were smaller twisted trees with roots that crept forward into the water as if to sip from the precious clear liquid. Water trickled into it continually from panels in the walls from the sides.

But where was the Dragon King?

I frowned, looking at Kahmel. My voice echoed through the room, making a whisper bounce back like a shout. "Could this be right?"

Kahmel looked equally as confused. "I don't know. Maybe there's something wrong."

"It's not like the Dragon King could be anywhere else," I said with a sweeping motion of the grand room.

"I was hoping if I stood still long enough, you would leave," came a female voice from behind the pool.

My mouth fell open as the gnarled tree behind the pool opened its eyes and moved forward, dark bark churning with every movement. It wasn't a tree at all. She was the Dragon *Queen.* Narrowing my eyes at the dragon, I realized that the gnarled features that looked like knobs and twisted branches were facial features and a neck that rested on the ground beside the pool. Where I thought one of the massive roots was dipped into the pool was her enormous tail. Her horns were shaped like branches that arched out and split like lightning bolts above her head. Her form was covered in scales that looked exactly like bark.

As easily as I realized she was a dragon, I could very well go back to believing she was a tree again. Like the dragons in the jungle behind the palace, unless she was moving, it was hard to distinguish her form from her environment.

I had to focus hard to realize that she didn't have two branch-like horns, but one. The other side of her head had an empty space, with a notch where it was supposed to be.

I guessed that was what the traitor of K'sundi stole from her, like Aithel's missing eye.

My gut twisted.

The Dragon Queen's eyes opened again, and only then did I notice she closed them often. She wanted to remain indistinguishable. With her eyes closed and thus the only discrepancy between her and the trees erased, I couldn't tell where she ended and the trees behind her began. Her eyes were red as roses and piercing like thorns.

"I felt Aithel awaken his power over K'sundi," her voice rumbled out again. *"I could scarcely believe it. And for another K'sundii Half-Drac with pretty words, no less. Two of them, at that! You've even made the dragons in my region cautiously excited. You're selling a dangerous thing, you know."*

I frowned in confusion. "Selling?"

As soon as I said the words, I clamped my mouth shut, remembering what happened last time I did that in front of a Dragon King.

But the Dragon Queen only stayed her unsettling red eyes on me and said, *"Hope. It's a dangerous thing to sell to the broken, and it comes at a high price. How much will your hope cost me, Half-Dracs? And do you understand what I would lose should this gamble fall apart?"*

The Dragon Queen's entire being permeated sadness, a heaviness that made my lips leaden and loathsome to move because it would never be enough. I could never say enough to make up for her grief, her betrayal. It shone through the intensity of her eyes. And I knew exactly what she meant, coming from an orphanage. Hope *was* a dangerous thing to sell to the broken. It wasn't like we were foreign to the concept of hope. But we'd tried it before and failed. Every fall hurt more than the last.

To the Dragon Queen, we were nothing more than greasy salesmen peddling a dysfunctional product that would cost her everything to invest in.

Kahmel commented where I had no words to say. "I know we're asking for a lot, but—"

"*But?*" The Dragon Queen moved into her pool of water, making it splash everywhere as the ground trembled slightly under the weight of her movement. She reached her long neck forward and growled, her head a few feet away from where we stood. *"But nothing, Half-Drac. There is absolutely nothing you can say or do that will change the last few hundred years. Perhaps Aithel has chosen to forget about it, but I am not so easily swayed by—"*

Kahmel opened a flame in his palm to illuminate the marks on his arms better. "This is proof of the promise I made to Aithel, and it holds me to keep it. A promise that K'sundi will change how it handles its dragons. Right now, my ability is limited, but even with my limitations, my wife and I have made great strides already. We built a museum that has people asking questions about the standards Zendaal has set, and we now feel confident Gheres will back us and our policies. It will be even better when K'sundi separates from the Equalization."

It didn't matter what I knew now in comparison to a year ago. The words still made me shiver. Especially with what Kahmel showed me happened to countries outside of the Equalization. Somehow, the Zendaalans could manipulate the fruitfulness of the land with the stolen power of the Dragon Kings.

The fear continued to linger over my head, but Kahmel seemed confident it was a step we had to take, and I believed in him. He told me once that ever since he became king, he thought K'sundi might be in danger of being labeled a rebel country, so he started up storage drives where food and water were being saved for later. A percentage of agriculture, meat production, and water processing was taken and added to it every quarter. That knowledge made me feel a little better, but it was still a temporary solution that meant we had to accomplish what we set out to do quickly. Or K'sundi wouldn't last.

The Dragon Queen was quiet for a moment, considering what Kahmel told her. She closed her eyes again, her form beginning to look like a tree once more. She opened her eyes, startling me as she stared right at me.

"Your husband has spoken bold words. Surprising words, I must say. What say you, Faresha? Why should I buy your hope?"

I swallowed, knowing I was not an eloquent speaker like Kahmel, but knowing that while she was relatively calm now, the power of the Dragon Kings was not to be underestimated.

"I don't really have a reason, Your Majesty," I said, my voice faltering, but I went on. "Kahmel has a lot of ideas, and I believe in him, but you have no reason to. I know what it's like to be broken. I know how much hope can hurt when it lets you down. I think..." I bit my lip as her face remained unchanged. I had to keep going. "I think we need to prove ourselves and let our actions speak for themselves. See for yourself what we have done so far and what I believe we'll continue to accomplish." I pursed my lips and looked at Kahmel with a small smile. "I think we can do it. But I can't make you believe me."

The Dragon Queen made a low rumbling sound and closed her eyes again. Moving out of the pool, she shook the room with every step. I took a few instinctive steps back, but then I realized the low rumbling was chuckling.

"There is a very wise Faresh and Faresha in the palace of K'sundi." When her eyes opened, they were sharp with warning. *"I am still cautious of you, Half-Dracs. But I will go along with your proposition. You have my alliance. For now. I can sense you've made the dragons excited. They're multiplying and traveling all over Hemorah more than usual."* She gave a knowing wink, but I wasn't sure what it meant. *"With my approval, expect things to get even more...interesting with the dragons. Tamed and untamed alike."*

Kahmel and I looked at each other, neither with a suggestion of what the Dragon Queen could mean.

The Dragon Queen laughed, probably enjoying our confusion. *"You may want to find a way to establish a Drake Bond soon. It will help."*

I sighed at the mention of the term that I still couldn't quite understand.

"What is a Drake Bond?" I tried, earning another laugh in response.

"*Where would the fun be in just telling you?*" she said, a mischievous glint in her eye.

She was enjoying this. Kahmel was right. The Dragon Kings still didn't completely trust us. They would dangle the answer in front of us, making us work and research if we wanted to find it out in its entirety. Nothing would come easily.

Kahmel asked, "What is your name?"

"*I never told you, did I?*" The dragon contemplated. "*Gaiena is what the humans called me. And I am not so cruel as not to give you a little bit of help, as I predict you will need the Drake Bonds soon. Your new alliance with Gheres will prove very profitable to you. As the K'sundii retained their history in texts, the Gheresans also retained a part of themselves, partly unknowingly, in their art. If you look close enough, you might find a clue.*"

With that riddle hanging in the air, Gaiena turned her back to us, her tail nearly batting us like an enormous log as she waded back into her pool and settled in the water, resting her head on the ledge and sighing.

"*Now go away.*"

A black vortex opened in the floor beside us, and Kahmel and I looked at each other and jumped down, knowing how it went last time.

Surrounded by blackness, a white claw broke through and clutched both Kahmel and me. The dragon of in-between carried us away and into the darkness.

FARESH AND FARESHA

Days later was the morning we were scheduled to leave Gheres. The emperor had lived up to his reputation of holding extravagant parties, filling our week with festivities until the day we planned to leave. We'd found Gaiena just in time. We almost didn't have a spare moment to ourselves until today.

I was normally exhausted after the kind of night we'd had, dining and socializing with members of the emperor's court all evening. However, despite the long day, I felt charged. My body thrummed with energy—*excitement*, even.

We had found the second Dragon King—or Queen, in this case. And she was on our side, albeit grudgingly. But a yes was a yes. What was more, Daoliu liked Kahmel, and Cirssa liked me. I might have even dared to call her a friend.

When we went to the party last night, I ventured to hold my head up high. There were some who didn't have anything good to say about me, but I let the comments fall on deaf ears, knowing that Kahmel's stares would silence any further remarks.

Especially now that he wasn't wearing his glasses.

Kahmel and I silently reveled in the low murmur of crowds everywhere we went that night. The low click of hidden cameras went off whenever we stepped out into a public space, and Kahmel did nothing to stop it. He wanted them to know, and I was ecstatic about it.

After a quick check on my eWatch, I confirmed that there were already articles with zoomed-in shots of Kahmel's eyes and speculation about it. The sight brought an amused smile to my lips. The irony occurred to me that Kahmel and I were both dragon tribe, but then so was Cirssa, it turned out.

The world was led by more savages than it wanted to admit.

I put my eWatch back and turned over to lay on my back, looking up at the ceiling from the bed. Kahmel was still asleep. Out the window to my side, I could see the temporary stable for Huntress and Comet being taken down, the two dragons being led away by T'shan and a few others as the sun arched overhead.

Now to go home. According to Kahmel, a group of rebels would take T'shan away to a hiding place they used for smuggling immigrant families. It was a cabin house in the snow-capped mountains of the south with the nearest town a couple dozen miles out, and even that was a small town with a population in the tens of thousands as opposed to the millions in most cities of K'sundi.

I hated that we'd have to separate, but, for now, it was for the best.

Now all that was left to do was to sit around and wait for rebels to find more information so we could find the next Dragon King.

And all the while, we were losing time.

"What are you thinking about?"

Kahmel had turned to face me, eyes awake and alert, arms propped up on the barrier pillows.

He wasn't asleep after all.

"I don't like just sitting around waiting for something to happen," I said in a low voice. "It's going to be nerve-wracking."

"We won't exactly be sitting around doing—can I move these pillows, please?" He was pushing the pile down with his arms to see me better and struggling as the foam pillows fluffed themselves back up.

I laughed at the display, slipping my hand under my head and propping it up. "I don't know; can I trust you? Rumors say you can be quite the brute, Faresh."

"Rumors say you're pregnant with triplets, Faresha," he

countered, pushing the pillows to the floor. "They're not always accurate."

"Fair point. Unless I am—"

"Can we move on, please?"

I laughed at his expense, and he cleared his throat to underscore his changing the subject. "As I was saying," he continued, "we won't be sitting around. I'm going to be pushing harder for much more lenient dragon laws. I'll be more insistent. With Gheres backing us, we can be bolder. And, since you're always eager to go, maybe I'll make sure you're assigned a few more *tasks*."

With a warm feeling in my chest, I enjoyed the fact that I was someone Kahmel could rely on for the rebel stuff. I'd come a long way in a few months.

I nodded eagerly. "I'd love to."

"Good," he said, a small smile on his lips. I liked not seeing that dark mood settle in every time we talked now.

There was a small smile that spread on my own lips as I thought back to our conversation in the catacombs of the palace. When he gave me the option to leave, and I realized that the dark shawl was all because, for months, he thought I would go. Heck, until he asked me, I thought I'd leave, too. But then he asked, and I realized that I didn't want to. And now that we had it out of the way, our conversations were so much easier. So much lighter.

"Hopefully, you won't go too stir crazy," Kahmel said, taking me out of thoughts I didn't even realize I was submerged in. "Besides, you'll be able to see Nana more."

I beamed. "That would be nice."

Kahmel looked out the window, and I followed his gaze to see Arusi, Rand, and Asan leaving the estate with their luggage, servants milling about them, carrying ours.

Kahmel traced a finger on my arm. "Before we leave," he murmured, "I have a surprise for you, remember?"

In all the commotion and searching, I'd completely forgotten about Kahmel's promise to surprise me and the secret that Asan almost let slip earlier.

I chuckled, turning back to him, only to be taken aback by the intensity in his fire-colored eyes as he stared back at me. I found myself squirming without knowing why. Suddenly his words felt like they meant something completely different, and I was all at once aware of the fact that we were lying together in the same bed with his touch on my arm and no barrier in between.

"I'd completely forgotten," I said, distracted by the heat in his eyes but trying to shake it off.

"Good," he chuckled. "Otherwise you would have bothered Asan until he told you."

I wanted to laugh, but the way he was looking at me scrambled my thoughts and smothered the laugh, and all I could think about was the fact that as many times as I'd said it for other people, I was suddenly aware of the fact that Kahmel was my *husband*. And despite how I felt about the arrangement, he always treated me like his *wife*. He refused to let anyone talk about me; he let me be as "improper" as I liked, and he defied anyone that told him otherwise. His eyes lit up when I came into the room, and he'd made it clear that he was willing to wait however long it took for me to feel the same way he felt about me, marriage or not. I thought back to what he murmured in his sleep the night I left all those months ago as he subconsciously pulled me to his chest. *I love you.*

The words resounded through my head to the point that I only realized Kahmel had gotten up when he took my hand to get me out of bed.

"Come on, get dressed. We're going somewhere," he said with a smile on his lips. I liked the way his eyes twinkled when he smiled like this, the sun kissing the curls in his hair from the window behind him. "Wear something you can move around in. We'll be taking the dragons."

I raised an eyebrow, still trying to shake the feeling of being melted by his stare. But something about his heat made me want to respond with a feisty heat of my own. I crossed my legs, aware of the way my nightdress exposed my legs and upper thighs with the motion. Something he was aware of as well. "Dragons? We're taking both?"

"Absolutely," he said, dragging his eyes back up to meet mine. "I don't think we've ever had the opportunity to fly side by side one another. It's about time we rectified that."

I stood up, starting for the closet. The servants left me a few outfits to choose from, so I had options. "All right, I'll get dressed, then. Any hints to where you're kidnapping me to?"

He faked an offended look. "How can I kidnap my own wife?"

The way he said *wife* somehow felt different from all the other times he said it, and no matter how far away I walked, his gaze followed so intensely, it was like he was on my heels.

I slipped into the closet and closed the door behind me, enjoying the slightly disappointed look on Kahmel's face as I did.

Enjoying? What had gotten into me? I'd never sought this kind of attention before. I hadn't thought about it—I hadn't wanted it.

But...

I didn't dislike it.

"I don't know," I called out to him as I peeled off my clothes and tried to decide what to wear. "They say you're always bringing up the strangest archaic traditions. K'sundii men used to kidnap wives, you know. Went around grabbing them from other tribes all the time. Thanks to you always making me read, I read a few stories like that in the library at the palace."

"So now who's the historian here?" he said, chuckling. "One discrepancy, Faresha. They kidnapped *other people's* wives, not their own."

I finally settled on an orange outfit that wrapped like a breezy jumpsuit, with billowy pant legs and a wrap that crossed one shoulder and left the other one bare. Still suiting for a royal but easy to move around in. I pulled my hair back with a patterned scarf, tying the knot askew rather than in the middle because I liked the way it looked with the fabric cascading to the side. Feeling a little coy, I also played with a light application of mascara and a rouge that made me feel fiery.

"If you say so," I responded as I dabbed my lips with red. "Just so long as you don't sling me over your shoulder."

When I opened the door, I found him leaning over the doorway. Leaning over me, a smirk on his lips. He was already dressed, similar to me, in something semi-formal. He had on a red silk vest with a neckline that exposed part of his chest, with matching red slacks that both hugged him and moved loosely about his body. A leather bracelet was on the wrist that he had perched on the door hinge. He must have slipped his clothes on in the bedroom while I got dressed in the closet.

"You're determined to peg me as some kind of brute, aren't you?"

"Well, you know, they call people like us savages." I challenged his stare with one of my own, tilting my chin to look up at him. "Maybe there's something to it."

"Oh?" Light danced in his eyes, and he took a step forward to reduce the space between us. "Does that make you savage, too?"

"Ha!" I threw my head back as I laughed. "I think you and I are the worst of them."

The look on his face turned smoldering, his gaze dropping to my lips. He moved to eliminate the space between our faces, but I swerved, ducking under his huge arm and pretending I didn't notice as I adjusted my hair a little and made to look for my eWatch, unable to resist the smile that tugged at my lips. I wondered when exactly this had become a cat and mouse game and why I was enjoying it so much.

My eWatch was on the nightstand next to the bed, and I could feel Kahmel's stare following me without having to turn around to look at him. After fixing it on, I turned and smiled at Kahmel, not quite able to understand the flutter in my chest as I did so, and watched the way he looked back at me. Wanting.

Wordlessly, he nodded at the door and offered his arm. I slipped my arm through his, feeling the way his muscles bulged. We came to the outside, where servants still milled about preparing for us to leave.

"I have to get the dragons," he said. "I'll just be a minute." He walked away and came back a few moments later with Comet and Huntress in tow, both dragons following obediently, without reins, I noticed. "Ready to go?"

"No saddles?" I questioned, observing that those were also absent.

"Much more fun without, isn't it? Besides, you've proven you know your way around your dragon. I don't need to be overly cautious if you're already good."

I beamed at the compliment as he handed me an earpiece. I took Kahmel's hand, and he helped me on Comet. Then he slung himself on Huntress. Now that she was used to it, she raised her whiskers up to meet his hands, and he flicked them like reins to get her up into the air.

I had to be a bit more strategic, but Kahmel had shown me how it was done before. I adjusted my position so I could grab Comet's ears. Excitement buzzed from him, literally. My hairs stood on end, and the air buzzed with static. My fingers gripped scaly flesh that felt like leather as I tugged Comet's ears, and he eagerly took off into the sky to join Huntress.

SECOND DATE

The two dragons streaked the sky with black and yellow like thunder and lightning. The ground raced below like a carpet being pulled from under us. Comet flew above Huntress, then Kahmel pulled Huntress up above Comet, smirking at me from above. Then we weaved about each other, swapping between top and bottom, trying to pull ahead by a hair, turning it into a race. It felt like a race, but it looked like a dance, bobbing and weaving, and we laughed as we maneuvered our dragons around each other.

Then Kahmel suddenly dropped with Huntress and dove toward the ground. I followed, Comet's muscles churning beneath me as he flapped his wings to catch up. Huntress roared, and Comet roared louder.

Even the dragons could feel the competition.

We landed beside a stream at the bottom of a waterfall. The stream seemed deceptively deep. Some ends of it had rocks jutting out of it, the water cascading over them just barely, leaving them in a permanent state of shiny wet. But upon looking down, I realized the rocks weren't at surface level. They were huge stones that emerged from deep in the water. The waterfall dropped off into a pond just beyond where we were, where the water was dark green and full of river fish scurrying through and occasionally bobbing at the surface.

Ruins surrounded us, wooden structures with walls and fallen columns. The wood was stained with colors of green and red, the accents echoing certain features of Daoliu's palace. These were relics of Gheres royalty.

I inwardly laughed at myself, noticing architecture like this. Kahmel was getting infectious. We dismounted from our dragons, and I started to instruct Comet to stay, but Kahmel stopped me. "Let them roam. They deserve it. We can call for them later. They won't get into trouble."

Looking at the way Comet stomped the ground excitedly, I agreed. They hadn't even had "playful" free-falls during our rides with the Gherenan royalty.

I patted Comet on the head and stroked his snout, feeling him relax beneath my touch, and then he and Huntress took to the air to continue chasing each other as soon as Kahmel and I turned away.

Kahmel slipped his hand into mine and gestured to the area. "What do you think?"

"It's beautiful," I said, chuckling. "But what are we here for? We already found Gaiena."

"I told you it was a surprise, not a mission." He led me to a spot next to the waterfall. Kahmel crouched behind a fallen pillar and pulled out a small metallic box with a glowing button in the middle. He pushed it, and the box opened and released little misty clouds of cold air that brushed against my ankles.

"It's our second date," he said, pulling out a champagne bottle, two glasses, and a container with chopped up pieces of raw meat in it, speckled with herbs and spices. "I wasn't sure when we'd get a spare moment to come, so I had to ask Asan to bring this ahead of time. He made sure there'd be an excuse to clear my schedule if something comes up while we're here. Those were the preparations he was talking about when he let it slip the other day."

Kahmel proceeded to pull out a checkered blanket for us to sit on and another container with vegetables in it, along with an expandable contraption that looked like a portable fire pit with a metallic grid on top, which I realized was the same thing Arusi used when she cooked for us in the cave.

Kahmel heaped a pile of wood on the bottom. "I see the way your eyes light up every time there's grilled meat around, so I knew I had to include that. It's been a few days, but the picnic container should have kept it pretty fresh. Rand and I used to use these all the time back—er, well, they're reliable."

I pursed my lips as I thought about how hard he and Rand must have had it when they were on the run but followed his lead in moving on from the dark subject. Though they had a bleak past, I was proud of their present and was confident about their future. They had evolved into so much more, and so had their bond with each other because of what they went through together.

Besides, it wasn't like I didn't have enough background of my own to feel sorry for.

Kahmel poured two glasses of champagne and handed one to me. He gestured at the stack of kindling, then stopped himself and looked at me. "Actually, would you do the honors?"

Smiling, I chuckled thinking that now that I was put on the spot would be the moment I wouldn't be able to do it. But I took a deep breath and pushed my palm out to the wood. Energy raced through my body and flowed to my arm, fire spilling from my palm and licking up the wood. When I clenched my fist, it stopped like it was a faucet.

Kahmel grinned. "Look at you; you're a natural now."

"I wouldn't say all that," I said, ducking my head and smoothing imaginary wrinkles out of my pants.

"I wish you wouldn't be so hard on yourself," he said softly, surprising me. He poked the kindle with a stick to make the flames roar hotter, then eased the meat onto the metal grid, letting it sizzle. "You've accomplished a lot in a short amount of time. You should be proud of that."

Straightening my back and sipping some champagne, I allowed myself to be reminded of that, warmth spreading through my chest from the drink. "Thanks."

Kahmel went back to cooking, and he took a few sticks out of the picnic box and skewered the vegetables with them, laying them on the grill as well. I marveled at how Kahmel was a man of few expressions and simple words. But he was at the same time warm, gentle, like a giant handling tiny things with the utmost care and appreciation.

"Now that you know how to control your flames," he said after a few moments of silence had elapsed between us, "there's not much more I can teach you to do with your fire. You basically know as much as I do now. There may be a few clever uses here and there, but you're also smart enough to come up with your own uses for your fire, and I'm sure with as...*creative*...as you are, you might come up with uses I've never thought of."

I chuckled. But I was a little sad to know our lessons were over now. With a start, I realized that it had been, what seemed like a lifetime ago, the only reason I wanted to stay with Kahmel. It felt odd thinking about that now.

Kahmel's tone sobered. "Things are going to get more dangerous the bolder we become."

I nodded. "Yeah. With every step we take forward, it makes us more vulnerable to *them* pushing back."

"Precisely," he agreed. "We can't forget that the last Faresh and his family were assassinated."

That thought did wander through my mind now and again. But I knew Kahmel took so many precautions about everything, and even though I complained about it, I knew it was because he had to be careful. That was why we couldn't trust anyone in the palace that Kahmel or I didn't already know we could trust.

"I think Daoliu gave me a good tip," Kahmel pondered aloud.

I looked up at him. "What do you mean?"

"He mentioned that what happened to the last Faresh happened from within."

"What do you think he meant by that?" I asked, taking another sip of the champagne.

"It's like what the Zendaalans did with you. They use someone they could manipulate. Someone they could send in unnoticed to act like a poison that works ruin from the inside."

"Are you saying you suspect someone?" I asked, suddenly worried. Hearing what I very nearly did to him still made me sick with shame.

"No, no, no," he assured me. He pushed my hair back, a gesture that gently soothed me. "Just noticing a pattern. I'm going to try to have our people investigate the assassinations a little. Look for who may have been a traitor in their midst when they didn't notice. It'll give us insight on how to better protect ourselves."

"Good thinking," I complimented, and I observed how Kahmel's mind seemed like that of a war general at times.

To be completely honest, the only thing that kept me from panicking about the danger of living in the palace was that I knew Kahmel was doing everything in his power to prevent anything from happening to us. And even when I'd been working with the Zendaalans against him, I'd been afraid of what they would do when he *wasn't* around, not when he was. Even then, I knew he'd never let anything happen to me while he was around. So now, as guilty as it made me feel, I sometimes forgot about the dangers because even when Kahmel wasn't around, he made me feel safe.

Now, with the threat of K'sundi being marked a rebel country, I knew how adamantly he protected me and how adamantly he'd protect K'sundi.

Kahmel took the meat off the grill and put it onto plates along with the vegetables. He sipped his champagne and handed me my food, sitting across from me cross-legged to eat his own. Then he took the grill off the contraption, so we just sat and watched the flames as we ate. He'd cooked it to perfection, the meat just tender enough, and the vegetables with that slight charring I liked.

Everything was perfect. The water, the fire, the scenery, the food, the way we could just talk and laugh about anything we wanted here where no one could listen.

It was a nice second date.

The sun was high in the sky by the time we finished eating, but we sat and talked, lips warm from the drinks. I smiled as I saw Huntress and Comet arc across the sky like anxious puppies that just wanted to be around us.

Kahmel crawled forward and took my chin in his hand, leaning toward me, stopping for a minute, always leaving me room to say no.

He was always giving me an option out, even, as it turned out, with our marriage.

But I didn't want out.

His lips crashed into mine, soft, tingling with alcohol. I heard dirt scraping his knee as he slid into a sitting position, putting his hand onto the small of my back and pulling me closer into his chest. My arms wrapped around his neck as we kissed.

The dragons roared overhead.

PART II:

REBELS

LEGISLATION HOUSE

When we got back to K'sundi, the news, as expected, was exploding that Kahmel was dragon tribe. The members of the Council called for a meeting almost as soon as we got back, but, to my surprise, Kahmel blew them off, informing them, essentially, that he'd meet with them when he was good and ready and not when they told him to. The Council was infuriated.

Kahmel spent most of the days following our return to K'sundi with me. When he did have to attend meetings or events, he brought me with him. On our way to a political dinner in the limo, I asked why the sudden change, he chuckled.

"I only stayed busy to give you space and make sure K'sundi stayed on the good list." He scooted close to me and wrapped an arm around my shoulder, leaning in close. I laughed, pulling away. I was fine with it on the special occasion of our date that day, but cuddling just wasn't for me. An odd combination with Kahmel, who, despite his bulky frame and mostly stone face, was always reaching for my hand or pulling me in close and keeping me there. "But we're, uh, 'dating' now," he said, chuckling, "and as far as the other thing goes..." He shrugged. I knew what he was saying and nodded to indicate so. "So, I'd much rather spend time making you a priority for once." He settled for taking my hand and kissing my knuckles.

Eventually, Kahmel did acquiesce the Council, and, after being made to wait so long, they took the matter to the Court. With a grin, Kahmel invited me to come, and for once, I was glad to go.

I didn't feel as awkward at these meetings and events any more. I wore my royal sash with pride. When someone called for the Faresha, I didn't wince and think of a million people that would sound better answering back. I was eager to flex this new confidence at the Court with the people who hated me the most.

The Legislation House was where the Court took place, a huge building in Hashir that always had press buzzing around it, trying to catch a word from the officials coming in and out, because no cameras were allowed inside, and they all wanted a scoop on what was in talks before the decision was announced to the public. The building was round, glass windows sparkling with the desert sun. Steps went up from all sides, resulting in rings upon rings going up to the House. The Star Train had a stop nearby, so part of the rails snaked through the sky behind it.

The Court was the only entity in K'sundi with more power than the Faresh and Faresha with the authority to make us abdicate the throne if enough reason was found to do so. But despite how much they threatened it, they never had any real grounds as nothing Kahmel did was actually wrong. Annoying, yes. But not wrong. The only grounds weighty enough to abdicate a Faresh were things like sedition, fraud, or the like. Still, it wasn't like the people in power weren't desperate enough to falsify those things if they felt threatened enough. But Kahmel didn't think that was the case yet. So far, Kahmel was, at most, irritating and stubborn. He wouldn't be a problem until he was ready to be bolder.

Which we were, now.

But Kahmel was prepared. It would take time for them to work on a way to get rid of him, and the rebels would always be keeping a look out for any mischief the Court—or their unofficial superiors, the Zendaalans—was up to and alert us ahead of time. In the meantime, Kahmel work on presenting himself more openly to the people of K'sundi, something he was loathe to do, though he knew it was necessary. I felt that revealing himself as dragon tribe was a huge step toward doing that, but only time would tell if I was right. If all went well, the Court would have a hard time getting rid of a Faresh the people realized loved them as much as their previous Faresh had before he died.

And if there was one thing I knew about Kahmel, it was that even though he came to the throne with a certain goal in mind, he truly loved his people. If the people only knew the plans he had for our future, they would realize how suited to being Faresh he really was.

Maybe even see that I was suited to being their Faresha.

We climbed the stairs to the Legislation House, Rand trailing behind us for support, wearing a hood and hat despite the heat to appear to be just another entourage like the guards. The public knew little about Kahmel—they knew he had brothers but didn't know specifically that he had a twin, and Kahmel and Rand kept it that way. I was curious if that would change eventually as well.

Cameras and reporters surrounded us, almost all of them asking for a comment on Kahmel's eyes and why he'd hidden them for so long. He responded the same to all of them: *no comment*. I was sure they all missed the smirk that played on his lips as he did.

I smiled to myself. He may never admit it, but I had a feeling he liked not having his glasses on. More than he thought he enjoyed having them on.

Sliding glass doors welcomed us inside. We stepped on a plush velvet carpet in a room that hushed with silence in comparison to the noise outside. Arusi and Asan were already here. They waved when they noticed us walk in.

"Good morning, Your Majesties," Arusi greeted as we approached. Asan began filling Kahmel in on some tips and warnings about the various people inside and what to expect. I zoned out most of what was said but was attentive when Arusi commented to me, "I'm glad to see you here, Faresha." She smiled, and I smiled back.

Roving my gaze over everyone here, I realized just how much I relied on all of them. These were people I trusted with my life.

"So, are you ready to go in?" Asan was asking both of us, I realized.

"Yes, I am," I said, meaning that in a lot of ways.

We walked up some steps that went to either side and to a hall with a balcony on the edge that allowed people from above to see the people below. Before us was a huge round room that had entrance doors all around it. We went through the door closest to us and entered the House.

The House was filled to the brim with people—royal clans that had the right to know about the nation's happenings and give opinions on it as well as Zendaalan officials that had access to the House in the interest of Zendaal and could also voice opinions. The entrances all opened to aisles that separated the rows of seats. We walked past all of them, approaching a panel at the bottom of the room that was situated like a theater. Lining the panel were the elected members of the Court. In front of the panel was the podium the Faresh or Faresha stood at.

Arusi, Rand, and Asan all took seats in the front row as Kahmel and I stood up to the podium.

There were a total of twelve members of the Court. I tried to remember all the things Kahmel always told me about how the Court functioned, but there were just so many rules, terms, different kinds of rulings, processes that took months to accomplish... I knew it was a lost cause. But I knew enough to get through today because it was a petty matter.

The Court and the Council were two separate entities. The Council spoke to the Faresh on a regular basis, mostly to bring up matters and talk them through. And though the Council had a voice, the Faresh would always have the final word. K'sundi even had a Council in ancient times, so it was a structure that had existed for a long time.

However, with the relatively recent addition of the Court system, the Council could now bring up their matters to a higher power than the Faresh if they felt he wasn't listening to reasonable arguments. The Court could then force the Faresh into doing what they felt was necessary, despite his judgment. The Faresh could technically ignore the Court's ruling, but he risked seeming unfit to rule, and the Court would almost certainly act against an outright dismissal of their ruling.

One of the Court members stood, the one in the middle of the panel. I remembered what Arusi told me his name was. Roren Monoh, the Court member who directed most of the happenings of the House. He didn't have more power than the others, but he moved things along, and he did have a certain influence on the others. His opinion was well-respected. But he was a problem because most of his supporters were Zendaalans.

Monoh adjusted his glasses on his aged face. He, along with the other members of the Court, wore robes like judges. He brought up what called the meeting of today—namely, a complaint made by the Council. As the Council was here, seated behind us, the one who formed the complaint stood.

He introduced himself as Mr. Losan Odinbar. I'd seen him countless times before, but I always forgot his name.

I probably still wouldn't remember.

"We, the members of the Council," Odinbar began, "feel that Faresh Kahmel has been deceptive. In all the time that he has been Faresh, we have never known that he was dragon tribe. Of course," he rushed to say, for appearance's sake, "it has no bearing on his ability to lead. But we feel this represents a glaring gap of trust between him and his Council. One that is unfair and uncalled for. And such distrust can go both ways. What more could Faresh Kahmel be hiding, as elusive as he notoriously is?"

Monoh nodded, then looked to Kahmel. "And what is your stance on this, Faresh Kahmel?"

Kahmel stepped up to the microphone on the podium. "I understand the Council's position on this and that they were confused. However, as Odinbar has already stated, this has nothing to do with my ability to lead or my politics. I would much rather spend my time addressing pending issues in the nation that need more attention than this. My stance is that they didn't ask."

I had to keep myself from laughing. I wondered if this was new because he was in a better mood or if Kahmel was always this impertinent at his meetings, and I just never paid attention. It was a serious possibility either way.

Monoh pursed his lips in obvious displeasure, and, glancing at the seats, I noticed Odinbar with a look on his face that said, *You see what we have to deal with?*

Monoh allowed Odinbar to sit down, then addressed Kahmel. "Well, I suppose the mystery to why you always wore sunglasses in public is solved, then, Faresh." His tone was disapproving, like a condescending teacher reproving the kid shooting spitballs and leaning his chair back.

Another Court member, Hanis...Kodich, voiced her opinion. That was two Court members' names remembered—I was doing pretty good today. "You are very secretive, Faresh Kahmel. Even from what we've heard of how things are run in your palace—or I should say the lack thereof—we know that you are highly suspicious of others, even your own bodyguards. And access to you or your wife is extremely limited. Just a few months ago, you had a Zendaalan officer executed for treason for threatening your wife while she was visiting New K'sundi with no explanation for why she was there in the first place. You can understand that this situation only perpetuates how little anyone is ever allowed to know about you."

Kahmel nodded seriously as I clenched my fists nervously beside him. I hated that my involvement with the Zendaalans made things so complicated.

"Then I implore anyone curious to ask," Kahmel said.

"He's making a mockery of the Court!" Odinbar exclaimed, standing again as murmurs filled the room and they all wagged their heads.

"Settle down," Monoh said, slamming down a hammer to quiet everyone. "Please be seated, Odinbar."

"All right then, Faresh Kahmel," another Court member said. I blanked out on her name, but then I noticed the names of the Court members on little nameplates in front of them on the panel. Her name was Arera Nomali. I felt a little cheated, having remembered two whole names for nothing. "Then we're asking. What else are you hiding from this Court? What is it that you don't want the world to know?"

Something flickered in Kahmel's eyes as he put his hands on the podium and leaned forward. "*Hiding*...somehow the word doesn't seem fitting. Hiding implicates, as the Council's accusations are, that I intend to deceive you in some way. No, hiding is not the word. I am protective, Nomali. I'm protective of my palace, my people, my wife, and myself. I have demonstrated as much in this last war with Omani, something no one wanted to complain about at the time that you needed my protection most. And I protected K'sundi from Omani because before I came into the palace, it was vulnerable in all the time it spent without a Faresh. I'm protecting my home and my household for the same reasons. The *Court*," Kahmel said accusingly, though his face stayed perpetually firm, the whisper of a smirk on his lips, "never was able to find out who assassinated the last Faresh and his family. Forgive me if I take steps to prevent it from happening again."

The room grew eerily silent. Kahmel really was good at leaving people speechless. I could see the simmering anger on all their faces and loved it.

"What about you, Faresha?" Nomali finally said, face taut. "Are you hiding anything from this Court?"

"No, I'm good," I said, giving a polite smile.

A small turn of his lips, Kahmel leaned forward again. "See, all you have to do is ask."

GUN

I only had a few moments to use my eWatch's holographic camera function to snap pictures of the ancient artifacts I'd snatched from their hiding places in glass cases as the alarms blared. Seemed like rich people were tired of rebels breaking in and looking at their valuables and got smart. I was expecting the video cameras and the security pass to get to the office, but both were either handled or disabled. What I wasn't expecting was the infrared scanner inside the glass cases. One that was most likely disabled by unlocking the case, not cutting into it from the side.

It didn't matter; I was just about done anyway. Finished with my pictures, I ducked out the window, leaving everything in the office askew, and hopped from the house's second-story window and into the open air. The environment around me changed to the inside of the hovercar as I landed.

It was a little risky going on a raid in broad daylight like this, but we had little other choice. The owner of this manor was selling their artifacts to a buyer in Med Mali, and we wouldn't risk losing them.

I remembered that Gaiena said something about the Drake Bonds being found in Gheresan art, which was why I took an interest when I heard about rebels going on a raid involving a lawyer with Gheresan relics in his house.

Khes turned to me, shaking his head as he sent our hovercar

forward, sirens blaring behind us. "You know Kahmel will kill me if anything happens to you, right?"

"We'll be fine," I insisted. My robes and jewelry were already tucked away in a bag beside me, so I started changing as Khes turned his head to the desert, tapping a few buttons to help us lose our pursuers. Police were getting better at detecting camouflaged hovercars, but Khes was sending dispersal signals that would make us harder to track.

After I changed, I picked up my purse and sat next to Khes. Reaching inside, my fingers wrapped around a smooth round object the size of a pebble. I took it out and pressed the top, hearing it click as the surface under my thumb went in and glowed a faint blue. Then, I dragged the holographic images I'd snapped from my eWatch to the small device. I would hide it somewhere for the rebels to pick up and download to their database later. The small device had the ability to shift into the shape of a pen and appear benign to anyone who didn't notice the claw I would place beside it.

I continued to scroll through the pictures, wondering if something distinct would catch my eye. There were urns, the pictures taken at different angles to allow for seeing all sides of the patterns in their designs; paintings, boxes that were a puzzle that had to be solved to get inside. At first, I thought I'd have to take it with me to have time to solve it, but I found the solution was simple enough. I just had to slide a few pieces into the appropriate slots to get it to open. But there was nothing inside. I still took pictures, just in case, but it was disappointing.

Looking at them again, however, I noticed faint marks on the inside of the box that I didn't notice before. I squinted and zoomed in on them. They looked vaguely like old K'sundii letters.

I did a cross-search, tapping a few buttons on my eWatch to look for letters that fitted the faint markings on the inside of the box. It came up empty. I tsked. Maybe the computer couldn't detect the indentions I could see. Deepening the contrast on the image so the lines showed up better, I tried again.

This time I got something.

"Well, would you look at that," I mumbled.

"Did you find something?" Khes wanted to know. He finally slowed the hovercar as we lost our pursuers, the sirens blaring in the other direction.

The program I was running converted the letters to ones I could recognize.

Leh mani stepior

I frowned. They didn't make any sense to me.

I squinted at the text. "*Leh mani stepior*. Those words mean anything to you?"

Khes frowned in confusion. "Can't say that they do. Maybe it's in another language?"

"Maybe," I said, pursing my lips in thought.

"Don't worry too much about it. We'll figure it out eventually. In the meantime, better get ready to take the trainees out on their first recruit mission tomorrow."

I grinned. "Yeah, that's going to be fun."

Kahmel had ended up giving the rest of his trainees the recruit position. He got a report on some wild dragons flying close to the city, and he thought it was the perfect opportunity for the trainees to have their first mission. T'shan had a lot of fun rounding up the dragons in Gheres, so I knew the other trainees would have a ball. I wouldn't be participating, but I'd be watching from the sidelines while Kahmel took them out. I was looking forward to it.

Soon, Khes and I arrived at our drop-off point, and I climbed into the limo that was waiting for me—driven by a rebel member—as Khes went his separate way.

When I got home, Armeen, my friendly servant, greeted me as I entered the grand halls of the palace. "Did you have a nice evening with your friends, Your Majesty?" Armeen asked.

Taking off my coat and handing it to him as he extended his hands to take it, I smiled. "Yes, I did. Thank you."

"Faresh Kahmel is waiting for you in the dining room," he added as he walked with me.

"Has he been waiting long?"

"No, no," he amended. "The chef just finished with dinner. You're right on time."

"Perfect."

I was glad for Kahmel making more time for us to be together these days. I knew he'd get busy again as he started campaigning more for his ideal dragon laws, but for now, he still had to finalize talks with the rebels for what he was going push for. That reminded me—I had to talk to him about an idea I had, inspired by when Cirssa and I went out to find the entrance to the Dragon Realm.

Still, I was glad for the opportunity to be together more.

I came into the dining room to see Kahmel sitting at the table with Rand, Arusi, and Asan at his side.

They all stood as I came in, my friends giving slight bows for the sake of the servants standing around. Kahmel's lip turned up, an equivalent of a grin for him. "Glad you could join us, Jashi."

I could tell the servants were still off-put by seeing Kahmel's eyes, but I liked him this way much better—not having to stare at my own reflection in his sunglasses when I talked to him.

"The tables are turned now, aren't they?" I said, raising an eyebrow as a servant pulled out a chair across from him. Everyone took to their seats as well. "How does it feel waiting for me to get home for dinner all day, hm?"

Kahmel grimaced. "All right, I deserve that."

Chuckling, I sat down and started on what was set before me, a nice warm soup with beef chunks swimming with potatoes and carrots in a red sauce.

I turned to Armeen. "You see? He can't take what he dishes out."

Armeen chuckled uncertainly, probably conflicted between agreeing with me and his fear of Kahmel. Armeen shrugged and shook his head disbelievingly. As expected, the other servants stared at us strangely, unaccustomed to the royals talking to the servants like friends. But I had been in those invisible jobs most of my life. I'd be damned if I let a marriage and a title stop me from being human.

Asan chuckled. "I could have told you that, Your Majesty. If I ignored him as much as he does me, he'd have my head."

Kahmel rolled his eyes, and Asan gestured to him, giving me a look with his eyebrows raised. *You see what I mean?*

"We're all shocked you're still here," Rand said to me, shaking his head.

I laughed, and even Kahmel chuckled.

"How was your evening?" Arusi asked, a knowing look in her eye. "Did you and your friends have fun?"

I loved these moments, talking in code about the things no one outside of this table would ever know. I may not have been a good spy, but I adored being a rebel.

"We did," I responded, taking up another spoonful of soup. "I look forward to the next time we can get away."

Kahmel asked, "Did you see what the Emperor Daoliu Kun said on the news?"

I perked up at the emperor's name. It felt strange hearing the name of a political figure and knowing he and his wife were friends of mine, but it was something we were hoping would happen a lot more often. I wanted to start getting used to it.

"What did he say?"

"I don't normally like having a mini-HoloScreen out at dinner," he said, pulling it up on his eWatch. "But I'll make an exception this time."

Rand complained, "Oh, so you can watch the news at dinner when you say so, but I can't watch cartoons."

Kahmel shook his head. "Let's see if you can understand. News about K'sundi's allies, important. Crime-fighting cats, not." He swiped at the screen to send it to my eWatch, and Daoliu's face appeared on the screen. He was in front of an audience, making a speech in front of flashing cameras and eager faces. I smiled as I noticed Cirssa sitting on the sidelines, looking up at her husband with obvious pride.

I listened to the video as Rand tried to argue with his brother that they were crime-fighting cheetahs, not cats.

Daoliu's words were being translated, and they didn't match up with his lips. Kahmel had fast-forwarded to the point he meant for me to see. Daoliu was mid-sentence, his face as stone as always. "—rumors about Faresh Kahmel Omah and his wife Jashi Anyua-Omah. As many know, they recently visited this country. I was good friends with the late Faresh Adisoh Nodam, and I like Faresh Kahmel Omah." He said "like" with an unchanging expression, but I knew it was a high compliment, and I smiled at Kahmel to show as much. He nodded at the video for me to keep paying attention, waving off whatever Rand was saying. Daoliu went on. "As a matter of fact, I feel as though the world has underestimated him. They think his ideals are outrageous. His vision for the future unrealistic. But this is not a rash man. I believe he's going to prove to the world that they should have been listening all along. He and his wife are going to usher this age into a new future. I would watch those two if I were you. They're bound for greatness. And when that future arrives, I shall be standing on the sidelines, saying, 'I told you so.'"

I laughed in pleasure, and Kahmel took his screen back and flicked it off, his chest puffed with pride. "Daoliu is proposing that Gheres erect Dragon Towers so they can support having wild dragons."

My eyes widened. "Really?" I wondered how much of that decision was because of Cirssa's insisting that she wanted a dragon of her own like us with Comet and Huntress. I wouldn't be surprised if it were the only reason for doing it. "The Gheresan government can't be too happy with that."

"They're not," Asan acknowledged, "but the fact that K'sundi has been maintaining them successfully makes his argument more convincing. Thankfully, we haven't had the same issues from last year. The Dragon Towers have had no new incidents with dragons attacking surrounding cities. The Watchers still need to learn how to handle dragons with fewer kills, but even that has been improving. Kahmel's trainees are in the news, and they inspire Watchers to do better. Daoliu actually has a lot of good arguments to bring up." He looked at me as he said, "You and Kahmel have done that. Everything you're doing now makes it possible for Daoliu to push for this. You should be proud of yourselves."

I was. To see these fruits of our labor made it all worth it.

"Rand!" Kahmel yelled.

I turned to see Rand had pulled up a HoloScreen with cartoons of cheetahs wearing fedoras in a car chase playing on the display. He sipped his soup as he chuckled at something that happened on the show.

Kahmel looked to me for support. "Do you see this? We're trying to have dinner!"

I pulled up my own HoloScreen and loaded up an episode of *The City of Kohpal: Criminology.*

Kahmel placed a hand on his face and sighed as Arusi and Asan laughed.

When dinner was over, Rand went to his room, and Kahmel and I started back to ours. I felt wonderfully full and satisfied, thoroughly warmed by the soup in my belly.

"Well, thanks, Jashi. Now we're going to have *Alley-Cheetahs* on every night at dinner."

"You're welcome," I said, laughing.

Kahmel's wrist glowed momentarily, and he frowned at the notification that appeared on his eWatch, tsking.

"Bad news?" I asked.

"No, no," he said quickly. "It just looks like I'll have to leave tonight. There's an emergency with one of the Dragon Towers in the south, and the Zendaalans want me there by tomorrow morning for a meeting on what to do about it. It seems there's an influx on the population because a lot of eggs hatched recently, and the dragons are getting territorial. I guess we'll have to cancel with

Jemmorah, Ashed, and Kent. This would be too much for them to handle."

I frowned as we came to our bedroom door and entered our room. Kahmel set out his luggage to pack. "Aw, and I was so looking forward to their recruitment mission." I crossed my arms. "Why do they need you?"

Kahmel sighed and shrugged. "Looks like it's making people worried. But still, you're right, it's odd. Even more so for the Zendaalans to be involved." He started on a message, probably to the servants for them to prepare. When he was done, he put an arm around my waist and kissed my cheek softly. "Don't worry; I'll be careful," he whispered.

"Make sure of it," I whispered back. I tried to calm the worry that nipped at my mind, reassuring myself that if Kahmel wasn't worried, I didn't have any reason to be.

Kahmel pecked my lips, then went back to work getting ready for his trip. "I'll probably be out by around three in the morning," he said. "I'll be gone by the time you wake up."

I nodded in understanding, going into my closet to change. I peeled off my robes and slipped comfortable pajamas on, reassuring myself that Kahmel went on trips like this all the time; it was just now he was more transparent about it.

I climbed into bed and put on a sleeping mask so Kahmel could continue to prepare with the lights on. I eventually drifted off.

Buzzzz ashi...et up

 Buzzzzz get...p

My eyes peeled open, disturbed by the interruption. My first reaction was to assume it was from an alarm, but I opened my eyes to darkness; it was still night. There was stirring, and I figured it was Kahmel, so I closed my eyes again. But the buzzing was insistent.

There was more stirring, fumbling around with something on the nightstand. Frantic. Fumbling with my eWatch.

Then my thoughts collected as the disturbance continued, shaking the sleep off. Why would the alarm come from *my* eWatch? Kahmel was the one who needed to get up early. And why was he struggling with it so much? All he had to do was turn it off.

"Jashi, *get up.*"

The voice wasn't shouting, but it was firm and adamant. Was it talking this whole time? Yes, it was talking with the buzzing, I remembered. I was just too sleepy to notice. It sounded like Arusi. Her voice had the kind of sternness that was in control, but with the twinge of urgency that was disturbing enough to stir the grogginess from my mind enough to wake up. How was she talking on my eWatch, anyway?

"Shit!" muttered another voice. Not Kahmel's. Not Arusi's.

I shot up with newfound urgency.

A figure wrapped in shadow stood in the room. With a gun. Pointed at me.

"Jashi, get out of there!"

I didn't know how Arusi knew what was going on or how she was communicating to me through my eWatch, but the person in the room fumbled with the eWatch to turn it off.

The person threw the eWatch to the ground and pointed the gun shakily at my head.

Despite everything in me, I resisted the urge to scream. I needed no witnesses.

Summoning order to the chaos in my mind, I searched for my fire. It flared up in response, like a call to action. My hands went to my sheets, letting them light up in flames as energy and adrenaline pulsated through my body, knowing it wouldn't hurt me in the slightest. My attacker jumped back, startled. I threw the flaming covers at the silhouette and leaped from the bed as whoever it was wrestled with the covers to avoid catching fire.

I forced myself to concentrate. I reacted faster than my thoughts.

The flames were alive to me, aware of me. Ready for my call. I summoned them, prodding them to burn hotter. Larger.

The person jumped and flung their arms to be rid of the flames that blossomed all over their clothes and body like fiery lilies that wouldn't be suppressed, responding to my desperate call to resist the attacker's patting and grow hotter.

"Jashi!" Rand rushed into the room with guards at his side. I had enough focus left to find the flames again, eager and roaring with life, and silently whisper to them to finally fade. The fires died with a sigh, leaving smoking sheets and a smell like burnt rubber filling the air.

The lights flicked on, and I gasped as the guards hauled my attacker to his feet. Armeen's eyes were wild with a mix of fear and incredulity.

Armeen.

I would just have to leave it to Kahmel to handle him seeing my fire. He was the only one in the room when I used it, and he didn't even see me explicitly use it. He saw my covers set ablaze, and he saw them go out. Even if he questioned or suspected, he was *my* attacker, not the other way around. No one had to believe anything he said.

But still.

Now that the rush was over, it settled in how fast my heart was racing. My head felt light, my arms like noodles hanging at my sides. The room began to dip as grogginess and exhaustion merged into one. I must have faltered because one of the guards rushed forward to support me as I tipped to the side.

"Take him out of here!" Rand barked. Arusi was coming into the room at that moment. The guards started piling out of the room, but two stayed behind. Rand shook his head. "All of you, out."

"But, Your Highness, we have to ensure—"

"*Out.*" The murderous look on Rand's face silenced any further protests, and the remaining guards left, Arusi quickly replacing the one who was supporting me at my side. She helped me sit on the edge of my bed. My mind felt like pudding at this point, so I just followed whatever she was instructing me to do.

"Are you okay, Jashi?" Arusi asked, the firm look in her eyes completely devoid of panic, but a steadiness that helped me center myself and focus.

"I-I-I think," I managed. I didn't even know I was shaking until she reaffirmed her grip around my arms in a half-hug.

"I'm so sorry we didn't get here sooner. The security cameras in this room were producing a faulty feed, and it took us a while to mobilize the guards because they didn't think anything was wrong."

I still hadn't quite registered what happened. "Armeen…"

Rand pursed his lips, looking just like his brother now that he was properly angered. "We'll have to talk about him later," he said finally. "Right now, let's worry about you. I know you're shaken, but did you get hurt?"

"N-no. I didn't get hurt, but…" I looked at the sheets, charred and blackened where the flames had sprouted.

Rand shook his head. "Don't worry. Kahmel will handle that. You did good, Jash."

I breathed a sigh of relief.

Arusi stroked my shoulder, and that simple motion helped ease my mind a little more. My heart had only slowed by a fraction, but I felt calmer.

"How did you even know to come?" I finally gathered the mind to ask. I knew I heard Arusi's voice on my eWatch before. I still didn't know how she managed it.

"We have eyes and ears everywhere," she said with a look. The rebels.

Rand nodded as if to confirm that very thought. "Kahmel made sure there were separate defense systems all over the palace, outside of the guards."

That made sense. I already knew Kahmel didn't totally trust the guards. It seemed he made sure there was an extra security system only the rebels had access to. Which was probably why whoever arranged this attack didn't know about them.

"I heard the alert," Arusi went on to explain. "I used the special communicator we synced up to your eWatch right before I contacted Rand and the guards. As soon as Armeen entered the room, I could see and hear everything, so I know what happened. I hope you don't mind."

"Not at all," I assured her, trying to keep from thinking about what would have happened if she hadn't intervened.

Rand sighed. "I'm going to send a message to Kahmel and tell him to come right back." Lowering his voice, Rand leaned in. "I think this was a set-up from the beginning. They waited until Kahmel was away. We thought the Zendaalans calling him away was suspicious, but we anticipated them coming after him if anything. It looks like they specifically wanted to draw him away from you, so you'd be alone. This was a highly calculated move, and almost certainly orchestrated by the Zendaalans themselves."

Suddenly certain events clicked together in my head. Mira warned me before that the Zendaalans would do something about me being in the palace if I didn't agree to disappear. And then Daoliu's warning to Kahmel that the ones who came after the royalty in K'sundi always attacked from the inside out. Just like they used me. They used Armeen because he was on the inside as well.

It smelled like a Zendaalan arrangement for sure.

"They warned me," I mumbled, my voice sounding distant even to me. "They told me to take an out. Mira told me."

Rand hugged my other side. "Don't worry, Faresha. You're not going anywhere. We're going to make sure of it."

REVEALING

Kahmel Axon Kai of the Omah Clan, Faresh of K'sundi

My hands gripped the leather arms of my airplane seat as I went over in my head again and again how much I wished I'd never left Jashi alone. I wasn't wearing my usual suit; I was irritated and hot in the jacket, and thinking about what happened to Jashi made me even more irritated and hot, so I took it off. I only had the plain t-shirt that I'd worn underneath it, my arms bare.

Stupid!

Of *course* they were drawing me out. How could I be so *stupid?*

Rand assured me Jashi was fine but shaken. He brought Jashi to the caller, so I got to talk with her. She didn't sound good, but I was proud of her for holding her own. Discreetly, Rand let me know we had some covering up to do.

It didn't matter. We would figure something out. The rebels could plant evidence to make it seem like it was Armeen's plan to burn the evidence after he was done, and Jashi got a hold of his lighter and used it to defend herself. Something along those lines. For the moment, I told Rand to tell Jashi to say she found a lighter and used it to set the fires. We'd make it make sense later. My head was spinning too much to think clearly.

Before Jashi came to the palace, I found a lot of people working for the Zendaalans in the palace, the reason for all the executions that had to be done at the time. Several attempts were made on my life, or the rebels would find evidence of the plans being made for one. I was used to people coming after me.

It was another thing altogether for them to come after Jashi. My wife.

Normally, I had enough control of my fire to be able to contain myself, but this time, my arms itched, and my palms burned. I opened my mouth to breathe the fire out, but it had beat me to the punch, tracing all along my arms and hands with a painful bite, fire erupting from my limbs with a vengeance.

I took a deep breath. I needed to get back in control. I couldn't afford to lose it, even if I was alone on the plane. Slowly, the fire died, and I gritted my teeth at the familiar pain of holding it back that I hadn't felt in years. It had been a while since I lost control like this.

But I had other things to worry about. The Zendaalans were moving again. It seemed like their goal was to scare Jashi away. They probably understood what it meant for Jashi and me to be two Half-Dracs who knew about each other. They might have thought she would leave on her own eventually, seeing as she did everything she could to resist the marriage initially. But as she gave up on that, they now had to take more extreme measures to accomplish the same thing. My own mother warned her as much. Something it seemed Jashi remembered as well, as she'd mentioned my mother's warning on the HoloCaller.

I might need to pay another visit to dear old mom.

And as a matter of fact, I wondered where my father was these days. I hadn't heard from him in a while, and with this recent attack on Jashi, I wondered why.

Then there was Jashi herself. Something tickled the back of my mind as I mentally searched for possible breaches. I wasn't ignorant of the fact that Talad disappeared in the middle of his visit.

I also wondered how she'd react when I ordered Armeen's execution over this. She was royalty, and the price for an attempt on her life was high. I just hoped she'd be able to handle it.

I didn't know how long I was in the air. It was only supposed to be a few hours. All I knew was every second felt too long. When the plane finally landed, I practically flew to the limo and barked at the driver to take me to the palace.

Meanwhile, I calculated. The question was, how public should I let this get? I could smother any reports the police wanted to make and demand that it got no further than just us. But my recent promise to Jashi stopped me. I told her I'd be more open. Wasn't this the moment to do so? My instinct was to make sure no one knew our business, but then again, that was always because I was more concerned about getting the Dragon Towers established and making sure the dragon nest caves weren't destroyed than maintaining my image to people. Both of those things were accomplished now. Now I *needed* to make time for the people.

This attack was almost certainly conducted by the Zendaalans, and no investigation would ever yield those results. But I didn't have to do them any favors by covering up their attack, either.

The more I thought about it, the more apparent it was that the better solution was one I wasn't accustomed to. I found myself remembering the fear that always eclipsed everyone's eyes when they looked at me and how it always changed to a look I never liked: sympathy.

I never got it when I was younger, when my parents hated me for being born different. Nor when those same people turned into the very people that tried to kill me. When I joined the rebellion, they knew the situation I came from, but they didn't bother with niceties and just put Rand and me to work, which was what I needed. I didn't get sympathy from anyone, and by a certain point, I found I didn't want it.

What did that even mean? *I feel sorry for you.* What good would that do? I didn't want people being sorry; I wanted them *doing things.* But maybe the world didn't work like I did. Maybe they needed to feel that sympathy to inspire a reaction.

Something bit back that I didn't *need* anyone to feel sorry for me. That I could handle the situation on my own. But the truth was, I couldn't. Not this time. For the future of K'sundi, I couldn't. For Jashi's safety, I couldn't.

The Zendaalans had it easy because they could be so damn invisible all the time.

Maybe it was about time I made that harder for them.

I STORMED into one of the living areas of the palace where Jashi was lying down on the couch, leaning over the arm. She was with Rand and Arusi, both sitting in armchairs to either side of her. Rand had set up a HoloScreen with *Alley-Cheetahs* playing on it.

"Are you all right?" I asked, coming to her side in an instant.

Jashi looked up and gave me a weak smile. Her usually bright tangerine eyes looked glassy as if she'd cried and was still on the verge of tears. In spite of it all, she still held herself with that edge of regality I'd noticed in her lately. I had to admire her strength—her refusal to be broken. No matter how you looked at it, Jashi was a dragon at heart.

"I'm all right," she said in a small voice. She looked back at the television when she said, "Armeen is in jail. They say they're questioning him now. He isn't saying anything, though."

Rand looked at me with steel in his eyes. My twin liked to joke around and act light most of the time, but I knew he was capable of burning anger, thinly veiled by that last thread of lightness in his dark eyes. But that look was just as much of a mask as my sunglasses.

"It's clear he had help, though," Rand said. "The security systems around your bedroom were all being fed a false feed about an hour after you left the palace, showing nothing but still halls and a sleeping Jashi on loop. His gun had a silencer he most certainly couldn't have gotten on his own."

I looked at Jashi, a pang shooting through my chest as she wouldn't meet my eyes. She knew what I was going to say and that I was avoiding it, but I had to say it anyway. "You know what's going to happen to him if he doesn't talk, don't you?"

She just watched the cartoons with a dead look that wasn't remotely amused by all the quirky sound effects and cheetahs being smashed in the head. "I know," she finally said, barely audible.

Arusi said, "I'm not sure if we should increase security around her room or not at this point. Even the guards know someone on the inside had to have let this happen."

"Don't," Jashi said, snapping her eyes from the HoloScreen and looking at Arusi with a tenacity I wasn't even sure she realized was there. "There's no point. I lived this time *because* Kahmel already treats the guards with distance. We should just continue as we are. I just need to be more aware now."

"We all do," I admitted. "This kind of thing has happened before at the palace, before you showed up, Jashi. It just slowed down for a while."

"Well, not anymore," Rand said, breathing out.

Jashi frowned, her tired eyes on me. "Really? I'd never heard of any attempts made on your life."

Arusi supplied the answer. "He never let it get public."

Jashi nodded like she should have known.

"Not this time, though," I said, and all eyes in the room were on me. "I didn't let people know because I didn't think they needed to. I was the Faresh everyone was afraid of, and it was better for everyone to continue to think of me that way because I didn't have time to make them believe otherwise. But it's time for that to change." I took in Jashi and the perplexed expression on her soft face. "There will probably be more attacks, Jashi. But don't worry," I added quickly, thinking she would be scared, but instead I was met with a look of intrigue.

That was my girl.

"What do you mean, Kahmel?" Arusi wanted to know.

"It's about time we make it harder for these people to hide." I looked at Jashi. "Someone told me to be more open, and I think it's good advice. We make it convenient for them to stay unseen by shielding ourselves from the public."

Rand leaned forward. "You don't want this quieted."

"No," I said, breathing out, mentally lining up my plans and how they would interact. The dragon laws, the search for the next Dragon King, and now this. There had to be a way for them to all work together. "I have an idea for how to deal with this, but we'll have to talk about it later."

I took Jashi's hand, and her tired gaze rested on me. "I'm sorry this happened."

She didn't say anything. She just rushed forward and let me take her into my arms. I felt her sobbing gently into my chest.

"I know," I murmured into her hair, knowing exactly how she felt. Being betrayed, no matter who it was by, was never easy. Knowing that someone could be friendly to your face and have a dagger behind their back the whole time.

I hated to do this to her, but it had to be done. Gently, I leaned into her ear.

"Armeen's not going to talk. You...know what I have to do, don't you?"

She nodded but didn't look at me.

She just squeezed harder.

MOTHER

Kahmel Axon Kai of the Omah Clan, Faresh of K'sundi

It had been days since the attempt on Jashi's life. I knew I had to make this meeting quick because I was going to meet with the rebels later.

But what I had to do wouldn't take long.

I didn't bother with the limo. I drove down my parents' driveway in my own personal hovercar. Technically, I wasn't supposed to drive myself anywhere, but I didn't think one could break the rules any more than basically being a rebel king, so in comparison, the crime didn't seem severe.

The sun was setting on the evening, throwing wicked red light on the topiary bushes along the lawn. All kinds of memories seemed to float around the air and cling to me as I drove by. Moving here after the assassination of the Faresh before me. Coming home after escaping almost being killed at my "doctor's visit." Finding Zendaalans in our home, ready to take me in soon after. Escaping with Rand and beginning our life on our own. All my other brothers got to spend the rest of their lives here after we moved. Rand and I only got that small window of a few years to fill with as many traumatic events as I'd ever had in my life.

Coming back was strange.

When I became Faresh, none of that history mattered because, technically, my doctor's visit never happened; thus, neither did any of the events that followed. I just moved out with my twin and appeared seven years later as Faresh of K'sundi, and my family, therefore, became royals. They could no longer get to me because I was Faresh. I couldn't blame them for the past because they were covered by the fact the world didn't know my abilities existed.

So now we all just pretended none of that ever happened.

A few years ago, going down this same driveway would have meant almost certain death because my parents would have wasted no time calling back the Zendaalans to get rid of the child they were embarrassed to have in the first place.

The only other reason I might have gone down this driveway would have been for my parents' historical archives for information, but I would have left the car somewhere on the road and snuck up this way with Rand and a couple other rebels.

Today would have neither of those endings.

Today, they'd get something that was a long time coming.

I arrived at the home and got out of my car, rapping on the door until a servant opened it, looking confused.

He made a quick flourishing bow, quickly straightening and saying, "F-Faresh Kahmel, we weren't expecting—"

"I know," I cut him off, letting myself in.

It wasn't like he could stop me.

I strode down the cold checkered floors of the foyer, lit warmly by the standing lamps and chandelier. Not that it could make the place feel any less like a dungeon to me.

"Is Mother home?" I asked the servant.

"Ah, no, she's out at the moment with—"

"What about Father?"

"Business excursion." The servant shook himself, flustered. "Really, if you come back later to advise them ahead of time—"

"Oh, no need." I showed myself into the living room, sitting on one of the black leather armchairs. The tight leather made rubbery noises with every movement, and it made me remember how particular Mother always was with her furniture, seeing that old habits truly died hard. All the pieces in the room looked barely even used.

"Your Majesty," the servant objected. "You have to admit this is all somewhat improper."

"Improper?" I asked, getting up. I was used to people being afraid of me now. Even enjoyed it, somewhat. After living so long with my sunglasses, I never realized how much people would fear me even more without them.

And I liked it.

"I think as Faresh," I continued, taking steps toward him and watching him take just as many back, "I can do whatever I damn well please, especially in my own family home, wouldn't you say?"

This servant was only seeing a fraction of the anger I had stored up for this evening, and even that had him nodding vigorously and stammering an apology before he hurried away.

Jashi was right. Being without my sunglasses was fun.

Reclaiming my seat, I heard whispered voices in the hall, probably from the servant calling Mother to let her know I'd gone insane or something. Good. It'd make for less waiting time.

As I suspected, it wasn't long before I saw a dragon lowering down into the driveway. ZST trained, of course—its collar glowed a bright red in the middle.

Mother burst through the door, wearing a fur coat over a silk red dress. She must have been at a dinner event with some royal clan or other.

"Kahmel, what are you doing here?"

I stood, the corner of my lip dragging up. "Happy to see me? It's been a while since we've talked, hasn't it?"

She watched me with cautious eyes as I strode about the room lazily.

"What do you want?" she demanded.

I frowned and feigned ignorance. "I'm hurt. What makes you think I'm here because I want something?"

"Oh, stop your endless toying. You do love to toy with us, don't you?" She tilted up her chin in defiance, a smile crawling up her blood-colored lips. "How is your wife?"

I could feel the involuntary throb in my temple but kept my calm composure. Like she taught me how to do when I was younger. We were supposed to be "special" because we were clan. And clan families didn't show fear, pain, or weakness. The world could know little about us because we descended from greatness. Unfortunately for my parents, that greatness was mottled by me, the savage child. But all the same, that made me have to make up for it even more by being more perfect. Perfect grades, perfect career choice, perfect life.

Of course, when the Zendaalans offered them a way to blot out the imperfection, they leaped on it, and all those years of learning perfection were reduced to nothing. Until now. I needed it as a rebel and as Faresh. I supposed I should thank them for drilling two-sidedness into me because now I could don a royal sash as easily as I could don a mask and raid a house with the rebels. Just as easily as I could stand here and want to set the whole house on fire but instead show the face of composure.

"She's fine," I said. My smile didn't falter. "She had a bit of a scare, but she's stronger than her enemy thought." With pride in my chest, I said, "People have been calling her the Dragon Queen. Maybe her attacker should have taken that into consideration."

She narrowed her eyes at me. The frustration boiling up in her was palpable. But of course, she, also, was perfect. Her voice was level as she seethed and repeated her question from before. "What do you want?"

I leaned up against the wall beside the window, looking out onto rolling waves of sand that greeted the back side of the house. "Where's Dad?"

I knew her well enough to notice the split second in which she faltered, and I knew my hunch was right.

"What are you talking about?" she said quickly. She knew she messed up, too. "I'm sure the servants told you he's out on business."

I rolled my head to look at her again. "Right. There was some ancient bone buried somewhere he just had to see. How long has he been gone? His trips never took this long, and that was before he was a royal. So where is he really, Mother?"

Her jaw clenched. "I've told you all I know, son."

I chuckled darkly. "Son. How many years has it been since you were willing to acknowledge me as that, huh? Before I was Faresh, and we had to pretend the last seven years before never happened, I mean." I raised a hand to stop her as she opened her mouth. "No need to answer that. I know you won't anyway."

Her face twisted like she'd smelled something foul and said, "I don't know why you chose to show yourself to the public. It was bad enough your wife is dragon tribe; now the world knows you both are."

I nodded, going back to walking around the room. My hand traced the back of the leather armchair. "It's the start of them knowing a lot of things that didn't need to be kept secret so long. See, you and Father had it so wrong about clans. We descended from greatness?" I barked a laugh. "More like cowardice. They were traitors to their own people!" She looked at me with utter confusion, but I didn't stop to explain. "But that's okay. I'm going to bring us *back* to greatness. And it's going to start with knowing the truth." I looked her in the eye. "About everything."

Her eyes widened. "You don't mean...but the Zendaalans—"

"I said everything." I enjoyed the incredulous look on her face before I waved the matter away. "But that's not really what I'm here to tell you." I closed the distance between us, leaned into her, and spoke in a low voice. "I don't care what the Zendaalans told you they can do. I can do more, and I am relentless when properly motivated. I gave you a chance to leave my wife alone, and now I'm mad. I hope you've enjoyed your days as a royal because they'll soon be over." I sat back in the leather armchair and crossed my legs. "Now, are you going to tell me that Father and my brothers are conspiring with Zendaalans against me, or will I have to find them myself?"

DEVOTION

Jashi Anyua-Omah, Faresha of K'sundi

I couldn't think about Armeen, so I buried myself in the book the rebels had printed and bound for me. Even though the words just blurred together without any of them really sticking. I couldn't let myself drift, or I'd end up down the same path, fixated on the execution. Part of me wanted to stop Kahmel and tell him it didn't matter, but I knew it was a lie. It did matter, and it had to matter, or I'd be making a joke of my position.

But still.

It infuriated me that Armeen wouldn't talk. I didn't even want to know who he worked for or how he did it. I just wanted to know why. What price was high enough to betray me? What offer was so tempting that it was worth my life when I'd done nothing to him?

That road had no end, so I tried, once again, to focus on the pages in front of me, rereading the same paragraph for the umpteenth time.

I'd finally established the Bond with the dragon I'd taken a chance with, just in time since the battle was near. I will never tire of the wonder of dragons. How one dragon no different from the last can create a lasting bond with you that can transcend lifetimes if one manages to establish the connection. No two connections are the same or for the same reason. I pity those who never experience it and am glad that, in my position, I have Drake Bonds with several dragons. The heightened power will be the making of this next battle. I can feel it.

I quirked an eyebrow. This was important information. It still didn't tell me how one was made, but it alluded to the purpose of Drake Bonds. It seemed like it was a connection between dragon and rider that was unique. From the context, it seemed like it could be done with several dragons, but not *any* dragon.

I snapped a picture of the passage with my eWatch and scanned the important section of the page, storing the information for later.

Kahmel was calling a meeting of the rebels tonight. We would be meeting in the desert, hidden by camouflage technology from spying eyes. It was different from the area I had been taken to when Kahmel introduced me to the rebels. We'd used an abandoned warehouse then.

I closed the book on my lap and looked up at the sky that was turning the fiery colors of evening. Glancing at my eWatch, I noticed Kahmel should be back from his parents' house soon. He'd said he was going to pay them a visit. I appreciated how infuriated he was about it all, because I didn't have the energy to be.

Crossing my legs, I looked around at the little garden Kahmel and I had to ourselves, thinking about the memories we had here. I sat on the bench facing the three little winged statues chasing each other around. Brick walls closed in our little secret. Flowers bloomed all around the edges of the walls, and a small stone path went around the statues in the center.

This was where Kahmel and I had done my fire training in the beginning. None of the windows of the palace could see this area, and we used it to our advantage. This was also where I had made my escape that night when I betrayed Kahmel. One of the statues in the circle was the switch to the exit, and I'd found it and used it to leave.

I'd had good times in this garden. And heartbreaking ones. It had that sort of unspoken magic about it, where you knew everything important would happen here.

I thought about my mindset a year ago, realizing that all the executions Kahmel ordered that made me scared of him were probably because of attempts on his life like this one. At the time, all he'd accused them of was treason, without going into the depths about what that meant.

It was dizzying to imagine how many times it must have happened for Kahmel to have ordered so many executions. It must have slowed when we got married, probably because I was an extra witness they didn't want to deal with. Kahmel didn't sleep alone anymore. Even when they attempted with me, they waited until we were apart.

Kahmel always kept so much to himself, especially when it came to pain. I could tell by how embarrassed he acted after he told me that story about him and Rand to help me with my fire.

It was going to be healthy for him to finally let the nation in on how much he dealt with on their behalf. I understood why he kept it secret. He had this protective attitude that didn't want the people he loved to deal with his burdens. But he needed to learn how to share his burdens.

I smiled. I was glad he took my advice and was deciding to do just that. I knew how uncomfortable it must have been for him.

I checked my eWatch and realized how much time had passed. The dragon riders would be training now. Kahmel said I could participate if I wanted, but to otherwise take the day off. He was going to be conducting the class today.

Picking up my book, I decided that though I didn't feel much like riding, watching the class might do me some good.

I dropped the book off in my and Kahmel's private library, then headed for where the trainees were. The sound of dragons roaring and beating the air drifted through the halls.

I emerged in the training area to find Kahmel there, directing them as promised. He sensed my approach and turned.

"Hey, Jashi. Good to see you." He kept a calm composure, but I could tell he was still seething with rage. The throb in his temple gave him away.

To my surprise, the dragons in the air landed all at once, and the trainees piled off them and rushed around me.

"Faresha!"

"Are you okay?"

"We heard what happened. Are you all right?"

The honest concern in their eyes warmed my heart. "I'm fine," I said in a small voice.

Kahmel had walked over, watching as if to make sure I was okay but not intervening in his trainees checking up on me.

Wanting to change the subject, I asked, "Are you guys glad to have Kahmel back?"

Kent smiled. "Yeah, he's all right."

He earned a glare from Kahmel.

"Will you be joining us, Your Majesty?" Jemmorah asked. "You're the one we really miss."

The three of them laughed, and I smiled at them.

"Probably not this time, but I'll be glad to watch."

Ashed said, "We'll miss you, but we understand. Take care of yourself, Your Majesty."

"All right, now let's get back to the lessons," Kahmel interjected, and they all dispersed, albeit hesitantly.

Seeing them was just what I needed. To see I still had loyalty somewhere.

The dragons roared as they went back into the air.

And there was that. We would always have dragons.

TELLING THEM EVERYTHING

Jashi Anyua-Omah, Faresha of K'sundi

The fluffy coat I wore only partially helped with the cold. It still nipped at the bare skin on my face and the sliver of skin between my sleeve and gloves on my wrists every time my sleeves slipped.

The desert night brought a harsh chill, but the blanket of stars we were rewarded with was well worth the sacrifice. A crescent moon hooked the night sky above us. My boots gritted against the sand beneath our feet as the cold wind blew across our faces. The area around us shimmered slightly, the only indication that we were cloaked from prying eyes with camouflage technology that some rebels established here for the meeting.

But the flutter in my chest was keeping me warm. Kahmel told me what he was going to talk about. I could barely believe it.

He was going to tell the rebels *everything*.

A meeting like this was normally only called once a year, and we'd already had it. I attended it so that Kahmel could introduce me to the rebels. But Kahmel was making an exception for today's announcement.

So many rebels weren't usually gathered all at once, and it made me remember how big the rebellion really was. There were people from all over gathered, rebel countries included. I even saw a few from alien planets scattered in the audience. They murmured to themselves in a mixed melody of languages. White lights illuminated the people in a pale light that haloed them strangely like it was a gathering of people getting ready to be beamed up by an alien ship from old science fiction stories.

I spotted Arusi next to Rand and Khes, talking. She saw me at the same time and waved me over.

"I can't believe he's really doing this," she said.

Kahmel always told his closest friends everything, so they knew the basics of what he was going to say tonight.

I was just as shocked as she was.

I knew Kahmel was going to have to tell the rebels eventually, but the way he'd talked about it, it seemed like it would be some time in the future.

Rand rubbed his hands together and breathed into them. "About time, though. I think we're all better off being on the same page."

"I agree," said a familiar voice.

"Nana!" I rushed forward to hug the woman who raised me. The smell of cinnamon washed me over in nostalgia.

The older woman pulled away to look at me with a warm smile that creased her warm brown skin. Her curly white hair was pulled into a bun. "Look at you!" she said, looking me over like the motherly woman she was. "You look lovely, dear."

I grinned back. "I didn't think you'd make it."

"I just made it," she said, wrapping her scarf so it covered half her face. "Had to get Catlani to fill in for me, and you know how much I don't like to use her, but this was important. So many other rebel leaders are here, so how could I not be?"

I chuckled just as Khes came lumbering over. His huge form stood taller than even Rand, and he and Kahmel both made me seem like an elf in comparison. Asan was behind him, which was a funny contrast between one with a bulky frame and the other with a wiry one.

Khes grinned. "Didn't think this day would come so soon. I'm curious how they'll all react to it. Some part of me fears they'll just think we're going stark-raving mad."

Nana laughed. "If they can believe their Faresh is a fire-manipulating dragon rider who part-times as a rebel, I think they can accept anything."

"I guess we'll see for ourselves now," Asan said, pointing to Kahmel, who climbed up on a small platform that let him command a view of everyone.

The murmuring settled down without him even having to call for it, his dominating presence silencing the chatter. His orange eyes glittered against the night with their own luminescence. They scanned the audience until they found me, and he gave me a small smile.

Then he grabbed the mic in front of him.

"I'm not going to beat around the bush because I don't like taking a long time to get to the point. We've all been working hard on different tasks, between getting help to rebel countries, researching the dragons, and seeing what we can glean from the past to help us in the present. But you've also been working on a task you didn't know about.

"You know that the dragons are a big part of our plan to retake our sense of identity from the Zendaalans." Kahmel earned several indignant grunts in agreement. "We know they're powerful assets that were the turning point in K'sundi's war with Omani, and we're hoping for the same to happen when we challenge Zendaal. That's why we're always trying to learn more about them, because we know there's a lot we still don't know about their power.

"But today, I'm going to tell you something that isn't about the dragons. Not in the way we've been talking about them, like a clever battle strategy or a shocking innovation that will turn the tides. Today, I'm going to tell you about them like a dear friend. A dear friend that we, the K'sundii, have let down and betrayed. This story is going to sound strange. It's going to shock you, appall you, but, in the end, I want it to inspire you. I want you to understand the importance of what we're doing, how we're *making* the difference between what we were before and what we're doing now, and how it should have been done a long time ago."

Kahmel went on to describe what happened when we approached the Dragon King in New K'sundi. He told them everything, told them that the "Fire Bugs" were really Half-Dracs, how it took two to open the entrance to the Dragon Realm, the betrayal of the Dragon Kings, and the power that was given to the Zendaalans to manipulate prosperity in Hemorah. When he got to the part where the Dragon King made Kahmel promise to pave the way for a brighter future for the dragons in exchange for his cooperation, he pulled his coat off halfway and drew up his sleeve to show the marks, earning a collective gasp from all of them.

Beside me, Nana nodded, listening intently, pride in her eyes. I smiled to myself, realizing that she sort of raised us both. Me when I was younger, but Kahmel ever since he joined the rebels. And then she arranged our marriage, knowing exactly what we were capable of together. Earning her approval was something not just anyone could do, and I was proud to know that Kahmel and I had done that.

Kahmel then recounted what happened when we were in Gheres, and how we talked with Gaiena and mentioned briefly that they both alluded to the Drake Bond, which we were still researching.

"We've been doing a lot of research into the older ways to give us an idea of what we were like before the Equalization, see what we can glean from the information," he said. "But now, I'm asking you to put all of that away and focus on these tasks: We need to find out where the missing two Dragon Kings are, and we need to find them quickly. Next, I'm going to pass more dragon laws so that when we do talk to the next Dragon King, we'll have reasons for them to say yes to siding with us. But even that I need your help with. Some of you, very few of you, are royal clan members. You need to influence the others in your clan to take my side. Make your own family members your mission. This is more important than any information raid. I need people on my side because I can't do this on my own."

The crowd was silent as if they weren't used to Kahmel talking like this. They looked among each other unsurely.

"K'sundi people have been dividing among themselves for a while. We see our dragon tribe people as savages. Clans make themselves higher than anyone. If we're going to make a difference in the way things are now, while we unite everyone else, we need to join ourselves together as well.

"The Zendaalans rely on us keeping them a secret. As rebels, we're vocal about our opinions, but as soon as we're finished, we try to stay safe by remaining quiet. But now I'm telling you to do the opposite. Be loud about it. We need people asking questions about what we've quietly accepted over the past few centuries. Zendaalans work best when they can work from the inside. That's how they attempted the assassination of Jashi, and that's how they got in power in the first place. If we become a united front, they won't have anywhere to sneak in through.

"I'm not saying it's going to be easy, but we have to do it. Because we don't have any other options." Kahmel took a deep breath. "K'sundi will probably be announced a rebel country soon enough. They've been lying in wait for a while, it seems, and since Jashi won't leave and I won't change, my father and brothers are at the Zendaalan capital now trying to build a case toward forcing me to abdicate the throne. And I'm going to refuse to comply when they do."

Even though I knew it was coming eventually, it still sent an involuntary chill down my spine to hear the words. There was a nervous shuffle among the crowd.

"The former leader of the rebels, Khes, has been working tirelessly toward finding information that will illuminate where the last two Dragon Kings are, but he can't do it alone."

I looked to Khes, finding him nodding and pursing his lips, the scar over his eye glinting in the moonlight. I knew that Kahmel became the leader of the rebels when he became Faresh, but I had no idea Khes had been the rebel leader before him. But then it made sense that Kahmel would make him one of his most trusted generals during the war against Omani, and then one of the leading forces in finding the other Dragon Kings.

Kahmel went on to say, "I need as many of you as possible researching. We've seen the Dragon Kings referred to as the 'Trembling Ones' in certain texts. Great beings, paths where travelers have disappeared—all of those are key phrases that have helped us thus far. Search any ancient piece of text you can get your hands on.

"The Zendaalans can try to cut us off, but we already knew this would happen. It just might end up sooner than expected. But it hopefully won't be for long. Because after we have the alliance of the Dragon Kings, we'll go to war for the fragments of their power the Zendaalans acquired from us and return them to where they belong."

There was a brief pause, a heartbeat when Kahmel finished. He looked somewhat exhausted from emptying himself to his following, and his eyes roved over the crowd, searching. Maybe even afraid. Thinking they might not follow or they'd be unwilling. Maybe that they'd think he was crazy. I didn't have to read his mind to know because I felt the same way.

But it was only a moment.

In the next, there were roaring cheers.

I heaved a breath of relief, and Kahmel did, too. We looked at each other amid the crowd going crazy, and we smiled.

NEW LAW

In the middle of everything—acquiring Gaiena's alliance, coming back to K'sundi, the assassination attempt, the meeting with the rebels—I'd forgotten. I kept putting it off, and now I had *moments* before I had to make it to Kahmel at the House and tell him before he proposed his new law.

It would have been nice if I could have cracked the Drake Bond mystery before this, but he was pressed for time, and we had to make do. He would be presenting his new dragon laws today.

I pushed the driver of the limo to drive as fast as he could. When it slowed to park as we arrived, I darted out before it even stopped, ignoring the driver as he exclaimed something about my safety as I started up the stairs to the House. Cameras clicked and lights flickered around me, questioning reporters wanting to know.

I didn't bother to dismiss them, letting the door closing behind me be an answer as I came into the building. My eyes roved for Kahmel.

I walked around but couldn't find him in the halls, so he must have either already been before the Court, proposing law, or in the private chambers they provided here. Politicians often used the private chambers to prepare for their arguments, which was what I hoped Kahmel was doing because if he was already before the Court, it was too late.

I went up the steps to the mezzanine level, going around the circular path to where another one branched off to the side.

A pair of Court officers stopped me. "Do you have business to propose to the Court?"

I ground my teeth. "I'm the Faresha; I'm coming to see Kahmel."

"Faresh Kahmel isn't in the chambers, Your Majesty. He's already before the Court."

I cursed under my breath.

We were running out of time every day. These laws needed to be passed *now* while the rebels continued to search for where the Dragon Kings were so that the next Dragon King would agree to take our side. The Dragon Kings needed to see our dedication.

Well, Kahmel told me to be bolder.

I backed away from the halls leading to the private chambers and sauntered toward the main room.

"Wait, the Court is in session, you can't—"

I flung the doors open and started down the steps. There were exclamations to either side of me from those that were in the aisles.

"And so, I propose..." Kahmel trailed off as he must have heard the doors close and turned to watch me approach.

"Well!" Monoh said, looking at me incredulously from his seat in the middle of the Court members. "I hope you have a good explanation for this, Faresha."

Kahmel looked surprised, but the look soon faded, and he wagged his head.

"I need to talk to Kahmel," I explained matter-of-factly, stepping up beside him.

"If you wanted to talk to your husband," said an elderly woman, another member of the Court, with wrinkles around her pinched mouth, "you should have done so before we—"

"What is it, Jashi?" Kahmel asked me, completely disregarding the woman. His voice wasn't even disapproving. More like unsurprised and even somewhat amused.

"I need to—" I stopped, startled by my own voice echoing in the microphone bent toward us. The Court members grumbled and let out heavy breaths. I turned it away. "I need to tell you something important about the laws you're trying to pass."

"And you couldn't mention this earlier?"

"I forgot!"

"Excuse me!" The woman objected again. "This is not the time nor the place for your...marital spat. Is this really that important?"

I turned to her, squinting at her nameplate to see. Lenaris Finorin. Never would have remembered that one on my own. "It'll just be a minute, Ms. Finorin." I added a smile before turning back to Kahmel. "Come on, you'll hear me out, won't you?"

Kahmel laughed. "Do I have a choice? Just be quick about it."

"Faresh Kahmel!" Monoh exclaimed.

Kahmel ignored him as I lowered my voice and pressed myself closer to him. "Listen, I know you're going to talk about the dragon laws today. Basically, you want people to be able to ride trained dragons in the city and for people to have to acquire a riding license for them to be able to do so. And if I'm not confusing things, you also want the Dragon Towers to be prohibited from using lethal measures too many times a year, which you're hoping will force them to figure out how to tame and train more of them."

He raised an eyebrow. "You do listen when you want to."

I laughed softly and hit his arm. "*Anyway*. I didn't have any thoughts about dragon-riding in the city; I think your idea is good there. But I did have a thought about how the Dragon Watchtowers are run."

Surprised, he nodded for me to go on.

"Will this be much longer?" asked an exasperated Finorin.

"Just a moment," Kahmel insisted, then gestured for me to continue.

"It was inspired by when Cirssa and I went around those ruins," I said, words spilling out in a flood. "You know how dragons follow a hierarchical order, and Elementals are at the top?" I whispered lower as I noted, "Well, I used that to my advantage to protect Cirssa from the dragons that started to surround us. They wouldn't even come near Comet."

Kahmel kneaded the space between his eyes, opening his mouth to say something, but I had already gone on.

"It got me thinking—you essentially use Dragon Watchtowers the same way, right? You want to represent a form of command that keeps the dragons in line, but you use technology and force-field barriers to do it. I think there's a better way to keep the dragons from the city barriers."

"All right," he said, intrigued. "What do you propose?"

I grinned. "Use more dragons!"

Kahmel blinked.

"Just listen! Elementals keep all the other dragons in line. They demand respect. So put a bunch of Elementals along the city barriers, and the other dragons will naturally stay away."

"Okay...but Dragon Watchtowers still have trouble with their own dragons. What will keep their Elementals in line?"

"Didn't get that far."

Kahmel pursed his lips and nodded with a face that said he wasn't sure why he expected anything less.

But a thought occurred to me as I glanced at my eWatch, reminding me of the files I was looking at from my research. "Oh, I know! With Drake Bonds! They're a good way to establish a bond with a dragon, and therefore make sure it heeds commands well. If you can use Watchers that have established one with Elementals for the city limits, that should solve the problem."

His eyebrows shot up. "You figured out how to establish one?"

Using my hand to shield my eWatch screen from prying eyes, I pulled up the program I had running before. "*Leh mani stepior.*"

"And what does that mean?"

"Beats me. But! I'm sure it's key."

"Are you quite done?" asked Monoh impatiently.

I turned to him, my back straight with as much confidence as I knew would be irritating. "Quite."

Then I turned my back to the members of the Court, taking a seat in the nearest one available along the aisle.

Kahmel gave me a lost look. I gave him a thumbs up.

"Right," he said, returning his attention to the members of the Court and adjusting his microphone back to its proper place. "I think my point has been made clear, and I'll just summarize. I want people riding dragons in the city. I'm demanding that the Watchtowers be more lenient. I want people educated on a better way to be."

"You mean the way you've decided is better?" Monoh said, seething.

"I mean the way I've proven is better," Kahmel asserted, steel in his voice. "The excuse for the Zendaalan Standardized Technique has always been maintained because there was no other way to do it. I've won a war with trained dragons, I've protected the cities from my dragons, Jashi and I both use our dragons on a regular basis to set an example for others, and my trainees have exceeded even my own expectations. What more do I have to do for people to be willing to admit that there is another way, just no one's willing to consider it?"

"You seem to forget, Faresh Kahmel," Finorin said, her eyes glittering with warning, "that you may have a lot of pretty ideas, and we have entertained you this far. But now, you have crossed over into questioning the way the Equalizers have ruled, and this issue is above our heads. You want policies changed? Take it up with them."

"This doesn't concern them."

The words sliced through the air like a sword and left everyone deathly silent.

"Doesn't...concern them?" Monoh questioned, the other members of the Court clearly unwilling to even answer Kahmel.

"That's exactly right. Zendaal allows all the countries under its rule to pass their own laws as they see fit, so long as they don't break any of theirs. The ZST is a standard, but it's not law. Every principle the standard is built upon is based on dragons being under control and not allowed to destroy cities and civilians. I'm not abolishing the ZST, which *would* be against the law. But I'm offering another way."

Kahmel summoned Asan by waving him over with two fingers, the latter approaching the podium with a HoloScreen display in his hands. "I'm calling it the K'sundii Alternative Method," he said, reading off the screen and swiping to send it to the displays on the podium of the Court members. I knew what was on it. It was basically all the details of the things Kahmel was asking for and how they would work. "I've worked with my trainees enough to take the way we're training them and use it as a template to teach anyone how to train and ride a dragon. I'm going to start enforcing it in Watchtowers everywhere. And start implementing it being taught in what will be dragon-riding schools, where anyone can acquire a license to train and ride. And it's none of Zendaal's concern because I'm not contradicting their standard, only how it is regarded."

I could tell the entire Court was fuming, but, as usual, Kahmel had managed to dance his way into not being *technically* wrong, though he had angered everyone in the room on his way there.

"Very well," Monoh said, gritting his teeth. "I suppose we have no good reason to oppose you in this."

Kahmel stood taller, then he looked at me uncertainly but continued anyway.

"Also, following the tip Jashi just gave me, I'll have to send you an updated version of the document you have before you, including a trial-basis method to protect cities involving the use of Elementals."

The Court members gasped and looked at each other, but Kahmel continued before they could object.

"Don't worry," he said, waving as though to dissuade their concern. "The Elementals will be in complete control, but I know how nervous you get about these things, which is why it will be on a trial basis for now. Until you can see how it will work. But I assure you, once the Watchers are taught how to use the Drake Bonds, the Elementals won't be a problem at the city limits at all."

"Drake what?" questioned Finorin, her face scrunched up in confusion.

Kahmel sighed as if it was supposed to be obvious, and I hid the laughing smirk that had started to creep up on my face. He was completely bluffing. "I see once again I have stumped the Court on a term that they would understand if only they would research their own libraries more often. Perhaps we'll meet another day when I have time to educate you on what it is and how it works. It'll all be in the updated version of that document."

Yeah. Now all we had to do was figure out how to *do* it.

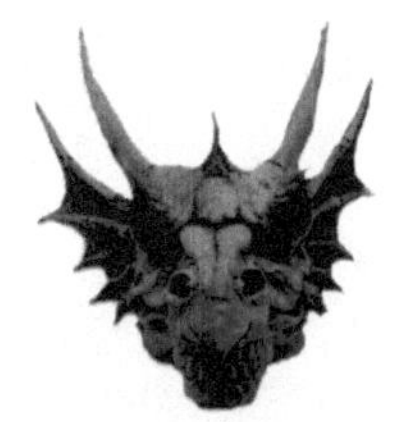

TWO HALF-DRACS ARE A WHOLE DRAGON

Kahmel had more meetings to attend because of the new laws he was proposing, so he'd be back late.

I walked along the moonlit path leading down the garden, my arms tucked, swaddling myself deeper into the fuzzy black shawl draped over me. Looking up at the stars, I wondered about the Dragon Kings and their realm. Where did it really exist? Did we visit someplace far away into the heavens? Or was it far in another sense? Like another dimension that paralleled ours, under a different set of stars, existing in a different set of circumstances?

I sighed. We had so much to do and so little time to do it. Still no word from the rebels on any significant progress on finding the entrance to one of the other two Dragon Realms. I felt better knowing they knew what they were looking for now, but still. Waiting was nerve-wracking.

I felt someone coming from behind me, and I suspected it was Arusi since Asan and Rand were with Kahmel.

But the voice sent chills up my spine. "Faresha."

My heart raced in my chest as I spun on my heel to face him. Dralus.

The Zendaalan's mismatched eyes took me in with calmness, but there was fire in them. Starlight danced on his chrome hand as he clenched it. His wispy platinum hair burned white from the glow of the moon, his hard face haunted in shadow.

"What are you doing here?" I asked, taking a half-step back.

Dralus cupped the head of a red flower growing from a bush instead of looking at me.

"'It's none of Zendaal's concern.' Those were Kahmel's exact words, Faresha. You know how dangerous they are. So does he." His gaze rested on mine, his red eye whirring lowly as it focused on me.

I felt like he expected me to succumb under his glare. To agree because it was easier. Because we were all safer playing nice with the Zendaalans. It was how they'd maintained their strength in the world thus far. Giving in was easier than fighting back.

But Kahmel was right. We couldn't take the easy route. I was Faresha now and a rebel. I wasn't going to be intimidated into backing down anymore.

"Kahmel only told the truth," I said, tilting up my head and straightening my back. "We aren't breaking any laws—why should Zendaal be concerned?" I narrowed my eyes at him. "Unless the problem you have with Kahmel has nothing to do with the law."

Dralus shook his head and chuckled. "You dragon tribe haven't changed at all over the centuries. Still the same brutish people you've always been, no matter how few your numbers may be." He stepped forward, but I refused to back up anymore, leaving no more than a few inches between us as he scowled over me. His voice came in a hiss. "Zendaal has been doing you a favor by getting rid of the Fire Bugs among you. But if you're going to be insistently stubborn like this, then heed my words, *Faresha*." He spat out the word like it was an insult to his tongue. "We're giving you a warning. Don't continue down this path. Or this country will face the consequences."

"On what grounds, Dralus?" I demanded, matching his tone. I enunciated my words. "We're breaking no laws. I don't care what Kahmel's family is telling you; they've got nothing."

A mocking smile touched his lips. "The people hate you as it is. They won't question how we get rid of you, only why it took us so long to do so. If I'm not mistaken, one of my subordinates reported even you questioned the logic in having yourself and Kahmel as

K'sundi's leaders. What makes you think the rest of K'sundi is any different?"

I clenched my fists at my side, gritting my teeth. The gloves were off now. He even admitted to being directly connected to Attican. The Zendaalans' web was well-woven, and it would take a lot to undo it. "I'll admit I was confused before," I said. "Because I didn't know how much Kahmel was always fighting for his people and for me. Against you. But if anything, I'm proof that when people realize who you really are, Zendaal had better watch its back."

Dralus pursed his lips together, his jaw working. "We will offer it one more time, Faresha. Leave Kahmel, and you'll finally serve the only purpose you have here, which is to discourage this foolish task of yours."

"Why?" I raised an eyebrow, cocking my head. "Why so adamant on stopping us if you're so sure of yourselves?" I tilted my chin up. "Unless we scare you."

Dralus's eyes flickered with danger, a vein throbbing in his neck. "I can assure you, Zendaalans fear nothing, girl. But we do make good on our promises. Remember this conversation."

I was so focused on standing my ground against Dralus, a strange mark in the dirt that caught my eye threw me off focus. I squinted, wondering why it felt important when I realized.

Then I smiled.

"*You* remember. I'm not a Fire Bug; I'm a Half-Drac." Fire puffed from my nostrils. "And dragons don't back down."

I turned and set him behind me, smirking to myself.

It was a claw scratch in the ground. If there was a message from the rebels within the palace itself, it could only mean one thing.

They found another entrance to the Dragon Realm.

THE MESSAGE in the garden was left by Khes, and we didn't find just one entrance to the Dragon Realm—we found both. The rebels discovered more artifacts that illustrated more clearly the meaning of certain terms and provided a more accurate picture as to the time frame in which certain documents were written—and therefore helped us understand what the maps looked like at that time.

One entrance to the Dragon Realm we needed to find was in Vahdel, which confirmed one of our concerns. But it paled in comparison to the last one, which was on Hemorah's moon.

According to Kahmel, there weren't a lot of ways he could manage getting us a trip there given that, though our moon was livable, it was mainly used for the research and development of about six Hemorahan nations. Not a lot of reasons a Faresh and Faresha would need to visit a place like that. Hesitantly, Kahmel told me there was another way, and it involved T'shan, who was a Half-Drac, too. Eyes of scrutiny were more on Kahmel than they were on me, and he mentioned that I could disappear on "a trip to the Malis Islands" and do the same thing I did with Kahmel with T'shan. But he was reluctant to offer that option because now he feared me going anywhere on my own, something I rolled my eyes at. We had to do what we had to do.

But still, it made me wonder. This information we were digging up was hundreds of years old, if not thousands. Ancient K'sundii certainly weren't supposed to be capable of space travel at that time.

So how did they possibly have the means to reach that Dragon King?

That question was still unanswered, and now we had bigger concerns. The most accessible Dragon Realm entrance was the one in Vahdel, so that was the first one we would pursue.

We wouldn't be able to go to Vahdel the same way we went to Gheres, which was on a diplomatic mission. Vahdel was a rebel country, and, for the moment, K'sundi was not. We would have to find a way to sneak over the border. It was going to be risky, and if we were caught, there would be irrevocable consequences on K'sundi.

I told Kahmel about my conversation with Dralus, and he told me the best we could do was just stay aware. For the moment, we had to stay focused on the Dragon Realm entrance.

But there was something Kahmel wanted to do first.

I breathed out, my fingers clutching my royal sash. The mark of the Faresha. The gold silk was bordered with red on either side, glimmering in the light with an almost radiant quality.

I never thought I'd want this so bad. To be K'sundi's Faresha. I wanted to be part of our learning and growing and rediscovering ourselves. I wanted to see what we looked like when we could be on our own, truly independent. I wanted to help guide us toward the tomorrow I didn't even know we needed.

And now, I was afraid. Because now that the feeling snuck up on me, and I wanted to be K'sundi's Faresha, it could all fall away. With what we were doing with the rebels, the dragon laws.

And what we were going to do today.

With a shaky breath, I pulled my sash over my shoulder and looked at myself in the mirror. The girl looking back at me looked like a Faresha for once. She didn't look like she was pretending to be something she wasn't. She had grown since I last saw her like this, and I was proud of it.

I just hoped she wasn't about to lose everything.

I adjusted the curls in my hair and added a few more gold pieces to the cornrows that came up to the crown of my head. Silver earrings that came down in spirals swung from my ears. A gold necklace with a circular plate in the middle sat on the collar of my red robes, like a golden drop of dew on a desert flower.

The thought of a desert flower incited a memory.

I searched through my jewelry box until I found it. Kahmel's wedding present from last year. It was how he'd found me when I needed him most. A chuckle slipped from my chest, and I didn't realize I was smiling until I caught myself in the mirror again.

Biting my lip, I wondered how he'd feel about not using the pillows tonight.

"Are you ready, Faresha?" a servant asked. She waited patiently at the door of the closet, refocusing me on the task at hand.

I looked at myself one more time and nodded. "Yes, I'm ready."

As ready as I'd ever be.

Kahmel was waiting for me outside our room, dressed in his best suit, a dark green one I liked him in. It brought out the broadness in his chest and complimented his warm eyes. He extended an arm to me, and I slipped mine through it.

I clenched and unclenched my other hand around my purse, trying to distract from the way my heart pounded against my ribcage and made me slightly lightheaded.

"Nervous?" Kahmel asked.

I swallowed. I knew I told Kahmel to be more open, but I never thought he'd take it this far.

But I wouldn't back away from this.

"I am," I admitted, throat dry. "But I know it's necessary."

Kahmel pressed his lips into an encouraging smile as we made our way to the limo. A servant opened the door for us, and Kahmel chuckled.

I frowned at him, stepping inside. "What are you laughing at?"

"Nothing," he said, shaking his head as he came in after me. "I was just reminded of something." The limo driver started on his way, and I sighed. The conference hall wasn't close, so this would be a long drive. Not to mention we had to show up a few hours early so we could prepare for the actual event.

"Reminded of what?" I asked, eager for a distraction from the speech. I needed a way to fill the hour-long drive.

"When you first came to the palace. I was just thinking about how you've far exceeded your initial promise."

My brow furrowed slightly as I struggled to remember what he was talking about, but the memory soon came to mind. It felt like an eternity ago now.

If I can prove to you that I know what I'm doing to protect this country, can you promise me that you'll consider being someone to stand by me?

Will you let me earn your trust?

I gave a sheepish grin. "Exceeded? I think you're forgetting the part where I ran away and almost ruined everything."

"You're right, I don't remember any of that. I remember you saving me and inspiring a quick victory in the war. And all the things you accomplished after that. The things *we* accomplished."

His hand found mine, and I squeezed it, accepting the strength and encouragement that came with it.

"You know," he said, brushing his thumb over my knuckles, "you've done such a good job with your promise, I think it's only fair you ask one of me."

"A promise?"

"Precisely."

I laughed. "It feels like we're making wedding vows all over again. Only this time, it won't be because the Zendaalans asked me to spy on you."

"And what a difference it makes." Kahmel's eyes danced. "Go on, ask for anything."

I thought about it, my cheeks warming as he stared at me. Something came to mind, but I couldn't say it while looking at him, so I looked at my hands, messing with the chain strap to my purse. I thought about all the ways he'd always come when I needed him last year, always there to fight for me and protect me when I couldn't protect myself.

"I want you...to promise not to stop believing in me, even when it's hard for me to believe in myself. And to keep being there when I need you..." With a pang like an invisible scar, I thought of Talad. "And that we'll always evolve together."

Kahmel took my chin in his hand, tilting my head to look at him and pulling our faces closer. "I promise."

"Are you going to officiate our marriage again?" I said, smirking.

"No, see, that's the great thing about conveniently being already married."

"Is that so, Kahmel?"

He chuckled, and from this close, I could feel how warm his breath was. "You know, back then, I never got to tell you how crazy you make me just saying that."

"Saying what?"

"My name."

"Kahmel," I repeated. His gaze grew intense as he pulled me to him, his lips fervently pressing against mine. His hands traced my back as my arms wrapped around his neck. Kahmel's hot touch blazed trails on my skin. Fire spilled between our lips and flushed our faces with heat. It had never happened to me before, but then again, I'd never kissed anyone like I was kissing Kahmel. My mind briefly flashed to all the emotions that triggered our fires: anxiety, anger, fear. But it seemed like the common trait was *passion*. And in this moment, we shared our passion. Our fire, as one.

The temperature in the car rose. The heat pouring from us felt like enough to set the car in flames.

Two Half-Dracs made one whole dragon.

My mind felt like a melted candle, but puzzle pieces fell together by accident in my head. About dragons and the way to make them spit fire.

"Command words," I murmured, pausing.

"What?" Kahmel's voice was thick and with a twinge of agitation.

But my mind raced. "What if the words are command words?" I turned my wrist to access my eWatch, but Kahmel put a hand on it, pulling it and my other hand back around his neck.

"Can't this wait until later?"

His eyes smoldered as our chests pressed together. But I smirked and pulled my arms back. "We are a little pressed for time, Faresh. Remember a certain document the Court has with a term in it that you don't have the foggiest idea of what it means?"

He tsked, pausing before he reluctantly sighed and gestured for me to go on. "You said something about command words?"

"This," I said, showing him the image of the box, the lines of the letters traced over, so they were more apparent. "*Leh mani stepior.* It's written in ancient K'sundi. Old like command words are. Is it possible it's a command word that somehow initiates a Drake Bond?"

Kahmel stroked his chin in thought. "You might be on to something. But how would it work? You say the words, and then what?"

I pursed my lips. "I'm not sure." Flipping through the other images I had and scanning certain pieces of text I'd saved, I said, "If I remember the passages from that book correctly, it does seem like you know when you've established a Drake Bond. And it doesn't work every time."

"Can you only create a Drake Bond once, or more times?"

"I don't think there's a limit," I said, checking with other references to verify. "The general I've been reading about seemed to be looking for *more* dragons to establish a Drake Bond with for a particular battle. Like when you were looking for dragons for the war with Omani."

Kahmel nodded. "Makes sense. So, we just try it and see what happens?"

"Can't hurt."

"Right," Kahmel said, clapping his hands together. "With that out of the way..."

"With that out of the way, you can start thinking about the speech." I checked my watch as he groaned. "We spent so much time..." I cleared my throat, my cheeks suddenly feeling very heated. "Anyway, we're almost there."

He wrapped his arms around my waist from behind. "Fine, then." He lowered his voice. "I'll get to you later, then."

"Promise?" I asked turning to face him with a raised eyebrow and a quirk in my lip.

THE WORLD WILL KNOW

We were surrounded by people and cameras. I thought I'd gotten used to it, but today, it felt like each one of those eyes was glaring into my very soul.

Today, the world would know.

There were several Zendaalan officials in the audience and behind us, as always. I'd never been afraid of them before, but I couldn't help the lingering "what if" that sat on my nerves.

"Thank you all for coming," Kahmel began. He paused as if considering his next words carefully. He hadn't talked much with the people here about what he was going to say, but he did talk it over with Asan and me. He knew how to start, but maybe he was just as nervous as I was, deep down. His jaw clenched before he continued. "Ever since I first became Faresh, I've done a lot of things in my campaign that have made me distrusted..." He drifted off, kneading the space between his eyes.

I frowned, turning to him and putting a hand on his arm. "Kahmel?" I whispered.

He just shook his head, then looked up at the crowd again.

"Screw this." He trained his eyes on the video camera in front of him. "I'm going to put it plainly. You don't like me." That wasn't what we'd rehearsed. "No one likes me. K'sundii citizens, the Equalizers, other countries of Hemorah. No one trusts me. You don't like Jashi. You think we're too mysterious, distrusting, dangerous, or under-qualified. But if you notice, no one complained about the way I won the war when we were the most vulnerable. Why?

"That's a question K'sundi asks too sparingly. If I were such a brute, why would all the officials against me decide to hold their tongues while I used the most uncommon way to win a war—the employment of dragons? But now that the war is over, they're against dragons all over again. Interesting. I, of course, remain the brutish Faresh no one likes the entire time.

"But I let it happen. I let you choose not to trust me because it was more important to protect you than for you to appreciate what I was doing for you. That's the way I'm used to carrying myself. You listened to me out of fear, and at the time, it had to be good enough because I didn't have time to ask for anything else.

"But now I am asking you to trust me. The K'sundii officials will tell you all kinds of reasons why you shouldn't. The Zendaalans will subtly imply it. A lot of words are going to be thrown around. Discussions, arguments. But I'm asking *you* to judge. I got you asking questions about the dragons. I protected you when you needed it most. The only problem you have with me is that you don't know enough about me. Which is fair—I allowed that to happen. I had bigger problems to address than whether you liked me or not. Mostly with the people who are going to try to convince you against taking my side.

"But all that has to do with a lot of things I've kept from you. And you may not trust me because of that. Because I keep too many secrets. Great Spirits know Jashi didn't trust me at first because of that." He said it with a chuckle at me, and my shoulders relaxed a little. "But I think I can safely say she trusts me now. And it's because she's gotten to know me better, to be able to separate the myths from the truth by what she sees. By what I've proven. And as she's wisely advised me, you all need the same opportunity.

"I've taken one step toward that by letting you plainly see that I'm dragon tribe. But I'm done taking baby steps."

Kahmel looked at me and nodded.

Breathe.

Fists clenched at my sides.

Energy rushed down my arm, blossomed in my hand, and erupted in flames. Fire danced in my hand, eager like it was happy to be exposed for the first time in my life. I clenched my fist and let the flame die, only then realizing the entire crowd was gasping and exclaiming in awe and maybe fear.

Kahmel opened his palm and let fire arc toward the sky. This time, people shouted, but amidst their fear was the twinge of amazement. It was how we all regarded fire, really. It was intense—dangerous, even. But at the same time, it was too beautiful to ignore.

"All right, show's over," spoke a man with a Zendaalan accent. Equalizer officers poured onto the platform from either side.

"We're shutting down this conference. Shut that camera off!"

Officers barked commands, trying to disperse the audience. People didn't seem to know what to do or how to react.

They needed a push.

Kahmel was being pulled away from the microphone despite his protests. I leaped forward before someone could take me, grabbing hold of the mic and shouting into it. "We know we're not the only ones. You know who you are." Metallic and human hands grabbed me, pulling me away. Cold chrome screamed against my skin.

"We said, 'show's over.' We'll deal with you later."

There were chaos and confusion everywhere, but I didn't stop, speaking over the officer trying to interrupt me. "You've hidden yourselves out of fear, and you were right to! There are not as many of us as there should be. Like Kahmel said, K'sundii people need to start asking more questions. Ask yourself why we had to keep ourselves secret. And I know you're young. You're all under the age of eighteen." I screamed as one officer yanked my hair, making pain light up along my scalp.

"Jashi!" Kahmel called, but he was halfway off the platform now.

"Someone shut off that camera!"

A Zendaalan officer was barking an argument with Asan.

Someone with a camera was trying to wrestle away from an officer. Rand and Arusi were being dragged away behind us. Our own bodyguards were immobilized as the officers had more power than them in this situation.

But I was going to finish.

I elbowed whoever had my hair and was able to lurch forward enough to reach the microphone again.

"We're telling you to come out of hiding now! They may come after you, but we'll protect you. We have ways. We're better united than we are apart. Don't let them stop this."

I was yanked away harshly, my shoulders aching with the constant pull. But I'd said what I had to say.

Kahmel and I locked eyes for a moment as we were pulled in opposite directions. It was a look that shared a thousand words. We weren't sure what Zendaal's next steps would be, but they were revealing themselves. Whatever they were going to do, we wouldn't let them do it in hiding this time.

Our shared gaze was broken as Kahmel was pulled away first. Someone started me down the steps off the platform. But we silently agreed. Neither of us would fight back. If the Zendaalans were going to treat us this way, we wouldn't let any violence on our part be the reason for it.

The Zendaalans taking me away were slowed.

By the crowd.

People started pushing against them from the bottom of the stairs.

"Unhand her!"

"She's done nothing wrong!"

"Let the Faresh and Faresha go!"

The Zendaalans didn't seem to know what to do. "Stop! Get out of the way!"

But the crowd came forward, unrelenting. The Zendaalans had no choice but to back up with me, going back up the platform.

The Zendaalans had switched to their own language among each other. I picked up a few words. "Crowd out of control," "This will be more difficult than we thought," "How do we proceed?"

I realized they had to be communicating over an intercom with some superior. Someone had given them an order to act. It made sense; that was why they'd all started interrupting at once.

Someone jumped onto the platform, Zendaalan officers shouting after them. With all the officers holding me, I could just barely turn my head to see.

A boy with tawny brown skin and a dusting of freckles on his face who couldn't have been older than sixteen stood on the platform in front of the podium. His eyes were the color of flames. He stood with a dark, lanky man who only could have been his father. An Equalizer officer was trying to talk to them from below the platform, but they weren't listening.

"If you're going to take them away," the boy said, "you're going to have to take me, too."

His arms burst into flames. I could tell by his pinched expression that they came because he couldn't hold it in any longer.

He was mad.

The Zendaalans who held me had loosened their grip, obviously at a loss. I couldn't see Kahmel, but it seemed like this audience was unrelenting. They continued to force themselves up the stairs, forcing the Zendaalans to bring me back to the platform. At this point, I could have wrestled away, but I didn't think it was wise. At least not yet.

It was time for the people to stand up for themselves.

Kahmel, Rand, Arusi, and Asan were all back on the platform, though still being detained. Their faces were like iron; they didn't fight back either.

One officer stepped into the middle of the platform and lowered his visor, revealing his half-steel face and murky green eyes. He used a voice amplifier to speak louder. "Citizens of K'sundi, please remain calm. We don't mean the Faresh and Faresha any harm."

Objections rang through the crowd.

"You wrestled our Faresh to the ground!"

"Did you see how the Faresha was manhandled?"

"The guards couldn't even do anything!"

"These are nothing but lies!"

The officer held up his hands to abate them, but it took several moments for them to finally quiet.

"Please, people. They were in clear violation—"

The crowd erupted in jeers.

The boy's father demanded, "We may be average civilians, but we know the law well enough to say they didn't do anything worth being treated like damn criminals. Now let the royals go."

The crowd slowly picked up momentum, chanting his last words until they all were saying them.

"LET THE ROYALS GO!"

"LET THE ROYALS GO!"

"LET THE ROYALS GO!"

The Zendaalan officer's jaw worked, his expression sour. Then he nodded to his fellow officers, and, after a reluctant pause, we were all released.

The crowd erupted in cheers.

Kahmel took me in his arms and hugged me tight, soothing to my biceps that ached from being gripped so tightly.

It was only once the rushing in my ears had slowed, and my heart wasn't racing so fast that I realized the crowd was chanting something new.

"Long live Faresh Kahmel!"

"Long live Faresha Jashi!"

I was so shocked I could barely move. My eyes stung with tears.

We started something today.

ROYAL CLAN

I normally hated watching the news, though these days, I honestly didn't mind so much. Because now it was a necessity.

News of what happened at Kahmel's conference exploded, not only in K'sundi, but all over Hemorah. At some point, the Zendaalans did manage to get the cameras off, but it didn't matter. People in the crowd started recording what was happening from where they were in the audience. Zendaal had yet to make an official statement, but judging by how people were reacting, they wouldn't be able to hold off for much longer.

People were outraged.

Clips of me getting my hair pulled and Kahmel being wrestled to the ground were replaying on every news channel, social media outlet, and gossip column. And so were the words we said.

People demanded to know what we did to deserve how we were treated, and the Zendaalans didn't have an answer for them.

And more Fire Bugs were coming out. When news outlets asked how it was possible for Kahmel and me to have done what we did, news of the boy who stood up for us discredited any accusations that we faked it somehow. And then more people, young people, were admitting they had the same abilities.

For once, it was the Zendaalans backed into the corner.

But we had a problem.

While the Zendaalans wouldn't answer how they felt about our fire abilities, claiming they were "still trying to ascertain what happened," they insisted that Kahmel and I be put under close watch. According to Kahmel, the Zendaalans had been dancing around the topic of rebellion or eradicating Kahmel for a while, but now they were outright saying it. They were keeping an eye on Kahmel and me on the grounds of suspicion of disloyalty to the integrity of the Equalization and that K'sundi's alliance status to the Equalizers was being scrutinized. We couldn't even go near our dragons during this investigation.

For the time being, we sent the trainees home. There was no point if they couldn't ride their dragons, and we wanted to make sure they were safe.

I wasn't sure if the people's rage was stronger than their fear of becoming labeled a rebel country. It was one thing to threaten Kahmel's position on the throne, but people were going to be scared if it put a threat on our position as an Equalized nation.

Hell, it scared me.

But we had to keep moving. There was nothing that could be done at this point, and we had too much to do. Our idea was to get all the Dragon Kings on our side before K'sundi was marked a rebel nation. That way, when it did happen, we could come out with *everything*. The Dragon Kings, our history, and what we needed to do to move forward. We were hoping it would be enough to convince the people to trust us even though everything appeared to have fallen away. To have confidence in the Dragon Kings to fulfill their word and to help K'sundi and other nations from completely being driven to ruin.

And ultimately, to challenge Zendaal's rule on Hemorah as a whole.

There were a lot of what-ifs involved, though.

What if we couldn't get the Dragon Kings' approval in time?

What if we couldn't figure out a subtle way to get to the moon?

What if we accomplished it all, and people still wanted my and Kahmel's heads for getting them kicked out of the Equalization?

There were no answers to any of that, so we just had to move forward. There was nothing else *to* do.

Kahmel and I couldn't get away to rebel meetings. Zendaalan officers were stationed all over the palace, and at least one was always in the number of guards who followed us everywhere. But it didn't matter. Everything was in place. The rebels had set up for us to meet with a transporter they typically used to smuggle immigrants from rebel nations. Of course, we would be doing the reverse. We would meet with the transporter in a few days.

We just had to figure out a way to leave the palace unseen.

In the meantime, we waited.

One evening found me strolling through the halls of the palace. To the guards, I was just on my way to the library, but I was really trying to calculate a route. Kahmel and I figured our best bet was to use the hidden passages in the palace to escape. It was unlikely the Zendaalans had accurate information on the palace's true infrastructure. The palace was simply too old for them to have any good data on it.

After we left, Rand would stay behind. With orange contact lenses and a mean face, no one would be able to tell he wasn't Kahmel. As for my cover, Rand, as Kahmel, would tell everyone I left to visit friends in Kohpal. If anyone asked why I didn't go with guards, my haphazard nature of always going out without anyone knowing came in handy.

The Zendaalans could always raise suspicion anyway, especially since they were in an unreasonable mood. But it didn't matter.

This was more important.

I passed the hall that led to the garden, shaking my head as I considered the possibility of taking that route. Kahmel had helped me learn how to identify the cameras hidden throughout the palace. The smallest black dot on a seemingly benign surface belonged to the eye of a camera. There were too many cameras leading down to this hall. Not only would we quickly be discovered, but the Zendaalans would also learn of the garden, and that was the last thing I wanted.

Continuing my walk, I passed by the kitchen. I hadn't considered the hidden door in the pantry. Obviously, during the day, it was bustling with people, but at night, it was quiet as a spirit temple. There were cameras down this hall and a few in the kitchen itself, but the cameras in the kitchen were more avoidable. The hidden passage from the throne room to here might avoid the cameras in the hall, too.

I had to run the idea past Kahmel to see what he thought. There was also the matter of how to get to the throne room unseen to accomplish such a feat.

I stiffened as Zendaalan officers came marching down the hall, not so subtle in their glares as they came by. It disgusted me to see the palace so infiltrated like this. It felt like an infestation of rodents had afflicted our very walls.

"Jashi," Rand's voice called behind me.

I perked up but frowned as I turned and saw Rand being followed by Dralus. Rand's expression was stern, but not at me. It was a similar face to the one I wore in the palace these days.

The face of being among the ones you love with an enemy always present.

"The chancellor says he has something to tell you that can't wait," Rand said.

Dralus had a faint smile on his face. "Yes, quite. And you'll be happy to know that I actually bring good news."

I gave a mock smile. "Have you come to tell us that Zendaal has finally decided to let this silly matter aside? We were attacked first."

Dralus's eyes flickered with danger. "I won't speak on that matter, and you know it, Your Majesty. We have no idea what you and Kahmel did that day." He gave me a look. He was lying; I knew he was lying. But there was nothing I could do about it. "And until we have an explanation for what happened, we will continue to keep an eye on things around here. In the meantime, I apologize if you were inconvenienced by the actions of the officers. They didn't know what was going on!"

Sure, getting my hair pulled was an *inconvenience.*

"No, what I have to say is on a much cheerier matter," Dralus went on. "Actually, it might even help you in your case with what happened that afternoon at the conference. It seems that after that... show you and your husband put on, it aroused the attention of some people who haven't seen you in *years.* Of course, we don't want just any ruffians in the palace, so we had it thoroughly checked out, and it seems it all—"

"Ruffians in the palace? What are you talking about?" My brow furrowed in confusion. Rand looked at him weirdly, too.

Dralus grinned. "It seems we've found your parents."

The words reached my ears, but I couldn't understand them.

My *what?*

"What are you talking about?" I said, wincing at how low my voice sounded at that moment. I was supposed to be keeping a defensive front. I didn't want to admit how much this was rocking me.

It couldn't be real, could it?

They had to be imposters of some sort. Crazy people pretending on the Zendaalans' behalf.

But even if they were, I hated how much it affected me just to hear the words. The way the entire matter with the rebels dissolved from my mind, replaced with a million and one questions.

"You heard me right," Dralus said as if he could read my thoughts. I detested the way his face got smug. "They're waiting outside to see you."

My head spun. "Wh-what, you mean now?"

I didn't even realize I'd grabbed onto Rand until I went with him as he moved forward. "Wait, you can't just invite strangers into the palace."

"I already told you," Dralus said, evidently enjoying this and wanting to drag out every minute of pleasure he could. "We've confirmed their identity, and I can assure you they're the real thing. The Kohpal police agree that they're the same people who left a note at the orphanage you were left at, Your Majesty. And it seems they've witnessed firsthand the abilities you and Kahmel displayed. Which is why it might help your case. They heard about you on the news since you became Faresha but thought it best not to say anything until you revealed your abilities on live HoloScreens everywhere. They've been moved to come forward now. We asked Matron Taias, and she recognizes them as well."

It felt like the floor was moving under me.

"Parents" was a term I only understood in concept. The only thing I had close enough was Nana. I hated how my mind immediately went to all the years I spent waiting and hoping for a miracle. That amid always trying to be available for adoption like an unwanted object on an "everything-must-go" sale, my parents would come back and change their minds after all.

I hated how mad I was. That if these people really were my parents, they only stepped forward now, after I was already grown up, married, and Faresha of the country. They had to have been being used by the Zendaalans for something.

But what? Why now?

Rand looked just as confused as I was, and I realized the worried look he was giving me was in question to how I was going to react.

And to tell the truth, I didn't know.

"Let's meet them, shall we?" Dralus said, his voice like silk. "I wish Kahmel could be here, but he'll see them later."

Yes, Dralus always seemed to find me at a moment when Kahmel wasn't around, I noted. Though my head was spinning too fast to really put much thought together, I just kept thinking, *It can't be real. They must be imposters.*

But the thought fell apart as Dralus led Rand and me through the front doors of the palace, and we saw them waiting. A man and woman who had to be in their fifties grinned when they saw me.

The woman had a few white strands in her curly hair, which was pulled away from her face in a ponytail that cascaded in curls down her back. Crow's feet edged dark eyes. Her face was long and somewhat sunken in, her cheekbones sharp and pronounced.

The man was darker than she was, with close-shaven hair and a beard that was dotted with white all over. Smile lines marked his lips, and his huge hands were wrapped around his wife's as they clutched each other.

I realized it wasn't the first time I'd seen these faces. It drudged up an old memory. One of a search through the folders in the room Nana kept telling me not to look through. Of pulling up my own file and finding the mug shots of the people who were found after an extensive search by the police after I was left at Nana's doorstep. They'd been initially blamed for the fire I'd caused as an infant and arrested as a result.

These faces were aged from the photos, but they were the same.

They were my parents.

Dralus said, "Jashi, this is Emanon and Zaranna Anyua."

Emanon, the man calling himself my father, stepped forward, astonishment on his face.

Everything these two did *felt wrong*. Their expressions and actions were flimsy, as if they'd peel away at any minute and reveal who they really were.

I stepped back instinctively as if a horrible disease would hop from his extended arm to mine if he came too close.

"We can't believe it's really you," Emanon said.

"The feeling is mutual," I muttered, waiting for someone to jump out and say "psych."

Zaranna said, "We can't tell you how many times we wanted to reach out, but just...couldn't find the strength." The way her face fell was almost convincing.

I tried to stay focused on rebel things, but angry words kept flying to the forefront of my mind. *Eighteen years of waiting for you. You left me. You made me wait for you.*

I didn't have to hide my fire anymore. When heat blasted through my body, I let it rush out my hands in two fiery pillars.

"Oh, and now you did, huh? I thought you left because you were afraid of my fire. Now you come back *inspired* by it?"

"Jashi!" Zaranna exclaimed, her hand over her heart.

Rand interrupted, "Listen, I don't know who you two are, but I don't think this is the appropriate moment for a family reunion." He glared at Dralus. "Especially in the midst of all these investigations we're under."

"Oh, but we would never go against K'sundii law," Dralus said, clearly amused.

I didn't like the way Rand's face fell. He understood something I still didn't, so I ventured, "What K'sundii law?"

Zaranna at least spared a moment to look hesitant. "Well, it does seem..."

"They have a claim to the royalty status," Dralus supplied.

AUDACITY

R oyal clan.

My parents had a right to be formally made into a royal clan.

We had things to do. We had an escape route to plan, a trip to a rebel country to think about, and a Dragon King to find and convince to take our side. I knew this. I knew this, and yet, I continued to pace the floor of my bedroom, flames shooting from my nostrils like a bull huffing its breath. Kahmel could only sit on the bed and watch me because every time he tried to say something, I'd cut him off with a look that told him I was *not* in the mood to be reminded of what I already knew.

We'd been like this for the past fifteen minutes.

"Eighteen years," I growled with another puff of flames.

By this time, Kahmel understood that my outraged commentary was to myself and to do little more than nod in understanding in response, if at all.

"Almost nineteen now. They had all this time to pretend to care about me. *Now* they want something to do with me? I thought my fire was a curse to them! Now they want to help us prove our case? On top of it, to prove what the Zendaalans already *know* but are going to lie through their teeth and say they don't!"

Again, Kahmel nodded, clearly wanting to say something but, wisely, choosing not to.

He told me that he'd have his people from the palace and whatever rebels he could spare look more into it but so far, it looked like it all checked out. They were my parents.

I knew he was mad too, but for once, I was madder.

"This has to be a ploy to use me. Why else would they come back like this? And only after I became Faresha, obviously. I only wonder why it took them so long to come out with it! If they were going to use me for their new position, why not just come out and do it as soon as I got married?"

"Because the Zendaalans were hiding them."

I was so lost in my own rampaging that it took me a minute to understand what Kahmel was saying. At first, I bristled, thinking the first thing he was going to say would start with, *I think you should calm down*. I settled down when I realized he hadn't. "What?" I said, fire erupting from my mouth.

Kahmel looked up at me with his hands clasped together, still seated in the same position on the edge of the bed. "Do you remember what I asked you shortly after we got married? I asked about your parents."

Vaguely, I remembered the conversation he was talking about. It was when we were playing a game of questions. Then I remembered more clearly. He was right. I'd been surprised by the out-of-the-blue question about my parents while we were trying to get to know each other better.

Well, I was asking questions to get information for the Zendaalans, but whatever. The memory was the same.

"What about it?" I asked, too tired to draw conclusions.

"Knowing your background, I already thought about the possibility of parents showing up out of nowhere. Instantaneous success often draws the attention of normally uninterested family members. I couldn't find them."

I frowned, confused. I knew my parents didn't want anything to do with me, but when the police had to find them years ago, they eventually did. That was how I knew they weren't dead.

As if reading my thoughts, Kahmel went on to say, "You know how extensive of a reach I have to find someone if I really want to, and it was important to know about any family members you might have had that would rise up to claim their right to become a royal clan. But I couldn't find a trace of them. It was like after they were arrested for arson they just vanished. Information about where they worked, lived, or made their lives was either too vague to go on or grossly inaccurate. However, now that they've surfaced, all that information is readily available again, like the hiding of it never happened."

He still wasn't making sense to me. "But how can that be?"

"The Zendaalans. I think after you became Faresha, they hid your parents away and messed up all records of them after a certain point just so they could pull something like this at the right time. I thought they might do something like this, but I wasn't sure. Now I see I was right. They've been saving them up as a trump card this whole time. That must be what my mother was alluding to and what Dralus has been keeping from you this entire time."

"Why?"

I hated how my voice cracked when I said it. How my eyes teared up when I didn't want them to. I hated how hard I had to try to stay angry instead of breaking apart into the nine-year-old girl who ran off and set a dumpster on fire because her parents didn't want her.

I hated how much I wanted to cry.

Kahmel stood and put his hands on my shoulders, bending his head down to speak to me softly. "They want to weaken us at the most crucial moment. They can feel how close we are, and they know just what to use to get to you. That's why we have to stay focused."

My fists clenched at my sides, shaking no matter how much I willed them not to. "But they're in the palace, Kahmel. They're *here* and —"

I stopped before I started crying.

"I know," Kahmel said, seeming to know the right moment to pull me into his chest, rubbing circles into my back.

But I didn't cry. I wouldn't. Not over them. Not anymore.

"We can still turn this in our favor," Kahmel whispered into my ear. "But I need to know you're ready for this."

Breathing deep, I nodded.

I'd been ready for years.

Now I KNEW how Kahmel felt about having embarrassing parents.

I pulled on a violet robe that exemplified everything I was now. Rich, lavish, and flowing. A silver sash wrapped around my waist, a dipped neckline showed a little more than I usually did, but I was feeling daring today. The hem of the robe flowed all the way to the floor and trailed behind me.

I picked up the skirt of my robe and left the room, going down the hall, enjoying the sunlight that poured through the pillars to the side of me. I looked at Hashir spread out before me and wondered how long I would be able to see it like this. Prosperous and happy. Strong.

If I had anything to do about it, it would stay like this.

Rand's room was on this side of the palace, the east wing. This was also where Arusi, Asan, and even Khes came to stay on occasion. If Kahmel's parents were to be so bold, they technically had the right to stay here too, but they weren't. At least not yet.

Right now, that particular audacity belonged to *my* parents.

I had dreamed of a moment like this for years. There were a thousand scenarios for how this conversation would go.

From the age of nothing to nine, it took place on a horse-drawn carriage, with an explanation of a horrible misunderstanding, simply forgetting me someplace, not leaving me on purpose. From ten to fourteen, it was an angry exchange, demanding an explanation before I eventually gave in and went home with them, where I belonged. Then there was that stage between fifteen and seventeen where it was just going to be an emotional reunion that would end in the both of us going our separate ways. Maybe it'd be on the HoloScreen or a talk show, but it wouldn't go much further than that. Too much of my childhood was gone for it to be much more than that. By eighteen, the fantasies were gone, except for in the dreams I tried to forget, where I wouldn't do any of the talking, and my mother would weep to me an apology in the hopes we could simply be friends in my adulthood.

But this was going to be sweeter than any of that.

The Zendaalans tried to time this perfectly. And by the look of things, they had. They couldn't possibly have known that this was the worst time to bring up these people.

Maybe if they had brought them to the Jashi from a few months ago, because she didn't know who she was. She had to grow up quickly in a harsh world and couldn't possibly slow down enough to realize how loved she was. By Nana. By Lora. Even by Kahmel and his friends. She was insecure and naïve because of it.

But this Jashi was Faresha.

And she wasn't to be trifled with.

Too bad the Zendaalans' intel wasn't good enough to tell them that.

I hadn't been to this side of the palace often since Rand and the others usually came to see me in the other part of the palace. All the rooms had access to this small living area, complete with a quaint bookshelf, two couches, and a HoloScreen projector.

Zaranna and Emanon were sitting on the couch—I refused to call them "Mom" or "Dad." Something was playing on the HoloScreen, but they weren't watching, instead talking to each other in hushed voices. They stopped when they saw me.

Emanon stood up. "Jashi."

Zaranna's sunken eyes fluttered as if she was blinking back tears. She exuded exhaustion. If I didn't know any better, I'd say she looked apologetic. Or, at the very least, sick.

I leaned against a pillar, crossing my arms. "So. All these years and you guys finally show, huh?"

"Obviously, words can't express—" Zaranna started.

"No, they can't." My words shut her up.

Emanon tried to be the peacemaker of the situation. "But we're here now, and we want to help you. So you can prove to the Zendaalans that your—abilities—are real." He tried an uneasy chuckle. "We have a burned-down house to prove it."

"So you do." I pushed off the pillar and sauntered toward them. "All out of the kindness of your heart, right? For the small price of becoming royal clan."

Zaranna looked hurt. "Jashi, that's not true." Then she faltered.

And there it was. The truth.

"But it *is* law," she insisted.

"We can use this position to help you!" Emanon added quickly.

From this close, I finally realized what I recognized in them—hate was behind this flimsy look of sorrow and repentance. I'd seen it in Talad on his bad days. Really bad days. It was the look he had in his eye when he would play nice for a while and then finally get to the point where he was going to ask for drug money.

I didn't know what mess the Zendaalans dragged them out of when they found them, but Zaranna looked like she hadn't had a decent meal in a while, and Emanon smelled faintly of beer and cheap cologne. There was a slight pink to his eyes, and it had nothing to do with crying.

These people were playing the role of those who knew how to say the right words to get their next fix.

Only this fix wasn't drugs or alcohol. It was attention.

Well, today, they'd get their wish. Kahmel had given me free rein to do as I wished.

I chuckled. "You're here to help. I guess I didn't need you growing up as much as I do now? Don't worry, don't apologize," I said as they opened their mouths to object. "Because you're here now. Tell me, how did it feel when you found out that the demon child you left behind could actually get you ahead in life?"

Zaranna looked appalled, and I laughed. "Oh, save the tears.

You'll need them for the camera. I'm sure someone will want to do a special on you."

Emanon objected. "Now that's no way to treat your mother."

"Mother?" I barked a laugh. "You don't show up for a few minutes and call yourself my mother!" My voice carried through the halls. A few guards were sure to have heard me.

"Take it easy," Emanon said.

"Easy! Sure, I'll take it easy. Nineteen years of being left behind on account of being a demon, but don't let me be an inconvenience. I'll take it easy!"

At this point, guards were coming into the room.

"Faresha, please calm down," one suggested.

"Don't tell me to calm down! I won't tolerate another minute of these people in *my* home."

"You don't get to make that decision," Emanon barked. His eyes looked more bloodshot now, an ugly vein throbbing in his temple. This was who these people really were. "The law is the law, and there's nothing you can do to change that. We have just as much right to be here as Faresh Kahmel's family."

"I don't care, I want you out!"

I made sure there was a lot of screaming going on, and I noticed one of the guards slipping away. Good.

Kahmel was brought in shortly after, and I caught the slight smirk on his lips that he hid behind a stone face as he walked in.

He played the role of the concerned husband who had to explain to his ignorant wife how the royalty here worked and that my parents couldn't just be willed away. I even shed a tear or two as I stormed off in frustration.

We did great.

Kahmel met me in the gardens as Huntress and Comet roared in their stables, still not allowed to come out. Kahmel smirked as he handed me a piece of tissue. "Feeling any better?"

I gave an extra sniff and pouted as I accepted it. "Not really. I'm so upset, I just might disappear under mysterious circumstances and leave you to handle it."

"What *am* I going to do with you?"

I wanted to laugh but had to stifle it as a guard walked by. I buried my face in my tissue and wiped at imaginary tears.

Kahmel bent down beside my ear. "I'll see you tonight."

RATS

From inside my closet, I pulled on a black bodysuit, the material sticky on the inside, smooth and elastic on the outside.

Kahmel was waiting for me, also dressed in black, standing as he looked out the window. He turned to me. "Rand should be here soon."

"Good," I said, breathing out. I joined him in looking out at Hashir, and I felt like we were thinking the same thing.

I put a hand on his arm. "They'll choose us over the Zendaalans."

Kahmel breathed out. "I can only hope."

"What's being done with the Half-Dracs right now?" It was hard to tell what was going on with all the confusion between the Zendaalans' silence and more Fire Bugs coming out every day.

Kahmel tucked a stray hair behind my ear. "For now, it doesn't look like Zendaal is doing anything against them. At least not yet, from what we can tell. People are just in shock." He sighed again. "Which isn't the greatest state to leave them in right before we leave the country to a rebel nation, but..." He shrugged.

"Not much we can do about it," I finished for him.

I jumped as Rand's face appeared in the window. Even more disturbing, with orange contact lenses that made him look like Kahmel.

Except for that stupid grin on his face.

He tapped on the window, and Kahmel opened it so he could climb in.

"How are you two lovebirds doing?" Rand whispered.

Kahmel chuckled, then patted his brother on the back. "Thanks for doing this."

Rand scoffed. "This is nothing. You guys got the hard part. All I have to do is sit around and be mad all day. Easiest job in the world."

I wanted to laugh, but Rand was right. This wasn't going to be easy.

"But seriously," Rand said, his expression sobering. "Stay safe, you two."

Kahmel nodded to him, then looked to me. "Let's go."

He went first, climbing out onto the ledge and flushing his back against the wall, sidestepping to get around the walls.

This ledge went all around the palace, and we would be going to a hall beside the throne room to avoid the cameras.

Still didn't make a four-story drop any less intimidating.

"Don't look down," Kahmel warned in a whisper.

I braced my back against the window behind me and forced myself to take Kahmel's advice. The cold air wrapped around me like an icy blanket, and the thin material I was wearing didn't help much.

Kahmel looked at me and nodded.

We sidestepped along the walls of the palace.

I gritted my teeth. I felt like a rat snooping around in my own home. But I had to tell myself that it was only temporary.

We were doing this to get the real rats out.

My heart pounded hard enough against my chest that it hurt. I kept my eyes on Kahmel as he moved forward, determined not to get distracted, inching along the edge and sucking in my gut.

My foot caught a loose piece of stucco.

I stumbled forward.

"Jashi!"

Kahmel caught me before I could tip over, giving me enough time to regain my footing, skipping over where the chip in the ledge had fallen. I made the mistake of looking down and saw the white piece of plaster fall to the sand below. My stomach lurched.

For a few moments, we just breathed. I couldn't even thank him.

Kahmel held my gaze, but even he looked panicked. "Are you ready to keep going?"

I didn't feel it, but I nodded. We had to get this part over with. There was much more to come.

We kept going, carefully making our way around a corner, and then continued around the palace. I only stole a glance down to check for loose points in the plaster. Kahmel kept a hand in front of me now as we went. I breathed a sigh of relief when we finally reached a window that would allow us access to the hallways.

Kahmel was first to go through, and I climbed after him. But we didn't have time to celebrate.

Silently, we treaded the palace floors to reach the throne room. Behind our thrones, there was a loose tile. Kahmel picked it up, revealing a smaller square etched in the ground. He stepped on it, and the wall behind the thrones gave, allowing entrance to the hidden tunnel.

The one we'd shared our first real kiss in.

Kahmel replaced the tile, and we darted through the passage, making our way to the kitchen, avoiding spots we knew we would be caught on camera.

The kitchen was vacant. A place that seemed to always have the bustle of pots and dishes clanging felt odd now that it was empty.

Why couldn't I shake the feeling that I was saying goodbye to it all?

Following Kahmel, I ducked into the pantry with him. There wasn't anything of note here, just spices and things like flour, salt, sugar, rice. If Kahmel hadn't told me ahead of time how to access this secret exit, I would have never guessed it.

We were surrounded by shelves, but one was on its own, separate from the others that had rows beneath it. This one floated on the wall with nothing but a jar of sugar and another with vanilla beans in it. I stood on the balls of my feet to reach up to it and pull it down, revealing that the sugar and vanilla beans were glued to its surface, and the shelf folded against the wall, clicking a switch, and revealing the wall to be a swinging door. Stairs led the way down.

Kahmel gave an *after you* gesture, and I silently chuckled at him as I went.

Trying not to be haunted by the feeling of saying goodbye.

🐉

I HAD BEEN through the routine several times in my head, but I repeated it over again to myself just in case.

There were no second chances here.

There were two types of transports that went on between rebel countries and Equalized nations: army vehicles from the Zendaalans and surveillance teams. The surveillance teams didn't have to be Zendaalans. They were usually sent from the governments of surrounding countries to ensure that no passing was happening from rebel countries into Equalized ones. They were placed along the borders.

Kahmel and I crouched close to the ground in a surveillance team truck. As these teams were sanctioned by the Zendaalans, it was harder to swap them out for rebels. The Zendaalans did thorough background checks on all its officers, so smuggling out an entire team would take months to accomplish, which we didn't have.

Camouflage tech was tricky. It took what was behind you and put it in front of you, so, for all intents and purposes, you were invisible. Which was especially effective when you were far away from those you were trying to hide from.

Not crouched in the same truck together.

Moving caused a slight flicker as the suit adjusted to project the right background, and from up close, it would be plainly obvious to anyone looking in your direction. Touching or bumping into anyone was also a dead giveaway.

The rebels managed to get us in the truck before the surveillance team by creating a diversion long enough for us to steal inside. From here, it was up to us to keep quiet and not let anyone touch us.

And the worst of it all—this was the relatively easy part. The high-security vehicle checks didn't happen on the trucks going out.

We had a whole other beast to slay on the return trip.

The truck was large, looking like an armored tank on the inside. There were rows of seats along the walls, eight in total, though only seven were occupied. The surveillance team was armored, enveloped in dark robotic suits, not unlike the ones the Zendaalan officers wore.

Kahmel and I crouched in front of a crate their weapons were stored in, next to a few other odd items lined against the wall, some backpacks, extra water containers, the like. It was as if they were packing for a camping trip rather than a stakeout to make sure the haves and the have-nots stayed apart.

My legs cramped from being pulled up against my chest this entire time, and there was still an hour left in the trip. Kahmel's hand was clenched in mine. I couldn't see him, but feeling that squeeze was enough. My body was sticky under the skin-tight camo-suit, the see-through fabric of the mask that covered the entirety of my face making me feel claustrophobic.

But I wouldn't move a hair in the wrong direction.

This was just the beginning.

The location of the entrance to this Dragon Realm was much clearer than the other two we'd found. Normally, information regarding rebel countries was hard to come across because the Zendaalans restricted any information that had to do with rebel countries. But having all the members of the rebellion know what we were after helped us out.

A lot of rebel members were Vahdelan, and there were local myths that sounded like what we were after. They told of the Vahdelan deities that resided in a lake that was once considered sacred. It was said that when the deities were angered, they shook the lake with awful tremors that made the area non-traversable, so the ancient locals forbade passage through that way.

The stories matched what seemed to be a common pattern with the other places we'd found Dragon Realm entrances. But getting there would be no easy feat.

There were a lot of variables, and nothing was certain. Every step of this journey was going to feel like scampering across the walls on the outside of the palace, with one foot over the edge. I had to summon a kind of courage I'd never asked of myself before. The kind that could put aside Jashi.

And do it as K'sundi's Faresha.

INTO REBEL COUNTRY

The truck finally stopped. The bones in my knees felt locked in place and they ached, but as the men in the truck piled out and closed the door behind them, I could stand at last, rising slowly and feeling blood rush back into my limbs.

The air flickered beside me, and Kahmel took off his mask, making him look like a floating head in the darkness. I stifled a giggle as I took off my mask so he could see me, too.

"Let's go," he whispered, barely audible. He opened the back door slowly so that the click made as soft a sound as possible. He looked through the crack, then put his mask on again, gesturing for me to come slowly. Slipping my mask back on, I crept up behind him, and we ducked out of the truck together, closing the door behind us.

We were outside in the darkness of night. Surveillance officers swarmed the area, but in the dark, they wouldn't notice the way the camouflage suits buffered.

Lights cast a glow on the area, spaced far apart, making it hard to see how it looked. The ground we stepped on was dry and gravelly. There were other trucks lined up behind us, and the surveillance officers were being transferred to other vehicles and dispatched to different locations.

Kahmel somehow found my hand and pulled me along. We avoided walking too close to anyone. Though the darkness helped, we still couldn't risk anyone recognizing the way camouflage technology reconfigured itself from up close.

The crunch of gravel beneath our feet turned to the sturdier sounds of asphalt. We'd walked far enough away from the camp of surveillance officers to reach the road, and the darkness was near-absolute. But we couldn't risk using light because it might be noticed by the people behind us.

We could, however, take off our masks, at least for the time being. Hitting a button on the nape of my neck, I turned off the camouflage. A floating head was more suspicious than anything else, and if no one recognized us in the dark, we would be fine.

My eyes slowly adjusted to the darkness, helping me at least recognize where the dirt ended and the road began.

Kahmel and I followed the road until we reached the point where we couldn't see where the surveillance officers were camped. By then, the sun was coming up, turning the sky a pale gray. Looking back, I was finally able to see where we'd come from—a building plated with windows on all sides that glinted in the weak light, making it look like a slate of white against the gray. There was the border, where a wall stretched from one end to the other as far as I could see. A vehicle's check station marked the only way through it. Given the nature of the coming and leaving, it didn't happen often, but I knew that the check coming out was going to be thorough. That much was clear by the soldiers in robotic suits standing guard at the wall in a line, laser shotguns in tow.

Looking around made me catch my breath.

Vahdel had only been labeled a rebel country less than a year ago. But the effects of Zendaal's power over Hemorah was clear.

All this time, we'd been walking on dry ground, hearing a crunch that I was used to, coming from a desert. I wasn't thinking.

Vahdel was made up of forests.

Around us, the trees were withered and spindly forms of what they must have been at some point. A few of them still had green leaves hanging on the skinny twigs. But most were bare, leaves scattered on the ground, brown and dry. The ground was almost completely bald, dusty enough to be blown by the wind when it stirred. Where grass did grow, only a few patches were still green, though most of it was dry and brittle, a sickly yellow.

I was struck with newfound horror as my shoes crunched against the dry ground, feeling like I was treading on a graveyard.

"It happened so quickly," I muttered.

Kahmel looked at me. He didn't have to ask what I was talking about. Instead, he returned his gaze to the road. "It doesn't take long for the effects to set in." His voice was firm. Hard. "That's why we're relying on the Dragon Kings to help K'sundi when the time comes. If not..." he trailed off. There was no need to finish the sentence.

I preferred he didn't.

Not long after, I saw the marker for the arranged meeting point. The rebel contact told us to look out for a spot on the road where a large tree had fallen over, and we saw it. As described, it was a rotten tree with its roots sticking up out of the ground.

From here, Kahmel and I were to go off the road and keep walking until we met with our contact.

We didn't walk more than a few feet before we heard a car going down the road. I turned and stiffened. It was a Zendaalan military vehicle, clear by the insignia of their flag on the side: white, gray, and yellow. We ducked behind the fallen tree until it passed.

When it did, Kahmel took me by the arm and moved a little faster with me. "Let's keep moving."

I agreed.

My eyelids itched from not sleeping all night, and my legs were still tired from being crouched in the vehicle. The walk took longer than I expected, but it made sense. Being caught anywhere near the main road would have been suicide for any rebels, especially so close to the border.

Just as my calves were starting to feel like cement blocks, we found an old hovertruck parked behind a huge gangly bush. The red paint was chipping in several places, and one of the hoverports was offline, indicated by the way the light flickered instead of glowing a solid blue.

A man with a beard and a scar on his tawny cheek waited for us, leaning against the hovertruck with a dead expression. He was tanned, the skin around his eyes a lighter color from wearing sunglasses. He chewed a piece of grass between his teeth.

Without a word, he opened the door of his hovertruck and pulled out two sleeping bags and thermoses.

"Rest," he said. His translator made his voice sound like a robot, and there were a few seconds of delay between the words he said in Vahdelan and the voice repeating them in K'sundi, but we got the message. "You're going to need it."

"Thank you," I said, accepting the thermos and then a bottle of water as he handed them to me. The thermos was still warm to the touch, and opening it up and taking a sip revealed it was filled with a simple stew of a few vegetables and meat. I felt a little guilty taking it, knowing that I could very well go home and enjoy these same luxuries easily. Not like here, where there were surely shortages.

Kahmel laid out the sleeping bags, and the man went into his truck without another word, crossing his arms and resting his head against the back of his seat. He might have gone to sleep.

"We'll only stay here a few hours," Kahmel said as he took a long drink of water. "How are you holding up?"

I breathed out, crouching down to sit on the sleeping bag and letting my legs stretch out and rest for the first time in hours. "I've been better, that's for sure."

Kahmel pursed his lips, twisting off the top to his thermos. "This definitely isn't anything I ever wanted to ask my Faresha to do."

I chuckled, pulling my legs to my chest and wrapping my arms around them. "Your Faresha is fine." Looking out at the landscape, I sighed. "Much more than I can say for the people here.

Kahmel sat down and looked up at the sky, which was getting brighter by the minute. But even the sun seemed harsher here. Even for someone used to K'sundi heat, it felt unnaturally hot for being so early in the day, the rays feeling intense on my skin already. "We're so close. If we can just get past this part in time..."

"We'll make it," I said, scooting over next to him. I managed to smile at him. "We're Half-Dracs, remember?"

Kahmel smirked and pecked my lips, running his hand through my hair. "Let's not waste time. We need to eat and rest so we can head out again."

We ate our stew quickly and finished the bottles of water before resting on top of the sleeping bags—sleeping under them was out of the question in this heat. It didn't take long for sleep to settle in.

When we woke, the sun was high in the sky and making me sweat. Thankfully, the need for the camouflage suits was over, and the man turned around so I could change into the clothes he'd prepared in the back of his hovertruck—a pair of shorts and a t-shirt that had a few holes in it but served well enough. Even that felt too hot, though, and I ended up tying the end of the shirt into a knot, so my stomach and back didn't feel so sticky. Kahmel got dressed in more casual clothes, too, wearing a tank top and shorts.

The man, whose name we'd learned was Inero, handed us faceless black masks.

"It's what the rebels around here wear. You're safer with our faces than your own."

I was reluctant to wear anything over my face in this heat, but he was right. It was better for anyone who might see us to assume we were rebels rather than K'sundi's royalty.

Kahmel and I piled into his truck. The only relief from the heat the car could offer was in its broken windows slid all the way down and the breeze of being in motion. Otherwise, winds didn't stir much here.

Inero set off into the air but stayed low to the ground to avoid detection. We rode in silence, tilted slightly to one side on account of the busted hoverport. I wasn't sure how Inero knew where he was going because we weren't following any road or GPS, and all the dead trees and foliage looked the same to me, but he didn't flinch.

Finally, we came upon a road, and Inero went down it. This one had more activity, but only by a little. The cars that passed made

Inero's look like a luxury model. Most had odd char marks on the sides, the original colors long-forgotten with decay.

"Why are they all burned?"

"Equalization militia attacks," Inero answered. I couldn't understand what he'd said in his own language, but the lag in the translator let me hear how gruff his voice became. "The Zendaalans send troops to 'enforce the peace' but mainly harass civilians. It often ends in laser fire. The lucky ones make off with burn marks."

I bit my lip, drawing blood since it was already chapped from the sun.

"Speaking of—duck!" Inero shouted.

I didn't understand what was going on but obeyed dutifully, bending down so my head wouldn't be seen through the window. Kahmel was sitting behind me, but I heard his body shift into what I assumed was a crouched position.

At the sound of laser fire I braced myself for the impact, but it never came. However, Inero did start driving faster, pushing the rickety machine to its limits, the car shuddering until he finally slowed down again.

"You can get up. I was worried they'd seen your masks, but no, they were targeting someone else."

Ahead of us, two Zendaalan military cars were speeding after someone, the soldiers leaning out of their cars, firing.

"Good," I breathed, then clenched my fists, watching the pursuit. "Or relatively so."

Inero didn't respond.

He told Kahmel and me to duck several more times from military vehicles passing, and the more we did, the more I noticed Inero's lips press into a line.

Something was wrong.

By the fifth time, Inero was muttering to himself in Vahdelan. He'd turned his translator off a while ago, probably to save energy.

"What's going on?" Kahmel asked, leaning over the seat to look at him.

Inero only shrugged, eyes trained on the open road and his rearview cameras.

Turning to Kahmel, I asked, "Why do you think there are all these militia vehicles going this way?"

"I have no idea," Kahmel muttered.

So far, only the first ones had been firing. These cars were just driving in the same direction and passing us up every so often.

We topped a hill that gave us a view of the valley below—and we got the answer to our question.

In the middle of the valley was the lake. It looked like a historic spot, the lip flanked by two ancient statues standing erect. The road leading up to the statues passed through a town first, but it was small enough to drive through in maybe half an hour, most of the buildings looking abandoned or impoverished. The statues portrayed clothes that were typical of the era at the time it was built, gaudy necklaces etched into the stone against bare chests, with masks with spikes coming out of them that looked like beams from the sun. The statues stood tall enough to be seen clearly from afar, making the valley look like their playground.

And at their feet stood dozens of Zendaalan soldiers armed to the teeth.

DRAKE BOND

Inero stopped the car, parking it on the side of the road as he shook his head and slammed his hand against the wheel, muttering to himself in Vahdelan.

I frowned, turning to Kahmel and Inero, the former also mumbling a couple curses.

"What's going on? Why are they here?"

Kahmel breathed through his teeth, grabbing his hair in clumps. His eyes were trained on the soldiers in the valley before us. There had to be at least a few dozen standing there at the ready. "They know what we're after."

"How? We barely knew where to come."

"I think they've known for a while," Kahmel speculated, his gaze finally resting on me, but I could tell he was more lost in his calculations than concentrating on me. "It's just never been relevant until we started uncovering things. That's why they didn't want me at war with Omani. They couldn't tell how much I knew. With the war, our latest trip to Gheres, and our announcement, they must have figured out we know a lot more than they anticipated. Damn bastards probably know where all the Dragon Realm entrances are. Or at least the higher-ups do. They almost have to." He rubbed a hand over his face. "It makes sense."

"What do we do?" I asked, but neither man had an answer.

I slouched in my seat, glaring at the soldiers keeping us from the lake. We still didn't know where *exactly* the entrance was. We would have to get by them to look for it, most likely while being fired upon. And that was assuming we could get past them in the first place.

I bit my lip, iron filling my mouth as it bled more. A thought occurred to me, but I didn't know if it would be too risky to try. But we didn't have another choice.

"Kahmel, how resistant are dragons to laser fire?"

Kahmel looked up at me, obviously submerged in his own thoughts as well. "Very. But there wouldn't be any dragons out here, not even with collars. Once the Equalized status was taken from Vahdel, they extracted all their business from here, and dragons only come from Zendaal in regions outside K'sundi and Omani."

I nodded. "Yeah, I know that, but you remember there were dragons at the entrance in Omani where there wasn't supposed to be, and again in Gheres."

He stroked his chin. "True. So, you're saying you think we'll find a dragon if we get closer to the entrance?"

"That's what's happened so far."

"Even if that's true," Inero joined in, apparently having turned on his translator again, "any dragon around here isn't going to be a healthy one, and you'd still have to tame it enough to ride."

I looked at Kahmel. "You've tamed dragons before. We just need to get close to one."

Kahmel looked dubious. "I don't know. A hungry dragon is usually the worst kind, especially out here where food is scarce."

"What if we have a surefire way to tame it?"

At first, Kahmel looked at me in utter confusion, then realization slowly dawned on him. He shook his head. "Only you would call using the Drake Bond when we aren't even sure we know how to use it 'surefire.'"

We drove through the small town on the way to the lake. It was clear that it had been abandoned in a hurry. Personal effects were strewn across the streets; kids' bicycles lay on their sides, rust creeping over. Cars were parked haphazardly in the road, one with its lights flickering and the front dented as if it had been in a crash, and the person inside had to get out and run.

I supposed that when resources were scarce, small towns like these were the first to be abandoned for the bigger cities, where, if there were resources, there was more of a chance of finding them.

The ground rumbled, sparking hope in my gut that what we were doing wasn't completely crazy.

We drove close to the road, going down side streets and keeping an eye on the sky. We were trying to get closer to the lake without running into the Zendaalans just yet. So far, we'd seen dragons appear close to the Dragon Realm entrances. It even helped lead us to them. It stood to reason that if we could only get close enough to the entrance...

"There," Kahmel said, leaning over the seats and pointing.

Sure enough, there was a dragon behind a house...walking into the wall?

"What the hell?" I looked at Kahmel, who appeared just as confused.

Inero stopped the truck, lowering it to the ground before we all stepped out. I caught myself before I stumbled when the ground shook again, stronger this time. We were close to the entrance.

The dragon had seen better days. It was a Draconian, the scales a dull red, almost brick color. Some parts of its body had lacerations, blood crusting in jagged lines. It was frightfully skinny, several ribs showing, its stomach sunken in. One of its horns had been broken off. It walked into the wall of the house like it was on a treadmill, undeterred by the fact it wasn't going anywhere, it kept walking, like a character in a glitchy video game.

I took a cautious step toward it, but a hand on my shoulder held me back. "No, look. It has a collar."

I didn't even notice it, but Kahmel was right. A grimy black collar was around the dragon's neck, a faint red light glowing in the middle of it, showing the dragon was "on."

"There's nothing we can do with a ZST dragon. Their minds are too far gone," Kahmel said with a grimace. "It's probably stuck on a forward command from a remote we have no hope of finding. Not that I'd do anything but put this poor creature out of its misery."

Inero barked something to us in Vahdelan, pointing. I followed his gaze, surprised to see another dragon, a Wingless, coming toward us, trotting stiffly in one direction, tripping over anything in its path, probably, like Kahmel said, stuck on a command. But then I noticed there was another behind it, limping, but on its way.

"Where are they all coming from?" I asked.

Kahmel stroked his chin. "They all look like adolescents. They might be coming from a temperament warehouse. If the Zendaalans withdrew their finished dragons, they might have abandoned the ones that were still in the middle of being trained. They're no use to anyone because their consciousness is subdued, but they still haven't been programmed with commands outside of a few basic ones because they aren't old enough yet."

Like "move forward," it seemed. But I did notice these dragons were smaller than Comet or Huntress, and he was probably right about them being younger.

"Still," I pondered, "why would they all be moving in the same direction like this? I'd get it if they were all on different commands, but they all seem to be on the same one."

Kahmel looked around. More dragons headed this way as we spoke, a few flying, even more crawling, but they were all going in the same direction, albeit awkwardly as they didn't seem to know how to avoid obstacles in their path. As Kahmel said, their programming probably wasn't advanced enough to understand basic pathfinding.

"They're going toward the entrance," Inero noted, nodding in the direction of the main street.

It was true. I hadn't noticed before, but they moved in the direction of the lake.

It sparked something in me that I wasn't sure we'd ever considered before.

Were ZST dragons truly lost?

Clenching my fists, I hopped over the fence that parted the backyard from the street and walked up to the dragon that was walking into the wall in front of us. Kahmel looked at me strangely.

I tried to remember the words. "*Leh mani stepior.*"

The dragon blinked but didn't otherwise react, continuing its treadmill walk into the wall of the house. Finally, it got a claw on the low roof and managed to climb on top, then crawl away in the same direction as the rest.

I pursed my lips, not ready to give up yet. I looked at the next nearest dragon, an orange-scaled one trying to make its way around an overturned car. Dust covered its arms and legs, making the orange look more like sand. I hopped back over the fence, jogging toward the dragon, heart in my throat. If this didn't work, I had no idea how we were going to get by the Zendaalans blocking the entrance to the Dragon Realm.

And we *had* to get to the other two Dragon Kings before Zendaal announced K'sundi a rebel nation.

What was happening to Vahdel...no one would trust Kahmel if this happened to K'sundi before he had enough time to win them over.

We had to succeed.

"*Leh mani stepior.*"

The dragon didn't even glance at me, continuing its path mindlessly.

My throat tightened.

Behind me, I heard Kahmel moving, and I turned to see him walking beside the dragon that had walked away from the house. "*Leh mani stepior.*"

Inero looked around and found the dragon that was limping, not fast enough to walk ahead like the others had. His accent was thick, but he pronounced it like Kahmel and I had. "*Leh mani stepior.*"

It lit the flames of determination in me all over again. We were going to figure out how to get this Drake Bond. And we were going to get past those Zendaalans.

A crash got my attention. It was another Draconian trying to make it over a fence, falling over as it brought down the entire chain link with it. This one was steel blue with muted grey eyes and a gash across its snout. One of its paws was missing a claw, and it was even smaller than the others. The creature had seen better days.

I walked toward it, taking a deep breath and staring it in the eyes. Eyes that were dulled, the bright intelligence I saw clearly in Comet and Huntress long gone, buried under torture and neglect. I reached for the hope that it wasn't gone for good. That the Zendaalans couldn't take everything from it forever, just like they couldn't take K'sundi's heart and soul before it eventually found its way back.

I felt a click. The dragon blinked, pausing for a moment—just a moment—before it continued on its way, but I noticed it. This one was different.

This one was mine.

"*Leh mani stepior.*"

The dragon stopped.

It looked at me, breathing, air pushing from its nostrils.

Then its eyes *glowed*, bright orange. Like my eyes. The glow faded, and the dragon roared. A deep, guttural roar that lit something in me that screamed out too.

Its roar cut off, an agonizing scream taking its place. I jerked back as the dragon swiped its head across the air, scraping its neck against the chain fence. Then it clawed at its neck.

The collar.

The red light in the middle turned bright and flashed, and a low buzzing sound filled the air.

Electrocution.

Kahmel leaped forward and grabbed the collar, fire blasting from his hand. The collar whined, the pitch going higher until its form warped and bubbled, then broke under his grip, falling to pieces on the ground.

The dragon sighed as soon as it was off, and its eyes trained on me, a low growl erupting from its throat like a purr.

Thank you, it seemed to say.

This was a huge victory, but we didn't have time to celebrate it. I slung myself on its back, and Kahmel jumped on behind me. As we leaned forward on the dragon, it moved toward Inero.

"We'll be back," I called to him, then grabbed the dragon's ears. We leaped into the air, the dragon flapping its wings hard and rocketing forward at a speed I didn't think it was capable of.

I could barely believe it.

ZST dragons could be restored with the Drake Bonds. That was why it was so important for us to know. This changed everything.

But right now, we had to face the Zendaalans. They wouldn't keep us from the Dragon Realm. Not today.

AVERTON

The air erupted with the sound of laser fire.

It was time to take everything I learned from Kahmel and Rand about dragon-riding and apply it here, now.

Taking a deep breath, I tilted up my rebel mask far enough to expose my mouth and channeled my overflowing energy into a puff of fire. It seemed like a coincidence—though it didn't feel like one—as the dragon breathed fire, too, roaring into the air as flames poured out in waving arcs into the sky. It wasn't old enough to have roars that ruptured eardrums, but the noise still left my ears ringing.

The Zendaalans were firing, an entire line of soldiers letting loose a reverse rain of laser fire from below.

First, the zig-zag flight pattern.

I threw my weight to the side, the dragon following seamlessly with the motion as we dived diagonally, then completed the dive to the other side, weaving through the air. The air was hot with laser fire.

The dragon jerked and roared as it got hit. Once, twice. The air sizzled where red fire grazed my leg, the skin there left tingling. But I didn't falter. I kept diving to either side, determined to protect this dragon and us as much as I possibly could. We got hit a few more times, at least. But I had to focus on what was in front of me. The lake was up ahead, the sun dipping white light into the surface as it rippled.

At the lip of the lake were the two huge statues, standing against the sky almost as if in defiance. Like there was a part of Vahdel that could never truly die, and the statues knew it, their arms crossed against their chests, waiting for their day to come.

At their feet were two pedestals with metal bowls on top.

The Zendaalans were surrounding them.

"Damn," Kahmel cursed behind me. "We can't use our fire against them, but the dragon can. You think you can manage?"

"I'm sure I can."

I dove to the side, letting the dragon lower itself toward the lake, the tip of one wing grazing the water and letting it splash behind it, sparkling in the air. We turned to face the Zendaalans head-on. I pulled on the dragon's ears just as the Zendaalans fired, hearing the lasers burn against the trees behind us as their shots flew below. Fire roared behind us as the trees ignited.

My heart was already racing, but it seemed to race even faster, my head starting to swim. Energy pulsed through my body, like the first time I controlled my fire on my own, but this was different. It felt like a raging river rushed through my body. My fingers twitched, my limbs buzzed.

I felt excited as if I was stretching muscles that didn't get used much. An opportunity to do what I'd been waiting to do for some time now. Energetic wasn't the word for it. This was a juvenile kind of excitement, like the happiness a child felt at something as simple as candy. But this wasn't candy—this was purpose. This was being used for something more than just being trained like a vehicle—

I flinched.

Was that *the dragon's thoughts?*

I didn't have time to think about it because the dragon flapped its wings and soared impossibly fast. The air itself seemed to part for us, whirling around us and tossing the water from the lake up in the air. The Zendaalans were startled, and that moment of hesitation proved to be fatal.

I didn't even get to say the word, *"K'mhet."*

As soon as I'd wanted it, *thought it,* the dragon responded, blasting flames across the Zendaalans that I'd never seen in an adult dragon, much less an adolescent. The air exploded with heat, and the Zendaalans screamed in horror as they were rained on with greedy flames that licked up everything they touched. Several jumped into the lake; others ran, attempting to take position somewhere farther and fire at us, but soon realized that the flames could reach them there, too. The dragon was unrelenting in its downpour.

The dragon landed on the ones left standing with a crushing slam; it clawed and swiped at them, flicking others with its tail.

What's more, all of this happened as quickly as I could *think* it. When I noticed a Zendaalan getting away, the dragon noticed it too, smacking them with its barbed tail. When I saw someone getting in position to fire, the dragon breathed fire on them first. It was like we were in sync, using each other as easily as we would our own limbs. But it wasn't abusive, like the control of a collar. This was a bond.

This was the power of the Drake Bond.

I slung off the dragon, Kahmel following behind me.

"Wait, but the Zendaalans. If we leave, what will happen to the dragon in the meantime?" Kahmel asked.

"She'll be fine. She can handle them," I answered, not even having to think about it. In fact, I felt like if I did think about it, the feeling would dissipate. It was like using muscle memory. You had to trust your body, your instincts, more than your mind, or you would lose it.

"It's a she?"

I didn't even realize I'd said it, but it felt right, and I went with it. "Yes. Now let's go."

With the Zendaalans detained, it would be easier to use our fire without fear of being recorded or reported. I lit my hand in flames and threw it into the bowl, and as Kahmel did the same, the fire roared into the sky.

My dragon roared with it.

The ground trembled with enough strength to knock Kahmel and me to the ground. I tasted dust and iron as I bit my lip. But I saw something white and glowing slithering our way and grinned.

We made it.

I felt myself being taken into its claws, and we soared up into the air. The dragon of in-between roared, then dove down toward the water.

I clamped my eyes shut and held my breath, ready to be taken under. There was a splash and then an explosion of water, but when I opened my eyes, we were surrounded by blackness and completely dry.

And in the distance, amid sparkling stars and swirling colors of the galaxy, was the palace of the Dragon King.

This one was opulent, a castle of white with spiraling pale colors glowing against it like opal stone. The tops of the towers were squared, with rectangular windows and bright green lines blazing across the walls at angles that accentuated the geometrical shapes of the building.

The dragon of in-between dropped us at the foot of the palace before it roared again and flew off into the ether.

This time there was no need to look for the Dragon King inside the palace.

It was draped over one of the castle's towers, its tail crawling up the wall behind it, falling between the battlements at the top. Its scales were a pale blue, reflective like a mirror. Its white horns twisted above its head like a gazelle's. When it rose to look at us, its scales rippled like water, shimmering and waving to the point it looked like its form blurred out of focus.

"*Absolutely amazing,*" the dragon remarked in a rumbling voice.

My face was drenched in sweat. I took off the rebel mask. "I'm glad you found all that entertaining."

As hesitant as the Dragon Kings acted, this was the third time it seemed as if they'd been closely watching my and Kahmel's movements. They may not have wanted to admit it, but I felt like some part of them wanted to believe that Kahmel and I could accomplish what we'd set out to do.

The Dragon King's face spread into a coy smile. *"So, you finally remembered the Drake Bonds."*

Kahmel cut a look at me, a sparkle in his eye. "Thanks to her quick thinking and wit, yes."

"What are you here for, Half-Dracs?"

Kahmel took a breath. "We already have Aithel and Gaiena on our side, and we were hoping—"

"Yes, yes, I agree. Now listen, you two have a lot of work to do."

Kahmel and I looked at each other in confusion.

"You mean that's it?" I blurted.

"I am Averton," the Dragon King introduced himself, *"and I can see the trouble you went through to get here, so I'll be brief. I will admit, I was wary at first, but it has become clear to me now that if you were willing to come all the way out here after Zendaal has used its stolen source of our power to devastate it, you must truly have spirit if nothing else."* As Averton leaned lazily to one side to see us better, I realized that his scales *were* wet, glistening with water that poured from his body and trickled down to the floor in little currents. In the star-lit darkness, I didn't see it at first but then realized that the trickling noise had been there all along.

I also saw what the K'sundi traitor took from him—where a claw should have been, a rounded off foreleg ended abruptly instead.

"But what kind of work are you talking about?"

The dragon's silver eyes rested on me, a silencing effect, even without him trying. *"Oh, the Zendaalans are quite angry with what you've been doing now that they've caught on. Like your ancestors, you're very battle-minded. Take a moment to leave the battle behind and look around you, Half-Dracs."*

I frowned, not knowing quite what the dragon was referring to until I took his advice, looked around, and gasped.

We were surrounded by dragons swimming through the air.

Wingless, Draconian, Elementals—all kinds of dragons drifted in peaceful flight around us, in vibrant colors I'd never seen before. They were hard to see because they drifted in and out of sight; there one moment, vanishing into thin air the next.

"This is the realm of dragons, after all. But lately, they haven't even had the mind to come. You've inspired them to come home to us. Even the minds that have been beaten into subjection have been stirred to come home. That's why you saw so many that couldn't manage many thoughts but knew what direction to go—home. All Dragon Realm entrances have that effect. It's like a beacon of sorts, both to dragons and Half-Dracs alike. That's why you just know when you're close to one."

"You're very forthcoming," Kahmel noted.

Averton chuckled. *"Am I? Though I'm quite convinced you two just might have what it takes to convince the other dragons to come back. The ones with golden eyes and golden hearts who enchanted us so long ago. I can feel their collective consciousness reawakening now that you've exposed yourselves to them. That's another reason the dragons have been inspired to come home."*

Tears burned at the back of my eyes.

"You mentioned that we have a lot of work to do and that the Zendaalans have been angered. What do you mean?" Kahmel asked.

Averton sighed. *"Yes. Though part of me is gone,"* he lifted the foreleg that was missing a claw. *"I can still feel it. I see it at all times."*

"You can *see* your claw?" I asked, raising an eyebrow.

"I see a lot of things, Half-Drac. And yes, the Dragon Kings are ever living, and that includes every part of us. That's why the power that was stolen centuries ago still lives on. The Zendaalans keep our parts in their central city, always close to them. However, it also gives us the ability to always see them. A blessing and curse, as it were. That said, I feel in my bones that they're planning something, knowing full well what you intend to do. And they'll do anything in their power to prevent it. They're going to stir something that should have never been disturbed." Averton's gaze was distant. Before either of us could ask, he shook himself. *"Just know that you are in a race, young Half-Dracs.*

Who will make it first—you arriving at your destiny, or the Zendaalans crushing it before it could even see the light of victory? Only you can make the difference. Now go. I give you my word that I will do what I can for the lands of Vahdel and the surrounding regions. With my power cheapened, it can only do so much, but it will help. Use the strength of the combined Dragon Kings allied to your side already to rally support, because I fear you might not have as much time as you suspect."

Kahmel's face twisted into a confused grimace. "What do you mean?"

Averton looked at me, a touch of sadness in his eyes. *"You are very brave, especially for your age. You will need that courage. Your enemy has plans for you, and I don't think you'll be able to avoid them."*

What the hell did *that* mean?

Kahmel's jaw clenched. "Maybe you can help us. If we knew how to get to the last Dragon King—"

"Queen," Averton corrected. *"Obellana is not normally so trusting, but with the three of us on your side, I'm sure she will be convinced. And yes, I can tell you—the way to her entrance is a touch more unconventional than the rest of ours have been; however, the K'sundii of ancient times knew the technique to find her. There is a place in your own country that bridges the gap between space and time and connects to the entrance of her side of this realm instantly. Quite similar to how the dragon of in-between brought you here. K'sundii have used it for centuries to get to Hemorah's moon, though the Zendaalans have done well to get rid of most of the evidence, the dragons have never forgotten, and they'll lead you there if you let them."*

It was obvious that Averton wasn't being *completely* forthcoming, leaving a lot for us to figure out on our own. And with his ominous warning on top of that, a newfound sense of dread had slipped down my belly. But we could at least work with what he had given us.

Kahmel swallowed, his Adam's apple bobbing, but he nodded in thanks. "We appreciate your help, Averton."

"Yes, yes, now be quick about it. Or it will all be for naught. And ask Aithel to help you find the Half-Dracs. The Zendaalans are out to kill them now. Especially with the new ones popping up."

"What?" I asked, but the question was left unanswered as the ground beneath us fell away with the swipe of Averton's hand, and the familiar grip of the dragon of in-between took hold of us.

As I suspected, we would be on our own to figure out all the riddles Averton left for us to solve.

If we survived getting out of Vahdel.

SMUGGLED

I blinked, and we were back in the middle of laser fire and screaming.

But there was an added element to the mix.

Dragons—with their collars still on—were fighting the Zendaalan soldiers. It was clear they still didn't know what they were doing, swinging blindly and ramming into things along with the soldiers, but it was effective in preventing the soldiers from being able to do anything as the dragon of in-between dropped us off in our places beside the pedestals.

They were creating our getaway.

Kahmel and I both had our masks on again. I scanned the crowd for my dragon, and, as soon as I spotted her, her eyes went to mine as though she could feel my gaze. She moved away from a Zendaalan soldier she was stepping on and ran to Kahmel and me like a puppy that missed its owner.

Fluidly, I slung myself on her back, and Kahmel followed. The dragon didn't need to stop, continuing as she beat her wings against the air and took to the sky.

A few shots went out, but most of the soldiers were preoccupied.

We were going to make it.

Still. I couldn't shake the warning Averton gave us.

What were the Zendaalans planning for me? And why wouldn't Kahmel and I be able to stop it?

Kahmel squeezed my waist. "Let's not stop. Inero can meet us back in the same place we met him. From there, we'll head to the hideout where we'll lie low for a few days before going home."

I pressed my lips together. I *felt* how much this dragon was straining to keep us on her back. She was still young, not as strong as an adult dragon. But I also felt that she knew how much we needed her right now, and she was willing to do what it took to help us.

"Is there anything we can do for her?" I asked in a small voice.

Kahmel paused. "I'll figure something out. It'll be hard, but luckily, since she's young, she doesn't eat as much as adults do."

I took some comfort in that but still wasn't sure how much help we could really be. Or if there was even a way to bring her home.

"Don't worry about it," Kahmel assured me. "I'll think of something."

I decided to believe him and concentrate on the task at hand. Below, I saw Inero watching in awe of the battle around him.

"Hey!" I called to get his attention. He pressed on his ear to turn on his translator. "Meet us at the same spot from before!"

He nodded and climbed into his truck.

Behind us, we left the battle to the dragons.

It twisted my gut, but I reminded myself that Kahmel and I had a bigger battle to face and that these little battles had to be won first, or we'd never make it.

Like Averton said, we were in a race.

KAHMEL and I had to wait a week for a way to open for us to go back home. We were essentially in the same position as immigrants, and between K'sundi and Vahdel, there was already a transport system. Rebels from K'sundi spent months placing themselves in surveillance vehicles undercover. They snuck into the ranks slowly so as not to draw suspicion. Then, when the time was right, they arranged for a seemingly random assembly of rebels disguised as Zendaalan agents in one truck, so there wasn't a single actual agent in the vehicle.

Then, the rebel-operated surveillance vehicle would go out and pick up however many immigrants they were assigned to smuggle across the border. To avoid detection, they separated the trips sporadically, sometimes arranging for a handful of trips a month, only one, or even skipping a month entirely. These happened at every road going from Vahdel out to another Equalized nation.

I didn't like knowing that we were taking a trip from some Vahdelan family that would have to wait who knew how long for another opportunity to leave.

But at the same time, I noticed a difference in Vahdel since we left the Dragon King.

It was still hot, but the air carried a refreshing breeze. If I didn't know any better, I'd say the trees were budding with new growth rather than decaying. It was slow, as if the progression had been halted somehow, but it was like the land itself was fighting to live again, instead of allowing itself to die.

The words of Averton rang through my head. I could tell it was bothering Kahmel, too. We were hiding out in an abandoned warehouse while we waited to be transported. The night we arrived at the warehouse, Kahmel gripped my hand.

"I won't let them get to you," he said, fire in his eyes.

I knew he would do everything in his power to protect me.

But somehow, I felt like Averton knew what he was talking about.

We were able to sneak Ocean—that's what I'd called my dragon— to the warehouse with us. Inero knew how to get to the warehouse without following main roads, and it prevented us from being spotted.

Inero couldn't stay with us long because he still had other things to do for people in the area, distributing resources and the like. But he visited us every now and then to check on us.

Kahmel came through on his promise to find a way to feed Ocean. There was a field of grass beside the warehouse where wild coyote went hunting for anything dead, and now that Ocean had a mind to hunt for herself, she was filling in, to my relief.

Now if only we could sneak her home with us.

There were so many things to panic about. We had no way of knowing how things were in K'sundi. We didn't know how to prepare for Averton's warning. There were so many things that could go wrong.

But I found myself looking up at the stars one night in the open field, taking a moment to appreciate the solitude. Though the situation forced us into a place of frustrating stagnation, it also meant it allowed a rare moment of stillness. Ocean was hunting around me, so I didn't fear the coyotes. I heard footsteps and sat up to see Kahmel striding toward me.

He lay next to me, crossing his arms behind his head.

"We should be able to leave soon," he said after a few minutes of restful silence.

I turned to my side. "How do you know?"

"The signal the immigrants use when it's time for a convoy to leave. I just saw it—a rebel walking with a backpack with a red handkerchief tied to one of the straps. If he stops for a minute, it's leaving in a day. Two minutes, two days, and so forth. My guess is they'll be ready tomorrow night."

"That's good."

As if answering my unasked question, Kahmel said, "I think I know how to bring Ocean. She's small enough to ride with us in the truck. It'll be a squeeze, but it might work. As long as you think she can keep quiet."

The way he was looking at me, he was asking if I thought it was even possible. I bit my lip, uncomfortable with the position of being the most knowing party in our relationship. But since he hadn't established a Drake Bond yet, he had no idea. And frankly, I couldn't be sure, either. But I felt like if she could detect my urgency, Ocean wouldn't make a squeak.

I nodded. "I think she can, but is it worth the risk?"

It hurt me to ask, but I knew the responsible thing was to do so. If she could survive on her own, taking her to K'sundi wasn't as important as us making it over the border safely.

Kahmel turned to look up at the skies. "I think we can make it work. It certainly seems like she's quite obedient to anything you want. I've never seen anything like it." He chuckled as he turned to me. His eyes were tired, but they warmed my heart. They were tired from always taking care of me, his people, the dragons. It was a tired he had earned. One of his most attractive qualities. "You're quickly becoming a better dragon rider than I've ever been."

It felt like gravity pulled our bodies together, our lips finding each other like it was natural. Kahmel's hand ran through my hair as he pulled me deeper into the kiss. But then something twisted in my stomach that made me pull away.

"What's wrong?" he asked, and I could tell from his voice he was afraid he'd done something wrong.

I shook my head. "Nothing, nothing. Just tired. I think I'll go to bed."

I got up and left him there.

I couldn't explain to him what didn't make sense. But Averton's warning still rang in my head.

And that kiss felt too much like a goodbye.

THERE WAS nothing but the sound of the engine running as we drove over the wilderness. I didn't know when we crossed over to the road as the truck had no windows, but not knowing made me even more nervous. Now on the road, the truck could be checked at any time, especially now that we were going in the direction of the border.

We were wearing surveillance team suits, along with other rebels in disguise.

Kahmel had a brilliant way to bring Ocean over. He assured me that bringing her was important as we weren't sure how or when either of us would establish a Drake Bond again, and he wanted to make sure the rebels were able to study our relationship.

Now that she was more filled in, we would pretend to be a surveillance team that found a good dragon that could be sold in Equalized country for a good price. It was perfect, as surveillance teams also scavenged for goods Zendaal could benefit from; it was believed that rebel nations were undeserving anyway. We found an old collar to put on her, and as long as she kept her eyes closed and pretended to be asleep—a thought I made sure was in my mind at all times—they would assume she was turned off.

We remained in silence, clad in armor as Ocean sat in the middle of us, closing her eyes obediently.

Then the truck stopped, and my gut clenched.

It was time for the check.

The Zendaalan officers stepped into the truck, along with Inero, disguised.

Inero was in the middle of telling the officers in broken Zendaalan that such a good dragon shouldn't be wasted on rebel nation people and that it was better suited for distribution in Equalized nations.

The Zendaalans grunted a reply as they came into the vehicle, sizing us all up. My mind flashed to the families who had to do this just to make something of themselves in Equalized country, thinking of how children must feel having to squeeze into crevices, hidden by smuggled cloaking technology, holding their breath.

I had a palace to look forward to. They had nothing. In comparison, my job was easy.

But my heart hammered against my chest as a Zendaalan soldier looked me in the eye, opening his palm. "Badge, please."

Attempting to smother my fear, I pulled out the item he'd asked for and handed it to him.

The officer held my stare a moment more, and, for a split second, I almost feared one of my contact lenses had fallen out, but his gaze broke away, and he handed it back. Turning to the rest of the rebels in the row, he followed the same procedure. Another officer was opening Ocean's mouth and examining her teeth, then moved to check her ear.

As they turned away, her ear twitched, and I willed her not to do that again. ZST dragons didn't move on their own at all.

For a breath, I was afraid someone had noticed, but no one did.

The officers stepped out of the truck and told us we were clear to proceed, and to keep an eye out for rebels, as they'd been more active in this area as of late. Inero assured them that we would be, and we headed off.

We were on our way home.

SUMMIT

Kahmel and I returned to a K'sundi thrown into confusion. Rand was able to keep things from spiraling into chaos, but the state we were in wasn't too far from it.

The Fire Bugs—or, rather, Half-Dracs—were popping up everywhere. They were fighting for Kahmel and me to be released from these ridiculous investigations.

As we still weren't allowed around our dragons, we had to send Ocean to where T'shan and his family were hidden. But I felt better knowing she was in good hands.

But "better" was relative.

The Zendaalans weren't pleased with my disappearance. Especially since I ignored warnings that I should come back. Warnings I had no idea were being issued since I was in Vahdel at the time. But we couldn't exactly tell them that.

K'sundi was being threatened with either getting rid of Kahmel and me or losing its status as an Equalized nation. And with the amount of research we still had to do on getting to Obellana's Dragon Realm entrance, we wouldn't have enough time.

There was only the question of if K'sundi wanted its Faresh and Faresha more than it wanted its status in the Equalization.

I could tell Averton's words still weighed heavily on Kahmel. He hadn't left my side since the moment we got home. At this point, pleasing the Court was pointless because there was nothing that could be said or done to change their opinion either way. Besides, the

Court was at a standstill. Even royal clans were coming forward and demanding an explanation from the Zendaalans for why they still had no answer for all the people rising up and saying Kahmel and I weren't the only Fire Bugs. Zendaal still only gave vague replies, and the Court couldn't decide one way or the other.

Then there was the issue of my parents.

It still felt strange even addressing them. Much less seeing them every day in the palace until Kahmel could get rid of them. He told me that until K'sundi was a rebel country, he couldn't order them out for the same reasons he couldn't order his family out—the law protected them. K'sundi law prevented him from making any decisions like that without permission from the Court, which they most certainly weren't going to give him.

They didn't do much more than smile at me and try to start conversations, but I didn't like it. I did not, nor did Kahmel, trust them, but there was nothing we could do about it.

I had talked with Lora only once since I'd been back. It was the first time since Kahmel and I revealed our fire that we'd spoken. It was a short call. We looked at each other in the HoloCaller, her eyes full of tears. She only said two words.

"I understand."

That was all I needed, and she seemed satisfied after having said it to my face. And I went back to worrying about all the matters that were still up in the air.

Finally, after weeks of nothing being quite settled, Zendaal made a public announcement.

Apparently, it was very official, and Kahmel and I were to receive it in our throne room. Cameramen recorded our reactions. Kahmel, dressed in golden robes that made him look regal and like a lion protecting his pride, grasped my hand at my side. I was wrapped in violet robes the color of passion, the silky material draping over my legs and over the floor. He nodded to me in confirmation, then looked to the presenter—Dralus. "We're ready."

The president of Zendaal appeared on a screen in front of us.

The leaders of Zendaal never appeared anywhere in person, supposedly because they ruled too many nations to visit them all. I suspected the rulers were too sick to leave their country. Zendaalans were notorious for being ill, but their bionic parts always accommodated their weaknesses and made them just as functional as anyone else. Sometimes more.

But the presidents of Zendaal were a special kind of ill. They all came from the same super-rich society, usually, and somehow it seemed the richer they were, the worse their illnesses.

As they could afford it, the especially rich of Zendaal granted themselves cybernetic parts that made them more than human. The president of Zendaal had a chrome mask over his mouth and nose, fused into the skin of his face. Where a nose should have been, a circular black filter stood instead, filtering air on his behalf. His arms were folded over, the extra metallic arms also folded on top. He had six arms in total, including his natural ones.

Well, as natural as they could be. His arms were covered by his white draping sleeves, but on his hands and along his wrists, glowing red lines poked out, which kept his blood system flowing where his veins had given up in a glimmering, pulsating rhythm.

What was left of his hair came out in stringy tufts brushed back behind him. Cold green eyes glared through the screen.

"President Eruvin Nodic," Dralus presented.

Kahmel and I nodded to acknowledge him and encourage him to speak.

The president breathed out—an action that made systems whir to life before dying back down when the breath was completed. "We are inviting His and Her Majesty to a summit in Zendaal to discuss these strange abilities that have sprouted up among the K'sundii. We must make the safety of the Equalization top priority, and there is no assurance that these strange abilities will not endanger it. There is also the matter of you keeping it secret all this time, as well as your identity as dragon tribe. This opens the possibility of your abilities being the result of an infection. An unnatural mutation, even."

"Our powers—" Kahmel objected, but the president cut him off.

"If you wish to argue your case, you will do it in Zendaal."

Kahmel bit down his comments, his jaw clenched. "Very well."

"Failure to comply will result in K'sundi's immediate expulsion from the Equalization."

"We understand," I said, swallowing the rage pulsing in me. Now wasn't the time for fire, so embers flushed from my nose.

The president nodded, and the transmission ended.

We exchanged niceties with Dralus, and Kahmel brought his lips close to my ear as the Zendaalans left.

"I don't like it."

"But do we have any other choice?" I whispered back.

He paused. "Until I know the people trust us? Not really. But I'll make sure the rebels come."

I nodded, but it twisted my stomach.

This didn't feel right.

FEAR OF LOSING SOMEONE

Kahmel Axon Kai of the Omah Clan, Faresh of K'sundi

I ran through everything in my head a million times. I checked everything a million times. There were rebels packing our bags to make sure they didn't get planted with trackers. Rand, Arusi, Asan, *and* Khes were coming on this trip. I had my private plane ready to head to Zendaal with no other choice but to go. I wasn't planning on leaving Jashi's side. Not with what Averton said. It was all I could think about since he'd said it.

We were at the point to leave, and I had just left Jashi in the living room to send the rebels a message in my room about the plan I'd made for them to check the palace thoroughly after we returned.

I left part of an advertising poster of a claw, programming the message to display with my eWatch.

When I stepped out, a servant came to meet me. "Your Majesty, there you are. The Zendaalan officials are here."

I frowned. "What do you mean, they're here? What are they doing here?"

"They're here to escort you to your plane. They want to make sure you attend. *Theirwordsnotmine,*" he finished quickly when met with my glare.

"Well, tell them to wait. We're not quite ready yet," I said, moving past him.

"But they've already left with your wife."

Those words made a creeping urge worm through my throat. My mouth went dry, and Averton's words ricocheted through my mind.

"Take me to them," I told him.

"But they've already left, Your Majesty," he objected. "And in quite the hurry. I suppose they wanted to make sure you met with them as soon as possible."

But I had already started moving.

I left her for *two seconds*.

Last year when this happened, Jashi left of her own accord, to a certain extent. If I thought that feeling was bad, this was so much worse. Jashi wanted to save K'sundi as much as I did now. She *loved* me now. And more importantly, she was a threat now. Before, the Zendaalans wanted her to think they were on her side. They wouldn't be so nice anymore.

I moved, not as if my life was in danger, but that the love of my life was in danger. Because she was.

But I didn't know.

I didn't know the fear of losing someone that meant so much to you made you blind to the steps you were taking that made sure you did lose them.

TRAP

Jashi Anyua-Omah, Faresha of K'sundi

I waited.

After ten minutes had passed, crossing and uncrossing my legs on the couch in the living room, I tried to suppress the feeling of ice that climbed up my gut. Thinking I had been spoiled by Kahmel never leaving my side and that it'd left me jumping at shadows when he was away.

I decided that I was only going to settle my irrational fears by checking on him. I pulled up the ends of my turquoise robe and walked toward my room.

Now I knew I was being paranoid. My very footsteps echoing in the halls were unnerving me. The way they bounced back at me made my skin crawl.

Then that feeling of unease turned icy. It was too quiet. There was nothing. No sound of guards, no shuffle of feet, no servants milling about.

My walk turned to a jog, my steps bouncing back at me, and then the jog turned to a run.

I ran down a corridor of silence.

When I got to our room and found it empty, I knew. I knew Averton was right. They'd detained Kahmel somehow.

I turned to go find somebody, anybody. I jumped when I saw who was standing in the doorway.

Talad and Attican.

My body trembled as I took a step back. "I-I thought—"

"Your husband had me executed?" Attican jeered, cold eyes making my spine shiver. But he had changed. His skin was already pale, but it seemed paler now. His eyes were an unnatural green, and his hands were traced with glowing red lines, like President Nodic. "Well, my people made sure I wasn't. Good thing about being presumed dead—people pretty much stop looking for you after that."

My eyes went to Talad, tearing up with rage. "And you. How could you do this to me? How could you even get in here?"

Talad's gaze held no love. No memories of what our friendship used to be. No regard for where we came from. "The Zendaalans, your parents, take a pick. Funny how everyone seems to want you gone." He narrowed his eyes. "You changed, Jash. And what's more, you're a freak. Maybe now you'll know your place."

Attican tilted his head up, sneering. "Good thing your friend has some sense about him. And he'll help us appeal to those of you that don't."

Before I could try to figure out what that meant, Attican lunged.

Since the moment I saw them, my mind had been racing. Averton didn't warn us so we could be paranoid. He warned us so we could prepare. And I would have to turn my knowledge into an advantage.

Fire pushed from my hand, flaring in Attican's face. I only needed a second.

Talad pounced on me from behind, knocking my head into the dresser. Pain danced in my skull, but I collected my thoughts enough to take what had fallen to my side and slip it into the curls of my hair, clipping it in place, knowing it was long and full enough to be hidden out of sight.

A white cloth was pressed against my mouth as makeup and jewelry from the dresser fell around me, and I held my breath for as long as I could. My hands were above my head. I didn't think they could see me typing on my eWatch or scratching against the wood of the dresser. I only prayed Kahmel would understand the message.

Burning for air, my lungs sucked in oxygen involuntarily, and the world blacked out of focus.

GONE

Kahmel Axon Kai of the Omah Clan, Faresh of K'sundi

When I arrived at the plane and Jashi wasn't there, I knew exactly what had happened. The "servant" who told me she left was nowhere to be found when I turned around. The staff around me had no idea why I was so enraged that my body burst into flames.

I called Rand, Arusi, Khes, and Asan and got back to the palace as soon as I could, but even before I got there, I knew I was too late.

It was confirmed when I arrived, and no one could tell me where my wife was.

What was more, all of them seemed to have just arrived at the palace, each of them having been given different instructions—ones no one remembered sending out—that their shifts were to start later than usual, assuming other staff members were working later.

Jashi had been alone in the palace. When I realized she was gone, I couldn't hear or feel anything. My body went numb. Rand was barking instructions around me, Arusi was demanding explanations, Khes said something to the security team. I didn't even know what they were saying.

My feet seemed to move on their own to our bedroom. The horror continued. The dresser was a mess, things knocked to the ground, drawers pulled out. It happened here.

Jashi wasn't taken because I left her for a second.

She was taken because I was stupid enough to let her get taken. This was my fault. All my preparations, all my planning, it meant nothing.

Among all the chaos, a Zendaalan officer demanded to know when we would be leaving for the summit.

Something snapped.

"Can't you see my wife is gone?" I roared. Fire shot from my hands and caught on my robes, but I didn't care. I tried to find the will to care about anything. "You can stuff that summit down your throats, you hear me? Now get out of here, get out of my palace!"

"If you do not show," the Zendaalan officer insisted anyway, iron in his tone, "it will indicate rebellion."

Everything was falling apart. All my planning wasn't enough. Nothing mattered anymore. "*Leave,*" I growled.

The officer scampered away, and Rand appeared in the doorway, pursing his lips. Everyone else must have left.

Wordlessly, my brother wrapped his arms around me, ignoring the small flames on the ends of my clothes, and for once, I didn't stop him.

The reality came crashing down.

Jashi was gone.

A sigh pushed from my lungs. My chest felt like lead. I was empty.

I closed my arms around my twin and shut my eyes.

"Hey, wait," Rand said after a moment, pulling away. He crouched to the ground, looking at something.

"What?" My voice was hoarse. I collapsed into the chair by the window.

I couldn't be bothered to notice what he was looking at until he said, "There's a message. Here, in the bedroom."

I thought he was talking about mine until I saw him crouching on the ground, looking at a mark on the wood just above the floor.

"There's a claw scratched into the wood here."

Standing up, I closed the door to the bedroom and opened my eWatch, using the decoder to look for hidden messages.

One showed up. It was riddled with typos, but I understood.

Cpme finnd me,like yu did befo8re. I lo4ve yopu.
   Yiur desrt floeer

My mind was such a mess, I didn't understand the ending at first. Then I realized.

Desert flower.

"Rand. Check the tracker on her hair pin."

He looked at me, and his eyes filled with understanding. "On it."

Acknowledgments

I have so many people I want to acknowledge for being part of my community and inspiring me to make *Rising* the best it could possibly be.

First, my family. My mom who's always been an inspiration to me, my dad who helped culture my love of fantasy and sci-fi, my brother for being the one I told stories to when I was little. They've always been supportive of my many interests and hobbies, and eventually became the biggest cheerleaders for my writing career, and I'll always be grateful to them.

Then there's my writing community, who's insight I couldn't be without. Kat, Em, and all the friends I've made in the Melanin Chat on discord, especially Porsha, Chelsea, LaKase, and Tristan. I don't know where I'd be without them. Probably curled up in bed, avoiding my unfinished projects. They're always holding writing sprints when I need them most!

And finally, I'd like to thank you, reader, for taking a chance on this wild journey of fantasy and futuristic worlds. As a Black writer, I always struggle finding a time for my stories. The past is so hard to look at, and the present can be so frustrating to focus on. So I craft for you, for us, a place to escape to. A world where things are different. An idea of what that might look like.

Fiction is all about possibilities. About finding your truth by sharing a "what if."

I'll always be grateful for each and every one of my readers, because for me, they make one of my "what ifs" come true.

If you've made it to the end of this book and you enjoyed it, please consider giving it a review on Amazon. Reviews really help authors like me that are with smaller publishers, even if it's just a single sentence! A little goes a long way.

ABOUT THE AUTHOR

Celeste Harte is an African-American writer living in Spain. She loves reading and writing sci-fi and fantasy, and is obsessed with all things mermaids and dragons.

When she's not building worlds and getting lost in her own fantasies, she's probably dancing to random music or watching (yet another) Korean drama. In addition to her native language, she speaks Spanish and Catalan almost fluently, some French, and would love to learn Korean.

This has been an
Immortal Production